PRAISI
TALE O

"I LOVE Fiona, and I found her to be extremely engaging."
– advanced reader for To Condemn a Witch

"I loved it... I could not wait to see the villains receive their comeuppance. And man, was the resolution satisfying."
– Amazon reviewer for To Rescue a Witch

"Quickly became my favourite read so far."
– Amazon UK reviewer

"Spunky and sassy, cunning and clever..."
– advanced reader

"The child, Annaliese, stole my heart."
– Jansikes.com

"The historical detail is spot on."
– Goodreads reviewer

"One of the best historical fictions I have read."
– Amazon reviewer

"Love found family, dark tales of hope, and a world that offers second chances"
– BookBub reviewer

"MacLeod was so very human in his desire to always protect everyone."
– Advanced reader

"My jaw dropped open in shock because of the plot turns."
– Amazon reviewer

Created in the United States of America

ISBN: 978-0-9833441 5 5

Visit www.lisatraugott.com for more information. You can read the first three chapters of *To Rescue a Witch*, part of the Tales of the Witchborn series plus exclusive previews of future books by subscribing to her newsletter.

To Condemn a Witch

LISA A. TRAUGOTT

BOOKS BY LISA A. TRAUGOTT

Tales of the Witchborn series

To Rescue a Witch
To Condemn a Witch, Prequel

Fitness books

She's Losing It! A quirky little memoir
The S.L.I. Method

Children's books

Mind Your Manners Minnie Monster

Thank You!

Thanks so much for reading my book! If you like it, please leave a review and tell a friend. To continue the adventure, I've provided an exclusive preview of the first three chapters of *To Rescue a Witch*, delivered to your email by signing up for my newsletter at www.lisatraugott.com. Be the first to receive exclusive previews, special deals and book contests.

Quick Glossary

Please note: Many of the spells include Scots Gaelic words that are translated by another character in the next sentence. Below are some of the most common words and phrases used.

I dinnae ken – I don't know
Dinnae fash – don't worry
Eisd rium a Dhia – hear me God
Cailleach – witch
bean-ghlùine – midwife
bairn – child
canna – can't
couldna – couldn't
dinnae – don't
feille – (funeral) wake
haena – haven't
handfast – marriage
isna – isn't
ken – know
shouldna – shouldn't
willnae – will not
wouldnae – wouldn't
wheest – be quiet

For Aunt Phyllis

Chapter 1

MATILDA

Scotland—1707

A hot sting from the executioner's slap jolted Matilda back to life, the noose still tight around her neck. Now gasping on the ground, she curled in a ball, wishing she could raise her tingling old hands to her head to stop the earsplitting ringing, but they were tied behind her back.

"Reckoned you'd get off that easy, witch?" the executioner said, yanking her to standing and removing the noose. His hot breath reeked of ale. "Dinnae fash yourself. The witch hunter's got something special planned for you."

Her blurred vision slowly focused beyond the crumbling castle, where she'd been imprisoned for weeks, to the tar-covered stake awaiting her. Her body felt weak, and the sound of her heartbeat thrashed in her ears. *This canna be happening.*

Staring into the crowd, the smear of color refocused. Wee Fiona, barely seven, held her trembling fingertips against her open mouth, unable to blink her amber eyes. For a fleeting instant, they were brave for each other.

Until there came an overwhelming rush of villagers chanting, "Burn, witch."

Skinny fishwives fingered bits of iron to protect themselves from Matilda's spells.

"She said herbs were for 'healing.' Lying hag. How many people died from her charms?"

"Matilda's been a troublemaker since her husband died."

"She helped my bairn survive the fever..." whispered a woman in a homespun shawl. "You dinnae reckon she used dark magic, did she?"

Clansmen in green plaids grasped Matilda's armpits, dragging her to the stake as her neighbors spit on her. Reverend MacDonald, a small, knuckly man clenching a large Bible, rambled incessantly about Christ as he walked beside her.

Matilda tried to orient herself. Admiral Goring's manor stood nestled in the forested hills to her right, looming as large as the man himself. Directly in front was the stake, with the entire village, plus neighboring clans, surrounding to watch. To the left were the worn stone steps leading to the water gate, where an older woman leaned against a cane.

Elspeth. Her traitorous coven sister hovered on the crowd's edge, ready to escape.

Admiral Goring, in his powdered wig and expensive frock coat, smugly counted eight pounds and four shillings for the executioner as the admiral's pretty wife rubbed the cross around her neck. "Money well spent," he said to the witch hunter, a mysterious English nobleman.

Matilda had never seen the witch hunter's face in the village until her arrest and torture.

"Thou has put down many with the fever," Admiral Goring called. "It would have been better for the good people of Kirkhaven if they had knit a stone about thy neck and drowned thee at birth."

The men bound Matilda to the stake, then shoved faggots of wood beneath her bare feet, while the elders of the Kirk lit their torches from within the castle ruins, and started their solemn procession to burn her alive.

"I'm a healer. I'm innocent," she called out, voice even raspier now than the day of her capture.

The witch hunter's lips curled into a sickening grin. "I know," he hissed just loud enough for her ears.

Dressed in a dark-colored coat that shimmered when he moved, he winked at Admiral Goring, then slipped into the crowd like a snake slithering through the grass.

Beside her niece, as if in mockery, Admiral Goring's two sons stood tall, laughing and joking, enjoying the display of their family's dominance over hers. Matilda's stomach soon churned as she watched the witch hunter weave towards Fiona and realized the men's plan.

"No," Matilda gasped. "Fiona!"

A break appeared in the gray clouds as a murder of ravens flew from the partially collapsed castle roof, shedding black feathers. Rage bubbled inside her. *Did Elspeth use Fiona's life to pay for her own freedom? Was my life not enough?*

Her temper exploded like a struck match, hotter than the approaching torches. Raising her eyes, she called out. "*Eisd rium a Dhia.* Beira, Queen of Winter, first *Cailleach*, Goddess, Destroyer, Protector." The price of her soul would be steep, but worth it. "May your ancient power annihilate mine enemies."

An icy wind answered from the mountains.

Elspeth desperately shape-shifted into a raven to escape.

"Flying back to London, traitor? *Losgadh, fear-brathaidh!*" Matilda's curse burned a sigil above Elspeth's heart, forever marking her betrayal to the coven, as the raven cawed in agony and flew haphazardly away.

Panic swept through the villagers as they stepped back, gaping at each other. The witch hunter inched closer to Fiona. The torch bearers rushed forward, quickly setting ablaze the wood beneath Matilda's feet. Curling her toes at the intense heat, Matilda cried out as her skin blistered. Each muscle cramped, making her body writhe in a sick dance.

"Enjoy your last dance with the Devil," Admiral Goring shouted. "Thy tongue shall never abuse these people again."

"Witches take your wit and grace from ye," she hissed.

The left side of Admiral Goring's face dropped, then froze. The villagers watched in horror as Admiral Goring's knees gave out and he collapsed, his massive jowls quivering as a dribble of saliva slid down his cheek.

Sunlight flashed against a dagger the witch hunter pulled from his damask waistcoat, bounding forward to Fiona.

"Run!" Matilda shrieked into the chaotic fury.

Fiona stared at her, not understanding all that was going on, not realizing how close she was to death.

"Your sons shall die yet, Admiral," Matilda shouted.

Another cold gust blew. Admiral Goring's eldest son, dark blond and handsome, collapsed at Fiona's feet. The younger son, pale, freckled, still growing into his limbs, held his brother's arm before a crimson line of blood wet his own cravat.

Did they think they could betray me without consequence? That Beira wouldnae demand her due?

Straightening to full height, her eyes locked on the witch hunter as the flames licked up her dress. "Evil tidings come upon ye. It would be better for the women of the burgh if ye were castrated."

The witch hunter stopped, instinctively cupping himself, then fled to his waiting horse, past the shrieking crowd dropping their belongings as they stampeded to safety.

For an instant, Matilda connected with Fiona's devastated eyes, willing her to understand. *Protect your magic.*

A coppery taste of blood filled her mouth as she bit down on her own tongue. Exhaling her last, furious breath, Matilda's vengeful spirit ripped from her charred body, floating above the flames.

Alone.

A trapped ghost, cursed to relive her death for eternity until justice could be served against all who betrayed her.

Chapter 2

Fiona

Scotland, Present Time, 1729—Imbolc fire festival

Fiona watched the sun set over the exact spot where Auntie Matilda burned over twenty years ago. How odd to no longer be a little girl, a crofter's daughter in the crowd, but to find herself now seated indoors as the lady of the manor, married to Admiral Goring's grandson. Not even Matilda could have predicted such a twist in fate.

Tap.

Martha MacPherson, sixteen, tapped the window again and flicked her gaze over her shoulder. Her swollen, red-rimmed eyes could only mean one thing.

Fiona nodded at the back door and joined her, careful not to draw the servants' attention.

"Lady MacLeod, I'm not meaning to bother you, ma'am, but I've got myself in an awful fix and my gran said you've knowledge of herbs."

The intense colors of the sunset were still fading into softer shades of violet, but there was enough time to help before moonrise. "Walk with me." Fiona led her into the courtyard. A novice might think it an ordinary garden, but from the second floor, the circular layout of the garden was apparent, just as Auntie Matilda had taught her. "How far along are you?"

Martha swallowed, toying with her long, plaited hair. "I'm six weeks late and my breasts hurt something terrible when my shift rubs them the wrong way."

"Who's the lad?"

"That's the problem. He's left to join the Royal Navy and willnae be back for months. If Reverend MacDonald finds out," her voice cracked, "he'll whip me in front of the whole village. 'Twill shame my family."

Fiona pulled her in for a hug. "Shh. All will be well."

Reverend MacDonald was quick to punish 'the weaker sex', which is why Fiona made it her mission to secretly empower them. She led Martha into her greenhouse and pulled out a sachet of pennyroyal from a top shelf. "Brew as a tea and drink before bed. Your stomach will cramp, but the blood should flow by morning."

"My gran warned me there would be a price and said your Aunt Matilda would curse anyone who dinnae pay. I've only got a thruppence, but—"

"Keep your money, lass. My aunt grew as bitter as the ale she drank in her later years and paid with her life. I'm not her." They left the greenhouse as the first stars appeared in the sky. "Tell no one what I've given you."

Martha's eyes welled. "Thank you, Lady MacLeod. Gran said you werena a witch like Matilda, but a wise woman. Thank the Lord she was right."

"We were both wise women." Her sigh was tinged with sadness. She gave the girl's hand a final squeeze and watched her leave. In the distance, the Firth of Clyde became a dark, glassy surface reflecting the decrepit castle as the moon rose above the forest.

It's time.

The tight knot in her chest unraveled. Grabbing a bucket, she headed to the clootie well. Alone, Fiona raised the water, smiling at Matilda's reflection in the pail. "I've missed you," Fiona said in her mind.

The wonderful thing about having an aunt who was both a ghost, and a witch, was that it allowed for much more private conversations—at least during the eight annual fire festivals when the veils between the worlds of the living and dead stretched thin.

William allowed ye to come to the clootie well? Matilda said in her mind.

"He's not home." Fiona tightened her plaid shawl against the wind.

Thank the goddess, Matilda said. *I'll never understand what ye see in him. Your marriage is the curse of my afterlife. How can I protect ye? How can ye protect yourself without magic? Damn Admiral Goring's grandson.*

"William had nothing to do with your burning. He was seven and living on the Isle of Skye on your death day. He loves me, and works himself to the bone for us. Do you think the roof mends itself? And unlike the admiral, William is fair with all the tenants, and is the first to defend anyone unable to stand up for themselves, whether in court or at the Kirk. Plus, you helped William's mother, Elise, elope with his father, for goddess' sake. You ken William is from the good side of that family."

Love or not, ye should have never married him out of respect for me.

"Why do you constantly make me choose? I love you both. And he sacrificed so much to protect me—our best land, his chance to move closer to being King's Attorney—all to keep me from arrest. How many men do you think would do that, and still remain a loving husband? We agreed I shouldna practice magic anymore. It's just too risky." She lowered her eyes. "I dinna realize then the cost of my promise. Anyway, my marriage shouldna have surprised you too much. We both predicted I'd marry a rich man from Skye."

Aye, but I dinnae think he'd earn his wealth by being Admiral Goring's grandson and inheriting everything. Dinnae fash yourself, I've no intention of coming between ye and your husband. She muttered under her breath. *Even if he wants to take away your magic. Tsk-tsk-tsk. Supposes he can outwit a goddess.*

Pooka, Fiona's black cat, curled around her legs and let out a good stretch.

Fiona took a deep, calming breath. "I'll not spend Imbolc cursing the man who holds my heart. He may thunder like the sea at times, but he's my safe harbor all the same. Come inside to see the boys. They've grown since the last fire festival."

Aye, that's what lads do. Now, tie a ribbon around the clootie well, make a wish to Beira, and let's be off.

Fiona smirked. "I missed you, even if you are a curmudgeon. I miss our talks." Closing her eyes, Fiona held the ribbon, focusing on her intention. *I wish things could return to the way the used to be with William. Ever since what happened in London...Beira, please show me how to save my family.* She tied her ribbon on the clootie well.

"Fiona," called Reverend MacDonald, ambling up the path.

"Did he see me tie the ribbon?" she asked Matilda. Imagining the worst-case scenario of getting caught again, her limbs began to shake.

A sour taste filled her mouth as she remembered her punishment, done privately under the reverend's judgmental glare, to avoid a witch trial.

Well, dinnae draw attention to yourself staring into the water. Gods forbid he gets curious to see what you're looking at, although seeing my sour puss in the pail might literally scare the man to death, and wouldnae that tickle my witch's heart? Matilda joked in an obvious attempt to calm her.

Fiona plastered a smile on her face as she greeted the preacher.

"I was coming to meet with William. Is he home?"

"Not yet, Reverend."

Matilda jumped her soul from the well water to inside Pooka, who let out a disgruntled meow. *Ah, pipe down, cat. I dinnae want to be inside you either, but it's the only way I can feel the tangible earth.*

Reverend MacDonald eyed the cat, then spotted ribbons adorning the well and nearby tree. "*Tsk-tsk-tsk*. I'll have to speak to William about your influx of Irish tenants celebrating Saint Brigid's Day. One would expect the remnants of Popery's decline by now."

Fiona sighed, relieved he hadn't seen her tie a ribbon, too.

'Twas Imbolc before the pope tried to change it into a Christian day, muttered Matilda in a form of a *meow*.

"Is it colder than usual?" Reverend MacDonald said, shivering. "I get such a strangling sense of dread at this well."

I tortured Admiral Goring seven years before he succumbed to death. It only takes one time when the veils are thin when I find the reverend with neither cross nor iron in his pocket, and I can have my revenge.

"Matilda, stop. It's been over twenty years. Are you going to hold your grudge for all eternity? How will you ever get to the light?"

Forgiveness is for the weak-willed.

Reverend MacDonald rubbed his neck. "Where did you say William was?"

"London, serving Lord Hallewell. Did you need something?"

"I caught wind there might be a bonfire and dancing. I dinnae ken if they use this night to pay homage to the old ways or as an excuse to behave lasciviously. Either way, I'm against it. As laird, your husband has a responsibility to ensure his tenants follow godly ways. Why he takes their side against the Kirk's often as he does is beyond me. His grandsire, the admiral, wouldna have allowed it."

"Mm."

Let me scratch the preacher's eyes out, Matilda hissed. *I can complain about William, but he canna.*

Fiona picked her up, stroking her fur while speaking in her mind. "Are you trying to get me burned at the stake as well? Control your temper, lest he grow suspicious. Walk away and drink the milk I've placed at the door for you, or waste your limited time among the living drinking in bitterness instead."

Fine. I'm a patient witch. Matilda left Fiona's arms, giving a parting hiss at the reverend, and pranced to the manor with her tail held high.

"I suppose I'll be walking the village alone tonight to ensure no candles are burning past curfew." He looked down his nose. "That includes at your manor, madam."

Heat rushed to Fiona's cheeks. "We are a godly household, sir, whether William is home or not. Haena I proved that?"

Holding each other's stare, Fiona broke the gaze first. A strategic retreat.

"I can commend you for how well James kens the Bible," he conceded. "I see him reading it to wee Broderick all the time after church. You could learn a thing or two from the piety of your eldest son."

"Aye, Reverend. I'm proud of his virtuous nature."

"Proud? A godly woman shouldna show pridefulness. We ken where that leads."

Fiona's fingers curled into fists. *My time with Matilda is fleeting and this self-important man sucks away precious moments.*

The reverend stood taller. "William needs to—well, I suppose that's a discussion meant for his ears, not yours. When he arrives, see that he visits me."

Be humble. He'll leave faster. Fiona's nails clawed her thigh as she lowered her eyes. "Aye, Reverend."

Tipping his hat, he ambled back down the road. Fiona spit on the ground. Shivering as much from her conversation as the wind, she was happy to return home. Moving to the hearth, she rubbed her hands to warm them.

Matilda licked her paw by the fire. *Och, the reverend talks so much he could fill the sails of a ship with naught but his breath. Are ye being a goodly wife, bowing before the reverend?*

Fiona twisted away.

You've followed his sermons for months, now pay homage to the old ways. It dinnae take much to do a wee bit of scrying, just look at the flames. Ye only have eight fire festivals per year when ye can call visions on command.

Fiona's eyes rested stonily on Matilda's. "How did scrying turn out for you?"

Matilda stretched her claws out in front of her and raised her wee arse to Fiona.

"You dinnae have to be rude, Auntie."

Come now. Help me find the mysterious noble witch hunter. I'm sure he's in London, plotting with Elspeth. Gods, I wish I wasna chained to this village but for fire festivals. I'd have more time to hunt them down. I want him to tell me to my face why he burned me despite my innocence. I never caused the sickness. And there's a special place in Hades for witches like Elspeth who betray their covens.

Fiona had no desire to stir up trouble. Hadn't she already dealt with her own horrors in London? But she faced the flames to placate her aunt, certain they'd never find the mysterious witch hunter. And Elspeth was long gone. Only the goddess knew where she went.

A loud pop from the fire drew in Fiona's gaze and held it. Heat intensified and the world around her buzzed, then grew mute. She looked around, realizing her soul was now inside the misty dimness of the Otherworld. She wandered through a forest with unfamiliar trees. *What land is this?*

A baby cried in the distance. Fiona touched her fingertips to her lips with a revelation. *A daughter. That's what will bring William close again.*

Tracking the sound, she discovered a blonde maiden in chains holding a newborn. The sun rose and set five times as the bairn morphed into a little girl with wild red hair wearing a wreath of flowers. Her face was pure innocence.

"Are you a fairy?" Fiona called as the girl skipped beneath a giant tree.

A wintry wind blew. The fairy girl reached for a fallen crown as a raven cawed. Dark shadows of a large viper fell over the child as she cowered from it.

"Only the coven can protect the girl from the witch hunter," said the woman in chains.

"Mam? Are you all right?" James stood directly between her and the hearth, drawing her focus back to the tangible world.

Fiona's soul reunited with her body.

"You were staring into the fire, Mam. Reverend MacDonald warned doing that can be dangerous on certain days."

Fiona wiped the sweat from her brow. "Just warming my hands, son."

Ye look like you've seen a ghost beyond me, Matilda said. *Have you found my traitors? I've pondered long and hard about my revenge against their miserable lives.*

Fiona shook no, shutting her eyes against the disturbing images from the Otherworld. Seeing the future was both a blessing and a curse. Was the vision a cautionary tale or a glimpse into a condemned fate? Who was the blonde woman? Why was she in chains? What child needed protecting, and why did she reach for a crown?

I canna stay long. I have to search for Elspeth and the witch hunter, but I had to see my wee grandnephews first. Matilda curled around James' legs. *When did he get so tall? He reaches your nose.*

The butler, Mr. Murray, entered with a full basket of peat bricks as the other servants gathered their coats. "Thank you for giving us the evening off, my lady."

"Be warned that Reverend MacDonald is on the lookout for bonfires and dancing. Not that any of you partake in those kinds of things," Fiona said with a wink.

"I canna speak for anyone else, but I'm taking Monsieur Laurent with me to visit my sister so he can have some proper haggis."

"I canna wait until William comes home to taste your latest recipe."

"*Oui,*" he said with a wry smile. "Everything is better with salt."

Ack, stop blethering with the help. I'm only here a few hours before the veils close.

Mr. Murray threw another peat into the fire as the scullery maids wrapped their green tartan arisaids around their heads. "When will the laird be back, ma'am?"

"Any day now, and then we're going to visit Matilda."

The maids gasped. Mr. Murray's hunched body straightened, pulling back from the flames as though her words burned him.

James looked mortified. "Da says we're not to speak of your dead aunt."

"Gracious, what a silly slip of the tongue. I meant to say we're going to visit my sister, Mary." Fiona's cheeks flushed. "James, go check on your brothers."

He left as the servants glanced at each other awkwardly. Matilda offered a *meow*, then walked like a queen into the back parlor, clearly thrilled she still had an effect on people.

Fiona faked a smile. "Enjoy your night off."

After they left, Fiona walked into the parlor. "Auntie Matilda, it's been a lovely visit, but get out of my cat's body. William forbids witchcraft, and you're going to cause a rift in my household if I act too suspiciously."

James and David were already roughhousing in a whirlwind of red and blondish-brown hair while Lachlan, her youngest with sandy blond curls, toddled nearby, tugging Matilda's tail.

Where's Broderick? asked Matilda, scanning the room.

"Boys, where's Broderick?" Fiona said.

David pushed up his glasses on his nose and shrugged.

Fiona left the parlor and strode into William's book-lined study. "Good heavens, what happened here?"

Broderick swiped his black hair behind his ear and lifted his brown eyes to her with a determined look on his three-year-old face. All that was left of Admiral Goring's grandfather clock, William's most prized heirloom, was a pile of cables and mechanics scattered across the floor.

Och, this is bad, Matilda said.

"Da said the clock is the key to our family's greatness. Where's the key?"

Fiona covered her mouth in horror. "There's not a literal key. He was using flowery language. Oh, Brod, you've positively destroyed it."

"No, Mama, I'll find the key and fix it."

Fiona cringed at Matilda. "William will be home any day. Of all sons to damage the heirloom, it had to be Broderick?"

Hearing the fuss, her other sons piled into the room.

"Are you mad, boy?" James said. "That was great-grandsire's clock. You ken no one is supposed to touch it. Da's going to kill you."

Lachlan toddled in. "Uh-oh."

Even beyond the grave, Admiral Goring strikes fear into innocent hearts, said Matilda, jumping into Broderick's lap.

"Oh, stop. Your father's temper is quick, but his heart is quicker still," Fiona said. "He'll be devastated the heirloom is broken. His mother said on her deathbed it would define his legacy." *Yet another thing Broderick ruined.*

David gave Broderick a quick hug. "Dinnae fash. Let's see if we can figure this out together. We can all help you. James, do you see where he put the pendulum?" he asked, cleaning his glasses on the corner of his shirt.

Meow. Matilda walked to the spot.

"I've got the weights and pulleys," James said on his hands and knees, pulling parts from beneath the couch.

"Who ken there were so many pieces?" said Broderick, raising his hands.

"Everyone," said James.

Lachlan tugged Fiona's skirt. "Bad Broderick."

"Wheest, Lachie." Raking her fingers through her hair, Fiona's mind raced. Who could fix a century old clock, and how quickly can they do it? "James, ride over to Uncle Malcolm's. He's handy." She hoped.

Your brother kens how to fix mill wheels, not an ancient clock.

James headed out the door, shaking his head at Broderick while muttering, "You better pray Da gets held up in London so we have time to fix it."

As David and Broderick worked together with Lachlan looking on, Fiona slipped away to the now empty kitchen. She lit a candle as Matilda jumped onto the table.

"William loves that clock. It might take days to find the right person in Glasgow or Inverness—and what if it canna be fixed?"

Meow.

"I promised William no spells. You ken that."

Meow, she screeched. Matilda left Pooka's body and spiraled like mist on the moor into a ghostly, semi-transparent version of her stocky frame. *This isna proper spell casting with burning mugwort leaves, or stones, or gods forbid a salt circle. People make wishes on candles all the time.* As she flew beneath the ceiling rafters, she stopped mid-air and shook her head. *Ooch, Fiona, do ye ever pay attention to my lessons about healing? Ye hung these herbs completely wrong.*

"You haena taught me lessons in years. Besides, I canna cast a spell to fix the clock, it's too risky. You ken my situation." Fiona bit her lip. "James had a good idea. Canna you cast a spell to delay him in London until the clock is repaired?"

He isna even home. Cast your own spell. And while you're at it, say a protective charm, so your servants dinnae go gossiping about the village, telling everyone ye mentioned me. Ye can trust no one these days.

"Aunt Matilda, I gave William my word I wouldnae practice proper witchcraft. Visions are out of my control, but actual spell casting with ingredients is a step too far. If I get caught again, there'll be no more mercy from the Kirk...But you can cast a spell for me."

Matilda's fists landed on her hips. *If ye keep denying the powers the Cailleach granted to ye, there's going to be a punishment. Ye dinnae want a goddess like Beira on your bad side.*

"Auntie, please. I'm trying the best I can to protect my magic, like you want, without practicing magic, like what he wants. You've put me in an impossible situation."

Matilda floated down. *You're lucky it's Imbolc, so I can help.*

Pooka tried to escape, but Matilda went back inside the cat. Pawing at the lower cupboard, the door flung open, and a wee bag of salt dropped to the floor. With her teeth, she hauled the bag, spilling the white crystals around them in a circle. *Eisd rium a Dhia. Protect this family from chattering servants.*

Jumping from the floor to the cupboard, Matilda cut the hanging herbs from the ceiling rafters in a sharp diagonal with her claws. Juniper twigs dropped into the candle flame and the brittle brown needles released a crisp, piney scent with hints of citrus.

Matilda stopped for a minute, panting. *Och, I haena walked the earth in decades, but ye have me cramming myself into a feline and jumping like a mountain lion.* Matilda sneezed, scattering the salt to the four corners of the room. *May the wind be at William's face until Fiona is ready to call him home.*

"No, Auntie, I canna call him home. That would require conjuring. You have to do it. Oh, please. I promised I wouldnae do any magic."

Och, you're such a pain in the arse, Fiona. Fine, I'll do it, but ye must burn a candle on your windowsill all night for the Cailleach.

Fiona nodded.

Delay William's return with three obstacles. Matilda jumped into the knitting basket on the floor and unspooled a ball of red yarn, chasing it until three knots formed, then splayed on the ground, panting. *With harm to none*...gasp...*so mote it be done.*

Fiona picked Matilda up and cuddled her. "Thank you."

Matilda's transparent body separated from Pooka. *The things I do for ye,* she grumbled. But Fiona detected the hint of a smile. *See ye at Beltane, ye pain in the arse. Wish me luck finding the nobleman witch hunter and Elspeth. Be on the lookout for ravens. Elspeth loves to transfigure into her familiar.* Matilda disappeared into the fire in the hearth, just as Fiona remembered her vision.

"Wait," she called.

"Mama?" Broderick said.

Fiona pocketed the yarn quickly. She pinned her arms against her stomach, now queasy not only for remembering the disturbing vision of the blonde woman in chains warning of the witch hunter, but for dancing on the edge of breaking her promise to William about practicing magic. "How's the clock repair going?"

"No key, but look what I found inside a chime." He giddily held a yellowed scroll.

"Hopefully it's the instructions to put the clock back together," she said, unrolling it. She squinted, recognizing the handwriting immediately. The letter was from William's mother, Elise.

1699

My dearest future son,

Tonight, I escape my father's grasp to elope with your father, Rory MacLeod. Greatness awaits you and your heirs. This letter—with the help of the right person—is the key that unlocks the mystery.

Love,

Maman

Did William realize the scroll was hidden in a chime? Is that why he said the clock was the key to their family's greatness? And who was the 'right' person to unlock the mystery? Fiona rolled the parchment and tapped it against her lips. There was a potent scent of enchantment about it. "Did anyone else see the scroll?"

He shook no. "What if we canna fix the clock?"

"We'll fix it. Besides, I have a feeling your father's going to be delayed."

A look of pure relief fell over his sweet face.

"No need to trouble anyone about this paper, it's nothing," she said, pocketing it with the knotted yarn. That's a lot of bewitched things to handle when you're trying to avoid magic.

A short time later she tucked her younger sons in bed and lit a candle in her bedchamber window to pay homage to Beira. She flipped the scroll over, smelling a faint citrus scent. *Rather cryptic message. Why not tell William outright why our family is destined for greatness? Am I the right person to unlock the mystery?* There were a few hours left of Imbolc to scry for the answer.

Voices echoed outside, and she peeked out the window. James and the servants were coming home...along with Reverend MacDonald. *Shite.* Quickly blowing out the candle, she hid the scroll and yarn beneath her bed and went downstairs. "Reverend MacDonald. What a pleasant surprise."

"I'll have tea." He made himself quite comfortable indeed, as though he owned the manor.

Fiona and the servants exchanged looks, and the maid said she'd fetch him some.

James took off his coat and warmed his hands. "Uncle Malcolm said he dinnae ken anything about fixing grandfather clocks but will send word to his friend in Glasgow in the morning. I'm going to bed. I'm pure done in."

"Thank you, love." She kissed him goodnight. "I am too," she said for the reverend's benefit.

"I hoped we might read the Bible together this evening. I'm sure William would approve."

All night? What wrath will Beira bring on me if a candle isna lit? "Aye, Reverend. Let me check on that tea."

Fiona mixed an extra dose of chamomile and lavender in his cup, but five hours later the man was still wide awake. No point feigning an excuse to go upstairs. They both knew she wanted to light a candle for the goddess. Silently she prayed. *Eisd rium a Dhia. Beira, please have mercy on my situation and forgive my disrespect.*

Her stomach twisted in knots with all that could go wrong. If the servants gossiped about her mentioning her witchy aunt... if the reverend searched her bedchamber and found the suspicious scroll and yarn... if William came home early and learned Broderick destroyed his family heirloom... It was the perfect witch's brew of potential reckoning from her husband, the Kirk and society at large.

When daylight finally broke, the reverend left, and Fiona raced upstairs to light a candle, but the sun already shone through the window. *Ah, damn. Now I have to face the wrath of an ancient goddess too?*

Retrieving the scroll, she sighed, wishing she could scry on command. She'd have to wait until the next fire festival when her powers were stronger... and hope the good reverend wouldn't try to thwart her magic again.

Chapter 3

William MacLeod

London, Present Time—1729

William MacLeod didn't plan on picking a fight with a witch hunter, but he didn't regret it either... At first. The whole thing started at The Old Bailey prison, when he was dealing with a situation decidedly not witch-related.

"I have one rule, and one rule only," said MacLeod, letting the silence stretch. "Dinnae lie to me. Understand?"

Across the worn table, a blond lad slumped lower in his seat, eyes on the floor. Outside the grimy room, a guard jingled his keys as he walked the corridor.

"Answer him, boy." Sir Jamison landed a hard blow against his son's head.

"Yes, sir," Charles muttered, lip trembling. "I've told you everything."

He dinnae. "To convict you, they have to prove—" MacLeod paused, glancing at the father, "both penetration and ejaculation, and two witnesses are required. Beyond the two we ken about, did anyone else see you?"

"Maybe?" Charles stared out the barred interior window, looking ill.

"You mean there're more mollies to pay off?" Sir Jamison boomed.

"Wheest," MacLeod whispered. "They listen."

Sir Jamison brushed aside a loose strand from his grizzled wig. "If my only son is executed for unnatural acts, it ruins us. Who's going to buy Bibles sold by the father of a..." Growing frustrated, he pounded his fist on the table, making his son flinch. "Why is the Earl of Blackmere and his Societies for the Reformation of Manners coming after my boy? When the king appointed him to clean up all the prostitutes and riff raff at Covent Garden, I applauded it. But my son? I'm a peer, for God's sake."

MacLeod nodded in understanding, if not sympathy. People were always quick to praise a firm hand until it was applied to them. "Sir, if I'm to defend your son I need ink. Perhaps the sheriff?"

Grumbling, Sir Jamison left, the bolt clanking behind him.

"Now that he's gone, I need the truth, lad. I canna get the charge reduced to assault with sodomitical intent if multiple witnesses testify." Reaching his long arm over the table, MacLeod squeezed Charles' shoulder. "Look, I dinnae care if you like a good buggering or not, but Lord Blackmere does. If you want to avoid a noose, give me something useful. Can the witnesses name your lover?"

"He wore a mask." Tears spilled down the youth's cheeks. "I've destroyed my entire family."

"Cry when you're locked in your cell. Right now, I need you to focus. Charles, I'm the only one on your side. Lord Blackmere is a snake, using you to get to your lover. He's looking for a splashy scandal. Let me help you. What's your lover's name?"

The lad sat taller, rolling back his shoulders and wiping his nose on his coarse prison sleeve. "When I die my family will celebrate. My lover is raising his sister's children. His execution will condemn them all to poverty. I'm not only protecting him, I'm protecting them."

"You seem resolute."

"Yes, sir. I love him."

MacLeod steepled his hands, touching his fingers to his lips before placing his palms down on the table. "Look at me: I'll only say this once. Tonight at nine o' clock the door will unlock. Take the coat hanging on a hook. Inside the pocket will be a key. Use it to exit the stairwell. Outside a man will be waiting. Tap your chin twice. He'll mimic it back. Follow him to the dock and board the waiting ship."

"Where am I going?"

"Away. Say nothing to anyone, unless you have a death wish. Someone will send for you when it's safe. I'll keep your things locked at my law office."

"My father arranged this?"

MacLeod hinted a smile. "No, lad. Your lover did."

Unbolting the lock, the guard let Sir Jamison inside. "Here's the ink."

"Thank you, I believe we're done here. I'll see you both in court next Thursday. Good day, gentlemen," he said swiping the ink jar from Sir Jamison's grip.

Charles exhaled in relief. "Thank you, sir."

MacLeod walked the corridor flanked by jingling keys and slamming doors. He tossed the ink to the sheriff and exited the prison.

Outside, the bitter cold slapped his face as he passed drunks, immigrants begging for work, and a coach coming from the county gaol with half-frozen disorderly girls shackled to the outside.

Digging his hands into his coat pockets, he veered into a desolate alley where Stephen Rose's coach waited. A window curtain drew back to reveal the gentleman biting his lip as he rocked a baby over his shoulder, while two young boys battled with toy soldiers across the seat.

MacLeod climbed inside, and the boys hugged him. He nodded at Stephen. "It's done."

Stephen looked ready to cry. "Thank you, Mr. MacLeod. Whiskey?"

"I'll hold her," MacLeod said, bouncing the baby on his knee and grinning. "What a bonny one you are. I've only got sons."

Stephen pulled a bottle of whiskey and a wad of paint-smeared cash from a satchel. "Sorry, I've been painting to stay calm."

"A word of legal advice: Stay away from the molly houses. Lord Blackmere is on a cold-blooded mission. You've got your sister's bairns to protect."

"When will it be safe to send for Charles?"

"When Lord Blackmere gets bored with his new role and slithers off to something else." MacLeod handed back the baby. "Now if you'll excuse me, I have to move onto the next task: find a new laundress for Lady Hallewell."

"Isn't that the butler's job?"

"Not when it's the fifth maid in as many weeks. My lady requested my personal intervention." And by that he meant the bitch demanded he find another unsuspecting woman who'd tolerate being screamed at over wine stains. Sometimes he truly hated being the family fixer.

MacLeod waited inside the formidable Saint Marks workhouse, wrinkling his nose at the profoundly bleak surroundings. A whiff of lye from the courtyard burned his nostrils, and he loosened his silk cravat to allow for deeper breaths.

Women in groups of six stood shredding ropes into large buckets under the strict supervision of matrons. No one spoke.

Mrs. Badger, a grim matron in a muted brown dress, sturdy linen apron, and plain cap over her graying curls, greeted him with a stilted curtsey. "How may I help you today, Mr..."

"MacLeod," he said tipping his tricorn hat. "I'm looking to hire. I need a laundress who can properly clean French gowns for Lady Margaret Hallewell."

"I'm surprised you'd hire someone from here. I imagine girls from good families would queue to work at Astwick House if you advertised the position."

Another advert in the paper would fuel gossip. "Hiring people isna the problem, it's keeping them. My lady has impeccable standards," he said diplomatically. *Ack, that woman roils through servants faster than a milkmaid churns butter.*

"Of course, sir." Snapping her fingers, the matron directed a somber girl in gray to fetch the unlucky prospects. He was preemptively guilty about subjecting anyone to her ladyship's authority.

The door opened, revealing rows of clotheslines in the yard crammed with dripping shirts and petticoats. Nearby, old men broke apart boulders with mallets to make backfill for the roads.

"Look," said MacLeod in a confidential tone, "the lass needs to be skilled, but more importantly, she needs to stay out of Lady Hallewell's presence, and for God's sake, she needs to be suitably obsequious." The matron blinked blankly. He tried again. "She needs to kiss her ladyship's arse."

"Understood. We'll find you the perfect match for Lady Hallewell. We drill order, cleanliness and discipline into our girls' lazy little brains. They follow the highest moral standards."

He scoffed. Half the tarts at the brothels Lord Hallewell frequented were former residents of Saint Mark's. As he absorbed the stark, joyless room, a musty woolen smell filled the air. His gaze fell upon a line of young women in ill-fitting dresses. "They dinnae look very happy."

"If we made it too comfortable, they'd never leave, would they? I'm very proud we teach these incorrigible poor girls industry."

"Seems like they're being punished for being unwanted and alive."

Girls ranging from eight to eighteen stared straight ahead, unsmiling, save for one pretty blonde. Tilting her head back, she took in his entire frame.

"The laundress will need to be brawny," he said. "Lord Hallewell hosts fifty to sixty guests on any given day and throws even larger balls. That's a lot of linens."

The blonde girl rolled up her sleeves in an obvious attempt to show off her muscles.

He spoke to her directly. "Do you ken how to clean silk versus linen? Lady Hallewell is very particular about the treatment of her gowns."

A blush rose to the blonde's cheeks. "Aye, sir. Boil and pound linens for at least fifteen minutes using a bat and only use a wee bit of water for silk."

MacLeod's ears perked. "Are you from Scotland? I detect a burr."

"Thank you, sir, for noticing." She curtseyed deeply. "I'm from near Inverness."

"Eleanor barely knew any English when she came to us," Mrs. Badger said. "The only phrase she knew was, 'Thank you, sir.' Unfortunately, the only person who knew Gaelic spoke in Scots rather than the King's tongue. It's bad enough she's an orphan, but she's got an awful Scots accent too and, quite honestly, I haven't had the time to beat the burr out of her."

MacLeod crossed his arms over his chest staring icily until the matron's eyes went wide realizing her own rudeness. "No offense, sir. You seem a well-educated Scot."

"I hope my law professors from Oxford would agree," he said with a wry smile.

The matron smoothed down her apron, as if to regain composure and authority. "Now, before you get too wrapped around Eleanor's little finger, I should warn you that she is impulsive, and tries to charm her way out of work. It cost her many a meal, I can tell you that, sir."

Sighing, he said, "I dinnae have time for laziness. Is there another girl?"

"With respect, sir, I'm not lazy. In fact, I'm one of the hardest workers. I taught myself how to lift the toughest stains with vinegar and to use a cloth when ironing to protect expensive fabrics. The parish hires me out all the time and gives me nothing. Mrs. Badger kens this, which is why she wants to trap me here."

"You will be silent," Mrs. Badger bit out. "You're here for bed and board at the taxpayers' expense, not for your own profit."

Eleanor bit her lip. "Yes, matron."

"Ignore her, sir. She's always had more tongue than sense." She faced the group. "You other girls will do well to distance yourselves from the likes of Eleanor Cameron." Mrs. Badger put her hands on a timid brown-haired lassie's shoulders. "Here's your girl. Very obsequious."

Bells interrupted the conversation as a flock of matrons swarmed the barrels of shredded rope to inspect the workmanship.

The brunette girl stared at her feet, as though the workhouse had already killed her inside. Honestly, she'd be perfect for the job.

"I'll work twice as hard to prove my worth, and I'll never pester anyone to ask for help."

"No one is speaking to you, Eleanor," snapped Mrs. Badger. "Perhaps a night next to the dead room will cure your rebellious nature?"

MacLeod waved his hand at the matron to silence her harping. "Never ask for help? That's a fairly large promise to keep, and not one that's in your best interest either. Everyone needs help sometimes."

"I've learned I can only depend on myself." Her blue eyes begged a chance. "I promise you sir, I promise, I'll be the best laundress my Lady Hallewell has ever met."

"You have quite an ambitious nature."

Eleanor's blue eyes pleaded. "I will do anything to avoid being here another day."

MacLeod chuckled at her feistiness. She was hungry, and hard, and the fact she stood up for herself made her an awful candidate for the position.

But still.

Lady Margaret had been nothing but a pain in his arse. Sod that aristocratic bitch. This could be fun. "I'll hire this one, Mrs. Badger."

Everyone gasped, and an enormous grin crawled across Eleanor's face. "Thank you, sir."

MacLeod noticed Eleanor subtly make the sign of the cross as the coach steered onto the private road. In the distance, Lord Hallewell's three-story palace with gray-white columns loomed large as flurries fell.

"It's hard to believe such a grand estate hides in the city, sir."

He flipped a page of his newspaper. She kept leaning over to squint at the satirical drawings, which grated on his nerves.

"I've only ever seen people read Bibles. Is it interesting?"

"Yes." He turned to a page with no pictures.

Eleanor took the hint and pressed her hands against the window. She waved at a group of stable boys putting stallions through their paces, then tilted her head at the enormous sculpture of a soldier on a rearing horse. "My lord is a military man?"

"No. That was Lady Margaret Hallewell's first husband. He was a general."

"Hm. Sounds like old Maggie's the one with the cash." She covered both hands over her mouth, immediately recognizing her mistake.

"Look at me, Eleanor Cameron. The Hallewells trace their ancestry to the country's oldest noble families. If you want to last more than a day, keep your gob shut and heed my advice. All servants are to be discreet, loyal to the family, and chaste. Is that understood?"

"Yes, Mr. MacLeod." Eleanor's cheeks flamed. "T'was only looking out the window, sir," she mumbled.

They crossed an arched bridge over a winding pond that led to a mansion tall enough to block the winter sun. Servants assembled, shivering in formation. Men wore livery distinguishing their jobs, and the women dressed better than most ladies in town, save for their unpowdered hair and stark white bib aprons.

MacLeod faced her. "Welcome to Astwick House. This place will test your mettle. Do your job, and we willnae have a problem. Cross me and

I can be quite the devil." It was important to make the servants a wee bit nervous to keep them in check.

Swallowing hard, she nodded.

The footman reached for her hand, giving her the once-over as his hot breath steamed the air. MacLeod rolled his eyes as he shoved past them. The butler stepped forward and bowed. "Is this the new laundress, Mr. MacLeod?"

"Aye. Her name's Eleanor Cameron." To Eleanor, "This is Mr. Belmont, the head butler. He'll get you sorted out." To Belmont, "Is his lordship inside?"

"Yes, sir. Her ladyship would like a word with you too."

He sighed, about as happy as a man getting his tooth pulled. Tucking the newspaper under his arm, he strode inside. "I have an important matter to discuss with his lordship first."

MacLeod held out the quill pen, but Lord George Hallewell hesitated to sign. His lordship's face was the epitome of the clashing harmonies he liked to play, a hidden discord behind the polished surface.

"My lord, the investment is sound. Not to brag, but even I'm impressed I convinced the marquess to agree to such favorable terms. As soon as you sign, I'll file it with the court."

"You? Brag?" Lord Hallewell smirked, leaving his enormous walnut desk to visit the decanter stand. He poured himself port while MacLeod stayed by the desk, wondering what his mercurial friend was thinking.

Lord Hallewell seemed distracted, avoiding eye contact and swirling the liquid in his glass. "While I'm pleased, I'm also — what's the word? — suspicious. Why would he agree so quickly?"

"He dinnae. I've been working for three months on this deal. The time is now. This opportunity is fleeting, and I need to get home. Reverend MacDonald must be working himself into a lather that my tenants are getting up to pagan rituals again."

Lord Hallewell smirked. "Do you remember when you and Fiona took me to my first Beltane festival?" His eyes grew animated. "I'd obviously danced around a maypole before, but to see the bonfire sparks escape into the night, and the dancing, and all the couples sneaking off to christen the fields…" Lord Hallewell poured MacLeod a whiskey. "While I was minding James, you and Fiona were off for a particularly long time, I recall."

"Well, I wanted a good harvest," MacLeod chuckled, taking the dram. "I planted David in her belly that night."

"One must follow traditions." Lord Hallewell raised his glass. "To the King."

"Slàinte Mhòr." MacLeod drained the drink, enjoying the quality whiskey George always kept for him.

"I vividly remember Fiona carrying a torch from the bonfire to build up a new fire in your hearth, and did those saining rituals while whispering incantations in Gaelic. It was so primal, and raw, and I felt alive. I cherish that time, even though I didn't realize it then." Lord Hallewell swirled the port in his glass. "You should head home, before the good reverend grows suspicious of your wife's witchy inclinations again. That was a costly mistake for everyone."

They shared an uncomfortable silence.

"Aye, lord." MacLeod's jaw tightened, longing to change the subject. He held out the quill again, sliding the contract in front of Lord Hallwell.

Lord Hallewell's eyes danced away from it. "This purchase isn't opportune. I've lost interest."

"As you wish, my lord." He put the contract away in his satchel. *Why is George suddenly risk averse?*

Lady Margaret barged in like a hailstorm.

"My lady." MacLeod bowed at her entrance. "I've hired the new laundress you requested."

"Do shut it, Mac *Loud*." Waving a letter she addressed her husband. "How long were you going to keep this secret? You assumed I'd never find out?"

A blush crept across Lord Hallewell's face. "You've ransacked my desk?"

"It pales compared to your ravaging of my household."

"I'll wait outside."

"No. You should see this." Lord Hallewell looked sheepish. "I've gotten myself into a bit of a jam. Well, show him the letter, darling," he said with an acid tongue.

MacLeod read.

My Dear Hallewell,

I hope this note finds you less forgetful than you've lately shown yourself around the tables at Branton Club. You owe a hefty sum, my friend. £666, to be precise. An amount, I dare say, that harkens back to less savory episodes in your family history. We wouldn't want a repeat of your father's misfortunes, would we?

I've also heard troubling murmurs regarding your private affairs. Allegations of bastards born to common women? Providing legal aid to sodomites? One wonders what your esteemed wife makes of it all.

Let's dispense with this unpleasantness swiftly, shall we? Do be a good man and settle your accounts by Friday lest I arrange for you to reside in the same cell where your father died. As head of Societies for the Reformation of Manners, I am clearly concerned about debts, both moral and monetary, for the good of the realm.

Ever yours in keen anticipation,

The Right Honorable Richard Atthill, Earl of Blackmere

MacLeod lowered the letter. *Ah, shite.*

"Six hundred sixty-six pounds, husband? That could buy a row house. And what, exactly is he implying about sodomites and bastards?"

"You're one to talk about illegitimate sons."

Her eyes widened at the reprimand, but she stayed put. "Beyond brothels, am I to assume you're frequenting the molly houses too?"

"Heavens, no. It's nothing, Margaret. An acquaintance got caught up in a scandal and I suggested MacLeod help with his legal defense."

"I handled it this morning, by the bye."

"Why on earth would either of you help the dregs of society? I say 'brava' to Lord Blackmere for cleaning up our streets. I read in *The Tatler* he arrested dozens of men at Mother Clap's, and three witches in London. Hang them all, I say. But focus on the matter at hand. What of your gambling debts?"

Lord Hallewell swirled his drink like a sullen child. "Margaret, I'm handling it. These are none of your concerns. Go embroider something. Your constant harping hurts my ears." He drained his drink.

Mr. Belmont entered. "My lord, your new harpsichord arrived. You bade me to fetch you when it came."

"How much did that cost?" she said.

Lord Hallewell strode past her like a rogue in the key of D major to inspect his latest toy.

Facing MacLeod, Lady Margaret unleashed her fury. "That idiotic coxcomb thinks this is none of my concern? Is he mad? If you want any funds left to be trustee of, you'd best rein in your friend promptly. Fix it, MacLeod."

"My lady, I will sort it."

"Will you? You're the one who put me in this precarious situation."

"Begging your pardon, my lady, but you got yourself into hot water long before we met."

She slapped him hard enough to leave a mark... not so hard to make him blink... which clearly infuriated her even more. "You put my son's fortune at risk, you odious Scottish extortionist."

Hold fast, MacLeod. "I'm on your side, my lady. Please stop yelling. It makes you look unhinged when obviously, you're in the right."

"Don't use that condescending tone with me. My ancestors were dining with kings while yours were herding sheep in the mountains," she snarled with ever-increasing volume. "He spends my money left and right on the most ridiculous things imaginable. We have an entire room dedicated to musical instruments from Italy to Africa. Is he trying to assemble a bloody orchestra?"

"Your money, my lady?" said Lord Hallewell reentering. "Mr. MacLeod, has the king changed the rules of coverture?"

Lady Margaret bit her lip, averting her eyes.

I bloody hate being in the middle of their spats. "Not to my knowledge, my lord."

"Perhaps if you weren't such a frigid woman, I wouldn't need to escape as often." His eyes were glassy. He moved close to her, invading her space but keeping his voice barely above a whisper. "Do not go through my things. Do not disrespect my authority in front of servants. I will handle this. Understood?"

I'm merely his servant now?

Dipping into a curtsey she nodded then left, crushing Blackmere's letter in her fist.

Lord Hallewell poured himself more port, scowling into his drink. "Looks like my wife used your cheek as a proxy for me. Her imprint is as red as your hair."

"What happened at the club, my lord?" He removed the decanter to a side table.

Lord Hallewell slumped on a couch in front of the fireplace. "Ever since Lord Blackmere was appointed head of the Society for the Reformation of Manners, he's been positively insufferable, making thinly veiled jokes with a forked undertone of malice about my father, trying to ensnare me into a duel. I only joined the game to shut him up. He cheats. And he has no manners. You know I speak the truth."

"Aye, he's a bastard, but you ken that and played the game anyway," he said sitting in the armchair kitty-corner. "Why have you gotten yourself on the wrong side of a powerful earl? Just because he tore down your father dinnae mean you should let him do the same to you."

"What are you implying? I'm the victim here on all counts. My wife shouldn't go through my desk, searching for reasons to fight. Why can't she be more like Fiona? I know the circumstances of our nuptials weren't based on love, but I hoped we'd become friends. I'm raising her sons as though they're my own, after all. She doesn't even want to hold our daughter. Why isn't she a normal, loving woman? I can't understand her."

"Six hundred sixty-six pounds, George?"

The slip into familiarity was only half accidental, and it didn't escape Lord Hallewell.

"You condemned me to this loveless marriage, so yes, *William*, yes, I like to play cards to take my mind off my miserable existence." He left the couch to reclaim his decanter then sloppily poured himself another. "God, I wish someone would come into my life and rescue me." He banged the glass down. "I was one card away from a royal flush. I knew he was bluffing. I'm sure he slipped the queen of hearts up his velvet sleeve. There's a reason people call him Supple Dick."

Multiple reasons. MacLeod closed the door and locked it. "Shall we face the music?"

"God, no. Don't make me look at it." Lord Hallewell flopped onto his leather chair and laid his head on the desk. "The room is spinning already."

MacLeod strolled behind the desk and removed the five-foot-tall portrait of Lord Hallewell on the wall, still smelling of fresh paint, and opened the lockbox hidden inside the wall. "You might vomit soon enough," he said, opening the ledger on the desk and updating the columns with his quill. "Six hundred sixty-six pounds due to Richard Atthill, Earl of Blackmere, four pounds to pay for the upkeep of your most recent ex-courtesan's bastard, plus whatever you paid for the harpsichord. That's quite a month of expenditures, my lord."

"Too bad you didn't pay off my ex sooner. She's the one who ran her mouth off to Lord Blackmere because I refused to triple her allowance."

"I will address it." MacLeod held his stare. "My legal advice? Pay Lord Blackmere what you owe him. Now that he's head of Reformation of Manners, he can use the law like a weapon against any real or perceived enemies. It's a losing battle. My advice as your friend? Rein in your spending, ease up at the brothels, and pull yourself together, man. Canna you lie with your wife more often? It might put her in a better mood. Besides, bastards are costly, and you risk getting the French disease. You willnae find what you're looking for at the bottom of a bottle of port."

Lord Hallewell tuned him out, staring into the fire.

"I best finish packing. Have a good evening, lord."

"No." Lord Hallewell pointed at him. "Before you leave, get Supple Dick Atthill off my back."

"Fine. Give me six hundred sixty-six quid."

"I'm not paying that self-righteous hypocrite one penny. Sue him for being a cheat. Let's see if you're as good a barrister as my father always said you were. Although, he died in Newgate Gaol, didn't he?" Lord Hallewell poured another drink. "Fix it, MacLeod."

I hate it when he gets like this. "Aye, I'll handle everything, as always, but what about the next time? How much money do you intend to squander this week?"

"People owe me money too, if you ever collected it. I don't pay you to be liked. Rough, MacLeod, otherwise I'll be an easy mark for anyone seeking money."

"You already are an easy mark, my lord."

"Fuck off." Slowly Lord Hallewell finished his drink as MacLeod waited to be dismissed. There was a modulation in Lord Hallewell's manner, as swift and startling as a key change. His arrogance softened into vulnerability. "Am I becoming my father, gambling as much as I do?"

"You take risks I'd never take. It's like you're begging for a scandal."

An angry spark flashed over Lord Hallewell's face. "You dare speak to me about scandal? How's your wife doing?"

A chill fell between them.

"I'll send letters to Lord Blackmere and your debtors on my way out of town."

"You'll go home when the job is done, and my strong boxes are full of coin again."

MacLeod bristled to be put in check. "Aye, lord. I'll tame your shrewish concubine, collect all your debts, and get Supple Dick off your back forthwith." *How did everything go to hell so quickly? Now I have three new knotty problems to fix. Fiona is going to be furious with my delay.*

Lord Hallewell walked him to the edge of the room then grinned. The new girl was staring at the ceiling with her mouth agape.

Oh bugger. MacLeod forgot one vital detail when he hired the lass: Lord Hallewell had a known weakness for blondes.

Chapter 4

ELEANOR

London—Astwick House

A chandelier stuffed with beeswax candles had drawn Eleanor's eyes up thirty feet to the most stunning image she'd ever seen. Painted on the ceiling was God himself half hidden by a cloud, and surrounded by winged angels with wee fat arses merrily playing on harps. Eleanor had to cover her mouth to stifle her laughter. *Who would ever paint such a thing, and on a ceiling no less?*

"Are you lost?" asked Mr. MacLeod. He quickly closed the door to the private study, but not before she glimpsed a handsome nobleman holding a drink.

I get to look at the likes of him every day? Eleanor's stomach fluttered in anticipation of her improved future. *The witch of Pye's fortunetelling was right. I'm walking among the nobility.*

The footman was still flirting with her something awful, finding a reason to trail her partway into the hall. She didn't pay him too much attention. She wanted to focus on moving up the ranks to become a lady's maid, the most powerful position someone like her could attain, rather than dallying with a fart sucker whose face was always in the path of a nobleman's bum.

"I was just taking her inside, Mr. MacLeod," said the footman.

"Well, you've done it. On your way."

Mr. MacLeod reminded her of an enormous bull, slow and powerful, built for impact.

"Follow me. I'm Mrs. Clark," said an older woman dressed in black with an enormous key ring tied round her waist. The crone shook her head and tsk-tsked. "We need to get your mismatched clothes sorted before Lady Hallewell sees you. You represent Astwick House now."

"Yes, ma'am, thank you ma'am."

Astwick House was bigger than a city block and more beautiful than a cathedral. Gripping the handle of her carpetbag, Eleanor noted its emptiness. Eight years in a London workhouse didn't give her much beyond one nightshirt, an old comb, and a rag to rub her teeth clean.

A flash of Da's haunted face climbing the ladder, leaving her alone in the dark orlop made goosebumps crawl up her arm. *'Stay hidden,' he said. 'I'll be right back. Everything will be better in London.'* She shook her head, interrupting the memory. *His musings willnae spoil my day.*

She stared at the grand marble stairwell and imagined herself standing on it, dressed in a ball gown as wealthy men vied for her attention.

"Get a move on, girl," Mrs. Clark said.

Each step echoed as they traveled the long hallway lined with suits of armor. "This is the loveliest place I've ever seen, ma'am."

"Indeed. But touch nothing unless specifically directed," Mrs. Clark said. "Women sleep on the third floor east wing and the men stay on the west wing. Don't even try sneaking to the wrong side, that door remains locked. Only Mr. Belmont, Mr. MacLeod, and I have keys. You're a pretty girl, so heed my warning."

"Thank you ma'am, I'm a good girl," she said as they climbed the servant stairwell. "What job does Mr. MacLeod do, ma'am? He's rather young to be so important. What is he, just shy of thirty?"

"He's Lord Hallewell's personal solicitor and is not a man to be trifled with. Honestly, he does whatever the family needs no matter the task, even something as low as hiring a servant if required. If you see him on the servant side, it's never a good sign."

They moved down the main hall towards a second set of stairs. Like a fireball barreling towards hell, a lady in a most fashionable gown of red silk and golden threads flew up the grand stairwell at the opposite end and down the hall with petticoats billowing. Mrs. Clark gasped, pushing Eleanor toward an empty room, but it was too late. The noblewoman crashed headfirst into Eleanor, knocking them both to the ground.

"Who is this godforsaken wretch before me?"

"I'm Eleanor, ma'am," she said rubbing her head. A letter had fallen beside her, and she picked it up. The lady quickly snatched it from her hand.

"Don't touch my things. How dare you?" The lady whipped off a finely heeled shoe and bashed the side of Eleanor's head.

Scrambling to her feet, it took every ounce of Eleanor's might to not throw a punch and lose her job the first day.

"My lady, this is the new laundress Mr. MacLeod hired."

"MacLeod can bugger off to hell."

The 'lady' slid her silken weapon over her foot and stormed into her bedchamber, letter in hand. Eleanor rubbed her forehead above her brow and discovered blood, then stared down the hall. "Who was that?"

"Lady Hallewell." Mrs. Clark moved quickly toward the end of the hall, making all the keys tied around her waist rattle. Eleanor hustled to keep pace as they climbed a narrow staircase to the attic. They entered a small room with two beds and a trunk. "We often refer to Lady Hallewell as a weather report. 'Approaching tempest with gale force wind,' or 'sunny skies at the moment.'"

"I'll be sure to avoid the tornado next time."

Mrs. Clark chuckled. "You're fearlessly optimistic, aren't you? I daresay you'll be gone within a fortnight." She pulled a handkerchief from her pocket and softly dabbed the cut. "Lady Hallewell can be...Working for a noble family requires great discretion. Even if you only last a few days, your loyalty is required for a lifetime."

"Dinnae fash, I've been treated much worse, and stayed mum."

"Haven't we all, dear?" she sighed. "Jane," she called.

A mousy girl, perhaps fifteen, appeared holding a brush darkened with shoe polish.

"You'll be sharing the room with Jane, the scullery maid. Your livery is in the trunk. Always keep yourself presentable. Breakfast is served at six o'clock sharp; your duties begin immediately after. Besides the washing, you'll be required to complete the mending for the family. Lord Hallewell's valet will supervise, obviously. I'll leave you to dress. Jane will show you to the laundry room."

"Matron, is this room only for two people?"

"I'm not the matron, and this isn't the workhouse. You get your own bed here, Emily."

"It's Eleanor, ma'am."

Mrs. Clark squeezed her hand. "No disrespect, dear, but I won't bother to learn your name. I'll write you a good reference letter, though."

When the door closed, Eleanor dropped her carpet bag and waited for Mrs. Clark's footsteps to disappear. "Tell me true, Jane. How do you like it here?"

"Fair enough," Jane shrugged. "Food's good. Lord Hallewell's quite kind...and handsome," she giggled, pretending to fan herself. Jane squinted at Eleanor's forehead. "I see you've met Lady Margaret. Stormy skies turned bruise-purple already? Are you alright?"

Eleanor peered out the small window overlooking a meticulously maintained, albeit frozen, garden with a glimpse of the city and the Thames winding beyond. "My head throbs a bit, but nothing a swig of gin canna cure. Ken anyone who drinks around here?"

"Mayhaps." Snickering, Jane checked the hall. When all was clear, she dragged a bottle from beneath her mattress, took a sip, then offered it to Eleanor.

Eleanor took a swig. "Tell me about MacLeod. It seems like he's the real one in charge."

"My god, he's scary," Jane said.

"But he's got a nice arse."

Jane laughed. "True enough, but I'd stay away. His wife, Fiona, is a witch."

Eleanor thought the music was a dream, but it continued after she rose from bed. Soft moonlight spilled into the room. Outside, the frozen garden glistened, reminding her of tales of the fae calling her to their secret, magical world.

Earlier, she had opened the window, despite the cold, because she'd never been allowed to touch the windows at Saint Mark's. How refreshing to have a measure of control over the air.

Notes carried on the wind, and she realized it came from the open window on the ground floor three stories beneath her room. Who would play music at this hour?

Peeking out of her bedroom, the empty hall echoed with the typical sounds of slumber. Barefoot, she padded softly. Mrs. Clark's door was closed, but the volume of her snores left no doubt she was asleep. Eleanor removed a hairpin and easily picked the lock—a useful trick learned at Saint Mark's.

Dinnae go, Eleanor. You'll get cast out your first night.

Sneaking down the narrow wooden stairs, she strove to be light as a kitten to not make anything creak. Soft carpets paved the second-floor hallway. His Lordship and Her Ladyship's bedchambers were separate but adjacent, apparently. Mrs. Clark warned repeatedly to never walk down that hall, nor visit the children's nursery, nor look directly at Her Ladyship, nor appear in her presence. Indeed, all servants must work like the devil, then bugger off like ghosts into the shadows when high society persons arrived.

As she descended the portrait-lined stairwell, it felt like a hundred nobles were watching her take outlawed steps. Polished marble chilled her toes, and she gripped the banister in thrilled anticipation.

A full moon shone through the main entryway windows, casting odd shadows against the end tables as she stood on the shining floor, staring at an enormous family portrait visible in the parlor to the side.

She snuck out of the workhouse before, which was fun, but nothing like this. How delicious to do the forbidden?

Also, how risky?

The notes grew louder, almost violent, and she made the sign of the cross. The hall ended with a slightly open door. Dim candlelight gave off a yellowish glow as music floated from within.

If someone catches me, I'll say...what? We've been told to use the chamber pots in the room. There's no plausible reason for me to be wandering. I'll say I'm sleepwalking? Should I go back?

Almost as if in answer, the music grew softer, barely loud enough to hear. A few more steps would solve the mystery. Creeping forward, Eleanor glimpsed inside.

Lord Hallewell's finely embroidered blue coat hung over a chair. A powdered peruke rested on top of a nearby globe, exposing an inch of his thick auburn hair. Masculine and strong, Lord Hallewell's silhouette was striking. Blinking at his state of partial undress, she stared at his open shirt tucked into his dark breeches, noting his back muscles spread and flex as he played.

His relative youth startled her. It was astonishing he was only in his late twenties and at the pinnacle of everything in life—looks, wealth, stature. Despite that, he appeared as approachable, vulnerable, and human as any man strolling in the park. Light from the candelabra revealed a glass of port and a nearly empty decanter beside it. Why would a man who had everything play such haunting melodies?

Eleanor became mesmerized watching his long fingers teasing their way across the length of the harpsichord keys and grew lost in the music, captivated by its sheer beauty. As he rocked, his eyes remained closed, as if he were telling a desperate story, spilling secrets in the night.

The notes stopped abruptly, and he swiveled to face her, squinting into the darkness. "Margaret, is that you?"

Eleanor bolted, which was clearly a stupid thing to do, but she couldn't think straight. Lifting her shift to avoid tripping, she scrambled upstairs, with her heart nearly thumping out of her chest. From the corner of her eye, she glimpsed him in his open shirt, holding his drink, staring.

As quietly as possible, she launched up the second set of stairs to the attic, grateful she left the door propped open, and jumped into her bed. Every inch of her body tightened.

Shite, fuck, damn. He's going to have Mr. MacLeod turn me out tomorrow.

A week later, Eleanor searched for an escape route but had nowhere to hide once Lady Margaret entered the laundry building. *What was the weather report? Twister on the horizon? Has Lord Hallewell told her I snuck out of the maids' quarters and went into a forbidden room the other night?*

Aware of her ladyship's disapproving gaze, Eleanor lowered herself into a curtsey.

"No one knows how to fold linens properly these days."

Am I to answer? "Apologies, m'lady. I dinnae ken how to fold it in a grand house, but I'll fix it to your liking, aye?"

Lady Margaret slid her hands to her hips. "Bloody goddamned hell, you're Scottish? Is that why MacLeod hired you?"

Eleanor blinked in shock at the noblewoman's language—crude as any sailor's. She reckoned only riffraff like the Saint Mark's girls spoke that way. "With respect, my lady, I never lain eyes on the man until he hired me at the workhouse, and from what I hear I dinnae ever want to cross him."

An exasperated snort escaped Lady Margaret as she pinched the flesh between her brows. "The workhouse. Of course, he found you there. Well, your prayers have been answered, I suppose. It is a privilege for someone of your sort to work at Astwick House. The last idiot barely lasted a week. If I suspect the hint of a stain on any of my gowns, I'll beat you myself before casting you out."

"Yes, m'lady. I'm very grateful for the opportunity indeed." Eleanor's knees grew sore staying in a curtsey and her head still carried a shoe-shaped bruise, but she didn't dare rise unbidden. After all, a hot iron sat on the table, and the lord in heaven only knew what this bitch might throw next.

"You may rise," Lady Margaret said, plucking a folded napkin and tossing it on the table. "Linens should be folded in thirds with a crisp line. Everyone knows that."

"Aye, ma'am. Thank you, m'lady." Eleanor briskly folded it as instructed, even pressing the iron over it to remove wrinkles. With a gulp, she moved efficiently, refolding the entire stack, doing her best to please the lady, who supervised with fists on hips.

Eleanor guessed at her age. A wee bit younger than Lord Hallewell. Twenty-two maybe? And living in a palace, married to the most handsome, talented, and worldliest man she ever met. *If Lord Hallewell were mine, we'd be making our own midnight music.*

"Who told you not to cross MacLeod?" Lady Margaret probed casually.

Is this the eye before the storm? Clearly, this is a test. I'm supposed to show loyalty and discretion to the family, but is MacLeod part of the family? "He warned me himself, m'lady. He said he could be the devil if I crossed him."

Lady Margaret cracked a smile. "Of course he did. He'll be the first person to tell you how important he is."

Ah, Maggie dinnae like MacLeod. "Thank you, m'lady." Fold, fold, fold into thirds, iron out the wrinkles. *Let's see if she likes flattery.* "What an honor it is for a girl like me to work for such a fine, upstanding family from the oldest noble lines."

Lady Margaret nodded, raising her chin. "I'm descended from the Habsburgs."

Eleanor gave a wicked grin. "I wonder who Mr. MacLeod's ancestors might be?" *Come on Maggie. Let's see if you're willing to take the bait.*

"Shepherds, no doubt."

Eleanor giggled. Fold, fold, fold into thirds, iron out the wrinkles. "Perhaps his wife descends from the land of the fae."

"What do you know of his wife?"

Fold, fold—hold. Eleanor peeked over her shoulder. "'Tis gossip, m'lady. I shouldna have spoken." She wasn't exactly play-acting out her fear, but it did add to the liveliness of the conversation.

Lady Margaret leaned in. "Don't be afraid. I'll protect you from MacLeod, providing you speak the truth."

Clear skies and sun shining. Looks like I'm keeping my job after all.

"It's more a slur than a truthful description, I'm sure." The pit of her stomach grew queasy. *What if the rumors about his wife are true? Do I really want to pick a fight with a witch? Still, if I can win this impossible noblewoman to my side, perhaps I can move up in the household. Maybe even become her lady's maid, and she'll take me on all her travels, or give me her discarded gowns.* Checking over her shoulder again, she lowered her voice. "Some say Mr. MacLeod's wife is a witch." Eleanor studied the noblewoman's unreadable face.

"My husband mentioned someone in Fiona's family had been burned at the stake."

Eleanor gasped, making the sign of the cross. She hadn't heard that part.

Lady Margaret chuckled. "Is witchcraft hereditary?"

"Aye, m'lady, I'm sure of it. But sometimes a witch will invite a new maiden into their coven to worship Queen Beira. My mam warned me all about it growing up."

"Whom? Is this a Scottish queen? Is she related to the Stuart line?"

"Beggin' your pardon, m'lady. Beira is the Queen of Winter. She has skin blue as a dead man's corpse, and rust colored teeth, and she's a vengeful old hag that keeps the wind and snow blowing through the mountains. She's the most powerful goddess in all of Scotland, and some people still worship her in secret to this day."

"Oh," said Lady Margaret, decidedly unimpressed. "Pagan rubbish. I was curious if Fiona was a proper witch, one that sold her soul to the Devil. Now that would be deliciously interesting gossip, as well as felonious. Can you imagine Mr. MacLeod, a barrister no less, having to watch his own wife condemned to burn?"

As Lady Margaret covered her giggling mouth, Eleanor's discomfort spread.

"What else have you heard, Eleanor?"

Gossip could have deadly consequences. She didn't even know Mr. MacLeod's wife and after all, wasn't he the one who took her out of the workhouse in the first place? As raw ambition collided with morality, she hedged her bets. "I'll be sure to keep my ears open, m'lady."

"The linens are looking better. I'm off for tea."

Chapter 5

WILLIAM MACLEOD

London

William MacLeod barreled inside Jonathan's Coffee House squinting past clouds of pipe smoke as he searched for The Right Honorable Richard Atthill, Earl of Blackmere. Too bad it wasn't a tavern, it had been a long week detangling three knotty situations before he could escape London.

First, he had to dispatch Lord Hallewell's gold-digging former mistress. After a firm but courteous conversation—and a binding agreement severe enough to make the devil blanch—she swore eternal silence about the affair with Lord Hallewell. MacLeod pledged to find her bastard child a decent home, pressed forty shillings into her hand, and secured her passage back to the Paris theater from whence she came. One nuisance down.

Second, he collected all past due debts owed to his lordship. While trained in the law, he found a swift punch to a debtor's gut was just as effective and less time consuming than legal proceedings.

And now, he reached the third and final task before he could return home. *If only I could have a wee dram before dealing with this venomous man.* "Lord Blackmere," he said standing across the table. "Well done on your new role leading the Society for the Reformation of Manners, my lord."

"I serve at the pleasure of my sovereign." Lord Blackmere's eyes gleamed with cold, slitted malice. Blowing on his coffee he took a sip and offered MacLeod a seat. "Let me guess, you want whiskey?"

"Just because I'm Scots dinnae mean I only drink one beverage. I'm surprised you wanted to meet here instead of the club."

"My dear MacLeod," said Lord Blackmere, "I wonder at your astonishment. You possess neither the clout nor the peerage to get into the gentlemen's clubs I attend."

"It's interesting that the king selected you as head reformer. With respect, my lord, I never considered you a moral crusader." MacLeod discreetly slid him the cash hidden inside a folded newspaper.

Lord Blackmere smirked. "Don't you believe peasants should behave in a godly manner? Honestly, they're merely children in want of a strong father to keep them in check." He sipped his coffee. "For as much hobnobbing and legal work you do for the nobility, a title from the king seems overdue. That must sting."

"Such is life. But we're not speaking of me, we're speaking of you."

"Are we? I thought we were speaking of Lord George Hallewell."

"With respect, my lord, kindly stop needling the man. You ken he's notoriously thin-skinned about his father's arrest."

"Why do you think I bring it up so often?" His laughter was a dry rattle, void of warmth or mercy. "His father's condiddling left many a man bankrupt. Had I known, I'd have never gotten involved with the investments with him."

Hints of horse shit wafted in from the street, mixing with the smell of rain-soaked wool coats as men came inside to escape the sudden downpour.

"If there's nothing further, my lord, I'm off to Scotland."

"You're going home? Isn't Thursday your court date?"

Shite. "Yes, of course. I'm leaving after Thursday."

"Perhaps you'd already heard your client escaped the prison?"

"Escaped?" MacLeod kept his face still.

"Mr. MacLeod, you appear quite amused with yourself. People like you always laugh and shrug off efforts to bring about order, and then wonder why London has become a cesspool of crime and debauchery. Have you walked Pye Street lately? Because I have. It's crammed with drunks, thieves, whores, violent immigrants, and witches ready to take the margins of society down even darker paths." Blackmere allowed his words to sink in. "How's your coffee, Mr. MacLeod?"

"Bitter."

"A man like you who carries a claymore with the inscription *Justice* seems an unlikely friend of a libertine like Lord Hallewell."

MacLeod glanced up.

"Surprised I've heard of your weapon's name? You carry a clan code of honor yet defend sodomites? I suppose all men have their secrets," he said with provocative calculation. "I never see your wife in London."

MacLeod took a long sip, weighing the danger level of the situation. "I note you've avoided marriage all together. But I suppose your work investigating the molly houses keeps you busy." *What did this arsehole want?* "You see me in London because Lord Hallewell pays me exorbitantly well to handle his legal matters, which helps support my lovely wife and four sons."

"That explains what Hallewell wants. I queried what you want. You're quite the contradiction. A barrister and a brute. A Scot who spends his time in London. Are you a hero or villain?"

"Just a man."

"What a terrible answer. Aim to be a hero."

Like you heroically cheat at cards, Supple Dick?

"George Hallewell is like his fraudster father—his reckless nature will bring about his demise. Apparently, the only reason he has any stature at all is because you arranged his marriage to a wealthy widow. Rather than throwing your lot with a gambling, whoring, rake like Lord Hallewell, you should expand your clientele."

MacLeod narrowed his eyes. "Whom should I include, my lord?"

"Every time you represent a person we arrest, he gets away, either literally or because the witnesses have a change of heart. I note the scars on your knuckles. It seems you're as skilled with your fists as a quill."

MacLeod sipped his coffee.

"How can I entice you to switch sides? I could use a man like you."

MacLeod sat taller despite himself. "A man like what, if I may ask?" It had been a while since Lord Hallewell bothered to notice his intelligence, hard work, or character.

"You know, a man willing to dirty his hands to get the job done. Every nobleman needs an enforcer."

Blinking, he leaned away. *Is that how everyone sees me nowadays? A brute for hire?*

"Let me teach you the art of interrogation, Mr. MacLeod. I come from a long line of witch hunters, and I daresay I'm quite skilled at making vermin confess."

MacLeod's muscles tensed at the phrase *witch hunter. Did Blackmere know anything about Fiona?*

"I sense not only would you excel at it, you'd probably like it, dear boy. There's something exhilarating knowing you have complete domination over a person, watching him squirm then submit. Help me return the realm to her former glory. I'd pay you better, get you in front of the right people. You're an ambitious man, right? I heard they called you King's Attorney at Oxford."

How much does he ken about me? "That's an old nickname." His broad shoulders slumped ever so slightly at his failure to climb the rungs of society. But at least Blackmere didn't seem to know, or care, about his wife.

"It's a real possibility. My guess is the only reason you help these dregs of society escape is because you do your master's bidding. Expose Lord Hallewell's secrets and advance yourself."

Had it been any other man sitting across the table, MacLeod would have charged and gored him for even suggesting such a dishonorable thing, but considering MacLeod had his own secrets to keep buried, there was no point in provoking an earl newly appointed to round up witches. "Lord Hallewell has no secrets to expose, and I couldna possibly abandon my favorite client to work for the government, but if you're looking to expand your estate holdings further, I can set you up with a sweet deal my lord rejected. I'll require a hefty fee though."

"I can see you're no man's beast to be bowed. Consider the estate purchase done and done. In fact, I have quite a bit of legal work I can throw your way. Ponder my offer Mr. MacLeod. We're better yoked as allies than adversaries."

MacLeod waited in Lord Hallewell's study, hands clasped behind his back. He smelled Lady Margaret's narcissus perfume before he saw her.

Leaning close, she spoke in an icy hush, her expression darkening like black-bellied clouds before a storm. "What of Lord Blackmere's threat to investigate my husband's love life? How will that impact me and the children? Will the earl threaten my son's inheritance every time George loses a hand of cards?"

Lord Hallewell came in giving a side-eyed glance at his wife. "To what do I owe the pleasure of your visit, good wife?"

"I was on my way out."

"Wait. I suppose you deserve to be updated too." Lord Hallewell poured a glass of port. "Have you settled everything?"

"Aye, my lord."

"You're sure I didn't pay Supple Dick a penny?"

"The people in debt to you paid the six hundred sixty-six quid; you dinnae pay a thing."

"I don't appreciate your self-serving wit, MacLeod."

"Aye, but neither of you would appreciate facing the Society of Manners snooping into your various sexual exploits."

Lord and Lady Hallewell avoided each other's eyes.

"Lord Blackmere is a fork-tongued man with legacy hatreds. He's the menacing sort who only feels powerful when he's threatening lesser prey. Dinnae allow him to get the upper hand, stay out of his way, and all will be well."

"It better be," she said with a frosty snap of her fan, leaving sans thanks.

He exhaled to be done. "I'm off to Scotland."

"Before you rush off..."

Ah, shite. What now?

Lord Hallewell poured him a dram of whiskey. "We left on poor terms. Too much port can loosen my tongue to say unkind things."

"Ah. It's the port's fault you disrespected my wife?" Each word was deliberate, like a warning that preceded a charge.

"I meant no harm. Truly." He offered MacLeod the whiskey. "Friends again?"

MacLeod took the drink. He'd forgive, for now, but he'd never forget. These instances of Lord Hallewell throwing the Colonel Wilkes situation in his face resurfaced increasingly often. "To the King."

"To the King." They both drank. "Tell me about the new scullery maid," Lord Hallewell said shifting modulation.

"You mean the laundress?"

"I mean the blonde maiden," he said sitting on the corner of his desk grinning.

"My lord, I just found a home for your last bastard. Do you really want to create a new one?"

"That was purely accidental."

MacLeod chuckled. "Oh? You accidentally fell on top of a naked woman when your cock was hard?"

"I'm never going to get mixed up with an actress again. They're too dramatic," he said, moving to the couch with a flourish.

"Eleanor Cameron is eighteen—"

"What a delightful age."

"Originally from Scotland—"

"No wonder you hired her."

"Grew up in Saint Mark's workhouse—"

"All my favorites at the brothel spent time there."

"Do you think it wise to pursue a mistress in the same house you share with your wife?"

"Who said anything about me pursuing her? She walked in on me playing the harpsichord the other night and piqued my curiosity."

"That's odd. The laundry room isna close to your music room. She shouldna be anywhere near that part of the manor." He pinched the bridge of his nose in annoyance. *Did the butler ever do his damned job?*

"I was playing with the window open, and the music must have woken her."

"What time was this?"

"Two in the morning." He swirled his port in his glass. "Blonde hair cascading down her back. A trace of her nipples showing beneath her nightgown."

MacLeod grunted. The blonde was a headache in the making and now that Blackmere might throw more business his way, he'd have less time to deal with Lord Hallewell's messy love life. *Play on his vanity.* "Sure you want to fuck a servant? It's rather unoriginal."

Lord Hallewell frowned. "I merely said she appeared interested in my music. Anyway, safe travels. Give your little sprite, Fiona, a hug for me."

MacLeod finished his drink, bowed and headed for the door. *Should I deal with the Eleanor situation now, or go home?* His delay was already significant, but this could become a mess if left unattended. “Belmont, a word.”

The butler came over.

“You need to check the locks in the servant quarters. Remove the culprit taking midnight strolls. There’s nothing I hate more than someone sneaking to places where they dinnae belong.”

Chapter 6

LADY MARGARET

London

Dinner parties were a chance for Lady Margaret to sneakily collect secrets from people she cordially detested. As a girl, she learned her role in society was to be beautiful and silent. With her Habsburg chin, she never fully pulled off beauty, but silence was her dominant weapon.

Ignoring the lies streaming from aristocratic mouths, she concentrated instead on their bodies telling the true story. Lord X stood beside his wife, but his right toe pointed at Lady Y, his mistress. As a youth, it didn't take long for her to crack the coded messages, and she longed to grow up and have her own lovers.

When women exited the dining hall to allow the men to smoke their pipes, drink scotch, and discuss pressing political maneuvers, she used to sneak back to an adjacent room to eavesdrop. Men became more interesting once women departed. Liquor loosened their tongues. They were funny. And disgusting. And weak in their constant struggle for power.

Silence was her greatest tutor indeed.

But now grown, and several years into her second unbearable marriage, she had to suffer dinner sitting next to an old duke droning on about the War of Spanish Succession. Who cared? She certainly didn't. *Smile. Nod your head slightly. Offer the occasional 'my goodness,' to show engagement.*

Her husband sat at the table's head, distant yet visible. Their marriage was a well-rehearsed madrigal. Everyone played their part. Too bad escaping him wasn't an option. He was the worst. Needy. Overly generous. Always believing he was somehow unique. Always trying to detach himself from his father's arrest, which honestly was the only interesting thing about his family.

Glancing at the table full of peers, she envisioned herself laughing as everyone at the table drank poisoned goblets and died a slow, torturous death before her. *Control your urges, Margaret. Such musings aren't helpful.*

Lord Hallewell raised his glass. "To my lovely wife, Margaret, the mother of my heirs and strength of our family, may your grace and virtues continue to shine brightly."

During the toast, the intellectually empty duke beside her spilled his wine on her new French gown. "Oh, I'm terribly sorry, my lady," he said, grabbing a linen in his knobby hand to help.

She willed herself to contain the thunder inside. He outranked her, after all. "No trouble, your grace. Accidents happen. Excuse me." *As though I'd ever allow another hideously wrinkled man to touch me again. Wasn't my first marriage enough?*

Blasting down the servant stairwell, she found the lazy wretches playing cards. "Is this what I pay you for? Lounging? Get my maids now. That goddamned bag of bones spilled his wine all over my new gown. It's ruined."

Panic ensued like a blizzard. Cards lay scattered as servants fled, leaving her alone with the new laundress, who quickly grabbed a brush and vinegar. "Let me clean the stain for you, m'lady, while you're waiting for your new clothes."

"I said it's ruined. Get away from me." Lady Margaret's voice rose in a pitch that would have made the wind shriek in retreat.

Disregarding her orders completely, the laundress scrubbed and blew on the fabric.

Lady Margaret rubbed her temples, as the pressure rose. "What's taking them so long? Where are my maids?"

"Aye, they should be here waiting for your beck and call, as I am, m'lady."

Lady Margaret rolled her eyes. Did this servant expect a pat on the head?

"Too bad Mr. MacLeod's wife, Fiona, isna here," the servant said keeping her head bowed. "She might cast a spell to clean your petticoats."

That caught her attention. "What was your name again?"

"Eleanor Cameron," she said, alternately blowing and scrubbing on the stain.

Lady Margaret chuckled. "I'd rather Fiona cursed the old duke to die."

Eleanor subtly made the sign of the cross. "The stain's gone, m'lady. It only needs drying now." Eleanor curtseyed and backed away, checking the window.

Her reaction was fascinating. "Is my bold talk frightening you?"

Eleanor curtseyed again, "No, m'lady. It's...just..." Eleanor scanned the room.

"What are you looking for?"

"It's been told Mr. MacLeod's wife can transfigure into a toad. I hope she isna listening."

Lady Margaret burst into laughter. "Do you believe in fairies, too?"

Eleanor's cheeks flushed bright pink as she stared at her shoes.

You need allies. Act like you care. Touch her arm. Lady Margaret did the comforting gesture people seemed to like. "You're frightened of witches? Is that your deepest fear?"

Surprised, Eleanor looked up with those eager blue eyes. "My deepest fear, m'lady? Not pleasing you, I suppose."

It was a safe answer for a servant. Maybe she dreaded a beating. Who knew? "Why does not pleasing me frighten you?"

"If I dinnae please you, I'll be cast out," she said holding the brush and jug over her chest, as though they were shields.

Fascinating. "And why does being cast out frighten you?"

The girl was positively crawling out of her skin and her eyes welled. Lady Margaret had scratched the surface of something and hoped it would bleed. "Perhaps it would be reminiscent of your workhouse days? Unwanted, unloved, and entirely disposable?"

Biting her lip, a deep flush came to those lovely cheeks before Eleanor closed her eyes. "What's your deepest fear, m'lady?"

A shrewd grin crept up her face. "I fear nothing, but I want a great many things."

Eleanor's eyebrows rose.

Such an absorbing face. So expressive. What other reactions can I learn from her? "Does that shock you?"

"Yes, m'lady. Friends called me fearless too, and I've always been ambitious." She nodded too eagerly, as if they were equals. "We're two peas in a pod, we are."

Lady Margaret bristled. *How dare this low wench compare herself to me?* She snatched a sticky wooden spoon from the table to poke the girl's eye out for such disrespect.

"You'll laugh, but even the witch of Pye Street said I'd rise above my station," Eleanor added with a nervous chuckle.

That blockaded Margaret's impulse, and she held the spoon midair. "Say that again?"

"Oh, not a real witch, m'lady! Just a daft old crone muttering in riddles. I helped her across the street by the Abbey, and she grabbed my hand and started spouting nonsense."

"What sort of nonsense?"

"She said, 'Are you a sinner, or a saint? Your choice has consequences.' She must have guessed I lived at Saint Mark's. A lot of girls from there end up working in the pleasure houses. But then she said something dramatic, like, 'Your daughter will bring down a king if she survives past Ostara in her fifth year.'" Eleanor laughed quickly. "Can you imagine? Me? With a daughter? And one bold enough to threaten a monarch? I nearly died of laughter. But she said it like it was some grand prophecy."

Margaret lowered the spoon. "Curious, indeed."

"Pure silliness. Likely she was drunk. But it made me wonder what kind of woman she imagined me to be. Fearless?" She dropped her voice. "Maybe I reminded her of someone like you."

"Have you returned to the witch?"

Eleanor's eyes were wide, with white showing around the whole iris. "No, m'lady. I'm a good girl and believe in Christ. I'd never openly seek a wise woman."

Lady Margaret gazed at Eleanor with newfound focus. "It would please me if you took me to meet the witch of Pye."

All color drained from the laundress' face. *How delightful.*

Visiting a witch was obviously illegal, and to do so with a servant she barely knew was utterly reckless, but that was the point. Danger was the opposite of numb. Not since her torrid affair with Colonel Wilkes had her body experienced such tingling electricity. Also, she found it entertaining to create an impossible situation and watch the worthless servant squirm.

"Well, I dinnae ken exactly where she lives," Eleanor said tugging at her ear. "I randomly met her in the street."

"Fine. Don't help me," Lady Margaret hissed.

Eleanor's shoulders rolled in as she pinched her bottom lip.

How scrumptious to watch the laundress have an internal battle between her deepest fears where every choice is dangerous. Will Eleanor go against Christ and the law to visit a witch? Or will she risk displeasing her mistress and be cast out? A laugh escaped Lady Margaret as she watched a bead of sweat form on the girl's forehead.

"I'll find the witch of Pye's home, my lady. If that pleases you."

Three maids burst in, tripping over themselves with a mound of petticoats, gowns, stomachers and assorted shoes in their arms. "We've come my lady."

"I feared you were lost. Eleanor remedied the situation. Perhaps she should be a ladies' maid. Which of you three should I replace? I'll have to ponder it over dessert."

Eleanor blushed with euphoria until the other girls darted daggers at her. Chuckling, Lady Margaret returned to the party. *As though I'd ever replace a ladies' maid with a workhouse laundress.*

"Have you gotten us lost on purpose?" snarled Lady Margaret as the morning sun cast a gloomy pall over the acre beyond the majestic Westminster Abbey.

"Beggin' your pardon, m'lady, I ken it's around here somewhere. I've only been once by accident."

"Yes, yes, I know, you're a good girl and such rubbish." Lady Margaret shunned her typical red gown and donned a black hooded cloak lest someone of importance see her as she followed Eleanor into the lawless part of town.

Prostitutes from the Irish rookery pawned themselves to passing sailors. Neglected children wandered past listless vagrants propped against squalid cadging houses with empty bottles of gin at their feet.

"Careful, m'lady," Eleanor said, holding out her arm to stop Lady Margaret as a chamber pot was dumped out the window, splattering its sulfurous stink everywhere. "It's over there."

A one-story hovel was tucked into the shadows of taller buildings. The roof served as a refuse catch-all from its impoverished neighbors and was covered in fish bones and trash.

Lady Margaret covered her nose but not even her perfumed handkerchief blocked the stench of the commoners inside. A mother with red eyes rocked a young boy who looked to be dying of consumption. Eleanor knocked three deliberate taps, and the inner door opened into a smoky room that smelled like wild herbs and grave dirt.

A lone candle dripped onto a wooden table, and an old woman, perhaps seventy, hobbled forward leaning on her cane. She was taller than Lady Margaret imagined a witch might be. The hag sized them both up with eyes black as obsidian, sharp and unblinking, with a glint suggesting she saw things others missed. "You brought coin? Readings ain't free," she said in a voice as weathered as her cloak.

"How do I know you're worth the price?"

The witch of Pye chuckled and moved behind the table, her cloak seeming to catch the wind. "You don't bargain with spirits, lady. You owe them."

Her fingers curled like talons around Margaret's hand, with a tight grip as she traced the lines of her palm. "Stop lookin' for your lover. You'll never see him again."

Colonel Wilkes' handsome face flashed in Margaret's mind. The last time she saw him was on her wedding day. "I don't have a lover."

"Not anymore," she said with a knowing grin. "Several sons and a daughter, but the lines are split. Different fathers."

Pursing her lips, Lady Margaret eyed the woman skeptically. Lots of woman had former lovers. *Admit nothing.* "I know how many children I have. Tell me something I don't know." *Will I ever control my life?*

"Control comes at a steep price, lady. Power can shift like a raven's wings through the air."

Did she read my mind? Lady Margaret leaned in. "Why are you speaking in riddles? What price? And how powerful? I'm powerful already."

"You're a pawn. But even pawns can kill kings, right love?" she said, shifting her beady eyes to Eleanor. The hag winced, rubbing in a circular motion above her heart. It seemed as though—but it couldn't be—that the skin she rubbed glowed like embers in a dying fire.

The laundress gasped, making the sign of the cross.

"Pretty prayers won't keep your guts in when the knives come out. A betrayal is coming."

"We should go, m'lady."

"Go?" said Lady Margaret. "It's just getting interesting. Tell me more of this betrayal."

The hag held out her palm for money and Lady Margaret gave a threepence.

"Beware the daughter of a red-haired man. If she lives past five, she'll be your downfall."

Lady Margaret smirked. "Well, that narrows it down."

"Lord Hallewell has red hair," Eleanor said wide-eyed to the witch. "Should m'lady fear her own daughter, baby Elizabeth?"

Perhaps Eleanor shouldn't be in the room, in case this charlatan proved legitimate. And how does she know my husband's hair color beneath his wig? "Go outside."

After Eleanor left, Lady Margaret eyeballed the grimy room. "You may live in a hut, but you certainly have power over the common folk. She hung on your every word."

"She's a peach, that one, proper treat she is. We both know power is a better gift."

"You dabble in the dark arts, I presume? Sounds dangerous."

"I only practice natural magic, lady, for healing. I read palms and moles and give clarity to dreams, is all. Want me to interpret your dreams?"

She snorted. *My dreams are as dark as the finest French chocolate, but far less sweet.* "What's it like to be a witch? To profit off people's hopes and fears?"

"No worse than a noblewoman tormenting poor servants so she can laze in red gowns. You don't scare me, love. Why're you really here?"

A raven in the rafters side-stepped along the wood.

Margaret's blood rushed past her ears and her skin tingled. "Can you wish someone away?"

"Yes, lady. For a time. For a price."

Should I purchase a charm? I'm sure it's all rubbish...but what if it works? No one would know. "My husband is grating on my nerves. I don't care why he leaves, but I want to enjoy the summer without him."

A broad grin swept the hag's face. "Bring me three strands of his hair and an unwashed shirt. It will be done before the next waxing moon."

"I highly doubt that, but you did provide a measure of entertainment," she said, dropping some shillings on the table then raising her dark hood.

If this charm works, perhaps I'll become a return customer.

Outside, Eleanor paced nervously.

Should I force the girl to bring the required items here? Better not. I'll do that myself. But I do want to toy with her. "Why would you bring me to a place like this? As soon as you left, she spoke of nothing but curses and the dark arts. Witchcraft is a crime. You better hope I don't tell Mr. MacLeod about this—he'll cast you out on the spot."

Eleanor's mouth opened. "But, you wanted me to take you."

Lady Margaret grinned. "I'm teasing. She's a charlatan. Look how frightened you were. Why you've positively twisted yourself into knots."

Chapter 7

Fiona

Scotland

Fiona clutched the red yarn in her pocket. All three knots had untied themselves. *William's coming home. The clock is fixed. The scroll is hidden.* But still, she worried. *Will the goddess Beira punish me for the unlit candle?*

Servants assembled in the blustering wind, standing to the left while Fiona and the boys shivered to the right. David gave a reassuring squeeze to Broderick's shoulder and James whispered to his brothers, "Remember, the clock is fixed, so no need to mention it, aye?" The boys all nodded.

William stepped from the coach, picked up Fiona and spun her, making her blush and laugh at his affectionate display. The tension left her shoulders, and she relaxed in his bear hug. "It's good to be home with you in my arms," he whispered.

"I missed you."

"Me next," Lachlan shouted raising his arms.

William tossed Lachie in the air until the lad burst into giggles, then sat his son on his shoulders. "James, David, are you keeping up with your lessons? The barrister path demands diligent effort, aye?" They nodded. "Good. I'll quiz you." He winked at Fiona as the boys swallowed. But then his gaze clouded with weariness. "Posture, Broderick," he said, snapping his fingers.

A deep flush came to the boy's cheeks as he cowered behind Fiona's skirts.

William rolled his eyes. "Jesus, Joseph and Mary, the lad's afraid of his own shadow."

"Just yours," she gently scolded as the servants shifted on their feet.

Handing Lachie to Fiona, William walked inside eyeing her. "Why must you always wear that tartan shawl? Dinnae misunderstand, you could wear a burlap sack and look good, but you're lady of the manor. I buy you a fashionable gown every time I visit London."

"How am I to don an English dress for you when I never ken when you'll be home?" she asked with a wry grin.

"Ack, I ken. It was as if God himself wanted to delay me."

She bit back a smirk. *Or Beira, Queen of Winter.*

"Did the money from Lord Blackmere arrive?"

"If you mean the strong boxes, they've been placed in your study."

"Excellent. James, David, go in there and grab volume two of *Coke's Reports*. I expect you both to read while I'm working." As they went inside, he kissed Fiona's cheek. "I'm swamped with court filings. I'll have to work until dinner, but there's a matter we need to discuss first."

Broderick lingered, glued to Fiona's skirts. "Dinnae stand there, boy. You've got chores."

As Broderick scampered off, Fiona put Lachie down and watched him chase after his brother.

William lowered his voice as the footman carried his luggage inside. "Reverend MacDonald sends word that Imbolc was relatively quiet, save a single candle lit in your window." He arched his eyebrow.

Busybody preacher. She wondered what the transgression might cost her. "It's difficult to see in the darkness," she said with a shrug. "He invited himself to stay the night."

"I ken you dinnae like him, but we have to be cautious. We need friends in the Kirk. Things are getting dodgy in London. Lord Blackmere, the backstabber whose testimony sent Lord Hallewell's father to prison, is now head of Society of the Reformation of Manners and wants to feather his hat by bringing outsiders to heel. It dinnae take much to initiate a witch hunt."

"Am I to be watched by the reverend for the rest of my life for magic I no longer use?"

"Fiona, I dinnae fear your magic, I only fear what others will make of it. Lord Blackmere seems the sort who would burn anyone to get ahead."

He put his warm hand on her cheek and pulled her in, pressing a gentle kiss to her brow. "There's a gown in the coach with silk that looks like mist. I thought of you the moment I saw it. Will you wear it for me tonight?"

"If you think a gown will make me forget your scolding, you're daft. But I'll try it on anyway."

He chuckled, then paused at the door. "I'll do what I must to keep you safe." He slipped into the study, closing the door with care.

Fiona flopped in her chair, tossing her favorite shawl on the couch. Every quarrel between them was rooted in the same truth: he loved her fiercely, if imperfectly.

"I've got the mantua, Lady MacLeod," said the maid carrying the large pasteboard box. "It's quite lovely."

Fiona trudged upstairs to her bedchamber. Unbuckling the belt around her waist she handed it to the maid, who then helped remove her wool plaid arisaid. The simple laced bodice was easy enough to untie herself. She tugged off her linen petticoat and kicked off her leather slippers.

She knew the gown was purchased with love, but dressing like an English aristocrat didn't sit right. Honestly, it still felt strange to walk the halls of the seventeen-room manor she once admired from a distance—as a farm girl hauling water from the clootie well. While she appreciated luxury, she sometimes missed living in a simple croft house. And she definitely missed her coven.

She missed the joy of learning the healing arts from Matilda and Elspeth. Her education was lost the same day as Matilda's burning, leaving her perpetually unprepared. Palmistry, tea leaves, dream interpretation—sure. But channeling true clairvoyance was tricky. What good was having second sight without having any control over it?

"Here we go, m'lady," said the maid, lacing a boned corset tightly over her torso. Fiona stepped into not one, but two petticoats over her shift, and tied them at the waist. She groaned as the maid tied the bum roll to extend the width of the skirts. "My goodness, the panniers keep getting bigger each time he returns from London."

The undergarments were putting her in a mood foul enough to impress Matilda. She loved her aunt, but Matilda was consumed by her own bitterness. Every fire festival divulged into a one-sided rant. Trying to learn any magic from her was impossible. When sunlight came ending the fire festival, Fiona often felt upset.

"Ready for the dress?"

Her torso now properly contorted into conical form, Fiona held the maid's hand as she stepped into the lilac gown with a pleated back. The low, square neckline made her blush. The maid pinned the skirt open to reveal the contrasting plumb colored underskirt. Fiona traced the embroidered flowers drifting across the lilac silk that glistened like a Highland mist.

Beyond a basic fog shield, she'd forgotten most spells. Both Matilda and Elspeth said she'd be able to control the weather if she practiced consistently. But after the disastrous salt circle incident after Lord Hallewell's wedding, she didn't want to tempt fate and draw any attention to herself. It cost too much. William stood by her, but they lost land, their marriage strained, and she felt spied on ever since.

The maid attached the engageantes at each elbow, letting the lace ruffles fall over her forearms. Fiona glanced warily in the mirror as the maid attached the stomacher, and a fichu over her neckline for modesty. She handed her matching silk-heeled shoes from another box as the clock stuck the hour.

Did William even know the scroll was hidden in the chime? Probably not, and if he did, he definitely didn't know there was a secret message made invisible through enchantment. It would have been helpful to confer with a sister witch during situations like this. Although even if Elspeth was able to unlock the scroll's message, Fiona would never seek out that Judas.

Fiona sat at her dressing table as the maid styled her hair and pinned it with combs that hurt her head. She winced with each twist.

The real darkness wasn't merely Elspeth's awful blood magic, it was her betrayal of Matilda. Both Elspeth and Matilda were arrested for causing the illness in the village, but Matilda burned and Elspeth flew free, never to be seen again. Her betrayal left their coven fractured, unable to heal, move on, or grow. But at least the next fire festival, Ostara, was around the corner, and she could talk with Matilda again.

Plucking the beautiful diamond and emerald bracelet from her vanity drawer, Fiona smiled at the memory of William purchasing it off the wrist of a duchess and clasping it onto her own at Lord Hallewell's wedding. But then she thought of Colonel Wilkes and her face clouded.

Should couldn't talk to anyone about what happened, so she kept it buried deep inside. Between the church, the law, her husband's overprotective nature, and Matilda's inherent distrust of forming a new coven, Fiona felt utterly alone. *Will I ever find another wise woman to confide in?*

An hour later, William emerged from his study, and dinner was served. They had barely taken their first bite when a post boy arrived.

"Apologies, laird," said the butler. "You have two urgent messages. One from Reverend MacDonald and the other from Lord Blackmere."

"I wonder what Supple Dick wants?"

"Who?" asked Fiona, as the boys snickered. She scratched at the lace bustline of her new English gown.

"Sorry—Richard Atthill, the Earl of Blackmere." William sliced open the red seal and read. "I'll be damned. He offered a personal introduction to the king. He's going to be at Lord Hallewell's ball, and wants to make arrangements there. Looks like I'm leaving for London tomorrow." William lowered the letter with a grin so wide his dimples shone. He took the other letter and dismissed the butler with a wave.

"You get to meet the king?" James' eyes sparkled with awe.

Fiona lowered her voice. "But dinnae you say Lord Blackmere is leading witch hunts?"

James held his fork midair.

"All the more reason to befriend him. We need powerful allies."

"But you just got home." Fiona sipped her claret to control her emotions. *Is this witch hunter meeting a warning to me? Is Beira punishing me for blowing out the candle early? Matilda warned she'd be angry. Och, these ancient goddesses have no understanding of modern marriages.*

"Fiona, this is a huge opportunity. I have to go."

"How long will you be gone this time?"

William threw down his napkin. "What do you want me to do? My path to power runs through London, and you constantly want me here. I canna be two places at once."

Everyone looked down at their plates. William broke the seal on the letter from Reverend MacDonald. His face soured with each line read. "Reverend MacDonald complains of ribbons on the clootie well. I can already hear his Easter sermon scolding us to put an end to the maypole celebrations."

"Will he shoulder the blame when the harvest fails, and our tenants starve?"

"You can discuss that with him personally. He's invited himself to our manor for Easter."

Ostara? If he's here all night, I'll miss my opportunity to speak with Matilda about the scroll. "I was hoping we might visit my sister, Mary, instead."

"Refuse a preacher hospitality Easter Sunday?" William took a bite of his smoked haddock and focused intently on the flavors. "This tastes different."

"Ah, the new chef, Monsieur Laurent, started a few weeks ago. Isna his cooking divine?"

William looked at James. "Bring Mr. Laurent in here, please." His voice was a low grumble.

A few moments later, Monsieur Laurent, all smiles, bowed. "*Bon jour*, laird."

"I taste salt. When you applied for the position, I specifically said no salt in my house. I made that very plain."

The Frenchman glanced at Fiona. He purchased the salt at her request. He used it for meals, but she needed it for other purposes. "*Pardonne-moi*, laird, it was but a pinch for flavoring."

"If you canna follow my wishes, you can seek employment elsewhere. You've been warned."

Fiona smiled in thanks at the chef for keeping her secret, as he bowed and left. William shot a look at Fiona, clearly reading her reaction. Only the chime of the grandfather clock striking the hour interrupted the thick silence. His eyes softened as he looked at his sons. "My mother always told me that clock was the key to our family's greatness. It represents our legacy."

"What does a clock have to do with greatness?" asked James.

"I think she wanted to remind me that time is fleeting, and to make the most of our brief stretch on this earth."

So he dinnae ken about the hidden scroll inside the chime...

Lachlan's citrine eyes connected with hers and a cold wind passed through the room. He pointed and said, "Bad Brodrick. Tick tock."

Oh, shite.

"Broderick touched my clock?"

Fiona took a deep breath. "Everything is fine. My brother found a lovely old gentleman from Inverness who sorted it out for a reasonable price. Problem solved."

"Sorted what out?" He lowered his fork staring directly at James who squirmed in his seat.

"Broderick was tinkering with the clock and accidentally broke it, sir," James confessed.

William raised his eyebrows at Fiona. "You let a three-year-old play with my family heirloom? Are you out of your bloody mind?"

Striding to the clock in his study, he opened the glass door and examined it, searching for dents as everyone followed. With his pocket watch in hand, he checked if the times on the faces matched.

Broderick peeked from behind Fiona's skirts as William stood over him, jaw tight.

"He's three, William. He meant no harm."

"What a ridiculous thing to say. The clock isna merely furniture. It's a testament to my family's status and history."

"It's not even broken anymore," Fiona said gently. *Eisd rium a Dhia. Beira, please. Dinnae punish the boy for my disrespect. Let me appease you,* she prayed.

"I was j-just trying..." Broderick's large brown eyes welled, "I wanted to find the key to our family."

William blinked, caught off guard. His jaw worked in silence, then reset. "That was a metaphor," he muttered, "not an invitation to take it apart." He wagged his finger at Broderick, clearly doing his best to keep his anger in check. "Dinnae touch my things. Do you understand, boy?"

Broderick nodded profusely, the harsh look enough to produce copious tears. James and David ushered him away.

William faced Fiona. "I should have locked my study. I canna turn my back without something falling to ruin thanks to the remnants of Colonel Wilkes."

"Broderick made a mistake. He just wants your love."

William waved her off. "That's fine. Defend him, like you always do."

"Maybe if you treated him like the rest of your sons, I wouldnae need to. Ever since the reverend butted into our affairs again, you've been in a foul mood. Why dinnae you go back to London and dine with your witch hunter friend, rather than snapping at Brod?"

"You think I want to be in London with that snake? You think I enjoy bowing to that hypocrite? Fiona, if I grow in influence, I can persuade people in the House of Lords to end the Witchcraft Act, or at least water it down so the penalty is no longer execution."

They stood in silence, the clock ticking softly behind them.

She moved toward the stairs, grabbing her plaid shawl and wrapping it around her shoulders. "You think all our problems can be solved from outside. They need to be solved in here first."

At the top of the stairs she heard David soothing Broderick. Peeking inside the boys' bedchamber, she watched James, looking very much like his father, scolded Lachlan. "You shouldna tattle."

Lachlan stamped his foot, defiant. The cold temperature of the room and the gleam of his eyes hinted that the goddess Beira might still be inside him.

"James, he's two," David said.

"He dinnae need to say, 'Bad Broderick'. I swear for a toddler he's great at causing trouble. Now Da and Mam are fighting."

A guilty knot formed in the pit of her stomach. "Boys, get ready for bed," Fiona said coming inside.

"I'll never find the key, will I, Mama?"

Oh, Broderick. Fiona didn't answer right away. She just opened her arms and hugged him. Magic didn't prevent bad tidings, it only delayed them. *Matilda was right. I'm a fool for getting on the wrong side of an ancient goddess.*

David kicked off his shoes and hose, leaving them in the middle of the floor. "I wish Da stayed home longer because if he got to ken Broderick, he wouldnae be mad at him all the time."

If only that were true.

James neatly folded his breeches, hanging them over a chair. They both climbed into their bed, and she kissed their foreheads, taking David's glasses off and placing them on the nightstand.

"Story," Lachlan demanded jumping on the other bed. "Please?"

"Which one?" she asked, tucking him in beside Broderick. If Fiona had any doubt about Lachie's possession, it ended with his answer.

"Beira. Old tongue."

A creak in the hall alerted her to William's presence. *Shite.* William mandated English-only at home, despite the village's Gaelic/Scots prevalence, but she'd not deny Beira again—not tonight.

Fiona wrapped her plaid shawl tightly around herself, settled on their bed, and prayed the goddess was listening.

"Beira, Queen of Winter, is as old as time itself," she began in Gaelic. "She created Scotland with her hammer, forming deep craggy glens and steep mountains by pounding on rocks carried from the center of earth. After creating the world, her white plaid became dirty, so she washed it in the sea, then laid it across the mountaintops."

"That's snow," David explained to his younger brothers.

Broderick raised a hand. "Is winter to punish us?"

"No, love. Winter reminds us we're under Beira's protection."

James frowned. "Isna she bad? She's a witch, aye?"

"That's one meaning," Fiona said carefully. "The English called her a hag. The Scots called her a wise woman."

Broderick snuggled closer to her. "Or a healer?"

"A goddess," Lachlan whispered, eyes glowing like citrine.

Fiona's breath caught. Beira was still with him.

"She's a hag," James argued. "Pet wolves, blue skin like a corpse, rust-colored teeth, only one eye—"

"What about, Bride?" David said. "She's bonny, no? She brings spring."

Fiona smiled. "At the end of winter, Beira wraps herself in her white plaid as the beautiful maiden, Bride, arrives. The two battle it out for a time, but eventually Bride brings the warmth, the flowers, and the light, but Beira always returns when the veils thin during Samhain."

"So, is Beira good or bad?" Broderick asked softly.

"She's both creator and destroyer. What's the most important lesson nature teaches us?"

"Balance," David said.

"Aye. Like all women, Beira has good and bad, ugliness and beauty, weakness and strength inside revealed through trials and time. A maiden has beauty but lacks confidence. A mother gains confidence but lacks wisdom. A crone is wrinkled but wise." Fiona kissed each son's forehead. "Each phase of life matters, not just the pretty one."

Broderick peeked from beneath the covers. "Should we leave nuts for her, Mama? So she's gentle this winter?"

"That's smart, love." *I'll place them beside the clootie well first thing in the morning, Beira.*

"Sounds like a stupid pagan notion," James muttered in English. "Reverend MacDonald says only God controls the weather."

Fiona's stomach clenched. *Careful, boy. Never mock a goddess.* Who knew what she might do next? Send a plague? "James MacLeod, have you had a direct conversation with the Lord Almighty?"

He scrunched his nose. "No."

"Then dinnae speak for Him. Just because our stories are old, it dinnae make them wrong." Her voice turned grave. "The last man who crossed Beira brought seven years of famine to our village."

That silenced the room.

When she reached Lachlan, the glow in his eyes dimmed, and the air warmed around them. Beira was gone. *I promise to honor you better going forward.* "Bedtime for real, boys." She blew out the candle, heart hammering as she stepped into the hallway—and straight into William.

"We need to talk," he said, sipping a cup of tea. They shared an uncomfortable silence entering their bedchamber. William placed down his cup and lit a candle. "You looked radiant telling the boys the ancient stories tonight. You have such an easy, serene nature, and I love that about you," he said, voice soft. "But the reverend wrote that you spoke in favor of the village fire festivals in town. You make it hard for me to defend you from the Kirk. I'm afraid for you, Fiona."

Her shoulders tensed. "Defend me from what? I've done nothing."

There was tension in the air, like he wanted to squeeze her hand in reassurance, but didn't. He moved to the fireplace, stoking the dying embers. Fiona's eyes drifted from the clean-shaven man in an overcoat and breeches in front of her to the portrait of a younger, bearded William standing strong in his kilt as she held baby James in her arms. She yearned for their former life. Every day, they drifted farther from their true selves, reshaped by the consequences of what Colonel Wilkes had done to them.

"I should pack for London." He tapped his index finger over his lips, tempering a smile. "Think of it. I'm going to meet the king," he said with wonder. "Perhaps...never mind."

She bit her bottom lip, second guessing whether to offer. "Care for a reading? Not magic, of course, just reading tea leaves like everybody does."

"Fiona, I'm not the one against magic, the law and the church are."

"It might help," she offered. *Oh, please let my magic help you.*

William tugged at his ear. "It's not like you're scrying for the villagers. I'm your husband, after all. And the boys are asleep. No one would ever find out."

She couldn't help but smile. It felt like her insides were buzzing as she grabbed the cup of tea. "Concentrate on your question while I drink."

"How do I narrow it down to one?" He tapped his foot against the floor. "All right. Will I have a promising meeting with the king?"

Finishing the tea, she inspected the bottom to read the leaves but found nothing. Not a single leaf remained. "That's...that never happened before. There's no fortune to tell."

He peered inside. "Shall I fetch another cup? Maybe read my palm?" He opened his hand.

She stepped back. The last time she read a man's palm, it ended with murder.

"Sorry," he said quickly. "This was a bad idea."

"No, no." She smiled. "I'm thrilled you want this again."

His finger tapped on his leg. "How about the fire? Maybe stare into it?"

She shrugged in apology. "It's neither a fire festival nor a full moon. But I'll try."

Kneeling before the hearth, she stared into the flames, trying to clear her mind, desperate for a vision. "*Eisd rium a Dhia.* Beira, Queen of Winter, first *Cailleach*, Goddess, Destroyer, Protector. Will William have a promising meeting with the king?"

Come on, Fiona. Concentrate. Her breathing grew unsteady. Heat flushed her cheeks. A buzzing filled her head—the way it sometimes did when a vision was close—but it faded. The fire only flickered, stubbornly mute. "There's nothing," she whispered, ashamed. She scratched her neck. "William, I'm sorry. I can only command visions during fire festivals."

William sat beside her, staring at the fire. "I hoped magic would help me just once."

Fiona tucked a strand of his wild hair behind his ear. "Did you want me to tell you lies?"

He shook his head. "No. But I suppose I hoped you'd see something. Anything. I'm blindly trusting Lord Blackmere wants to advance my prospects, but I dinnae ken his motivations, or if this meeting is a mistake. I canna afford to falter again." He stood, staring longingly at their family portrait. "You used to be able to do readings all the time. Maybe it's for the best you're losing your clairvoyance. It'll certainly make it easier to protect you from the long arm of Reverend MacDonald." He kissed her forehead. "I best get back to work. Dinnae wait up."

She sat alone in front of the crackling fire. Her gift failed. Her magic failed. And worst of all, she feared William stopped believing in her too.

Chapter 8

Eleanor

London

How could I have believed her? Eleanor berated herself for trusting Lady Margaret to honor her promise. Eleanor had asked when she should begin her duties as a lady's maid, but the shrew pretended the conversation had never taken place. *I risked arrest and God's wrath to take that wee aristocratic bitch to the witch of Pye and got nothing in return? Am I to be stuck as a laundress forever?*

Eleanor pushed her annoyance aside for the moment though, because tonight she was able to witness her first ball. The wealthiest, most fashionable people in the realm attended. Who wouldn't be excited to see such a gathering?

The serving boy told her Lord Hallwell gave at least ten toasts praising his wife's beauty, grace, and dedication to the Royal Benevolent Society of Orphans.

You'd think they were in love.

But Eleanor never needed to wash sheets soiled by lovemaking. Lord and Lady Hallewell shared an enormous fortune, but not each other's bed, at least not since baby Elizabeth was born, apparently. Helpful information, that. For as much praise as Lord Hallewell heaped on his wife, nary a compliment ever escaped Lady Margaret's crimson lips about him. It was hard to believe such a charming and kind man married a such a hellcat. Lady Margaret acted high and mighty and mean but couldn't wipe her own arse properly and Eleanor should know—she cleaned the shite-stained petticoats.

Exhausted servants counted the minutes until the nobles ended the ball. It killed her to be trapped in the kitchen under the watchful eye of Mrs. Clark while a party raged above them. Hours earlier, Eleanor's mouth watered at the scent of roast venison with rosemary and juniper berries, sizzling as it left the kitchen. She pictured champagne pouring like a waterfall into the French coupe glasses served to duchesses with shining gems dangling from their necks.

Then, finally, Mrs. Clark rested her head on the kitchen table and began to snore. Eleanor grew bold, sneaking upstairs into the grand hall. *Please dinnae catch me.* She just had to get a glimpse of the glorious guests in the mirrored ballroom before everyone left.

At this late hour, only the remnants of sipping chocolate in porcelain cups littered the dining table.

A hint of melody, different from the orchestra in the ballroom, rose above the din of laughter. Slipping through the perfumed air in the dark hallway, she hesitated outside the music room. *Should I go inside?* The stars twinkled in the indigo sky, lending an aura of magic. *I'll only stay a minute.* Tiptoeing into the edge of the room, she hid behind an enormous potted plant and watched.

A stout gentleman with a grizzled wig pounded his fingers over the harpsichord keys. What a difference from the gliding strokes of Lord Hallewell that first night she spied him. *Oh, please play, my lord.*

Powerful men swirled glasses of whiskey and told bawdy jokes. Lord Hallewell appeared disconnected from the pack, conflicted. His tight jawline was frozen in a smile, but his fingers tapped against his thighs as he eyed a tall man of obvious importance in a dusky bronze coat talking with Mr. MacLeod.

If I can just get a wee bit closer, I can listen. No one was looking her way. She furiously crawled to the next potted plant, closer to the thick of things.

"Lord Blackmere, finally, a chance to speak." Mr. MacLeod led the impeccably dressed man toward her in the darkened corner. The green and black embroidery on the gentleman's waistcoat twisted like coiled vipers, waiting to strike.

Shite, shite, shite. She crouched lower, hoping sunrise would take its sweet time, allowing her to remain hidden in the shadows.

"My lord, I'm honored that you'd arrange an introduction for me to the king. When and where will we meet?"

"Heel, boy," Lord Blackmere said in a tone meant to mock, "you're getting ahead of yourself."

Mr. MacLeod grimaced at being compared to a trained dog. His jaw, clenched and square, seemed forged for defiance. Watching raptly, she tented her fingers in front of her mouth to keep from giggling. *What fun to see MacLeod eager to impress his betters.*

"Of course, my lord. What matter did you wish to discuss?"

"Your client who disappeared."

"Could you please be more specific?"

The earl's lip curled. "That's right, you have a knack for being associated with disappearing gentlemen. Colonel Wilkes, Charles Jamison..."

Mr. MacLeod's body stiffened, and he crossed his arms over his barrel chest. "I met Wilkes once, that hardly counts as an association. Charles Jamison was the boy accused of sodomy. Whom did you wish to discuss?"

"Has Charles tried to reach you?" he asked a wee bit too casually, like he was more anxious than he let on. "I'm curious if young Jamison gave you any names of other men? Perhaps a painter?"

"I haena heard from the lad since his escape several months ago," Mr. MacLeod said, angling away, ever so slightly.

"You mean to say, neither the boy, nor his father, nor the lover, reached out to you about his self-imposed exile, in all these months?" Sarcasm dripped off his tongue like venom.

"I canna imagine he'd come back any time soon, what with your strenuous work reforming the molly houses."

"You disappoint me, MacLeod. Perhaps we can discuss that other vanished man, Colonel Wilkes," he whispered. "As head of Society for Reformation of Manners, it is my duty to tamp down questions about his disappearance," he said, striking a thinly veiled threat.

"Re-opening that investigation will keep you busy. It's my understanding Wilkes had plenty of enemies ready to challenge him to a duel."

She had heard the backstairs talk about the scandal but didn't put much stock in it. *Maybe there's some truth to it being more than just a man skipping town? Maybe I can work this gossip to my advantage. Ha! I'll be a ladies' maid yet.*

Lord Blackmere took a sip of his drink and made a sour face. "I need something stronger than this cheap swill Lord Hallewell serves." He splashed his wine onto the plant, thus onto Eleanor's face, eliciting a gasp.

Mr. MacLeod swatted aside the giant leaves. "Eleanor Cameron? You still work here?"

Swallowing hard, she backed away from the vegetation and wiped the drink from her face as all the men in the room gaped. "Beggin' your pardon, I'm a wee lost."

"Did you bring us a Highland lass, MacLeod?" Lord Blackmere kissed her hand then flipped it over. His grip coiled tighter as he stared at the lines on her palm. "The hag was right," he whispered, which left Eleanor completely unnerved.

Not noticing the ruckus, the man playing the harpsichord continued to pound away. As MacLeod took a step towards her with enraged eyes, she broke free from the earl's grip and raced to the middle of the room.

"I canna help myself, sir. The music makes me want to dance a reel." She danced a silly jig, startling the noblemen further. Boldy, she hooked her arm through Mr. MacLeod's and skipped in a circle as the aristocrats roared with laughter, then slipped away locking arms with another man, happy to oblige.

The men offered jokingly vulgar encouragement as she continued dancing throughout the room. When she reached Lord Hallewell, she stopped, tucking her chin and raising her eyes to him, curtseying deeply. He wore an amused expression, giving her the courage to speak. "Forgive me, my lord. I just wanted to hear you play."

The nobles elbowed each other, guffawing.

"Play for the pretty blonde, Hallewell," Lord Blackmere said.

Lord Hallewell's eyes twinkled with mischief. "What would you like to hear, Miss—"

"Cameron. Eleanor Cameron." Lowering her voice, she whispered, "I like what you played the other night."

"That's a private song," he said quietly. "How about Bach?" he solicited the crowd.

"Bach? Who wants church music? The girl said she wants to dance," Lord Blackmere said like the serpent tempting in Eden.

Eleanor surveyed Mr. MacLeod who had his arms folded over his chest, clearly unamused, then Blackmere. *Dinnae he say he headed the Reformation of Manners? Why would he want me to dance?*

"Please continue what you've been playing, while I dance with Miss Cameron," Lord Hallewell said to the stout gentleman at the harpsicord.

Heat flooded her shocked face. Never in her lifetime had she expected to dance with a baron, let alone Lord Hallewell. He bowed, and she blinked before coming to her senses and curtseying. "I dinnae ken any proper dances, my lord, but I'll aim to please you."

Fortunately, Lord Hallewell did know how to dance. Pressing his warm hand against her lower back, he increased and decreased the pressure to guide her through. Outside the elongated windows, the sky brightened to soft blue, interspersed with hints of pink on the horizon.

How long did they spin as men formed a circle around them, clapping and cheering? The gentlemen blurred into the background as Lord Hallewell trained his eyes on her. Her cheeks grew sore from smiling when the song broke off abruptly.

An icy quiet fell over the tense room.

Lady Margaret's silence vibrated louder than thunder on the moors. Instinctively, Eleanor bowed her head, waiting for the lady's cuff to warm her cheek. *I'm done.*

Her ladyship glided past, sending a chill up Eleanor's spine. "The Earl of Essex wanted to see your new harpsichord, husband. How delightful it's getting its full use."

"The new girl got lost, and we invited her in," Lord Hallewell said.

He's covering for me?

"Shall I loan her a gown and jewels to join the festivities?" Her cold smile had the warning signs of a deadly twister.

Mr. MacLeod's slow and weighted footfalls moved toward her, like hooves over packed earth. "We're on our way to the servant quarters, my lady."

"I can find my way back to the kitchen," Eleanor said, doing her best to escape.

"Why ever would you leave?" Lady Margaret said. "Please, dance for us. I find it charming how well they teach frolicking at the workhouse. They certainly put our parish poor rate taxes to good use, don't they? Go on, continue your merry little tune, Sir Griffin. Eleanor—is it? Dance a Scottish reel for your betters."

Peeking between Lord and Lady Hallewell, Sir Griffin decided it best to play.

Eleanor's face, neck and ears felt impossibly hot as she danced alone, not sure where to look. Lady Margaret clapped enthusiastically as Lord Blackmere joined in. His nostrils flared, and he recoiled subtly, as if Eleanor's mere existence was too filthy to touch. They cackled at her shame, transforming everyone's joyous laughter from before into mocking glee.

Mr. Belmont came in with a tray full of drinks and stopped short, clearly appalled.

"Belmont," Lady Margaret said. "Gather all the servants and bring them in to watch the laundress dance. Hurry, hurry," she said flicking her wrist.

Eleanor let her shoulders cave in, trying to hide behind the golden locks falling over her eyes. *I'm so stupid.* Her upset stomach gurgled as bleak visions of being sent back to the workhouse made her eyes grow wet.

In short order, every servant filled the music room, staring at her shame. Mrs. Clark fidgeted with her enormous key ring, probably worried about her own fate for falling asleep on the job and allowing a stupid laundress to get loose among the nobles. Some footmen sneered, applauding along. Scullery maids stared uncomfortably, perhaps in sympathy at such public humiliation. One maid wore an unkind smirk.

Ladies in their silken gowns and sparkling gems crowded the door to see all the commotion, barely bothering to hide their snickering and *tsk-tsks* behind their fans.

A sob was trapped in Eleanor's throat as she tugged down on her apron, as though she were naked. "I canna remember any more steps, m'lady."

"Ask the fairies for help. They like to dance, don't they?"

"Stop," Lord Hallewell said quietly, silencing the music. "You've had your fun, Margaret. You're irritated with me, not her." He faced his guests. "Everyone, come back to the ballroom. I'm sure breakfast will be served momentarily."

Guests shuffled away whispering among themselves.

"Such scandalous parties you throw, Hallewell, just like your disgraced father used to. It's atrocious that servants today don't know their place," Lord Blackmere said. Lord Hallewell cringed, following him to attempt social recovery.

But Lady Margaret remained. "Eleanor Cameron."

"Yes, m'lady."

"Is dancing a jig part of your duties?"

Eleanor stood quietly as the seconds ticked by excruciatingly slowly. Nausea consumed her, and she would have given anything to run away and hide.

"That wasn't a rhetorical question. Answer me." Each word stabbed like an icicle.

"No, m'lady. I shouldna have been dancing."

The slap came quickly, and knocked her back a step. Some servants winced, but most remained stone-faced.

She lifted Eleanor's chin. "And now your deepest fear comes true," she whispered. "Cast out forever, my worthless girl." On her way out, Lady Margaret called over her shoulder. "Take her back to the workhouse, MacLeod."

A physical pain struck Eleanor's chest as the dark realization of her future sank in. *If I return to the workhouse, there's no escape. What noble household would ever hire me?*

Lady Margaret's red gown spread against the floor like a trail of blood as she left. As much as Eleanor knew she was to blame, to be cast out forever while Lady Margaret lived happily ever after with a man she didn't deserve was beyond unfair.

I curse you, Lady Margaret. May you be humbled as publicly as you did me.

A cold wind blew through the hall as the horizon exploded into a dramatic sunrise with shades of yellow, orange, and red, spreading upward into lighter blues.

Only servants remained. MacLeod scowled furiously. "Mr. Belmont, I distinctly recall telling you to get rid of her for sneaking out at night."

Belmont's eyes grew wide. "Respectfully, sir, you said *someone* was sneaking out, and I did investigate. One of the stable boys confessed to going to a brothel after midnight, and I terminated him on the spot."

"Jesus, Joseph and Mary. Explain how a new washer girl is left unsupervised on an evening when every noble family within a sixty-mile radius is in attendance?"

Eleanor rushed to him. "It wasna his fault at all, sir, I—"

"No one is speaking to you, Eleanor Cameron."

Mr. Belmont stood ramrod straight. "There's no excuse, sir."

"I ken there's no excuse. How did it happen?"

"I was to supervise all the maids, sir." Mrs. Clark stepped forward.

MacLeod exhaled. "Please hand over your keys, madam."

Servants gasped and covered their mouths in shock. Mrs. Clark had been a loyal housekeeper for decades.

Eleanor stood in front of Mrs. Clark. "Please, sir. She did nothing wrong. I snuck out."

"Haven't you done enough, girl?" Mrs. Clark's eyes grew glassy handing over her enormous key ring. "I'll pack my things, sir." Raising her head high, the old dame squared her shoulders and left the silent room.

MacLeod squared against Mr. Belmont with the density of a mountain. "Must I assume all head butler responsibilities? Perhaps you should be on the chopping block next?"

Mr. Belmont grew crimson and snapped his fingers. "Everyone back to work."

MacLeod's anger flashed back on Eleanor as though she was his target to gore. "I took a chance hiring you, and you made me look like a fool. You caused a scandal in front of a hundred nobles, cost a good woman her hard-won position, and caused a rift between Lord and Lady Hallewell."

Biting her lip she whimpered, "I'm sorry—"

"Shut it. Pack your carpet bag."

Curtseying quickly, the dam broke, and Eleanor's tears flooded as she ran into the hall bumping into Lord Hallewell.

"Good heavens, please don't sob. I came back to apologize. My wife was terribly cruel."

Eleanor's whole body shook as she sunk to Lord Hallewell's feet. "I'm so...sorry for embarrassing," she gasped, "you, my lord." Inhaling she begged, "Please..." Her voice grew thunderously desperate, "dinnae send me back to the workhouse." Her sobs echoed in the cavernous hall, as if her cries were appealing directly to the painting of God on the ceiling.

Lady Margaret stepped into the hall from the ballroom at the noise. "What on earth is going on? Do I have to handle this servant myself?"

"Apologies, my lady, my lord. I'll handle this," MacLeod said, charging toward Eleanor with nostrils flaring.

Lord Hallewell waved him off and focused his attention on her. "There, there, darling. No one's casting you out." He raised Eleanor's chin with his finger, staring at her reddened cheek, then shot MacLeod a scathing glare.

"I dinnae hit her, your wife did."

"You're an orphan?" Lord Hallewell produced an embroidered handkerchief from his pocket and dabbed away her tears.

"She was an orphan," said Lady Margaret, raising her hands to her hips as she encroached. "Now she's a grown woman in need of employment. I'm sure Saint Mark's will find another situation for her."

Eleanor gripped Lord Hallewell's hand. "My lord, please dinnae send me back there."

Sunlight streamed through the windows. The passing servants gawked while strenuously pretending to be busy.

"Margaret, what's the point of raising money for the Royal Benevolent Society of Orphans if we can't show mercy to the wretched orphan in front of us?" he snapped. "She didn't mean any harm. She doesn't know any better." He squeezed Eleanor's hand. "Of course you can stay on."

Lady Margaret stood dumbstruck. A lord publicly siding with a servant over his own wife was an incredible rebuke. Lady Margaret's face turned as red as a slapped arse, and Eleanor enjoyed a flush of warmth to watch her ladyship's comeuppance.

Eleanor nodded a thousand times, wiping her nose. "Thank you, sir, my lord."

A silent conversation raged between Lady Margaret and MacLeod over the situation. Turning on her heel, Lady Margaret waved her hand, "As you wish, husband." She stormed off, all wind and fury towards a collection of guests.

"A word, my lord?" Mr. MacLeod said.

Lord Hallewell cast a stony expression as they huddled. Eleanor had mastered the art of eavesdropping, and kept her head down while she listened intently.

"My lord, you canna let her stay here. Beyond the marital tensions, consider the household discord. I've already let go Mrs. Clark over the incident, and you'll cause enormous anger among the servants if the older woman, whose only fault was to doze after a fourteen-hour workday, gets punished while the troublemaker is granted unwarranted mercy."

"Why should I care what anyone thinks?"

"Loyalty is earned. Justice must be dispensed fairly." He dug in his heels, unwilling to budge from his point of view.

Lord Hallewell rolled his eyes. "The servants can go to hell, along with my wife and you. Has anyone heard of forgiveness or mercy? Eleanor is young and curious, at most that deserves a slap on the wrist, not condemning her to a workhouse. For that matter, you've treated Mrs. Clark too harshly. Let her stay on as well."

Eleanor had to blink back her tears. She'd never known anyone to offer such kindness, especially a man in charge of everything.

MacLeod charged down a different path. "Consider the scandal. You think it was bad when your father went to prison? Mull over how they'll mock you for letting the servants run the household. Numerous guests will tell *The Tatler* about this incident."

Lord Hallewell's father went to prison? She hadn't realized aristocrats were ever held to account. No wonder he played such angry music in the middle of the night. There was so much more to Lord Hallewell than fashionable clothes and wealthy surroundings.

"What do you propose? I'm not letting Margaret win this battle. If anything, she put her capacity for cruelty on full display. That's the real scandal. The laundress stays."

"I'll handle things as you wish, but at least let me diffuse the situation."

"Fine. Fix it," Lord Hallewell said with a wave as he returned to the ballroom.

"Jesus, Joseph and Mary, it's like dealing with bairns all damned day," MacLeod muttered. Unsmiling, he walked to Eleanor, who was still rubbing her cheek. "Get your things."

"But Lord Hallewell said—"

"*Mr. MacLeod* said get your things."

"I dinnae understand?" She rose, shaking her head as she rushed up the double set of stairs, furious with the wrongness of it all. She'd put a curse on MacLeod too if she weren't afraid his witch wife would hex her back. Shoving her limited belongings into the carpet bag, she trudged past Mrs. Clark's room, not sure if the old woman was sacked or not. "I'm sorry," she whispered at the door.

Servants gossiped about Eleanor as they carried trays full of poached eggs and sizzling smoked kippers down the hall to the ballroom, not realizing she was on the stairs above them. As she reached the bottom, they met her with ugly sneers. *No one stood up for me but Lord Hallewell.*

Guests were beginning to leave, chattering as their coaches lined up. A duchess stumbled past Eleanor towards the exit clutching her slightly crumpled fan and laughing with unguarded glee. Her hair, once pinned in an intricate style atop her head, was reduced dangling curls that framed her claret-flushed cheeks. She charted her ungraceful path toward her awaiting carriage.

Lord Blackmere withdrew to his coach as well.

"My lord," MacLeod said striding out to meet him. "When did you want me to join you to meet His Majesty?"

The earl eyed Eleanor trekking outside with her carpet bag and tear-stained cheeks, as though she were Lucifer cast from heaven. "It appears you have your hands full with domestic issues, my good man. Bad things happen at Lord Hallewell's soirees, don't they?"

MacLeod kept a calm veneer on his face as his tensed body seemed to register a threat. A raven perched on a nearby tree.

Lord Blackmere faced her. "Don't look so forlorn, Miss Cameron. I've got a premonition we'll meet again." He held her hand and kissed it. It felt like a trap.

As his coach left, the raven clawed down the branch, as though it was listening.

"Are we going back to Saint Mark's, sir?"

"Get in the carriage, girl."

She climbed inside, feeling sick.

"Where to, Mr. MacLeod?" inquired the coachman.

"Grimbly Manor, then on to Scotland," he said climbing inside. "Fiona was right. Nothing to see with the king," he muttered.

"Not the workhouse? I'm still working for Lord Hallewell?" Grateful tears streamed down her cheeks. "Oh praise the lord in heaven." As they rode towards the sunrise, she searched the windows of Astwick House, wondering if she'd ever find herself beside her baron again.

Chapter 9

Fiona

Scotland—Litha fire festival

Fiona searched the firelight. If Matilda's ghost didn't come tonight, when the veil was thinnest, she might never unlock the scroll's secret.

A long line of villagers wove past the bonfire in front of the old castle, carrying chickens, rabbits, goats, and bags of coin. William mingled with the crowd, patting people's backs, cracking jokes, catching up on people's lives. As laird, his attention was in high demand from tenants wanting favors, clansmen talking politics, and neighbors seeking legal advice. David and Broderick helped take the livestock into the tower, while James recorded everything into the ledger.

Tables had been set up, and the servants prepared sweet meats and honey mead for the festivities.

At last, Matilda's ghost left the burning stake of her past life to join her. *For someone celebrating summer solstice, ye look miserable. Ack, Fiona, be happy—the veil between worlds is open tonight.*

Fiona spoke silently. "My family life went to shite since we last spoke."

I thought as much. I haena seen you since Imbolc. Did the delay spell not work?

"Reverend MacDonald has made it his personal mission to invite himself over every fire festival to prevent my scrying. He came during Ostara, then cancelled the village Beltane maypole dance and wonders why we're having a draught. As to the spell, it delayed William's return, but it dinnae help any. Beira possessed Lachie and told William that Broderick tore apart the clock. Then I tried to scry for William but couldna, and ack, I dinnae want to relive it. For a goddess, Beira can be quite unforgiving. Granted, I dinnae get to fully pay homage to her after your spell, but—"

Disobey Beira then act surprised? Ye were warned, lass, she snapped. *What's your husband doing now?* she asked, craning her neck.

"Collecting annual rents. They've been at it all day. The only reason there's a bonfire at all is because the tenants fear another bad harvest, and William convinced the Kirk it wasna pagan to do a blessing of the fields. I hope I managed to soothe Beira's ruffled feathers to protect the villagers from her wrath."

Matilda rolled her eyes. *They deserve a good famine for what they did to me.*

Fiona rubbed her temples. Sometimes it was easier to ignore Matilda's rants than to try to reason with her. "William's been in a foul mood since returning from London. He wanted me to foresee how his meeting with the king would go—"

William requested a reading? There's hope yet.

"But you never taught me how to command my clairvoyance outside of fire festivals. I foresaw nothing. Then his royal introduction was cancelled it made him even more irritated I dinnae warn him it would go badly."

If ye saw nothing, and the king's meeting never happened, it sounds like ye have more control over your visions than ye realize. Ack, he should be proud of your magical powers, even if he dinnae like the fortune told.

"If I had any control over my powers, dinnae you imagine I'd use it to read the scroll?"

Matilda looked bewildered. *Scroll?*

"Oh! After you left last time, Broderick found a scroll hidden inside one of the clock chimes. William dinnae even realize it's there. His mother, Elise, wrote it to him the night she eloped with his father. I'm positive it's enchanted. It has that smell."

Have ye tried to unblock it? Or did you search for a vision? You're both connected to William, so your prophecies might be entangled.

"Without magic it's hopeless."

How about now? I can meet ye wherever there's a fire or water to stare into. Make some excuse to leave.

Fiona nodded. She stepped up to William feigning a cough. "I feel something coming on. I need to rest."

He touched her forehead, brow furrowed. "It's not the fever?" he whispered.

"No, just worn down."

She kissed his cheek, and trotted past Reverend MacDonald still intoning a blessing in the field and slipped inside her empty manor. The servants were all at the festival. *Perfect.*

She lit a fire in William's study. "Matilda?"

Flames danced. Matilda stepped from them, her ghostly form already floating to the grandfather clock.

Fiona opened the glass case and unscrewed the false chime, and pulled out the scroll. She read aloud.

1699

My dearest future son,

Tonight, I escape my father's grasp to elope with your father, Rory MacLeod. Greatness awaits you and your heirs. This letter—with the help of the right person—is the key that unlocks the mystery.

Love,

Maman

Matilda smiled affectionately. *Ah, Elise Goring. I sold that lass more invisible ink than I dare admit. Kept her love letters secret. Her father, Admiral Goring, was such a bastard. She feared he would kill Rory if he caught them, so I made her a charm to protect her voyage to the Isle of Skye.*

Fiona pulled another letter from the Bible on the shelf. "Her writing looks...off. The spacing's different."

Och, Fiona, my eyes aren't what they used to be. Hold them side by side, in front of the fire, so I can see better.

As the firelight warmed the scroll, new letters formed between the sentences, faint and lemon-yellow at first, then darkening into legible script.

Fiona's breath hitched. "I ken it was enchanted. I suppose you're the 'right person' to unlock the mystery, auntie. It says, 'I told this dream to Elspeth.'"

Matilda's expression soured. *Elspeth? She told that traitor, not me?*

Fiona ignored her and read as more text appeared. "My father held a baby boy. He stepped toward the witch, Matilda. She held a baby girl..."

Matilda blinked. *I'm in her dream?*

"The letters are still coming," Fiona whispered. "They...the babies grew up, walked together, and formed a tree."

Lanterns flickered outside the window—William's wagon returning. "They're pulling up the private road. I have to hide it."

No. Hold it to the fire, so it heats up faster.

Fiona leaned in, the intense heat searing. "The tree bloomed with five blossoms...They held a baby..."

The lantern's getting closer, lass.

"A maiden, mother, and crone must form a coven to protect..."

Protect who?

"Can you stall him?"

Where's Pooka when ye need her? Cat, she called. *Where are ye?*

"Frost covered the ground. A blonde woman in chains... holding a red-haired girl...The sun rose and set five times." Fiona swallowed. "Then a crown fell."

What the hell does that mean?

The boys' laughter grew louder; their voices carried on the wind.

"I have to put it back."

It's almost done. Finish it.

"Dark shadows and a snake came to kill the girl and the coven, and then..."

The page caught fire.

"Bugger!" Fiona stomped it out.

Did the girl survive or not?

"I canna read the last bit where it burned."

Wagon wheels crunched the gravel as the wagon pulled in front of the front door.

Fiona scrambled to the clock, rolling the burned scroll and shoving it inside as Pooka padded in the room.

Here kitty, kitty.

William opened the door.

Meow, screeched Matilda, leaping with claws out.

"Damn it," he shouted, batting her away. "What's wrong with your cat?"

Fiona smoothed her hair. “Bad Pooka.”

“Werena you going to bed?” he said, rubbing a scratch on his cheek.

Words escaped her.

William touched her forehead with the back of his hand. “You’re still warm. You ken how these fever outbreaks can get dangerous. Best get to bed.”

As she climbed the stairs, the words from the scroll swirled in her mind. *A woman in chains. A fallen crown. Shadows threatening a baby. The dangers had only begun with no way to predict how it would end.*

Chapter 10

Eleanor

Grimbly Manor—Oxford

Eleanor dunked another tablecloth into the barrel and stepped into the cool, soapy water. The fresh air and picturesque views were a welcome escape from London's soot, and reminded her of Inverness, the only place she ever felt loved. Her truest escape was into her daydreams of the baron, of the way he danced with her once, of the way she dreamed he'd seek her out again.

Finally, the day arrived. A coach drawn by six thoroughbreds pulled into the graveled drive. Eleanor lined up with the other servants, bouncing on tiptoe. Lord Hallewell stepped down and peppered the butler with questions about the estate, ignoring her.

She wish cast. *Please, please look at me.*

He didn't.

Of course he dinnae. Why would a baron notice a laundress? Her heart sank.

Until he winked.

Lord Hallewell kept his distance at first, but whenever they passed each other in the halls, an energy sparked between them.

When Eleanor worked at Astwick House, everyone cast a sharp eye over her work, so she used a proper washboard and bat to remove the stains before bleaching. In Oxford, she did things as she pleased. The skeletal staff weren't watching, and the summer sunshine called her outside. Setting up a barrel near the well, she lifted her skirts and danced barefoot, the way her mam taught her. Eleanor swished her hips a little more, knowing he watched from behind a tree. Dressed impeccably in a powdered wig, gray velvet coat, and silk hose, the man was miles above the ruffians she once knew. "If you're going to stare, my lord, no need to be sneaky."

Caught, he stammered. Few challenged Lord Hallewell. "I was just—I beg your pardon—I was merely enjoying the fresh country air."

Eleanor didn't raise her skirts, but she didn't lower them either. "No need to explain. I serve you, my lord." She danced on, noticing his lingering gaze. *You danced with me at a ball, will you dance with me in a barrel?*

"I'll leave you to it." Instead, he walked closer, feigning interest in the process.

"You seem to be stayin' my lord."

"This is how laundry is done? I recall you using washboards."

"You recall?" she teased. He flushed. *I bloody made a baron blush!* "What are you reading, then?"

"A rather risqué novel. Perhaps you'd care to borrow it?" His eyebrow arched.

"They taught me laundry, not letters. You can tell it to me, though." She dragged a wet finger down her neck.

"Can't read?" he asked, stunned.

Dinnae remind him how stupid you are, eejit. Talk about laundry again. He's interested in that. "Dinnae tell Lady Margaret I'm doin' it this way. She'll have my head on a platter."

His lordship coughed at the mention of his wife. "Margaret's in London with the children."

"And you're alone in the countryside with me."

"Indeed. Well, not with you, obviously, but we are both standing here. You know, my solicitor, Mr. MacLeod, can teach you to read. His wife was a simple farm girl when they met. He taught her."

Back to reading again? Maybe I'm reading him wrong? Maybe he's not flirting, just kind. "Fiona, right?" She shivered at what MacLeod's witch wife might do if he was her tutor and Fiona was the jealous type. "No need to bother him."

Lord Hallewell insisted. "Oh, he's merely gruff. He's very loyal. It's settled."

Can you imagine? With the snap of his fingers, Lord Hallewell will make me literate? Not even a rich lord would pay for a servant's education out of the kindness of his heart. "Make yourself useful and hand me the soap."

His lordship acted startled. *It was a risk to speak to him impudently, but men like novelty, too, dinnae they?*

He fumbled the slippery stuff, and dropped it in the barrel. She bent low, giving him a good muse down her bosom. Before she found the soap, he found her mouth and kissed her.

Lord Hallewell tasted like wealth. Cream, and sugar, and wine.

He'll want a chase. Gentlemen like to hunt. She slapped him, watching his eyes grow wide, then she laughed and kissed him.

He realized she was toying with him, and a slow, masculine grin crept over his face. Anchoring his hand on her lower back, he pulled her forward. "You're a tease, Eleanor Cameron."

"Do you want to ken what I think, my lord?"

"George. You must call me George."

"I think you want a wife who's very clean, and a mistress who's very dirty. You're lucky I'm a laundress because I have knowledge of both. George."

Her urge to touch him overwhelmed her, despite her lowly status, the fact he was married, or the public location. A jittery feeling of excitement rose from within. *The richest, handsomest, most fascinating nobleman in London is choosing me?*

Lord Hallewell pulled down his breeches, and her eyes bulged, freezing for an instant to realize she was the reason it grew. She became aware of everything: his citrus and woody musk, the heat of his fingers as they dragged her petticoats up her thigh, the splashing of the warm soapy water against the barrel as he raised her dripping leg and wrapped it around his hip.

Holding onto him she felt safe in his sure grip. He entered her as she gasped through the burning, digging her fingernails into his back.

Her head was spinning. She hadn't realized people could couple standing up, or that her body craved this friction, or that a person could feel pleasure and pain all at once.

He shuddered inside then stilled, seeing blood. "It's your first time? Good heavens, I would never have taken your maidenhead like this had I known." He lifted her out of the dirty water as Giles approached on horseback.

She avoided his eyes, not sure of the right thing to say.

"Your guests are coming up the road, my lord. Take my horse."

"I forgot they'd be here today. Thank you, my good man." He squeezed her hand and left.

Awkwardly, she stood alone with the prissy old man who controlled her day. Pulling her arms into her core, she felt weak-kneed, crumbling at his scrutiny.

As Lord Hallewell rode off, Giles eyeballed Eleanor and spat. "Finish cleaning the linens, girl, then get yourself to a church and pray you don't get with child. Everyone knows how that story ends."

While the guests were visiting, Eleanor and Lord Hallewell avoided each other. There were rules. There were laws. Each passing day made her more anxious. *He's never going to speak with me again, and what if I'm left with a belly of shame?* Everything confused her, and she had no one to talk to. If only she could speak to him.

"Whore," someone whispered as she went outside to her laundry barrel.

Giles came out with a large basket of soiled bedsheets and dumped them on the ground. "You're behind on your work, girl. Lady Hallewell's cousins sweat through every sheet in the manor. Stop your damned daydreaming and get this done or I'll dock your wages."

"Yes, sir," she said plugging her nose.

As the guests pulled away in their coach, Lord Hallewell approached them. "Giles, my good man, could you bring some tea and biscuits? I'll take them at the gazebo."

"At once, my lord."

She started to work, but Lord Hallewell rested his hand on her own. "We left on rather abrupt terms. Let's take a stroll through the garden maze and talk."

The English yews were tall above their heads. She'd never wandered in a maze before. She'd never been in any situation like this before. *Is he going to turn me out now that he's had me? Or does he want another romp?* "Did you have a pleasant visit with your guests?"

"My wife's cousins. They're a quarrelsome lot. They've departed for London, thank God. Tell me about yourself, Miss Cameron. Were you always at Saint Mark's?"

"I'm from Inverness. I was orphaned at ten."

"I'm so sorry for your loss," he said squeezing her hand. He veered down a different path. "MacLeod lives up north too, in Kirkhaven. It's lovely but too rainy for my taste."

"'Everything's better in London.' That's what my Da said. I think Oxford is even better," she called getting turned around. Her cheeks warmed seeing him through the leaves, apart but still within her grasp.

"How did he die? You said you were an orphan?"

No one had ever asked her about her past before, and actually bothered to listen. "One day I was the happy fourth child of eleven. The next, everyone died of the pox but me."

"How awful. What a terrible burden on your heart, and then to end up in a workhouse. How did you get to London?"

She circled and backtracked, unsure how to navigate back to him. *Do I tell him? Or would telling the truth make him run from me?* "I dinnae wish to speak of it. It makes me sad."

"There you are," he said triumphantly.

She fidgeted with her apron strings, not used to anyone actively seeking her out. Most people used her and left. "Maybe I'll tell you everything someday."

He motioned with his arm to the opening, and she stepped into the sunlight. They continued strolling the gardens as servants peeked.

He dinnae mind servants seeing me, just not his wife's relations. Will the others get jealous and inform Lady Margaret to gain her favor? "Tell me about your music. When did you learn to play?"

"That's a bit of a sore spot in my family. I was always drawn to musical instruments and played everything—harpsichord, violin, harp. My father, the original Lord Hallewell, was a stern man, and dictated I should study law."

"You're a solicitor, then?"

He laughed. "Hardly. When it became apparent the law was beyond my grasp, he allowed me to study Moral Philosophy instead. I was twenty when my father was arrested."

Eleanor blinked, startled he'd admit such a thing.

"You seem astonished. I imagined servants knew all the secrets. I feel like I can trust you. Is that the case?"

She nodded.

"Do you remember the South Sea Bubble? My father was the scapegoat," he said, eyes fixed to the gravel path. "Lord Blackmere swindled just as many, if not more than my father, but slithered free and testified against him. It was as if someone had told him the future. That adder knew the exact moment to destroy the evidence against himself, and pin it all on my father. We lost everything overnight. Books, silver, portraits—gone. Blackmere even stripped the wedding ring from my mother's finger as debt repayment. We were left with nothing but the clothes on our backs, and a bill for my father's upkeep in prison. I threw it in the mud."

"No wonder you play such dark music in the middle of the night."

"I'm sorry, is this conversation too personal? I don't want to scare you off."

"I'm quite brave, my lord. Where did you go?"

"My mother moved in with her sister. William hired me."

"You mean William...MacLeod?"

"Strange but true." He chuckled. "When we met at Oxford, he already had land and a sweetheart of a wife, but I was the one from a noble family, and we were swimming in cash at the time. I took them under my wing. After the scandal, our roles reversed. It was humbling to be kept busy with paperwork for four long years while he grew in influence and stature."

"It seems he's in your debt now."

Lord Hallewell's face clouded with embarrassment. "I was incredibly jealous of his loving family. Then my father died in prison allowing me to claim the title of baron, much to the annoyance of Lord Blackmere. William arranged my marriage to Margaret and the balance of my and MacLeod's fortunes shifted completely. Quite a change from our Oxford days."

"What's moral philosophy, the thing you studied?" she asked, as they returned to her laundry barrel.

"The study of influential thinkers."

"Is that what you were studying in that risqué novel the day you claimed my maidenhead? Moral thoughts?"

His boyish grin returned. "Perhaps I should read it to you, Miss Cameron."

"Perhaps we should act it out," she dared.

Giles approached with a tray of tea and biscuits. She noted there was only one cup.

"I best get to washing all the sheets your wife's relations soiled."

He wrinkled his nose, taking a sip of tea from the tray. "I'm sure Giles can find someone else to handle that, right old boy?"

Giles stammered. "Of course, my lord."

Eleanor plucked a biscuit from his plate and took a glorious bite as Lord Hallewell took her by the hand and waltzed her inside.

The rest of the summer, Eleanor and Lord Hallewell lived a blissful open secret. Every night he played her a personal concert, his music becoming happier as they grew closer. They discussed everything from politics, to port, to sexual positions, of which they explored many. The man fascinated her, but even more interesting was that he truly cared to listen to her opinions.

She snuck into his bedchamber through Lady Margaret's passageway, luxuriating in the silk sheets and the orange-citrus scent of his peruke. Behind the rich velvet curtains of his four-post bed, she lay naked while prissy old Giles undressed him.

"Will you be needing any special travel attire for the duke's fox hunt?" Giles said.

"Oh bugger, that's this week?"

"Indeed, my lord. The last hunt of the summer."

"I suppose I'll have to go," he sighed.

"Very well, sir. The newest edition of *The Tatler* arrived, and you've received a letter from Mr. MacLeod. I've placed them on the nightstand. Sleep well." Giles closed the door behind him.

Lord Hallewell ripped open the curtain with a lascivious grin. "I thought he'd never leave."

"It's going to be rough returning to bleaching shirts while you're away." God only knew how she'd navigate going back to servant quarters.

"Can you read me MacLeod's letter?" he said propping the pillow behind his head.

"I canna read," she reminded him, stung that he'd forgotten his promise, but that's what men did.

"Oh darling, I didn't realize learning to read was important to you. I'll hire you a tutor." He opened the seal on the letter. "Oh, bugger. MacLeod can't go. He's busy with court cases."

"You need a solicitor to hunt? Are you afraid the foxes will sue?"

"No, silly. Every potential business opportunity requires a certain amount of...finesse, which MacLeod handles. If I want something another gentleman refuses to part with, MacLeod does due diligence to find what will properly motivate the man so I can get what I want. A baron, such as myself, requires distance from anything potentially scandalous that would reflect poorly on my good name. I should stop rambling on. You're a laundress, not well-versed in games of the aristocracy."

"I followed. MacLeod does your dirty work, aye?"

"You're smarter than you let on."

That caught her attention. *If he sees me as clever, not just pretty, maybe he'll keep me around longer.*

Playfully, he kissed her, tugging his teeth on her bottom lip as she giggled. "How about I show you my own dirty work?"

"Maybe MacLeod's not busy at court, but meeting the king with Lord Blackmere."

"Beg pardon?"

"I overheard them talking at the ball before we danced. Lord Blackmere wanted some information about MacLeod's client, otherwise he threatened to investigate the disappearance of someone named Colonel Wilkes. But if MacLeod did his bidding, he'd introduce him to the king."

Lord Hallewell pinched his eyebrows together. "MacLeod never mentioned any of this." He exhaled, and shrugged it off. "He probably deemed I wouldn't want to know until it was settled."

"He handles a lot for you," she said carefully. Every servant heard a rumor about the disappearance of Colonel Wilkes, but she never probed.

"I'd rather handle you right now," he teased, kissing down her belly. "I was under the assumption—a false assumption, clearly—that virgins were rather timid in bed." He lay beside her.

"Had you bedded many women before your marriage?"

"Ah...yes. I had a wild youth."

"Define wild, please, sir."

He rolled on his back and grinned. "Venice. Multiple women at the same time. Very drunk."

Eleanor studied him, wanting to please. "I might like to try something wild with you," she said tracing her finger down his chest.

He sat up. "Are you serious?"

She chewed on her thumbnail. "I like adventures."

Lord Hallewell fell back on the pillow. "Holy Christ, I'm the luckiest man alive. Where were you when MacLeod talked me into marrying the ice queen?" He picked up *The Tatler* and skimmed its pages. "My mind is positively brimming with ideas. Why are you pouting?"

"I dinnae mean to. It's just, well, I wish our romance wasna a secret."

"Agreed," he said flipping a page.

"I suppose it's just as well." She fidgeted with the edge of the blanket. "What would I do at the opera, or on a fox hunt, or at some table with eight different forks?" She grew quiet. "I dinnae blame you for being embarrassed of me."

"I'm never embarrassed by you," he said, lowering the paper. "You're the most authentic woman I've ever met but there are laws. I'm married, Eleanor. There are only four hundred noble families across England. We're all painfully aware of each other, and love to pounce if a personal scandal can be used for our advantage."

"Yes, my lord, you're right of course." She lowered her head on his chest, and he went back to reading. *He's going to his fox hunt, then back to London, and I'll never see him again.*

"Son of a bitch." Lord Hallewell sat up, snapping the paper.

"What's wrong?"

"I've been stabbed in the back, that's what's wrong. I need to get home."

"Can Mr. MacLeod help?"

"Fuck MacLeod. I'm the lord and he's my servant."

Alarmed, she reached for her shift, but he put his hand over hers. "Stay." He dressed.

"Did I do something wrong?"

"It's not you at all, darling. In fact..." Lovingly, he tucked a loose strand behind her ear. "You're the only honest person in my life, and I refuse to be separated from you for months at a time. Do you want to become my proper mistress?"

Her heart raced. "Aye, my lord," she squealed, hugging him tight.

He pulled her into a kiss. "I'll arrange everything. A fashionable address, an allowance. Say goodbye to your servant garb. You'll never work another day in your life."

She kept laughing.

"I'm going to the music room to think. Sleep well. I'll return in an hour or two."

But she was wide awake.

Leaving the bed, she strode naked through the secret passageway into Lady Margaret's room without hesitation, aware of the tingling sensations accompanying her newfound sense of power.

As Lord Hallewell's dark melody played, she unbolted Lady Margaret's wardrobe, luxuriating in the textures. The silky softness of a red Parisian gown stroked her skin as she pulled it on. The weight of the dress on her shoulders surprised her. Gliding to the vanity she rejected Margaret's narcissus perfume choosing her own. Jasmine and cloves—her own spell of seduction. A few drops on each wrist, behind her ears, a hint down the line of her cleavage as she imagined other ladies might do.

Standing before the looking glass, she pinched back the material in her left hand to see the curves of her waist. *That's me?* Her fingers touched her parted lips, shocked at the transformation one dress provided.

I was dressed in rags, and yet he chose me. He chose me.

She spotted citrine earrings and put them on. *Lady Margaret will never miss them—she wears red.* She smiled triumphantly at her reflection.

I am Lord George Hallewell's mistress.

Chapter 11

LORD HALLEWELL

London, Lord Hallewell's Wedding—The Past, 1724

Champagne in hand, Lord George Hallewell surveyed the sea of exquisitely dressed nobles from the bride-groom table. His eyes narrowed on Lord Blackmere. It was bold to invite him, along with Lady Margaret's secret lover, Colonel Wilkes, but tonight was a night for flexing his power. *What an incredible coup I pulled off.* He giddily sipped his drink, intoxicated with his newfound wealth and rediscovered prominence in society. Swaggering to his mother like an Allegro in a powdered wig, he kissed her cheek.

"Your father would have been so proud."

"Let's not ruin my wedding by mentioning him," he said with a strained grin.

Sadness clouded her face.

George leaned in. "Hold your head high, Mother, the stain of his scandal is washed away with my new wife's gold."

"Your wife is washing away her own thoughts with an uncorked bottle."

George frowned. *Margaret should be keeping up appearances.* "MacLeod will set up a residence for you by the end of the week. Nothing but the best from now on."

He kissed the top of her head, then strode towards his bride as onlookers raised their glasses in feigned congratulations.

They laughed at me, excluded me, mocked my family, and now they gaze on with jealousy at my palace, and drink the finest claret money can buy. Let them choke on it. Let them choke on their envy.

Lady Margaret sat alone, pouring wine, and staring into the packed ballroom floor.

"Searching for someone?"

She scowled into her glass.

With outstretched arms, he received Alexander from the nanny. George hugged his new stepson, bouncing him on his knee. *How drastically life changes in an instant.*

He spoke in a hushed tone to his bride. "You're upset I invited your lover to the wedding. True, I shouldn't gloat, but it isn't every day someone like me comes out ahead of someone like Colonel Wilkes." He leaned in. "The sooner you let go of him, the easier we can grow to love one another."

Young Alexander patted George's face with his chubby fingers. *How strange to have a son. I'll need to have my own children.* He swallowed hard sizing up Margaret's sharp nose, Habsburg chin and black hair. All his former lovers were blondes, but penniless barons couldn't be too choosey when the opportunity arose to marry a filthy rich widow.

"Careful my son doesn't sully your fine coat," Lady Margaret said flatly. "Did you buy that outfit before or after the ink on the marriage certificate dried?" she muttered refilling her glass.

"Ease up, Margaret. I'd hate to consummate the marriage with an inebriated wife," he half-joked.

With a slow sip of wine, she stared at the open doors leading to a long hallway decorated with paintings of her first husband, the old general. Couples scurried in and out of the ballroom, holding drinks and laughing. "You saved my reputation and son's inheritance, and now you get all my money for your pains. Don't make me pretend to love you, too."

An urgent tap on his shoulder made him spin. George smiled. "MacLeod, we should drink a toast to you for arranging everything."

Lady Margaret poured more wine.

MacLeod kept a stone face. "George—my lord—may I have a word?"

Handing Alexander to Lady Margaret, George rose, feeling uneasy. "Was the marquess trying to modify the terms again? The deal is signed. I've told my mother the house is hers."

"This is about something else, my lord," he said guiding George with his large hand on his upper back. MacLeod went quiet, and his gait seemed decidedly strange, like he wanted to bolt, but was restraining himself. Nodding at guests gossiping on the enormous staircase, MacLeod led him down a darkened hallway.

"I'll have to decorate these halls with suits of armor. Even if the cost means we'll go hungry, I can't bear to live in a palace lacking taste, or without suitably interesting decorations. Can you believe this is all mine? It still doesn't seem real, does it? I've been weighing a million different ways to invest my new stepson's fortune."

MacLeod spun, and held George's shoulders with an air of desperation. "I never meant for this to happen."

Hairs stood on George's neck. "What are you talking about?" MacLeod never acted like this. *Is this some jest to scare me on my wedding night? Are our friends from Oxford waiting to toast me in the back room?*

MacLeod glanced over his shoulder, and opened the door to the library, holding his finger to his lips for silence. Once inside, MacLeod bolted the lock, and moved a chair against it. Whimpers came from the darkness as moonlight streamed in through the elongated windows.

"Is someone crying?" George's eyes adjusted to the dimly lit room, until he discovered the unmoving body of Colonel Wilkes, drenched in blood, sprawled on the Turkish rug. Black patterns from the carpet looked like ravens flying from his wounds. "Oh my God," George said covering his mouth. An uncontrollable shudder swept through his entire body.

Red footprints glistened in the moonlight, and led to Fiona shaking in a ball in the shadows with bloodstained hands. MacLeod kneeled beside her, whispering in Gaelic as he rocked her in his arms.

George stood over them, gaping at the bruises around her neck. In her clenched fist was Wilkes' bronze medal. One of Fiona's fingernails had torn off. A painful lump formed in his throat. He wanted to help, but didn't know what to say or do.

MacLeod locked eyes with him. "I walked in on Colonel Wilkes raping her. I killed him."

Fiona gazed up, confused, then rested her head on MacLeod's chest.

A fog filled George's brain as he backed away. "You killed my new wife's lover?" Rubbing his jaw, his mind scrambled. "Margaret will think I killed him. I was just taunting her about him." His heel bumped against the dead body, tripping over it, barely catching himself from falling.

"Margaret hates both of us, Mac. She'll do everything in her power to see us hang for his murder. Oh fuck, Lord Blackmere is in the ballroom too. He sent my father to prison. He'll cherish the idea of destroying me."

MacLeod stood. "No. No one will ever find out."

"William, didn't you hear a word I said? Margaret is already suspicious, and the colonel's legitimate wife is in the banquet hall, too. Of course, people will find out! Don't you suppose she'll wonder where her husband went?"

"Wheest," MacLeod said, touching his finger to his lips. "There are over two hundred guests. No one will expect you to ken where Colonel Wilkes is, aye?" he said in a hushed tone.

"Jesus Christ, man, what have you done?" he whispered.

"He was raping—"

"Colonel Wilkes has the Order of the Garter. The king only bestows that honor on twenty-four men. Let's be frank, you're a nobody, and my father died in prison for fraud. Why would the king trust either of us saying his loyal friend is a rapist?" George gasped for air. "No. They'll discover Margaret had an affair with Wilkes, and everyone will agree I murdered him in some jealous rage, or that I put you up to his killing."

"No one kens about their affair but us," MacLeod said in a firm, steady voice.

"Nothing's a problem for you, is it? Not blackmail, not murder. I'll be arrested at my own wedding. I believed my father's imprisonment would be the biggest scandal of my life. I never envisioned this possibility." George loosened the jabot around his neck, feeling his chest itch. "Why would you do this to me? Why kill him in my home? Why not challenge him to a duel like any normal man?" His skin burned, itching with hives not had since childhood. "Lord Blackmere will ensure the king will have my throat."

He stared at Colonel Wilkes. He'd just seen him twenty minutes ago and now multiple stab wounds slit his shirt, and a shocked expression was fixed on his dead face.

"George, look at me." MacLeod grabbed him by his shoulders. "I. Will. Fix. It."

MacLeod's grip was rough and firm, the kind that left your skin bruised. His word carried weight, and George trusted him implicitly.

"Help me roll him in the rug, aye?"

They removed their coats, aiming to stay clean, but still bloodied their hands.

MacLeod surveyed the room. "I suppose, we can hide him behind the bookstack? I'll have to create a diversion to remove the body while avoiding the servants. Can you hide Fiona in a spare bedchamber?"

"I barely know the servants; I can't vouch for their loyalty or discretion." *How many times had MacLeod rescued me? I owe him loyalty, but enough to cover up a murder?*

Fiona rocked in the moonlight, dazed. Her diamond and emerald bracelet sparkled. "I'm sorry," she said meekly.

A flutter of guilt washed over him as he imagined what she went through. "Gracious, darling, you've nothing to apologize for." Moving beside her, he wiped a tear from her cheek with the back of his hand, fighting the urge to hug her, lest her blood-soaked shawl stain his waistcoat and further expose him for scrutiny.

MacLeod pulled off her shawl and wiped the blood from the floor. "You'll cover for me, aye? I need time."

George blinked. "Of course. I'll—I'll do a toast and draw it out. By the end, everyone will be too inebriated to remember who came or left, and no one will question your or Wilkes' whereabouts."

"I'll return to the wedding once I get rid of the bastard's body. If anyone asks about me, say Fiona fell ill, and I took her to the inn. I willnae forget this."

Neither will I. Trembling, he wiped his hands on the rolled up rug, then put his coat back on over his sweaty shirt, fumbling with the buttons, knowing that covering up his best friend's crime would forever damage their friendship.

Acid churned in his stomach as he stealthily left the library. Plastering a grin on his face he called to guests in the hallway, "Everyone to the banquet! Servants too. A toast! A toast to my beautiful bride!"

Chapter 12

WILLIAM MACLEOD

London, Present—1729

William MacLeod stared out the window at the blood red leaves on the ground while waiting.

Lord Hallewell strode into his study completely disgruntled. "What a lovely surprise to finally see you. I hear you had a busy summer, yet you still found time to double cross me." He opened his desk drawer and slammed down *The Tatler*. "Have you read this massive two page splash essay praising the moral efforts of Lord Blackmere's Reformation of Manners? Buried within the story it notes his ever-expanding land holdings. He's quoted as saying you arranged the deal."

"And?"

"That was my deal, MacLeod."

"You rejected it months ago because you dinnae have the money. I found another buyer."

"Who are you representing? Me or your new chum Lord Blackmere?"

"He's not my chum, and you're not my only client."

"Are you that hard up for money?"

"Are you that childish? You dinnae want the land but you dinnae want anyone else to have it either? He keeps pressing me to disclose young Charles Jamison's whereabouts, and I thought this land deal would be a peace offering to distract him. Was I wrong to try to protect your acquaintance's lover?"

"Why is he still concerned with Charles?"

"Do I ken how Supple Dick's brain works? I finally gave up the address. It took quite a bit of maneuvering to switch Charles to a new location mere hours before Lord Blackmere's men arrived to arrest him. At least I gave the appearance of helping while keeping Charles safe, but Blackmere keeps hounding me."

"Your dealings are purely altruistic, then? Bollocks. I heard you held audience with His Majesty."

MacLeod's blush betrayed him. "It was literally thirty seconds. I bowed and was soon escorted out of the throne room."

"You are here to fix my problems, as I have fixed yours with Colonel Wilkes, not to find ways to enrich yourself by aiding my enemies in exchange for an introduction to the king. When Eleanor told me about your conversation with Lord Blackmere I didn't believe her, but she was right."

Bloody eavesdropping piece of shite laundress. "Aye, I wanted to meet the king. Who wouldnae?"

"Your nakedly ambitious maneuverings are astonishing. Are you trying to make me the scapegoat for Wilkes, like Blackmere scapegoated my father?"

MacLeod's eyes opened wide. "No. I'd never betray you, George—"

"You will address me properly," he snapped.

He lowered his eyes, grimacing. "Apologies, my lord."

"I've more than proven myself to be your and Fiona's friend and protector. In addition to the Wilkes situation, need I remind you I pulled strings to keep Fiona from being arrested for playing at witchcraft? Sure, you handled the Kirk, but my connections prevented a trial. I couldn't get my own father pardoned, but I pulled some strings to secure clemency for her, didn't I? Then paid off the local constable and magistrate to quietly lose the paperwork so no one higher up heard about it."

His cheeks grew incredibly hot. "I'm aware, lord, and I thank you."

"I may not be the king, but I sure as hell rein over you. When I tell you to attend a fox hunt, it's not a suggestion. You come. Do I make myself clear?"

"Perfectly." *Hold fast, MacLeod.* His jaw ached from clenching in everything he wanted to shout at his friend-turned-adversary, realizing he was in the weaker position. *George would never seek to harm me, but what if he refused to help in a time of need? I dinnae have the clout or connections on my own to keep Fiona safe. I need him.*

Lord Hallewell poured himself port and drank unhurriedly while MacLeod stood still with his right arm holding his left behind his back, to pen in his fury at his dependance on this man.

MacLeod stared straight ahead, with a tightness around his eyes. "You ken I'm loyal to you, my lord. Lord Blackmere is a dangerous mutual enemy, and I like to keep my enemies close."

He chewed on his resentment like cud—over and over—never quite swallowing it down as Lord Hallewell enjoyed his drink, making him wait in silence as retribution for all the times MacLeod ignored him this summer.

"I know you're loyal," Lord Hallewell said at last.

MacLeod nodded.

"Good. Now that we've sorted that matter, I want you to set up Eleanor Cameron in a room near Covent Garden as my proper mistress. Oh, and one more thing..."

Chapter 13

ELEANOR

London, Present—1729

Eleanor squeezed the cold metal key pressed into her hand by MacLeod, and took a breath to take it all in. He toured her through her new home in the most fashionable part of London. She placed her carpet bag on the opulent couch, then opened the elongated windows. Her rooms had a commanding view over a private garden where beautiful trees, bright with autumn colors, muffled sounds of the city below.

"Lord Hallewell has a key, as do I." He made sure she noted that last part.

"And why might you have a key?"

"To check in on you at random times. It would be a terrible thing for a mistress to take on an extra lover."

"I'm a mistress, not a whore, Mr. MacLeod."

"Funny, I thought I hired a laundress." September sunlight bathed the room, giving everything a warm glow. "Your bedchamber is in the back. Servant quarters adjoin the dining room. They'll be arriving forthwith."

"Servants? For me?" She laughed, shaking her head.

He sat at the head of the dark cherry wood table. Silver candlesticks were on either side of an enormous bouquet of white lilies. "Sit. Please."

She kept a chair's distance between them. He pulled out a wad of cash from his waistcoat, counting it out in front of her. She blinked to see such a sight, grabbing for it, but he put his hand over the top.

"This is your allowance for the month. Dinnae ask for more because you willnae get it. If you try to get more by whispering in Lord

Hallewell's ear, I'll find out, and you dinnae want me on your bad side, aye?"

She rolled her eyes. "You can be quite the devil. I remember."

He lifted his hand lightly, and she took all her money. *My money.*

"The mantua maker and cobbler arrive in an hour. Lord Hallewell will stop by later this week. Do you have any questions?"

She put the money down her bodice. "How does it work?"

"I'm sorry?"

This man exasperated her. "Am I to stay inside all day? Can I walk the city?"

"May I. You're free to walk with an escort. Your lady's maid is named Gertrude. She reports to me. There are no secrets in this arrangement."

"Save from his wife."

The hint of a smile crossed his face. "Lord Hallewell tells me you canna read."

That's what he's like, MacLeod: Quick to put a person in their place. She sat taller because the hell with him. *I have power too.* "George says I will have a tutor."

"Aye. You're looking at him." He appeared about as happy with the situation as she did.

"Why you?"

"I'm not a threat. Lord Hallewell is jealous by nature, and he kens I love my wife. Married men are like butcher's dogs—we lie by the beef without touching it."

George is the jealous sort, is he? That's a useful bit of information.

Knock.

"Come in," he called, as though the place was his. Three servants entered, carrying their luggage. "This is Mr. Randolph, your butler, Gertrude, your lady's maid, and..."

"Jane? They let you leave Astwick House?" The girls hugged briefly until MacLeod coughed and addressed the servants. "This is your mistress, Miss Eleanor Cameron."

"My lady," they replied with a curtsey or bow. Jane kept sniggering.

Eleanor tried to stop them. "Oh, you don't have to—"

MacLeod's firm squeeze on her forearm silenced her. She didn't expect his touch. "Servant quarters are down the hall. Go settle in."

"Yes, sir." They left.

"Eleanor, you are his mistress now, his left-handed wife. You're not a servant. Those are not your equals. They are to address you properly, and you them. No blurred lines. We've had enough of that already." He looked like he sucked on a lemon.

"Mr. MacLeod, are you always hostile?"

"Yes."

"I'm surprised you aren't busier working for Lord Blackmere. Have you met with the king yet? Perhaps I should recommend George find another solicitor, one with a better disposition?"

"Aren't you cute?" He smiled, rubbing his bottom lip. "Lord Hallewell wants you to learn to read, so let's make this quick and efficient. This is a hornbook," he said pulling it from his satchel, and sitting at the table. "Have you seen one before?"

Shaking 'no,' she sat beside him. "Are those letters?"

"Aye. We'll start with the alphabet, and then combine sounds."

"Right now? Is this how you taught Fiona?"

He did a double take. "How do you ken my wife's name?"

"George told me."

MacLeod sighed heavily then tapped his finger on the hornbook. "This is the letter 'A'. Repeat it."

"A. Repeat it." Eleanor smiled and raised her eyebrows, hoping to get a rise out of him. "Fiona must be a saint to put up with you." *I dare you to yell at me now.*

MacLeod leaned away, resting his arm over the back of his chair. "I get paid whether you learn to read or not. You can focus and improve yourself, or you can remain an ignorant workhouse whore with a pretty face, and hope Lord Hallewell dinnae grow bored with your antics. It dinnae matter to me."

A flush crept across her cheeks, and she slanted away from him. *Obnoxious bastard. He reckons he's better than me?* "A. What's the next one?"

"B."

The lesson continued like that until he taught every letter and sound. Two hours had passed, and she shifted in her seat. "Will you be coming back tomorrow, then?"

"Who says I'm leaving?"

Eleanor rolled her shoulders. "I need a break. My brain is ready to split open."

"As you wish." He nodded, and the butler handed him his tricorn hat and coat.

"How soon till I can read and write?"

"It depends. Six months, if you're clever. A year, if you're lazy or stupid," he said staring down his nose at her.

"Are you saying I'm stupid? Is that what you're saying?"

"Prove me wrong. Our task is to learn the basics before I go home for Samhain. Dinnae waste my time fighting me tomorrow. Ten o'clock, sharp."

"I may not ken my letters, but I can read people, Mr. MacLeod. I've gone from a workhouse, to servants' quarters, to living in my very own London rooms, and I'm barely eighteen. George is enamored with me."

"For the moment," he said.

Chapter 14

WILLIAM MACLEOD

Scotland—Samhain fire festival

William MacLeod wrapped his arms around Fiona, pecking her cheek as she helped the boys carve turnips for Samhain. "Surprise," he said handing her a package.

"I dinnae need another gown from London." She opened the box and was shocked by the beautiful tartan arisaid, and another shawl from the Isle of Skye.

"These suit you better. Happy birthday."

"They're perfect. Thank you," she said with a hug.

He lowered his voice. "I'm looking forward to celebrating our anniversary too."

Her eyebrows raised. "Time for chores, boys."

Their sons groaned, setting aside their carvings.

Broderick had a panicky expression. "Not the chickens by myself, right, Mama?"

"Still afraid of the dark?" William tried for a teasing tone, but the weariness behind his words betrayed him.

"Take the lantern," Fiona said, then frowned at MacLeod as Broderick sulked off.

"You canna keep babying the boy."

He tried to kiss her, but she twisted away. "You're too hard on him. He's not the only bairn with fears."

"It's our anniversary. Please, for the love of God can we stop talking about him, and enjoy a few minutes of privacy before we head to the festival?"

"I have barmbrack baking I need to check," she said leaving him for the kitchen.

He wanted tonight to be simple. Just a kiss. Not another reminder of what they'd lost, and what they were forced to take in. He blew out air. *I suppose we can make love after the fire festival.*

He went to his chamber to freshen up. As laird he had a responsibility to lead the community. As Fiona's husband, he had a gnawing feeling the villagers looked at her askew, especially during Samhain.

Tugging off his shirt, he poured water from the ewer into the basin and washed.

He once thrilled to the idea of being married to a white witch. Then he discovered the costs. *If I dinnae have to protect Fiona all the time, I wouldna be beholden to George. I wouldna have to waste my time tutoring a workhouse whore. God only kens what she'll whisper in his ear to poison him against me and threaten my job. I'm trapped in every area of my life.* Patting dry his face, he put on a fresh shirt and waistcoat from the wardrobe, then grabbed his favorite overcoat and groaned. He came downstairs and held it out to Fiona. "Can you sew the top button? It's hanging and I need to appear presentable."

"In a minute." Fiona put down her plate of barmbrack. "Where's Broderick? We need to leave soon. James, have you seen your brother?"

James lowered his Bible. "No."

William exhaled in annoyance. "Dinnae sit there, boy, go find him."

"David," James yelled into the kitchen. "Do you ken where Brod is?"

"No," he yelled back.

William removed his coat and gave it to her. "Just a stitch or two."

"Broderick," Fiona called.

"What's so urgent you need to find him now? The celebration is an hour away."

"I haena seen him for a long time. I canna imagine him still feeding the chickens. It's cold outside, and you ken how he fears the dark."

"Aye, God forbid he linger near the haunted barn. He fears spiders, loud noises, dogs. Is there anything he isna afraid of? And his incessant Why? Why? Why? grates on my nerves."

James popped into the room. "I canna find him anywhere."

"As long as he isna tearing apart another family heirloom, he's fine. Can you please sew my button?"

"Can it wait five minutes? Are you leaving this very second?"

"Fine. Let's find the boy right now. Broderick," he hollered, storming through the house as servants scrambled to join the search.

"William, stop acting like a brute. I'll find Broderick then sew your damn button."

"Broderick," he shouted storming outside. He walked past the barn, its stone slab roof burdened beneath the weight of fallen leaves. MacLeod noticed dim lantern light reflected off the frost-covered ground and barreled forward. "Oh my God."

Fiona and the other boys piled behind, dumbstruck.

Dead chickens ripped to shreds littered the yard enclosure in front of the weathered chicken coop. Broderick was curled over his knees cowering beside the barn, its limestone walls splattered with blood.

MacLeod walked past the carnage, knocking over a tin pan with dusty grain left on the ground then knelt beside the boy. "Are you all right?" he asked, giving the sobbing boy a quick hug. "What happened?" He stood the boy up, quickly scanning for injuries and finding none. Broderick kept bawling, not even attempting an answer. "I said, what happened? Dinnae you talk, laddie? Or do words scare you, too?"

Broderick quivered with thick, damp lashes. "I saw a fox, sir. I...watched him kill all of them."

"Why dinnae you come get me?" MacLeod glanced around. "You just let the chickens get slaughtered?"

Broderick's mouth moved, but nothing came out as his eyes darted to the surrounding massacre. Tears rolled down his flushed cheeks.

"William, please."

The blood—Fiona's pleading—triggered the memory MacLeod fought so hard to forget. The copper scent of blood hit him like a wave. His hands trembled. He saw Wilkes again, saw the bruises around Fiona's neck and between her legs, her blood-soaked shawl.

And in Broderick's brown eyes, he saw Wilkes smirking. MacLeod experienced a pounding in his ears and his vision narrowed as he unbuckled his belt, ready to unleash, but the boy held up his hands. It took everything in his power to control his rage from the brink. His fist tightened around his belt and then he stepped away and threw it against the coop, grunting in frustration.

Then came the stares—Fiona's blazing eyes, his sons' disbelief.

Fiona picked up Broderick. "Walk away, William."

Rain drops fell, disorienting him. MacLeod put his thick leather belt through the loops, then surveyed the misery before him. Chicken entails were strewn across the yard and blood-soaked feathers floated on the wind. He left as fast as he could, ashamed for losing his temper, especially in front of his sons.

Striding down the uneven road he was drawn to the crumbling castle overlooking the Firth of Clyde. Cold air burned his lungs and steam rolled off his skin as he approached what had once been his greatest source of pride. The forest and the castle reflected off the glassy loch, smooth as a mirror.

He remembered his wedding night, when he vowed to shield her from witch hunters as they were handfast. But now his marriage was crumbling worse than the decrepit fortress before him. As he entered the drafty old castle, with its pitted stones and echoes of violent history, he stood in his own frustration.

Spying a web-covered chair on the floor, he picked it up and smashed it to pieces against the wall as he fought back tears. He dropped the broken chair leg. His hands were shaking.

I was supposed to protect her. That's all I ever wanted. I failed her. I failed them all.

"What in God's name is wrong with you, William MacLeod?" Fiona said in the doorway. "You need to attack a castle too?"

He ran his hand through his tangled hair. "Why does he have to look like Wilkes? I canna bear to see his face every day."

Fiona's fists moved to her hips, speaking in a clear, clipped manner. "You are not the victim here. Do you think I want a constant reminder of the rape? Like it or not, Broderick is our son."

"The rapist's son."

"My. Son. Too."

Her words hung in the icy air like mist as flurries fell through the partially collapsed roof. "His father wasna his choice, and I certainly had no say in any of it, just like the boy has no control over a fox getting into the hen house."

The heat of shame flooded his face. He moved to the winding stairwell, trying to regain composure. "This isna working, having him here." He rubbed his temples, taking another deep breath and blowing it out before facing her. "I ken the boy is innocent. It's just... He deserves better, and I canna give it." He couldn't hold her gaze. "I dinnae want to become the man who beats him." He glanced at Fiona, aching for how deeply he kept seeming to fail her.

She cupped his face in her hands. "If you let go of your anger, you could see him for the wonderful boy that he is and not the wretched pig who sired him." She sat beside him. "In any case, Reverend MacDonald proclaimed we're to raise him."

"Lord Hallewell sends his son to Lottington Hall. The lad is young, but he's already reading. Surely the reverend willnae object to the lad receiving a proper eduction."

"You want to send Broderick all alone to school in London? He's small and shy."

"It's for the best. For everyone."

Fiona rubbed her temples. "It's time to head to the festival. We'll discuss this tomorrow when you're calm."

He didn't answer. He thought about the arisaid and shawl he'd given her earlier for her birthday. Their anniversary. It was another day he meant to celebrate, destroyed by the lingering nightmare of Wilkes.

Chapter 15

Fiona

Scotland—Samhain fire festival

Sparks flew into the night air. Reverend MacDonald roamed a suspicious eye as the villagers walked their cattle between two bonfires to ward off bad spirits. The church disapproved of such celebrations, but superstitions ran deep, and no one wanted to risk another bad harvest.

William weaved through the crowd, chatting easily with her sister, Mary, and brother, Malcolm, while Fiona sat alone by the fire, tapping her toe as she waited for Matilda to appear.

Finally, Matilda's death manifested; her ghost departed the stake, passed through flames, and entered the land of the living.

Thank the goddess Samhain arrived. I've been mulling over that scroll with Elise's dream, trying to sort out what it all means.

"I dinnae even care anymore. William is sending Broderick away to school in London."

Why?

"He believes getting rid of Broderick erases the fact I was raped. I'm beside myself." Thunder rumbled through the sky as lightning struck the hills.

Ease up, Fiona. Control yourself before ye cause a storm.

Laughter interrupted them. David and James were dangling a yarn string in front of Pooka, trying to get her to walk under a defecating cow.

"What do you get if you lie under a cow? A pat on the head," joked David, doing his best to cheer up Broderick. Lachlan broke into giggles.

James headed to the harvest table. "Mam, do you want barmbrack?"

"No, you boys go."

James carried Broderick piggyback as David and Lachie ran beside them.

"I dinnae have the heart to tell them he's leaving tomorrow."

I'm sorry, dove. Do you want to focus on something else? Let's piece together the meaning of Elise's dream. It might reveal how I get unbound from Kirkhaven so I can hunt down Elspeth and the nobleman witch hunter.

"Matilda, enough with your revenge. Can you focus on anything besides your damned anger for once? Let Beira punish them in her own good time."

Lightning split the sky as thunder cracked in the distance. She closed her eyes, focusing on the angry clouds breaking apart and blowing away. "I dinnae mean to snap," she said after a moment, just wanting to make peace. "I ken William is trying to do his best to find a solution we can all live with, but it's just so hard...I suppose I could use a distraction. Let's talk about the prophecy. The dream said Admiral Goring held a boy, and you were holding a girl, and she told this dream to Elspeth."

Now I finally ken the true reason for my execution. Elspeth must have convinced the noble witch hunter I was going to bed Admiral Goring, god forbid, or one of his sons and bear a powerful witch. That's the real reason why he and Admiral Goring had me tortured and burned. But why stop with me? I was sure he'd come back for you.

"Maybe he dinnae believe the king was threatened any more, at least by you. After all, you cursed Admiral Goring and both his sons to death from the stake, leaving no one for you specifically to couple with, thus no chance of a wise child to be born. Or perhaps he only feared your daughter would marry one of the admiral's sons. I'm merely your niece."

You're more daughter than any child I might have born.

Fiona smiled at the compliment. "Perhaps he's too busy hunting the blonde woman in the prophecy to bother with me."

Aye, but what if the vision was misinterpreted by Elspeth, and she told the witch hunter the wrong thing? What if Admiral Goring wasna holding a son, but his grandson—your husband, William? And I was holding you?

"Do you think Elspeth made a mistake? Or lied to protect me?" Fiona covered her mouth.

Matilda looked particularly offended. *Goddess in heaven, you're not defending that traitorous hag, are ye?*

"No, of course not. You ken I hate her for betraying you." Fiona glanced at Reverend MacDonald, busy talking with the elders of the Kirk. "So you were holding me in the dream. It makes sense. The children grew up then walked together forming a tree that blossomed. That's got to be William and my family tree, aye? And the five blossoms are our sons? We're holding a baby in the vision. Is the bairn the key to our family's legacy? I should tell William about the scroll, and his mother's prophecy."

Och, Fiona, he'd never understand. Besides, we dinnae ken what it means with certainty.

"The five blossoms matches my prediction of having five sons. I still have another bairn to bear obviously, but it seems likely to prove true. That was one of the first visions I had as a lass, remember? But I had a more recent premonition too," Fiona remembered. "Back during Imbolc, I asked Beira how to fix my marriage. She showed a vision of a red-haired fairy girl, and I thought she meant I'd have a daughter. But then I stumbled upon a blonde maiden in chains protecting the girl as a raven flew overhead. 'Only the coven can protect the girl from the witch hunter,' she said."

Bloody hell, Fiona, why dinnae ye mentioned that sooner? Did the raven see ye?

"The vision came before we found the scroll, so it made no sense. In any case, you've said many times you'll never form a coven again."

Matilda paced. *If Elspeth located ye, and told the mysterious witch hunter, then what?*

"Who's the woman in chains? Only her daughter reached for the crown. And the crown means what? King George? King of the Fae? Someone with royal blood?"

None of this would have happened if Elise Goring spoke to me instead of that wormtongue Elspeth. I was always better at interpreting dreams than her. Why would Elise not confide in me, especially since I was the witch in her damned vision?

"Maybe she was afraid of you, after all, you did sink her father's ship, and everyone in the village feared your sharp tongue after a night of ale."

Och, shut your gob. Why would anyone be afraid of talking to me?

Reverend MacDonald walked through Matilda's translucent figure, and she cringed. He immediately crossed his arms over his chest as his teeth chattered. "I hate All Souls Day," he muttered walking to the barmbrack table decorated with carved, candle-lit turnips.

Matilda probed the sky. *Beira, when will ye let me have my revenge? Haena I paid homage to ye? Haena I been trapped in purgatory with no relief since cursing Admiral Goring?*

"Auntie, no. The only way to escape Purgatory is through redemption, not revenge."

Caw. A raven appeared inside the bonfire.

Son of a witch. Is that ye, Elspeth? Come to spy on me after all these years?

The raven flapped its wings in a wild retreat as Matilda's angry spirit flew after her into the flames.

"Matilda, no," called Fiona.

A cold breeze swept Fiona into a shadowy Otherworld, devoid of a light source. Damp mist wet her skin as she wandered the strange land. She found herself next to Matilda, inside the bonfire, looking into a torch-lit cave where some sort of religious ceremony was taking place.

"Where are we?"

Chapter 16

Eleanor

London—Samhain fire festival

"Where are you taking me, George?" Eleanor tugged at the nun habit over her hair. Dressed as a friar, Lord Hallewell gave no explanation for their required costumes, or why they traveled outside London after sunset on All Hallow's Eve.

"You'll see," he said, planting a kiss on her open mouth.

Six black horses pulled their decadent coach down a private road shadowed by a thick forest, then slowed to a stop. At the top of a hill, an abbey stood beneath the harvest moon.

"Based on our conversation this summer," he lowered his voice, "and your adventurous spirit between the sheets, I think you'll appreciate this wild place. I love that about you. But. We need to set some rules. If ever you feel ill at ease, say, 'My dearest George,' and I'll rescue you from the situation."

Eleanor's eyes opened wider as she crossed herself.

Lord Hallewell chuckled. "You don't have to pretend you're a nun yet."

"My dearest George, I'm not acting. I'm afraid the Lord Himself might strike us down with lightning for blasphemy."

"At least we'll go out with a bang." Lord Hallewell lifted his hood, then drew her into a protective hug. "It's time to leave heaven," he said.

Shivering as she left the coach, Eleanor craned her neck to scan the strange location, while inhaling the scent of chimney smoke. Dozens of footmen were joking among themselves, brushing and feeding their masters' horses as they waited.

How delightful to attend the party, rather than clean up afterwards.

George's warm hand gave her reassurance as he led her down a hill, and through a dark forest where owls *hoo-hooted* overhead. "Mac tells me your studies are coming along. He says you're quite bright."

"That's news to me. He's always grumpy," she said taking careful steps over gnarled tree roots. "But I can read simple sentences now, and write a few words. Soon we can send lover letters to each other," she said excitedly.

A clearing appeared at the hill's base, showing three decrepit church walls. She peered through the twisted iron gates blocking a cavernous opening where hushed whispers collided with boisterous laughter.

"Welcome to the Hellfire Club," he said with a boyish grin.

As the gates swung open, they stepped inside a chilly, damp cave lit by torches affixed to the limestone walls. The clay-laced scent of chalk clashed in a disorienting way with the rich aromas of roasted meat from deep within. Rounded archways led to various rooms, where lustful grunts echoed and reverberated.

"It used to be a monastery in the 15th century, but obviously fell into disrepair."

Two portly gentlemen wearing black robes and gaudy wooden crosses rustled past them. "Brother Hallewell," they said in greeting. After taking in Eleanor's full form, they nodded approvingly, then disappeared down a side path.

"How far do these tunnels go?"

"The chalk caves branch into different cells, and the last room, the inner sanctuary, is about 300 feet beneath the church on the hill. Can you guess what it represents?"

"Heaven and hell?"

"Smart girl. This is Judgement Pass. Saints go right, sinners go left. Remember, you need to return the same way, otherwise the ghosts will chase you. Which way shall we go?"

Fear struck Eleanor as she recalled her first meeting with the witch of Pye. *'Are you a sinner, or a saint? Your choice has consequences.' Did the witch know I'd be at the Hellfire Club one day?* She crossed herself, aware of the significance of her choices these last few months. "We must travel the path of the sinners, my lord."

Pressing her hand against the wall, she was surprised by the softness of the chalk and curious about the grooves beneath her fingertips. Upon examination, she gasped at the imprint of a man's face bearing an inverted cross carved into his forehead.

A stark-naked woman wearing rosary beads giggled wildly as she skipped down another passageway, and into a cell where Eleanor caught the glimpse of a gigantic bed with tangled sheets.

"My dearest George," Eleanor said, gripping his arm.

He hugged her. "It's silliness, darling. Sir Francis Dashwood took a Grand Tour in his youth, and came back from Rome despising everything to do with Catholicism. No one's really demonic. We're merely a bunch of bored libertine aristocrats having a good laugh at society."

A minute later, they passed a cell filled with friars gambling while nuns sat on their laps. A middle-aged man with a sharp nose nodded. "Brother Hallewell."

"Brother Sandwich," George said as they passed the room. "That's the fourth Earl of Sandwich," he whispered. "Gambles even more often than I do. He created a fantastic meal—roasted beef between two slices of bread so he could eat with one hand and play cards with another. It sounds preposterously awful, but tastes quite good. Now, we all say, 'We want a sandwich.'"

The din of chatter grew and commingled with the clinking of glasses coming from a banquet hall filled with hundreds of candles giving off a tallow scent. Beneath a huge domed ceiling was a long dining table loaded with roasted boar heads biting apples. At least thirty people—draped in a mix of satirical Catholic robes or pagan-inspired stag horns and animal skins—raised their glasses in a toast as they entered, then turned back to their debauched feast. Lord Hallewell pointed out his friends, "Member of Parliament, Member of Parliament, poet, actor, Regis Professor of Civil Law at Oxford, wine merchant—is it any wonder how he gained admission—Archbishop of Canterbury's son. Anyone of good taste is here."

"And you all go off in different rooms to roger women?"

"Well, not everyone. Many attend solely for the hilarity of the revelries and witty poetry after dinner."

A passing 'nun' traced her fingers across Lord Hallewell's chest as he grinned.

"Move on, bitch," Eleanor said.

Lord Hallewell's eyes grew wide. "Didn't you want this? You mentioned your desire for a ménage à trois with another woman."

I dinnae think that one through, did I? Eleanor believed a wild night meant they'd frolic with another man. She loathed competing for George's attention, but he seemed enthralled with the idea now. *If I say no, he'll find another girl.* There were dozens of other women here willing to do literally anything. She felt inadequate in every way. "I suppose I'll loosen up with some wine."

He grinned. "I never knew you had a jealous streak. I love it when workhouse Eleanor comes out." His face went serious. "I want to be perfectly clear; you don't have to do anything with anyone. We can go home whenever you want. But if you're curious to explore all things wild, this is the destination."

It was interesting when I pictured it in the privacy of our bedchamber, but do I really want to try an orgy?

A famous actor grabbed her hand and kissed it. "Surely the good nun will hear my confession?"

"Shouldn't you be at Drury Lane Theater dressed like a fairy?" Lord Hallewell said.

"And miss all the fun here?" A cocky grin played on the actor's lips. "By the bye, I play Oberon, King of the Fae, not just any fairy, thank you very much."

Eleanor giggled.

"Are you up for a game of cards, Hallewell?" The actor's eyes wandered over her body. "Perhaps the winner takes her home?"

Lord Hallewell's hand curled into a fist and his legs parted, as though readying himself for battle.

Sensing the tension, Eleanor stroked George's face. "Who needs cards? I can contemplate a million different games I'd like to play with my Lord Hallewell in one of these cells instead."

A satisfied grin spread across George's face, and all tension lifted from her. *He thinks I'm worth fighting for.*

The actor wandered off, and Lord Hallewell took a seat at the dining table, sliding Eleanor onto his lap. He fed her a single grape at a time, each bite of fruit bursting with sweet juice in her mouth. He drank from a golden goblet, then kissed her, leaving her lips tingled from spiced wine. Incredibly indulged, she drank enough illicit spirits to make her dizzy.

"It appears you have a wee bit of a jealous streak too, my lord," she teased. The near fistfight over her made an impression. She held her head higher, aware for the first time of her own budding worth in the eyes of men.

All around them, people disrobed, their mouths finding eager partners, hands gliding from one person's body to another's. Two masked men kissed; she gasped, then watched Lord Hallewell's reaction.

As he leaned in closer, she inhaled his woody musk. "There are no saints here, Eleanor, only pleasure seekers. Are you open to that experience? If not, you know what to say."

My dearest George. "Yes, my lord," she whispered, as he moved his expert hands up and down her body. Savoring each sensation, she particularly enjoyed the tall actor eyeing her the whole time.

A man with a dark blue coat and golden braid beneath his tricorn hat appeared holding a lantern that flickered in the cavern's breeze. "Brother Hallewell, I'm cox for the evening. Who is this pious nun accompanying you?"

Lord Hallewell gave her a wink, so she discarded her fears and played along. "Sister Eleanor, I suppose."

"Only, she's not pious at all. She's quite the wicked one, and requires an unholy baptism," Lord Hallewell said, pinching her rump.

"Sister Phoebe requires a baptism too," called another man.

"And so does Sister Mercy."

Eleanor gazed nervously at the other women, roughly her age. One bit at her lip, while the bitch who flirted with Lord Hallewell gave a quick, high-pitched laugh.

"Follow me sisters, to the River Styx," the cox said. "It leads to the underworld."

Eleanor glanced at Lord Hallewell, her eyes widening. *Are we going to the inner sanctum? Are we going to Hell?*

Sister Phoebe squeezed her hand as the long tunnel grew dark. Drips and splashes echoed, but pinpointing the source proved impossible within the cavern. A subtle mineral tang filled the cool, damp air as Eleanor's heels sank into the sand on a riverbank, where an ornate gondola rested beside the water.

Four men in white shirts and breeches each held a red oar. The cox led, Eleanor sat among the girls, and Lord Hallewell and the others filled the remaining seats.

Droplets of cold water fell from stalagmites to her skin. Eleanor's heart pounded with each splash of the oar; the boat's motion unsettled her. Her memory flashed to her childhood, rowing to the mainland with the captain, believing everything would be better in London. But he left her in a workhouse. A gnawing unease gripped the pit of her stomach. *Might Lord Hallewell abandon me too?*

Landing ashore on an island within the cave, the cox rose, lifted her and the other maidens onto a sandy bank opening to a large torch-lit chamber built inside a cave wall. It was so strange here beneath the earth. The spinning sensation from the wine didn't help either.

A red-cloaked, horned figure stood beachside, behind an altar. *Is this what the Devil himself looks like? What the hell have I gotten myself into?*

"Disrobe and kneel," said the horned high priest, pointing to a pile of leather and furs lain in the middle of a pentagram etched into the ground. Eleanor looked agape at the others. The noblemen from the gondola made a semicircle around them, covering their mouths to stifle their drunken laughter.

Lord Hallewell caught her eye and mouthed, "Are you well?"

Not really, but if Lord Hallewell is pleased, perhaps I should enjoy myself. After all, if the most powerful men in the world are taking part, what do I have to fear?

She loosened her nun costume until it dropped at her feet, leaving her naked save garters, and hose, and her black heeled shoes. Spinning to Lord Hallewell, she held deep and prolonged eye contact as she kneeled, feeling strangely strong as the eyes of powerful men ogled her plump breasts and rounded bottom with obvious appreciation.

Unnoticed by most partygoers, a tall gentleman dressed in a cloak of ash-dusted gold watched from the shadows. He wore an extraordinary Venetian half-face mask decorated with black and green snakes weaving around slanted eyes. Unlike most of the other men, the viper-masked gentleman wasn't interested in her body, and she had the creeping sensation that behind the safety of his anonymity he tried to penetrate her mind. The curl of his lip threatened violence.

She looked back to Lord Hallewell for reassurance, but he was busy joking with his friends.

Soon her female companions kneeled naked beside her on the furs. The men's panting grew louder. As she inhaled incense and musk, she noticed the crackling flames of a bonfire behind the altar casting eerie shadows on the chalk walls.

The high priest chanted in a deep voice and raised his left hand above her. "I baptize you with unholy water," he said while drizzling cold water over her head.

Goosebumps spread across her arms, and her nipples hardened. Crossing herself, Eleanor said, "Bless me, Father, for I have sinned." She noted George watching spellbound, giving her all the encouragement she needed. "And I intend to keep sinning."

Spontaneously, Eleanor turned to the girl beside her, and drew her head downward for a forbidden kiss as the men collectively held their breath. She'd never kissed a girl before, and found it interesting. Softer lips. A more cautious exploration of a wine-flavored tongue.

Heavy fabrics rustled as the men shed their robes, delighting in their games of no consequence. Lord Hallewell's mouth was soon upon her as he anchored his hands around her, squeezing her flesh with ever-increasing intensity. Soft strokes of lips and fingertips against her back, her neck, her thighs, came from multiple hands, and varied directions as she laid back on the soft furs, warmth blooming across her body.

"I'll be right back," George whispered, leaving to talk with two other nuns. Sister Phoebe soon clasped Lord Hallewell's hand, leading him to another cavern.

The cave seemed to shrink around her as she struggled to catch her breath. *Why would he leave now? Haena I done everything he wanted?* Eleanor rose to follow, but suddenly, the actor approached and kissed her, keeping her on the ground.

Her thoughts froze while her body heat rose. *Am I to kiss back?* The actor certainly had some skill, but would this upset George? *But he left, dinnae he? What if he came back and saw? Was that necessarily a bad thing?*

She moved her fingers through the actor's thick hair, smelling the whiff of his perspiration through his cologne. The actor kissed down her belly and before she could object, his mouth nuzzled between her legs, something only George had ever done to her. She laid back on the bear skins, noting all the strange pagan symbols shifting about the room.

The viper-masked man seized her wrists tightly above her head and tied them.

"My dearest George," she called, trying to sit.

George was nowhere.

A pair of otherworldly golden-amber eyes watched from the bonfire.

The actor grabbed her thighs tighter, continuing his ministrations. The viper-masked man's eyes darted between her and the actor, as though struggling with what to do next. His furtive gaze lingered on the actor's mouth. He abandoned her wrists as he moved behind the actor, hugging his back while she frantically tugged the rope to free herself. The actor looked annoyed, and shoved him off.

The glimmer of a dagger blade caught her eyes as she realized with increasing panic the masked man was readying to strike. Shaking uncontrollably, she wanted to scream or flee, but terror kept her rooted to the spot. She feared he might slice the actor's neck, but then his eyes narrowed onto her. Horror-struck, she watched him stealthily raise the dagger above her womb.

Bidh falbh, called a voice from inside the flame. A cold wind blew, knocking the mystery man back. The vipers forming his mask turned live, and slithered off into the cave. As he scrambled to hide his face, Eleanor was drawn into the bonfire flames.

She pressed her palm to her heart as tears welled behind her eyelids.

"Shh, you're safe," said a beautiful woman with golden-amber eyes.

Eleanor clung to her, wanting to be held by anyone as she broke down. "Was he going to...kill me?" she gasped, the words barely forming past the lump in her throat.

It's him, shouted a half transparent old woman. *The witch hunter who burned me!* The ghostly crone tried entering the cave through the flames, but some force yanked her back, preventing her from crossing into the tangible world. The ghost raged into the gray sky. *Beira, Carson a dhiùltas mi dìoghaltas?*

Eleanor scratched the back of her neck. *Beira Queen of Winter?* Eleanor hadn't heard Gaelic in years, but pieced the ghosts' words together—'Why deny me revenge?'

The ghost swept across the sky in a tangle of shadow and frost into a darkened forest.

It was only then Eleanor looked around at the misty nothingness surrounding her. *Where am I?* She wiped her eyes with the back of her bound hands. Now inside the flames she watched her body on the other side, entangled in a mass of hedonistic bodies, but the viper-masked man had gone.

Time felt slower. Naked and scared, Eleanor held her arms over herself. "How did I get inside the flames? Did the unholy baptism send me here? Was that a ghost? Am I dead?" Her voice grew louder with each panicked question. Thrusting her own hands in front of her face, she was relieved to discover they remained solid flesh, but confused why they were still tied together.

"You were right to be afraid of him, lass," said the woman taking a dirk from her garter and cutting off the bonds. "You've got a keen witchy sense."

"Witchy?"

"Shh. Calm down. You're very much alive, as am I," she said gently. "We dinnae usually pull people into the Otherworld, but you were clearly at risk."

"The Otherworld?"

The amber eyed woman drew her tartan shawl closer, peering through the flames into the Hellfire Caves. "What sort of brothel is that? My understanding of ladies of the night has expanded considerably." She offered her plaid shawl. "Dinnae catch cold."

Eleanor hesitated, but felt even more vulnerable naked, and wrapped herself in the shawl. "I'm a mistress, not a whore, thank you," she said raising her chin. "And it's not a brothel, it's a masquerade. Who was the man in the viper mask?"

"I dinnae ken, but he's clearly trying to harm you. Matilda—the ghost—seemed both terrified and furious."

"Who are you? Are you fae?"

"I'm a wise woman. And a mother." She smiled.

"You're a...witch?" The word hitched. Eleanor scratched the back of her neck. This woman looked nothing like the witch of Pye, nor any witches she'd seen in pamphlets. Why wasn't she an old hag with a hairy wart on her nose? Eleanor squinted between the woman, the fire, and the orgy beyond. "How can I be two places at once?"

"Your soul is here...temporarily," she quickly added, "while your body remains on the tangible world side. People will assume you're staring off."

"I'm very confused why I'm here," Eleanor said, rubbing her wrists where she'd been bound.

"Ack, honestly, I'm not sure why I'm here either," the wise woman said. "My Auntie Matilda can be impulsive, and I was trying to protect her from herself." She gave Eleanor's hand a reassuring squeeze. "Dinnae fash yourself. The veil will close soon. You can stay here and wait for sunrise to be reunited with your body, or follow me and meet Matilda. I'll not force you either way."

The wise woman walked into the misty forest with a quiet self-assurance that held Eleanor's attention. *I want that.*

She stared back into the flames. *My dearest George, where are you? Here I am, doing all sorts of things to please you, and you left me anyway?*

Eleanor strode into the forest where the trees scraped the sky. Neither dark, nor light, a dim grayness surrounded them. Where was the moon? Or the sun?

"So, you're a mistress? I dinnae mean to judge, but why not find an unmarried man? Is money your sole motivation?"

Eleanor looked away. "If only it were just about money." George alone listened to her, championed her education, and loved her in return. *But he left.* She flinched at her own thought.

"Ah." The wise woman's amber eyes penetrated Eleanor's walls, laying all Eleanor's hopes and fears naked. "Love can be frightening."

"I dinnae deserve someone like... It isna smart for a girl like me to fall in love." Her musings circled her failures. "Everyone leaves eventually," she said pasting on a fake smile.

"You sound like my Aunt Matilda. I understand though. It takes a leap of faith to trust people again," she said with genuine kindness. The wise woman lit a candle from her satchel and burned three mugwort leaves one by one. "This sains the air, ridding it of bad spirits."

"I never liked bad spirits myself," Eleanor joked, inhaling the woodsy smell, and becoming more relaxed. "Thank you for rescuing me from the masked man, whoever he was. I'm not used to being helped," she confided.

"Sounds like you've been hanging around the wrong people. Would you like to join me?" She pulled a bag of salt from her satchel, and started pouring a large circle around herself.

"Maybe?" Eleanor tentatively stepped inside the circle as Fiona continued to pour. "What's the salt for?"

Caw. A black raven circled above.

"*Ceòthach*," the wise woman called, raising her hand and creating a cloud between them.

"You can control the wind?" Eleanor's mouth gaped.

"It's a Druid trick for protection." Her eyes lowered to the pink marks around Eleanor's wrists. "Dark forces appear drawn to you."

"Why?" Eleanor pinched the skin between her thumb and forefinger, remembering the palm reading given by the witch of Pye.

The cawing grew louder from the treetops, as though it was searching for prey.

At the last minute, the old ghost joined the circle. *I've found ye now haena I, Elspeth?* she called to the raven, as the wise woman closed the ring around them. *Elspeth is within grasp in her raven form and the witch hunter from is hiding in the Hellfire Caves*, said the ghost with happy tears and shining cheeks. *At last, I can have my revenge.*

"Who are you?" Eleanor barely whispered.

A gasp escaped the ghost. She spun to the wise woman, her surprise quickly delving into rage. *Get her out of the circle. She's not part of our coven. We've no time. Curse him for me. The veil is blocking me.*

"A ghost and a witch forming a coven? My mam warned me about this." Eleanor crossed herself as the raven looped through pockets of mist.

Off ye go, honeylocks. The ghost tried to shove her, but her ghostly arms went right through.

"Auntie, if that's the witch hunter, then this must be the blonde woman from the prophecy. He bound her, ready to stab her womb."

"P-prophecy?" Eleanor stammered.

"It all makes sense now. Fate destined us to form a coven of maiden, mother, and crone to protect your child. That's why we're here." The wise woman called to the sky. "Is that right, Beira?"

An energizing wind, crisp as the first day of autumn, blew through the circle.

The ghost was positively appalled. *Bring her into our coven? Absolutely not. We canna trust anyone but each other. I'm not wasting my time on initiation rituals on someone I've never met while justice awaits. Are ye mad?*

The temperature dropped within the circle to an uncomfortable, almost burning cold. Frost gathered on Eleanor's shawl as her breath steamed the air. Her mind raced. "The witch of Pye said I'd have a daughter who would topple a king. Is that what this is about?"

"She *is* the one," said the wise woman, mouth agape.

Who's the witch of Pye? demanded the ghost.

Eleanor instinctively moved behind the wise woman, as though she were a child hiding behind a big sister. "An old hag who lives on Pye Street in London. She read my palm."

Aye, aye, but what does she look like?

"About seventy, walks with a cane, has a pet raven."

Elspeth, Matilda said as though the word itself was poison. She called to the clouds, *If ye imagine hobbling on a cane is bad, wait until I'm through with ye, Elspeth. I'll kill ye, then the witch hunter, then the reverend.*

A clearing in the cloud cover opened. *Caw.*

"*Ceòthach*," said the wise woman again, thickening the fog. "Auntie, no. I willnae be part of blood magic." The wise woman's tone deepened, locking a hard gaze on the ghost. "You ken when you do a curse it comes back to harm you three times. You're already trapped in Purgatory. Do you really want to pound on Hell's gates begging to get in? How will you ever reach the light?"

Eleanor almost tripped over a knotty root as she inched away from the arguing witches.

The three times rule is only for casting unjust hexes, said the ghost. *These wretches deserve every curse they get. Time is running out. Open the satchel and pull out some mandrake. Please*, she shouted, balling her ghostly fists. *Ye ken I canna touch things.*

"No," said the wise woman firmly. "Beira wishes us to form a coven. That's why we're here, not revenge. This maiden is chosen to have an important daughter. We have to protect her and her child."

Maiden? The old woman rolled her eyes. *She's playing rantum-scantum with an entire crowd.*

"You sound as judgy as Reverend MacDonald. Fine, she's a vixen not a maiden. Who cares? Beira wills this be done."

Eleanor's head was spinning. "Protect me from who?"

Caw. The raven punctured through a break in the mist diving towards them, flapping her ominous wings furiously.

Matilda raised her ghostly hands and shouted, *Gortachadh.* The raven dropped in a haphazard spiral as though her wing was clipped.

Eleanor tried to remember the Gaelic. *Gortachadh*—hurt? Eleanor slowly backed away, breaking the salt circle. "I want no part of this."

"Aunt Matilda, stop. Look—you're scaring off the maiden. Come inside, lass. It's dangerous out there."

Wait, shouted Matilda at Eleanor, then faced the wise woman. *What if the witch hunter presses her for information? We need a memory charm on her so she dinnae tell him about Beira's plan for a coven.*

The wise woman grabbed a fistful of herbs from the satchel and tossed them into the flame, but Eleanor dinnae wait to watch her finish. Sprinting at full tilt through the dark woodlands, she heard the raven flap her wings above her. Its caw morphed into a cackle as it flew low to peck at her head as she reached the bonfire.

Eleanor's soul was sucked back into the Hellfire Caves, back into her body.

Inside, heat intensified as the flames became royal blue. Fueled by her fear, the fire surged to the stalactites, then exploded. Hot ash fell on her, searing her skin, while the ghost and wise woman watched from the Otherworld.

Howling in pain, Eleanor swept the embers off as everyone stared. Scrambling to her feet, she raced to the water's edge, not knowing how to swim.

"My dearest George! My dearest George! George! George! Why did you leave me alone in this cursed place?"

The old crone's eyes grew panicky. She raised her hand behind the flames. *Na dìochuimhnich.*

Everything went foggy in Eleanor's mind. Slowly, both sets of witchy eyes receded, extinguishing the fire into smoldering ash.

Chapter 17

Fiona

Scotland—The Tangible World

Fiona blinked at the men furiously stamping out the bonfire embers that had jumped to a nearby field. It took a minute before she realized she'd been knocked to the ground.

"Have you ever seen such hellfire carry on the wind?" Reverend MacDonald shouted to the villagers. "We must halt these pagan rites. They're against God."

James stared between Fiona and the reverend with a worried expression as he stomped out a flame. David and the other children carried buckets from the well to the field.

William dumped water on the scorched heather, calling to the villagers. "Are all the embers stamped out?"

Broderick and wee Lachlan were on either side of her, rubbing her hands while Mary lightly tapped her cheeks.

"What happened?" Fiona asked her sister, gaping at the smoky remains of the field.

"It's a mercy you werena burned to a crisp," Mary said. "I've never seen the like. It was as though someone threw gunpowder into the bonfire."

Spotting Fiona, William rushed over. "Are you all right?"

Her brother, Malcolm, stomped out the final glowing ember. "I hope your cat survived. She was near the flames before the fireball."

William took a confused step back then narrowed his eyes glancing between Fiona and the charred earth. An edgy, twitchy sensation coursed through Fiona's veins as she avoided his gaze.

Mary looked between them and said, "Perhaps the boys can stay with me tonight?"

"Thank you," William said. Wearing a smile that dinnae reach his eyes he bade goodbye to the villagers as he and Fiona trekked up the rocky road to their manor. He used his most measured barrister's tone. "Is there anything you want to tell me?"

Yes. I want to tell you everything. I want you to wrap your arms around me, and tell me you'll protect us from these dark forces suddenly drawn into our life. "No."

He stood in front of her, forcing her to face him. "What caused the explosion?"

She looked away. "How should I ken?"

"The flames rose twenty feet, then blew in a sheet over the field. It wasna natural. It's a wonder no one was hurt."

"You'd never understand," she muttered striding away from him to gain her composure. "Auntie Matilda was right."

He cut in front of her path, stopping her movement. "Excuse me? Matilda, your dead aunt burned for witchcraft? In addition to everything else, you can talk with ghosts too?"

Shite. "I used to speak with them all the time as a child, but now it's mainly during fire festivals," she said more meekly than she would have liked.

"I canna leave you alone for more than two minutes without you dabbling in magic?"

"It's Samhain. I've no control over where spirits walk when the veil is pierced."

"My grandsire warned me Matilda might come back to haunt me, but I thought he was just addled with age and fear." William ran his hand through his hair. "That old, meddlesome witch wants to cause mischief in our marriage, aye? What poison is she planting in your head?"

Pooka appeared from the shadows and hissed at William.

Matilda, stop. "This has nothing to do with you. She's upset about being executed. Her best friend betrayed her, she dinnae cause any illness, yet the witch hunter condemned her to burn alive, while your grandsire showed no mercy. Wouldna you be furious in her situation? I tried to soothe her, guiding her toward the light."

They detoured into the forest.

"She's dead, Fiona. And you're not." His voice hitched. "It kills me that I can fight the Kirk and the courts, but I canna protect you once you walk through the flames. What if you get stuck between worlds? Fiona, you promised you'd stop doing magic."

She swallowed hard, thinking back to their wedding night when they were handfast in the castle. *'I've spent my whole life hiding my gift,' she'd confessed. 'You never need to hide your powers from me,' he said stroking her face. 'I was raised on tales of giants and fairies. Magic dinnae frighten me, Fiona; priests do.'*

"I haena done a speck of magic on this blessed earth in four years." *The Otherworld is a different matter. Did that memory charm even work on the poor blonde maiden? She looked terrified.*

He crossed his arms over his broad chest. "You're sure? No witchcraft?"

"Positive," she bit out.

"Would Martha MacPherson agree? I overheard her talking with her grandmother about the powerful tea you gave her."

Fiona swallowed, stopping in front of a babbling stream. "Herbs are different from spells. She's sixteen and had no husband."

"She should keep her legs closed. And another thing—did you ask our cook to buy salt?"

"Yes. And did you ever consider giving the same self-righteous advice to your friend Lord Hallewell? Every other month you travel to London to settle the scandals of his rakish love life. Have you gone to the brothels with him before? I ken they have wild orgies in London."

"Orgies? Why would I go to a brothel? Are you bloody out of your head? Do you think I want the French disease?"

"That's your sole reason for not going? Not your love for me, nor our marriage oath? You avoid whores so you willnae catch the pox?"

"What are we arguing about? I've never been to a prostitute, nor do I want to. You ken I love you." Their breathing quickened as they followed the stream home. "You want to talk about oaths? You make a mockery of our marriage. You suppose I dinnae ken you only speak English when I'm within earshot? Or that you teach our sons about the fae and the old gods disguised as bedtime tales instead of reading the Bible with them? Do you ken how often Reverend MacDonald and your very own brother have pulled me aside, suggesting I show you the back of my hand?"

Fiona stopped in her tracks. "Am I to thank you for not being a cruel husband?"

Pooka appeared from the forest, dropping a rat at William's feet. He stomped his foot near her, chasing her off. "I'm trying to have an honest conversation, and I feel like you only tell me half-truths."

How do I explain the Otherworld? Would he forbid me from visiting my coven because it's too dangerous? How can I go against destiny when I'm drawn to it? Shivering, she looked around. "Where did I leave my shawl?"

William took off his coat, putting it over her shoulders. "I love you, but it seems I worry more about keeping you safe from witch hunters than you worry yourself. You're not even trying to be careful. What happens if someone from the Kirk arrests you when I'm in London? Who would protect you? Lord Blackmere and his Reformation of Manners people are confined to London for now, but what happens if they travel north? I visit the prisons, I've been to the executions, I ken how they get confessions. He'll torture you and laugh while he does it, Fiona."

"I'm aware," she snapped.

"Clearly you need a reminder. They arrest you, parade you through the village."

"I ken this already—"

"Once the Kirk is assembled, you'll be stripped naked and shaved. A witch hunter will prick every mole on your body in the most sensitive places looking for devil marks as twenty men watch."

"William, stop."

"And if you dinnae confess, they'll lock you in a hole in complete darkness, interrogating you for hours on end. You're tired now? Try not sleeping five days in a row, completely isolated from everyone at the start of a Scottish winter. Did you ask your ghost witch, Matilda, what it's like to be tortured? Because that awaits you if you're not careful."

"I ken better than you ever will, barrister MacLeod. I watched my aunt, the woman I loved as my second mother, get destroyed for nothing by your grandfather and some witch hunter from London. Dinnae you think I'd give up my powers if I could?"

"No. I think you like your magic, and you tell me what you assume I want to hear. Am I wrong?"

Fiona bit her lip and looked away. "You ken who I was and you married me, anyway. Why canna you accept me as I am?"

"And you ken who I was too. I'm a barrister, yet I constantly cover your witchcraft. Look, I dinnae have a problem with your magic, the world does." He blew out a long breath to calm himself. "You said you'd give it all up after you were caught last time, but how can I believe that when you keep going back to it? I need to know if our boys come first. If I come first."

"What kind of question is that? Of course you do."

"Do you want them to experience the shame of their mother being called 'witch'? James has nightmares you'll be burned at the stake and he willnae be able to save you."

It was as if Fiona had been punched in the gut. "Why dinnae he tell me?"

"He loves you; he isna going to burden you."

"I'll tie a hag stone over his bed to stop the nightmares," she muttered.

"Jesus Christ, woman, stop. This is insanity. It's your birthday and our anniversary. We should be coupling, not arguing. I leave for London in the morning, and I dinnae want to spend my entire night discussing a dead witch. The reverend has been pestering me to end all Samhain celebrations from now on, and your actions tonight convinced me to agree. They're done. I canna risk losing you."

"But..." Now she had a whole new set of obstacles to deal with. Being cut off from fire festivals meant she'd never see Matilda again. They walked half a mile in silence as her mind raced.

William hated prolonged pauses and tried to fill the verbal void. "Ack, I never liked fire festivals anyway. The mead was always weak," he joked, trying to make her laugh. "Can we please just go to bed?"

She stopped. "I'm staying here."

"In the middle of a forest?" He slowly shook his head. "You're going to talk with her again, aren't you? Stare into another flame and fall into the Otherworld?"

"I'm not going to the Otherworld again," she muttered.

He caught her eye. "I canna hold this family together while you chase shadows. Every time you step into that world, I lose you a little more. I don't want to lose you, Fiona."

She looked away.

He folded his arms over his chest, his words growing increasingly sharp. "I dinnae have the time to sort this now. When I return for the holidays, we will have a long conversation. There will be a reckoning."

"Dinnae bother."

"What?"

"You love aristocrats and London so much? Stay there."

He recoiled in surprise, then became offended. He bowed. "As you wish."

They stood frozen as the heat of their words sank in.

"You're really casting me out, Fiona? You break the law, and I'm the one who pays for your crime?"

"I've paid a steeper price for this marriage than you'll ever ken. I have to give up myself."

"Being my wife is a burden to you?" His body stiffened at her silence. His voice sounded numb. "I wish the tangible world was enough for you."

"I love you more than breath, but I'll never stop hearing Beira's voice in the fire. It isna a a choice, William. I'm witchborn. It's who I am."

He reached for her hand, then clenched his fist instead. "Write me in London when we can find a way to live in the same world again." He paused before walking away, waiting for her to call him back. She didn't.

As he disappeared up the road, Fiona balled her fists. Lightning shot across the sky as a thunderclap shook the earth. Fiona wandered among the dead leaves blowing past her feet as the cold wind slapped her face and torrents of rain pelted the land. Sinking to the ground, she watched Pooka run into the nearby stream, and Matilda's face emerged from the water.

"Why, Matilda? Why do you constantly ruin my life?"

Fiona, come with me back to the Otherworld. Help me find the witch hunter so I can have my justice tonight.

"William is leaving me, and all you care about is your relentless pursuit of revenge."

Och, husbands always want to make rules over us. Ignore him. He'll come home when he wants a roll in the hay.

Another lightning bolt splintered the night. "Stop speaking of William as though he only married me for lust. He loves me, we love each other. He's trying to protect me, and all you ever do is bash his character and his intentions, and now I might lose him forever. I'm so tired of protecting my magic. Damn this magic to Hell."

Matilda's eyes grew wide with fear. *Dinnae say such things. You'll upset Beira.*

"What's the point of keeping her happy? She never helps me. Magic certainly never helps my marriage. I'm sick of all of it. I hate this 'gift' of witchcraft."

Hold fast to your powers. Once you close the door to the Otherworld, it's very lonely.

Fiona picked up a rock and threw it into the stream causing ripples across the water.

Matilda looked behind herself and gasped. *What the devil? No!* She was sucked away into the darkness.

Chapter 18

ELEANOR

London—The Hellfire Caves

Eleanor blinked through the flickering torchlight, disoriented. Her fingers trembled as she pulled a shawl tight around her bare shoulders. *Where did that come from?* Laughter echoed through the cavern.

"Darling, I never left, I'm right here," said Lord Hallewell, emerging with the bitch nun. Phoebe. who wore a self-satisfied grin.

Eleanor punched him hard on his jaw as the other men laughed. "You left me alone in this cursed place. Get me out of here," she screamed.

Even in the dim cave, Lord Hallewell's flushed face was apparent as he wiped the blood from his bottom lip. "Calm yourself."

"She found God, Brother Hallewell," snickered a man in pagan garb.

They dressed quickly with pinched expressions. He helped her step onto the gondola. The cox shook his head disapprovingly, but returned to the helm with his lantern. Lord Hallewell rowed with his lips pressed into a white slash.

Pointed stalagmites rose from the ground to meet stalactites clinging to the cave's ceiling, lit only by the cox's lantern. She rubbed her temples feeling like she'd woken from a vivid dream. *The viper mask. The chanting. The fear.* It all slipped away like mist.

Exiting the gondola, Lord Hallewell brusquely led her past the banquet hall towards Judgement's Pass.

"You told me we had to travel the same path, or a ghost would follow us," she said, tugging back against his pull. "We need to take the sinner's side."

He yanked her hand. "It's all bollocks, Eleanor. The saint's path is faster."

A frigid wind swept through the saint's tunnel, causing her teeth to chatter. Something shoved her. She stumbled, her lower back slamming against the jagged cave walls.

"Stop pushing me," she cried.

"How could I? I'm in front."

She spun, finding nothing, just swirling mist, and the faint sound of water dripping behind her.

Lord Hallewell pulled her forward making her sore wrists hurt even more.

When they finally exited the caves into the foggy night air and church ruins, she exploded. "You brought me here, then left me."

"You told me you wanted to try wild things, not that you'd transform me into a cuckold. I was arranging for a ménage à trois in a private room, but I came out to find that Shakespearean actor with his head buried between your legs. Are you using me to find your next lover?"

"How can you say that? Take me home."

"Gladly."

Each step up the hill proved difficult. Wisps of vapor hovered, then vanished in the chilled air, and she smelled wine and incense on his skin. At last, they reached the cemetery surrounding the abbey. He calmed himself. "I inquired multiple times if you were all right, and you never said, 'My dearest George.' Then you start screaming bloody murder? You made a scene in front of people who matter."

A raven circled the graveyard, making the hair on the back of her neck rise. She clung to him, trembling.

"Good heavens, what frightened you, Eleanor?"

"I dinnae ken, I..." Everything was on the tip of her tongue, but she couldn't quite remember. *Am I drunk? Was it a dream? Did I just get invited into a witch's coven?*

And above it all, the raven circled. Watching. Waiting.

Chapter 19

Elspeth—Witch of Pye

London

Elspeth rested her crippled leg on a stool as she pressed an herbal poultice against her aching shoulder. She forgot how nasty Matilda could be when she threw an indignant curse. With a longing gaze at her bed in the corner, she wished for a nap. Transfiguring into a familiar for a long flight left her exhausted, and it took everything in her power to stay focused on Lord Blackmere's ranting.

"I was about to kill the blonde from the prophecy in the Hellfire Caves until a spell pushed me away, and Eleanor disappeared into the flames. Why didn't you tell me living people can go into the Otherworld? I assumed you had to be a ghost or a witch."

"Gods and goddesses control the Otherworld, and their whims change with the wind. I did my end. The truth bore out, as I foretold. The blonde maiden was in the Hellfire Caves on Samhain night."

"Stop congratulating your scrying skills. We have a problem—that Scottish witch Matilda. The whole point of burning witches was to prevent them from returning from the dead to torment the living. How did she find me? What did you see as the raven? Did you kill her?"

"You can't kill something already dead, lord." She leaned in. "But what of the blonde maiden? She escaped your binding. I chased her back into the Hellfire Caves so you might kill her. Beggin' your pardon, lord, can't help but notice things turned a bit sour after that."

Lord Blackmere angled away, crossing his arms over his chest. "Matilda unmasked my face. I'd taken pleasure with multiple men earlier. I had to hide before anyone recognized me, lest her death day curse come true."

Elspeth bit back a smile as her raven, Jessop, flew down from the rafter and hopped on the table. "That's right. She yelled the world would be better if you were castrated. Terrible woman, she was. Though the penalty for sodomy is execution, not castration, I've been told."

"Tread lightly, Elspeth," he hissed.

Elspeth fed her raven crumbs as Jessop twisted his head, laughing silently with her. "I sense the goddess wants Matilda and Eleanor to form a coven. That's why she's back. Fear not, lord, it won't happen in this lifetime. Matilda minds her grudges more than her orders from Beira. Rather than doin' the initiation rituals, the damned old witch threw hexes at me. My branding hasn't sizzled like this since Matilda's death day." Elspeth lifted the poultice of herbs, revealing the scorched sigil above her heart. Smaller than a child's palm, the branding took the form of a Celtic knot encircled by a serpent biting its tail. In the center was an eye. "No salve will heal it."

"What does it mean?"

The sigil heated painfully, and immediately she regretted showing it to him. She was so exhausted, she wasn't thinking straight, and it could cost her if she wasn't careful. "The knot represents our coven." *Just enough truth to stop his questions.*

"Why are there three interwoven loops? I thought your coven was only you and Matilda."

Bugger. Elspeth did her best not to wince as her wound flared painfully. Matilda thought it clever to make the sigil burn if she attempted to betray the coven again. Elspeth might have betrayed Matilda, but never Fiona. She never told Blackmere the lass was part of their coven. So she lied. "It represents Beira—Goddess, Protector, Destroyer." The pain receded.

"Why is the serpent eating itself?"

Self-inflicted harm by betraying the coven, inescapable guilt, a cursed immortality where magical growth is never possible. I might live, but I'll never become a sorceress until a member of the coven forgives me. "The eternal bond of the coven—life, death, rebirth," she lied.

"And clearly the eye means Matilda's watching you, yes?"

"Clearly. At least durin' fire festivals." That much was true. At least she only had to avoid flames and water eight nights per year, when the veils were thin, and Matilda could visit the living.

"Tell me again about the prophecy."

Repeat the lie. "Admiral Goring held his son, and Matilda held her daughter, and they formed a tree."

"But I stopped the tree from blooming, didn't I? Matilda threatens no one, let alone the king, thanks to me. With a few Machiavellian moves, I was able to have the admiral and Matilda eliminate each other. No wise child could ever come from their union," he bragged. "She died a barren widow. All we have to do to break the prophecy for good, is find and kill Eleanor, and her baby. It would be decidedly easier if I could just hire a highwayman to slit her throat, and be done with it. You're certain the murder needs to take place during a fire festival?"

"With respect, lord, I ain't the one making the prophecy rules on how to outwit fate. Take it up with the goddess if you have a problem."

Elspeth closed her eyes, remembering Matilda get tied to the stake, feeling guilty but grateful it wasn't her. When Elspeth transfigured into a raven, it was the lightest moment of her life, knowing she saved her own body, not realizing then how little a wretched life was worth.

Blackmere steepled his hands, tapping his fingers to his lips. "My powers granted by the king only extend as far as the realm. How can I capture Eleanor if Matilda keeps pulling her into the Otherworld?" His eyes narrowed to glinting slits. "I need to learn real magic, beyond the simple palm reading parlor tricks you taught me."

The witch hunter wants to become a warlock? She chuckled. "Those parlor tricks saved you from gaol, didn't they? My fortune-telling told you when to pull out of the South Sea fraud, and pin the whole damn thing on Lord Hallewell's father."

"And I've paid you handsomely, have I not?" he asked, waving his arms around the dilapidated hovel he bought her. "Would you prefer living on the streets again?"

"I've got limits on what magic I can teach, see?"

"What limits?"

Elspeth inched away. "The price for betrayin' my coven, besides Matilda's sigil burned into me, was havin' my powers locked in time. I've still got 'em, sure, but they won't stretch further." *Unless a sister lifts the curse by forgiving me.* "I can only teach what I got."

"I'm not asking to become a wizard," he said, offended. "I just need to learn a little conjuring, you know, command the wind, read minds, transfigure. It's the only way to kill His Majesty's foes and protect the realm."

"Protect yourself from arrest for sodomy, more like," she muttered.

In a flash, a dagger pierced the wooden table between her two fingers. Lord Blackmere drew close, gripping the knife tighter in his fist. "I can hang you tomorrow, Elspeth, and no one would give two shits. Have you forgotten I spared your life twenty-odd years ago?"

"Mercy, lord, I meant no harm. Just sharin' a laugh." She cowered, holding up her other shaky hand to shield her face.

He backed off, keeping a narrowed gaze on her.

"I gave you the prophecy," she muttered. "I earned my life, lord." She winced as the sigil flared.

She'd fantasized about killing Lord Blackmere constantly, but the Goddess never allowed it. Neither poison, nor potion, would kill him, though Elspeth had tried. Her inescapable alliance with Lord Blackmere was a constant reminder, symbolized by the serpent biting its tail and burned on her chest.

She pressed the poultice against the sigil, fighting its heat. "I can teach you spells, my lord, but it takes time."

He bit his bottom lip. "What about the dark arts? Isn't that faster?"

"Blood magic you mean?"

He avoided her eyes. "Nothing so evil as that."

She studied his reaction with an eerie stillness. *A conflicted man is easier to control.* While she didn't relish her current life, Elspeth had no interest in joining Matilda's fate burning on a stake either. *I'll play it both ways, I will. Teach him enough to keep him docile while tryin' to win back the trust of my former coven sisters. Matilda will never forgive me, but Fiona might release me from the curse.* The burning lessened, leaving her skin raw.

"Eleanor wears chains in the vision, right? Don't need no magic for that, love. Arrest her. Hanged women deliver no babies."

"Won't Matilda pull her into the Otherworld again?"

Non-magicals are such lackwits. "No, my lord. A dead witch has limitations, like any other ghost. She can do spoken spells, and incantations, but can't mix any ingredients for a lasting spell since her body's transparent. Only during the eight fire festivals, when the boundary between worlds thins, can spirits cause harm. That also requires the living person to look into water or flames for them to talk. There may be eight fire festivals, but connections rarely happen more than a few times each year, especially with the church shutting down the bonfire festivities these days."

But if Matilda did add Eleanor to her coven with Fiona, that could be quite dangerous for me. Her sigil glowed bright, sizzling along with Elspeth's resentments.

Chapter 20

MATILDA

London

For over twenty-two years, Matilda's ghost had haunted the same miserable Scottish village. Tedious. Awful. Familiar. Then came Samhain—and Beira's blasted wind hurled her straight into a bond with the blonde maiden who ruined her chance at revenge.

Gone was the crumbling castle where Matilda had her rough interrogation in the dungeon. Suddenly she was in London, of all places.

As if being dead weren't annoying enough, now she was magically leashed to Eleanor.

For the past two weeks Matilda had followed Eleanor while she got fitted for gowns, gossiped with her lady maids, and generally enjoyed her pampered life, save for the constant pining away she did for Lord whatshisname.

She looked at the sky. *I ken you're upset I dinnae form a coven with the lass, but this punishment is a wee extreme even for ye, Beira.* It was driving Matilda mad to be tethered to the wee love-struck maiden when she should be hunting her enemies. She sat in the tart's London apartment like a mutt waiting for scraps. Grand, just grand.

She supposed she'd have to wait until the next fire festival to attempt any sort of disentanglement from the maiden. After all, Eleanor made it quite clear she didn't want to join the coven either.

A knock came at the door. When it opened, Matilda almost fell over. *William?* Now this was getting interesting.

He sat at the polished table. "Have you completed the lessons I left while I was in Scotland, or have you been lazy?"

"You're grumpy. Did you fight with your wife over Samhain?"

William's eyes opened wide.

Aye, William, it's obvious to anyone ye and Fiona had a fight. Wait, how does Eleanor ken about Fiona? How close are you two?

They settled into their roles of master and pupil while Matilda floated over the table and watched. William was very professional, focused on the task. "Concentrate on the sentence. Break it down into smaller parts. Dinnae rush."

"I ken, I ken. I suppose I'm distracted."

"You haena mentioned Lord Hallewell once this morning. Is everything well?"

Matilda leaned in. *Good question. I've been wondering about that myself.*

Eleanor bit her thumbnail. "He hasna visited since All Hallows Eve. Did he tell you anything? Is...is he angry with me?"

"I've only arrived yesterday, and haena seen him yet. What's happened?" William leaned back and rested his arm over the back of his chair with a wary expression. "Whatever it is, you best tell me, and dinnae even try to lie. I have four sons, and deal with aristocrats for a living. I can smell bullshit from a mile away."

Toying with the lace on her sleeve, Eleanor asked, "Is it true what you said during the first lesson?"

William was thrown off. "It takes six months to learn to read?"

Eleanor shifted in her seat. "That he'd grow bored with my antics. He gives the impression he likes wild experiences, but then gets upset. He says I was flirting too much with an actor at the Hellfire Club, but thinks nothing of both of us taking part in an orgy."

MacLeod's face flushed.

Matilda's eyes grew wide. *She's spilling Hellfire gossip to a married man?*

"I've never done such a thing, but I wanted to please him. Then, as soon as I began to enjoy kissing everyone, he acts completely jealous, and leaves me."

Matilda shook her head. *Och, what an eejit ye are, lass.* She looked to the sky. *Have ye lost your step, Goddess? This is the maiden to carry the chosen one?*

"I dinnae understand the man. I dinnae understand what he wants from me."

"I told you he's got a jealous streak."

She played with her quill. "There's more, but perhaps I shouldn't say."

Matilda slid on the empty chair. *More? Oh, do tell, I canna wait.*

The temperature dropped, and Eleanor shivered. "George and I had a terrible fight coming out of the tunnel. This sounds so stupid, I canna believe I'm saying it...ever since we came back through the wrong tunnel—the saints instead of the sinners—my life's turned upside down. It's like a rabid dog's tied to my waist, dragging me into walls. My lower back throbs, and I keep feeling... Judged. Like there's some nasty old scold riding my shadow."

Had the memory charm failed? Matilda spiraled in a panic like mist on the moor. As her circles grew wider, just beyond fifty feet, she was yanked back toward Eleanor, who yelped.

"There it goes again," she said rubbing her lower back.

"What do you mean you're being judged? In a court?"

"Nothing like that. I dinnae even hear specific words, I just get this overwhelming impression everyone hates me. Does George hate me? Am I still his mistress? I only wanted to please him." Her blue eyes welled. "Is he going to cast me aside?" she said, voice cracking.

Despite Eleanor's papered life, the lass's eyes seemed to carry the same hunger Matilda had seen in orphaned children—the hunger to be wanted.

William awkwardly offered his handkerchief. "I'm sure you'll work it out with Lord Hallewell. You're likely hearing your conscience, not some specter. Have you gone to church?"

"The Lord in heaven only kens what the Reformation of Manners people would do to me if they overheard my confession. I wish being with George wasna living in sin." She dabbed away her tears.

"There, there," he said, patting her hand. "Redirect your nerves into your studies."

Rolling her eyes, Eleanor laughed. "I'm opening my heart, and you want to talk about grammar? Is work your answer to all things?"

"You sound like my wife. Work distracts me, keeps me grounded."

"I never want to be grounded. Who wants to be a bird with a clipped wing?" Eleanor dabbed her eyes one last time. "I'll wash your handkerchief."

He smiled in surprise. "I canna remember the last time Fiona offered to wash my handkerchief. She acts like it's a hardship to sew a button."

Humpf. Matilda bristled at the dig toward Fiona. *Well, maybe she's too busy caring for your sons, and hiding all her powers to serve you as well.*

"You dinnae need to do anyone's wash from now on. You have your own servants. My advice is to be patient. He's probably busy with family matters and will call on you when he can."

"Bollocks. He's punishing me."

"I'm paid to tutor you, not to discuss my lord's love life. Back to the books. You've got a decent grasp of letters and sounds, but we need to expand your vocabulary. You like games, aye?"

"What kind of solicitor are you? You're impossible to speak with."

He dipped the quill into the ink and wrote something on the parchment. "What's this word? Sound it out."

"Win-window?"

"Aye." He blew on the letters, then ripped off the word. "Put it on the window."

She smirked, and stuck it on the glass. Soon, the room was littered with vocabulary scraps and laughter.

Matilda shook her head. *The lass is eighteen, going on five.* That said, it was a fun game. She'd never learned to read during life, and found it amusing she got to learn her letters in death, and William was a quite competent tutor.

Sliding beside him, Eleanor studied his face while he thought up the next word. "Did you play this game with Fiona—Mrs. MacLeod—when you taught her letters?"

"We played...other games." He laughed, flushing. "It led to our first son."

"Well, that sounds fun," Eleanor said. "Tell George I miss him. No, tell him if he doesna visit me in the next twenty-four hours, perhaps I should find new companions."

Matilda slapped her palm to her forehead. *Has jealousy ever kept a man loyal?*

Chapter 21

Eleanor

London

"I'm sorry," Lord Hallewell said, handing over a bouquet of winter jasmine tied with a string.

She waited an exorbitantly long time to respond while the butler took his drenched coat. *He made me wait two weeks. Let's see how much he likes waiting for my forgiveness.* "Thank you," she said coolly as the butler bowed off.

"What in heavens is going on in here?" Lord Hallewell said, trawling the room.

"You mean the scraps of paper? Mr. MacLeod is teaching me words."

"I mean the vases of flowers everywhere."

She eyed him casually, testing the waters as she dumped a wilting bouquet out the window and replaced it with his. "Several gentlemen from the Hellfire Club sent them. I would have told you, but you've been avoiding me. When was the last time we spoke? All Hallows Eve?"

"Those bastards," he muttered. "Have any of them visited?"

"I've no interest in any lord come calling, save you," she admitted, but noticed how rattled he appeared. "Oh, quit your pouting, and kiss me." Eleanor wrapped her arms around his neck. "What are we doing today, George?"

He smiled, kissing her. "We can surely devise an activity."

"Well, of course, but I mean...after. I've been trapped here, bored for days, waiting for your visit, and you want to keep me home? You promised you would take me to the theater on Drury Lane, but we still haena gone. I've never been to a play."

"I'm not sure that's the wisest decision. Margaret's friends patronize that venue. She mustn't learn of this. Darling, you know the situation."

She broke away from him, sniffing the flowers sent by other men. "Well, can I go by myself then? I'd love to see a play." *That'll get a reaction.*

"Yourself?" he laughed. "Why are you suddenly interested in theater? Are you trying to meet up with the actor from the Hellfire Club?"

"Of course not." *But if he's jealous, that's good.* The tightness in her chest loosened. *Press your power while you have it.* She put on her cloak.

"What are you doing? It's dreadful outside."

"Going to the theater. You can come if you'd like."

"Did you not hear a word I said?"

"Oh, I heard all of it, but it's bollocks. You dinnae give a rat's arse about Lady Margaret. I say, if her friends are there, let's give them a good show."

She twisted the door handle. He pressed his hand against the door, preventing her from leaving. Facing him, she stared him down. "George, I promise you I will not open my legs until I see a play, as you promised."

"Well, perhaps I'll pry them open."

Eleanor smiled. "Perhaps I'd like that. But not until after I see the play." She grabbed his bollocks. His eyes closed, and his breath stopped as she massaged them in her hand, then let go. *It's good to leave him wanting.* "Dinnae fash yourself. Even if the play isna good, I'll keep you entertained."

"Why are you so intoxicating to me?"

She laughed. "I'm the only person who tells you off."

He avoided her eyes. "Seeing you with another man in the Hellfire Caves...I didn't anticipate feeling...jealous. It appears you've cast a spell over me. I didn't visit because I was angry, but as MacLeod pointed out, I'm the one who brought you to the damned caves, so it's incredibly unfair to be angry with you."

A knowing grin slid up her face. *MacLeod must have told him I'd start searching for a new lover if he dinnae visit. I ken making him jealous would work.*

He held her gaze. "I'm sorry. For everything. Taking you there without fair warning, leaving you alone, not visiting these past two weeks...I've been quite an ass. I never meant to hurt you, but I know I did."

"Now that's a proper apology."

I win.

Eleanor soaked in all the sights, sounds, and scents of the Drury Lane theater, from the glorious costumes, to flicking candles lighting the enormous stage, to the odd assortment of perfumes worn by audience members.

Lord Hallewell kept his hands in constant affectionate motion, lightly stroking her arm, her hair, her thigh, as he explained the plot of Shakespeare's *A Midsummer's Night's Dream*, and a good thing too because the actors spoke in rhymes and used complicated words she'd never heard before. Titania, Queen of the Fairies, angered Oberon, so he made his trickster Puck sprinkle fairy dust, and somehow Titania fell in love with a donkey. What kind of play was this?

George affectionately wrapped a golden strand of her hair around his index finger. He glared at the actor playing Oberon, the same lad from the Hellfire Caves. "God, I hate Shakespeare. Such a common playwright."

The actor gave a confident grin before swaggering off stage.

George's lips were in a tight line, and it worried her. She didn't even care about the actor. "If I ever anger you, promise you willnae put a curse on me, like what happened to Titania," Eleanor joked in a hushed voice.

"I'd never curse you. I'd have MacLeod's wife, Fiona, do it."

Somehow, that answer didn't comfort her.

The players called an interval. Outside, the wet cobblestones glistened, but the rain had let up. Laughter erupted from the crowd as lords with powdered hair stretched their legs and bedazzled ladies discreetly reattached their cloth patches to conceal their pox marks. George scanned the crowd, not wanting to run into any of Lady Margaret's friends.

"Have you ever frolicked in an alleyway, George? Or rather, would you like to?" Eleanor whispered.

"Sounds highly illegal."

"And adventurous, right? It's private and public at the same time." Finding a quiet alley, she pulled him in, kissing his neck as feral cats and all manner of vermin dug through the scattered rubbish. "Don't you want to possess me, knowing the Oberon actor is only yards away from us?"

"Stop. If ever I possess you, it won't have anything to do with him. You don't have to make love with me in public, or believe coupling is the only reason I enjoy being with you. I genuinely relish your companionship, Eleanor, so please stop playing these games."

She glanced away, wanting desperately to believe him. He rested his hand at the nape of her neck and pulled her in for a gentle kiss. As it deepened, she relaxed in his arms, wishing she could trust the moment would last.

Light droplets fell sporadically, letting off a fresh, earthy scent. Holding hands, they dashed back towards the main street as a couple walked past. Eleanor bumped into a middle-aged military man wearing a red coat and a tricorn hat.

"Watch where you're going," he barked.

Eleanor blinked rapidly in a rush of confusing memories, as sparse drops fell cool and gentle on her skin. "Captain?"

The captain tilted his head, searching her eyes, trying to place her. "You?"

Eleanor impulsively hugged him, feeling ten again.

Lord Hallewell tugged her elbow until she took an embarrassed step back. "Are you going to introduce us?"

"Thomas, who is this woman?" his wife demanded, scowling at Eleanor.

A bell rang, signaling intermission had ended. Patrons crowded the doors, some glancing in their direction as they held up their arms to protect themselves from the increasing drizzle.

"You're the little stowaway, aren't you?" To his wife, "Remember the run I took to Edinburgh? We found a man wandering on the deck, and when we approached, he jumped overboard. Died on the spot."

Da killed himself? Everything began to spin, and she saw black spots.

"A day later, we realized the scoundrel had left his daughter in the orlop, poor thing. I took her to Saint Mark's, remember? When was that? Nearly a decade ago?"

As the drizzle changed to light rain, a steady, rhythmic tapping grew louder on the roofs.

"A Shakespearian play isn't enough drama for you, Hallewell?" asked a fashionable gentleman. "Who is this lovely creature who is decidedly not your wife?"

"Lord Blackmere, shouldn't you be hunting sodomites, scolds, and witches?"

"Oh, but my dear Hallewell, I am."

Eleanor felt a violent tug on her lower back, making her falter.

"Wait. I remember you." The nobleman laughed. "Eleanor is it? Last time I saw you, you dressed quite differently. I believe it was a servant's livery?"

She flushed at the memory of Lady Margaret publicly shaming her at the ball, while Lord Blackmere led the cheering. George protectively stepped in front of her.

"I do love watching you flounder, Hallewell. Yet another scandal? Perhaps my associates at the Reformation of Manners should stop by for a chat with both of you?" The earl's eyes narrowed on her.

A memory of a viper-masked man ready to stab flashed. She felt tugged in the opposite direction now, taking a few steps back into the alley. *What's wrong with my balance?*

Even the captain's wife shifted on her feet until she squinted into the depths of the alley. Her eyes bulged wide, then she lifted her petticoats and sprinted across the street, screaming.

A black cat screeched, and dozens of rats ran past them toward Blackmere. The cat jumped on some boxes then leapt, scratching his face, drawing blood. More rats crawled up his legs, inside his coat, into his wig, biting and clawing as if commanded by the screeching cat. As the rats tore at his skin, the captain and George tried to help swat them off, to no avail.

She had a sense of déjà vu, like something otherworldly had intervened once before.

Retreating across the street, Blackmere ripped off his coat and peruke, stomping on the rats as the cat pursued him like a lioness. A sudden tug sent the cat flying a yard backward. The cat spun and hissed at Eleanor, making her take a startled step back. *Is the cat protecting me, or trying to kill Lord Blackmere?*

He growled something, and the rats dropped off him, writhing and twitching in pain as they died in dirty street puddles. He and the cat exchanged an intense stare before he escaped into the theater, wiping his wounds.

"What the hell is that about?" asked the captain, as the rain grew heavier.

"Is there a full moon tonight?" Lord Hallewell asked, staring wide-eyed at the dead rats. "All the animals seem possessed."

"It's a good thing my crew didn't see this. They'd never step on another ship if they knew rats might swarm them like that." Before going, the captain squeezed Eleanor's hand, with kindness. "I'm glad you're well cared for. I best find my wife."

After the captain's departure, Eleanor's mind raced, struggling to comprehend everything. Cold drops wet her face, and her dress grew damp. "The play is starting," she said numbly.

"Bugger the play, Eleanor." Looping his arm through hers, Lord Hallewell strode towards their waiting coach, practically dragging her forward as the drops came faster. "God only knows what Lord Blackmere is going to do. Fuck, I hope he doesn't stick his morality inquisitors on us. I knew this was a bad idea. I'm sure he'll plague me with threats at every ball over the holidays. Merry Christmas, indeed."

The cat followed them with a disgruntled, yet resolved, air, keeping several paces behind them. Ladies wrapped shawls over their elaborate powered hair to keep dry from the rain, while merchants dashed between the growing puddles to find a dry place to hover with their carts.

A footman helped her into the coach, where she sat in a daze.

"Are you all right?" Lord Hallewell said, sitting beside her. The cat hopped inside the carriage, and no one bothered to throw it out.

"I'm fine."

He offered her a handkerchief to wipe her wet face, then quietly probed. "You told me your family died of the pox. Why didn't you mention your father abandoned you on a ship? How awful." He softly brushed his hand down her cheek, but she twisted from him.

Rain splashed louder against the coach as it pulled away. She stared at a stream of muck flowing down the congested street, as dampness spread deeper through her gown, making her skin cold enough to shiver. "Maybe we can see the second half of the play tomorrow. I'm curious to see how it ends."

"Why won't you let me in? Don't you trust me enough to confide in me?"

Every muscle in her body tensed, and a rush of anger broke loose like a torrent. "Let you in? For what purpose? I surely dinnae have your trust. You want to ken how I met the captain? You want to ken how I ended up in a workhouse?"

The coach hit a pothole, and they slammed against each other as the cat screeched.

"I was a child, and Da told me everything would be better in London, and he'd be right back. I never saw him again. He left me alone on a dark ship with a bunch of men who dinnae speak Gaelic. Do you ken how terrified I was? They yanked me from my hiding spot, and dragged me on deck to a horizon filled with waves. There was a sailor in a striped shirt. I'll never forget him. He had no teeth, and was balding. He undressed me with his eyes and squeezed me until the captain came up, punched his gut and made him spill his supper on the deck."

"The captain was your protector?"

The coach rounded a corner, picking up speed as they moved down a side street.

She nodded. "I learned quick to keep him happy. He taught me to say 'yes, sir' and 'thank you, sir' in English. Those few words had to mean many things. 'Did I clean the deck enough?' 'Can I have another bite of food?' 'Will you send me away where the toothless man will hurt me?' 'Thank you, sir?'"

The cat hopped onto Lord Hallewell's lap, watching intently.

"How did you get to the workhouse?"

Eleanor's hands fell into her lap, and she stared at them, swallowing a lump in her throat. "We arrived at a busy port. 'This must be London,' I thought, 'where everything is better.'" She scoffed.

The buildings grew hazy with the increasing speed and downpour. George was leaning towards her, listening.

"We got to the dock where the captain's wife and daughter waited. His wife dinnae like me then, either. I remember smelling tar, and wet wood while they argued. He took my hand, and we walked through the city. I supposed, stupidly, we were meeting Da somewhere. I had no idea he jumped. It's amazing the lies we convince ourselves to believe."

The horses trotted alongside a private park.

"We get to Saint Mark's. Go inside. Smells like burnt porridge and lye. Matron's there, unsmiling. Captain starts to leave, so I follow him. Matron rips me back. 'Thank you, sir,' I called desperately, but the words meant nothing to him now. 'Thank you, sir'—Take me with you," she said, gulping. "'Thank you, sir'—I promise I'll be good. 'Thank you, sir'—Please dinnae leave me here in this prison." Her voice broke. She pounded on the coach roof. "Pull over."

"What are you doing?"

"Go home to your wife. I dinnae need another ride to the workhouse." As the horses slowed, Eleanor pushed open the door, and jumped into the muddy road.

The cat followed.

Sheets of rain blurred her vision. Tightness spread through her chest as she sprinted, lungs burning, until she slipped through the slightly opened iron gates of a private garden. Sinking beneath an old maple tree, she collapsed over her knees.

After a minute, he caught up. "Eleanor, come in from the rain."

"Leave me alone. Please. I canna do this. I dinnae want to be a mistress, always hiding. Always afraid of losing you. I'm so tired of feeling worthless."

The heavens opened, and they were soaked.

Lord Hallewell kneeled in the dirt, pulling her against his chest. "Shh." Despite his drenched coat, warmth radiated from him, and she clung to him as the downpour roared around them. "I'll never abandon you."

She stared into his eyes. "Why did my da jump? I dinnae even ken he killed himself until tonight. It was a choice. He dinnae need to kill himself. I would have helped him find food. I would have found a job. Da was never coming back, because I wasna worth his effort to live."

"Eleanor, no, that's not true."

"Isna it? If I had bairns, I'd never leave them. I'd fight until the day I died to protect them and keep us together. But Da? He's so... What did I do so wrong to be abandoned as a child? What did I do wrong to have the captain dump me in a workhouse where everyone treated me like a dirty criminal? I'd never discard anyone, let alone my child."

She curled over her knees with her head in her hands. The cat appeared from behind the tree and crawled into her lap, warming her shivering body. The cat felt like home, like a hug from her grandmother.

George's prolonged silence made Eleanor fidget uncomfortably. She wished to flee, or hide, or get drunk. "I hope God punishes him for murdering himself. I hope he wanders outside the gates of Hell for eternity for what he did to me."

She calmed down as the cat offered a soothing purr. The rain lessened as the moon glowed above. Usually, a good cry lifted her mood, but today heaviness remained. "If I took better care of my family when they got the pox, they would have lived. That's why he cast me off."

"No, love. No one can outwit death." Lord Hallewell rubbed soothing circles on her back. "I wish I had the right words to say, but no one had the right words for me either. Remember when I told you my father died in prison? He hung himself."

Eleanor gasped.

"A scandal on top of a scandal." He gave a half-hearted chuckle, then sighed. "He believed I'd care more about gaining his title than losing him. I should have visited. I was his only son, and I left him to rot alone. If I hadn't been such a disappointment of a son, he might still be alive."

"Disappointment? You're a prize."

He shook his head.

"Am I a disappointment to you, George? I'm terrified when we go out, I'll embarrass you, or that your peers will shun you for being seen with me, or now Lord Blackmere and those stupid Reformation of Manners people will publicly shame us for our affair, and you'll leave. I'm trying so hard to please you."

"Eleanor, you don't need to constantly please me to earn my love. You already have it." His lips brushed against hers as leaves rustled in the light breeze, shedding their water. The cat disappeared into the night.

Eleanor stared into his eyes, shocked. "You love me?" Her chilled fingers caressed his face as the kiss deepened.

"I want to leave this godforsaken city and start a family with you," he said.

Would he truly give up everything for me?

Chapter 22

MATILDA

London

Matilda separated from the cat, and drifted like smoke on the wind above the trees, watching Eleanor and Lord whatshisname embrace each other in silence, creating a tranquil moment. Matilda's gaze softened. They were well-suited despite society's strict rules, and their growing love was obvious.

Flying in slow, deliberate circles around the tree, she tried to puzzle it out. *The mysterious noble witch hunter has a name: Lord Blackmere.* She spit.

He wasn't just any gentleman; he possessed power. The earl oversaw what, exactly? The Society for Reformation of Manners that hunted sodomites, scolds, and witches. She moaned aloud at the blatant hypocrisy. He's a witch hunter practicing dark magic, for gods' sake.

Blackmere had some powers now, even if he wasn't well-trained, but didn't have any at the time of Matilda's burning. He must have learned after the Hellfire Caves encounter.

A raven appeared at the other tree. *Caw.* "Had to see for myself to believe it," Elspeth said, interrupting Matilda's musings.

They held a stare.

Gortachadh, Matilda called with outstretched palm, but the hex bounced off the raven.

Elspeth laughed. "You didn't think I'd visit without casting a protective spell over myself first, did you? Difference 'tween us? I trip once, I don't fall twice."

Matilda soared towards her but got yanked back by her magical ties to Eleanor.

"Are we to continue hostilities indefinitely? Can't we put the past behind us? Can you ever forgive me, sister?"

Ash Sister, is more like it. Both of us burned—but ye warmed your hands on my pyre. I'll forgive ye when Hell freezes over.

Elspeth did a barrel roll over her head, as if to prove the curse hadn't slowed her, and landed on a branch on a nearby tree. "You preen like you're Beira's favorite, but you've got naught to show for it—same stale magic, same old tricks."

Seems like I do have new powers. I transfigured, and it's not a fire festival.

"The rules of magic changed, have they, love?"

How's your scorched sigil, love? Matilda smiled at the steaming wound beneath her feathers.

"Your shape-shifting just now was a fluke, not a new power within your control. That white-hot fury you felt seein' the witch hunter tore open the veil, and let you shift form, is all. Angry spirits do it all the time—haunting houses, knockin' things about. Unless you're furious, you'll have to wait for a fire festival like every other ghost." She ruffled her feathers smugly.

Rage didn't explain everything. She also transfigured into a cat to cuddle Eleanor, which the raven clearly hadn't seen. Matilda noticed a frost forming in a path around Eleanor. It dawned on her Beira must have granted her expanded powers, but only for Eleanor's benefit. *Beira, am I a guardian angel-witch now?*

Elspeth was still gloating. "Ain't got no powers you can control, but you do have a magical leash. That's fun. Reminds me of when Admiral Goring walked you through town locked in a scold's bridle like his little bitch."

A thunderclap echoed as Matilda rammed forward and got tugged back.

"Temper, temper."

I see the witch hunter allowed ye to return from banishment.

"Got me a bellyful and a warm fire. Can't ask for more."

Is your new life worth betraying your coven sisters?

"I don't owe you my neck just 'cause we broke bread once. And I never betrayed Fiona." She gripped the branch with her talons as she shifted back and forth. The former friends stared at each other, acutely aware of all that was lost between them.

Why, Elspeth?

Elspeth lowered her beak, averting her gaze. "I'm not strong like you, Matilda. He crushed my bones, kept me up for hours on end with no food, no light. I wanted the pain to end," she confessed softly.

You're a fool to teach Lord Blackmere dark magic. Do ye believe killing Eleanor's chosen child will end his thirst for power?

"You know about the prophecy?" Elspeth tilted her head. "How? The admiral's daughter told me her dream. I never shared it with anyone."

Save the witch hunter, Matilda snarled.

The patch of skin where the sigil would have been in her human form smoked as Elspeth cawed in sheer agony. The raven flew off.

We could have protected each other, Elspeth, she called.

Chapter 23

WILLIAM MACLEOD

London

"What's the urgent matter, my lord?" William MacLeod asked, entering the study overflowing with wrapped Christmas gifts.

Lord Hallewell held up a letter with a cracked black seal. "I received this today. My mother fell and broke her hip. I need to care for her over the holidays. I wasn't there for my father, but I'm damned and determined to be a better son. She's getting frail—I don't know how long she has left."

"I'm sorry, George," he said, squeezing his shoulder.

Lord Hallewell glimpsed down the hall before closing the door, then poured himself a drink with trembling hands. "I have a delicate request requiring your legal advice."

"What's got you so nervous?"

Pouring the liquid down his throat, Lord Hallewell wiped his lips with the back of his hand. "How difficult is it to get a divorce?"

"Why do you ask?" MacLeod said carefully.

"Every second on this earth is precious, and never guaranteed. The world tells me this is what I should want," he said, opening his arms to the room. "But I don't anymore. Epictetus said wealth consists not of having great possessions, but in having few wants. I want to marry the woman I love. I want to spend the rest of my life with Eleanor."

MacLeod rubbed his hands over his eyes. Eleanor was becoming a nuisance. "She already warms your bed, and her apartment is a welcome escape from your home. Isna that enough? Is she pressuring you?"

"Gracious, no. I want this, William. I want to marry a woman whom I truly, deeply love."

MacLeod noticed his sincerity—and grew jittery about the risks. "Divorce would effectively cut off your access to wee Alexander's trust. Seek a separation via ecclesiastical courts. This lets you live separately, keeping all income from your properties, claiming future earnings, and maintaining custody of the children, but you canna remarry."

"That's not fair to Margaret. You know I'm not a particularly moral man, but I'm not a complete cad either. Let her keep the money. I just want to marry Eleanor, and see my children. Tell me how to get a divorce. I know it can be done," he said, refilling his glass.

MacLeod sighed in exasperation. "Only a private Act of Parliament can end a marriage. It's slow, expensive and exceptionally public. Is that wise? Can you imagine what Lord Blackmere might say? What *The Tatler* will write?"

Lord Hallewell paced the room, deep in contemplation. At length, he stopped and faced MacLeod. "Perhaps it's time I stop caring what others think. Once I'm out of the grip of society, I can truly be free."

"Your brain is seriously deficient if you trick yourself into believing such simplistic nonsense. Freedom costs a lot of money, and last I checked, you dinnae have a job. Are you planning to play your violin on the street for pennies? Do you really suppose she'll find you quite so loveable when you canna take her to plays, buy her fancy clothes, or put jewels around her neck? Do you expect her to go back to being a laundress to support your gambling habit?"

"I worked well enough for you, didn't I? Back in the day."

"What about Margaret? Even if you gave her every cent, you'd nevertheless be leaving her vulnerable, shredding her reputation, not to mention causing a scandal extending to your children. You may not love her, but she dinnae deserve this."

"Margaret has never given two wits about what other people opine, which honestly sounds liberating. My moral compass might be askew, but she doesn't have one at all. Trust me, that woman will land on her feet. She's out of the house more than she's in it lately, probably prowling for a lover."

"Exactly. Why dredge up those rumors about Colonel Wilkes?"

"Are you protecting Margaret, or yourself?"

"Both—plus Fiona. You ken very well a title means nothing without money to provide clout. Why erode your own authority? Your romantic whims put all of us at risk." MacLeod scratched his hand through his wild hair. *Think MacLeod. How do I shut this down?* "Eleanor's barely eighteen and likes a good adventure. Perhaps any strapping young man might capture her attention at the Hellfire Club."

Lord Hallewell punched MacLeod's jaw, catching him off guard. "Do not disrespect Eleanor again. Why are you saying such awful things? She loves me. I love her. For once, I want to follow my heart instead of trying to live up to other people's standards. I assumed you'd grasp that."

MacLeod wiped the blood from his lip. He'd never seen George ready to fight over a woman. "What I grasp is you're reasoning with the wrong head."

"Fuck you, MacLeod." They glared at each other. "What happens when you file the petition?"

Dinnae sugarcoat anything. "Lady Margaret will hire the best barristers who will drag you through the mud in front of your peers. They'll remind everyone your father was a convicted fraudster who committed suicide in prison. Many men will queue outside Margaret's home hoping to marry her wealth, as you did. It will be easy to bribe any number of the servants to spill the household's secrets. Her first husband's relatives will file lawsuits over wee Alexander's paternity. Upon discovering the truth, they will take away Alexander's title and wealth. *The Tatler* will run stories about you being a cuckold. The Reformation of Manners people will arrest you, and me, and Fiona, and try us with circumstantial evidence for the murder of Colonel Wilkes, and we will hang. No one wins, George, especially not you."

Lord Hallewell's grip on his glass grew tighter as his breath grew ragged. "Goddamned this situation you put me in," he said, throwing the glass against the wall. A million shattered bits spread over the wooden floor.

"I put you in this situation? You were the one who begged me to find you a rich widow."

Flopping in his chair, Lord Hallewell held his head in his hands for a long while. "I suppose my love for Eleanor doesn't make any rational sense, but damn it, William, she's good for me. I haven't gambled in months. I'm at peace. She understands me better than anyone. Why wouldn't I want to commit the rest of my life to her?"

"I'll do whatever you want, but take a few days to mull it over. Your decision affects many people. A divorce isna to be taken lightly."

"Toys!" Young Alexander and Thomas ran into the room and headed straight for the Christmas gifts. Lady Margaret's face paled as she stood in the doorframe holding baby Elizabeth. "Divorce?"

Chapter 24

Elspeth—Witch of Pye

London

"Beggin' your pardon, lord, but mayhaps there's been a misstep?" she asked sipping tea as the frog tried to escape Blackmere's grip.

"Obviously," Lord Blackmere snarled holding the frog out with contempt over her table. "Even if I get inside, how do I get out? You're not going to trap me inside a toad, are you?"

If only it were that easy. "The frog will kick you out himself after a time, unless he's your personal familiar, like Jessop is to me. But first he has to allow you in. Helps if you ask. Stare at his eyes, and picture sharing space in his mind."

Blackmere's concentrated face resembled an old man with severe constipation. *This might take a while.*

Elspeth tasted the air blowing in from the window, lifting her chin to catch invisible currents he couldn't feel. She transfigured into Jessop, escaping up the chimney to see what was going on in the neighborhood.

A mishmash of tall, timber-framed houses, and shabby taverns with signs swinging on wrought iron brackets, flanked narrow, winding streets. Drawing deeper into the dark part of town, half-frozen vagrants held their dirty palms up for coins, but a hooded lady ignored them as easily as the rest of the refuse in the street.

Lady Margaret has come calling again?

Elspeth wanted to watch from a laundry line, but Jessop's stomach dictated it was time to eat. Swooping down, she noted Lady Margaret glance over her shoulder at the corner of Saint Ann's and Abbey Orchard streets. Elspeth paused her pecking on a decomposing carcass to stare.

The lady's heeled shoe caught on the icy road and as she stopped to pull it out, a thin man slid out from an Irish Rookery. Even in raven form, she could tell his stained, patched coat stank of unwashed body and gin. He inched closer with a hunger in his eyes.

Spinning, Lady Margaret faced him. "What do you want?"

Taking a startled step back, his eyes swept her up and down. "Top of the mornin'. Lost, m'lady? Spare a shilling or two?"

"Hey! You there!" A youth with platinum blond hair pulled his polished sword from its sheath, and crossed the street.

The beggar stepped back, hands raised. "I was only coddin' her. Merely taking a walk, lad."

"Walk somewhere else," the youth said, keeping eye contact until the vagrant ran. "Lady Hallewell, right?"

The noblewoman pulled the hood tighter. "And you are?"

"Your hero. Don't you remember me? I'm Viscount Percy Monroe. We met at the Bedlam asylum? You laughed heartier than I at the lunatics chained to the walls."

"Yes, yes, I remember you now. How fortunate you should be here," she said, exhaling.

"I was coming from an important merchant meeting."

A collection of prostitutes hanging out the brothel window waved their lace handkerchiefs. "Well done, Percy."

He laughed them off. "Why are you in this part of town? Here to visit the witch of Pye?" he joked, then stopped laughing at her silence. "Bloody hell, are you actually going there?"

Elspeth hopped closer, cleaning her feathers as flurries blew down the alley.

"You don't have to escort me. I'm sure your father wouldn't approve of you doing anything illicit." Her breath made puffs of smoke in the frigid air.

"Nor would your husband, I'm sure," he said with a cocked grin.

"Pretend to be my hired sword, will you? Perhaps we can scare the witch?" She weaved her arm through his.

A mind like spoiled bread, that one. Full of holes and stinking. Elspeth picked the flesh off the bone, then left her feast and flew over merchants pushing ox-carts, and down the chimney into the cottage. Her soul left her familiar, returning inside her body, still nodding. She cracked her neck, readying for the entertainment. It's not every day a witch picks a fight with a lady. "Lord Hallewell's wife approaches. Might want to leave now."

Lord Blackmere exited the frog's body, and scrambled to hide his face behind his hands. He rushed past Lady Margaret and Viscount Percy into the anonymous streets, as a very disgruntled frog leapt from the table to the open window and escaped.

"Jesus." Percy's eyes bulged wide, inspecting her cottage.

Tossing lavender in the flames of the hearth, Elspeth smiled. Her cloak flared at the breeze, as though she had wings behind her. "What is it you want now, lady? The veils between worlds will soon be thin enough to speak with the dead."

"I didn't enjoy speaking with my first husband when he was alive, why would I want to speak with his corpse? Sod your veils. You tricked me. I needed a respite from my second husband, and you delivered a scandal. He's fornicating with a goddamned servant now. Multiple people witnessed him with Eleanor at the theater on Drury Lane."

"He left you alone, didn't he?"

Jessop descended from the roof rafter and landed on the edge of the table. She stroked his head with her finger.

"She's his proper mistress now, according to gossip. Did you give Eleanor a love potion?"

"Eleanor's fun-lovin' and beautiful. Your husband don't need magic to be drawn to her, lady."

"I want you to make whatever charm required to terrorize that cunt."

"You must love your husband to crave such cruelty."

Lady Margaret snorted. "I don't care two shits about him, and I barely know the girl. What does it matter to you? Fuck him and his threepence lover. Why should either of them get unfettered joy while he keeps me trapped in a loveless marriage?"

"Trapped? Or trying to open the door of the gilded cage so you can both fly free?"

Lady Margaret's mouth gaped.

Elspeth collected secrets like shiny things, and since the first time she read Margaret's palm, she knew her husband would try for a divorce. "Forty shillings for an ill wish."

The lady signaled Percy with a nod. He held a dagger against Elspeth's neck.

"Enjoy using your hand while you still have it, love," she snarled at Percy.

"You'll do as you're bid, or I swear I'll watch you burn," Lady Margaret said with a self-satisfied grin. "I have friends in the highest of places, witch."

"I've buried people more powerful than you. But I'll make whatever curse you want."

Percy returned the dagger to its sheath, and wiggled the fingers of his hand, clearly disturbed by her quip. "I'll leave you women to it." He exited faster than his bravado would have suggested.

Elspeth snickered. "Looks like his gut's turned to jelly. You know, the charm I make for you won't help in the long run."

"Why not?"

"It's Eleanor's daughter you need to fear, and she ain't even made yet."

Lady Margaret pursed her lips. "You mean the daughter who's going to help overthrow the king? Oh wait, that's only if the bastard lives past five, correct?"

"Laugh all you want, lady, but I'm always right."

"Eleanor is the problem, not some future bastard. If my idiot husband goes through with his parliament idea, it will be a nightmare for me."

"For your son, you mean."

Lady Margaret bit her lip, doing her best to guard her secrets to protect her son. It was the only redeeming quality about her. "If your ill wish works properly, she'll leave before my husband ever plants a bastard in her belly. When will it be ready?"

"In a fortnight. Hide the charm carefully in her room."

Lady Margaret dragged a gloved finger over the bottles on the mantle. "What will it do, exactly? How long will it take to get rid of her?"

"I'll make an amplifier charm. Fear, wrath, envy, lust. Plays tricks on your mind, and makes you your own worst enemy. She'll be gone before the first crocus blooms."

"Perfect. Merry Christmas, witch."

Chapter 25

William MacLeod

London

William MacLeod sat at the tavern drinking as merrymakers sang Christmas carols and kissed under the mistletoe. James had written, begging him to come home for Hogmanay, as if it was his choice and not Fiona's directive. David sent a drawing with Lachie's handprint at the bottom. MacLeod nearly broke as he traced his finger over the lines, wishing he was home with his wife and sons.

Snow stuck on the windows. Outside, people rushed through the busy streets with gifts as church bells rang through the night air.

He felt hollow. *If only I'd protected her at Lord Hallewell's wedding, none of this would have happened. Broderick wouldnae have ruined our happy lives.*

As a peace offering, he hired a coach to take Broderick home from boarding school for the holidays, and sent mounds of gifts for everyone. He imagined them laughing around the hearth as he nursed another pint alone. *They'll probably be happier without me anyway.*

He'd written Fiona dozens of letters trying to make peace, but she never specifically asked him to come home.

All I ever wanted was Fiona by my side, and our sons muddy and laughing. I'd trade every drop of pride to hear her call me home. He took another drink. *She chooses magic. I wish she'd choose us.*

The tavern grew noisy. Someone played a fiddle, and the young blokes grew brash.

A pretty lass invited herself to his table. "Looking for love?"

"Aye. With my wife." He paid for his drink, and slept in the short, lumpy bed guaranteed to give him a backache.

Happy New Year.

The only brightness in MacLeod's bleak winter came from tutoring Eleanor. Lessons lingered longer each day as spring crept closer. He borrowed the sweet-scented pillow from her bed to ease his aching back. If only he had something to ease his unsettled mind. He couldn't stop ruminating about Fiona, especially whenever he went to teach Eleanor her lessons.

Why willnae Fiona lie with me? How long must I beg for scraps of affection from the woman I built a life with? What did I do so wrong, anyway? Try to protect her from arrest for witchcraft? Send the rapist's son to a top-notch school?

As the weeks passed, he guided Eleanor's hand to write letters, then words, then sentences, while she gushed over Lord Hallewell in ever increasingly emotional terms. And as he shifted the pillow, his mind fixated on George.

That fellow would be nothing without me. He acts as if he climbed a mountain when I carried him on my back to the peak. His quest for divorce puts everyone in jeopardy. Why should George get everything? A title, money, a bonny mistress who worships him? I'm sick of his unmerited superiority.

Today, he adjusted the pillow behind his back, then became drawn to Eleanor's touch as he corrected her penmanship. *She is rather pretty, for a blonde.*

Eleanor huffed, putting down the quill. "It's been excruciating waiting for George. All this back-and-forth to his mother's has interfered with our lovemaking to no end. Whenever we do see each other, we couple like rabbits."

He blushed. "Eleanor, your talk is too bold. Your passion is ten times a normal maiden's."

She bit her thumbnail. "Do you think I'm too eager? Too needy? I dinnae want to annoy him. I ken he was supposed to return from his mother's yesterday. Why dinnae he visit me yet?"

"Calm down. He's married with children. They need to see him, too."

"I grant he should see his bairns first, but not Lady Margaret. They dinnae even like each other. The laws are absurd. I canna wait until the divorce goes through, and we can start our lives."

MacLeod gave a half-hearted nod. Lord Hallewell had written him multiple times for an update on filing for a divorce. He tossed the missives in the fire. "Practice your reading, lass."

As she read Marcus Aurelius aloud, he only had to correct her once or twice. He nodded with satisfaction. "Your reading has improved a great deal these past few months. See what happens when you concentrate?"

"I suppose you're not the worst tutor a lass could have."

He smirked. "Such high praise. You should be proud of yourself. This skill remains yours forever. You've learned to read, now you can read to learn."

"Well, maybe I needed a push. And someone to challenge me," she said with a smile. "You should tell George to pay you extra for all these lessons." She tapped the book against her lips. "I'm sure your wife felt the same way. Enjoying a push."

He fluffed the pillow, noticing the heat it radiated. *The only thing Fiona wants is to push me away.* His gaze moved from Eleanor's neck to her plump lips, and he wondered how soft they might feel. A rush of warmth quickened his pulse.

A back door to the servant's quarters banged, startling him.

Jane, the scullery maid, moved to check the door. "That's odd. Is a window open somewhere? Why did the door slam so forcefully?"

Servants might have been in their rooms, but they were always nearby and listening. "I best be on my way. I need to get to the tailor to fix my coat. The button's loose again."

"Ack, dinnae be silly. I'll sew it," she said, grabbing a needle and thread from a nearby pin cushion. "Well, dinnae stand there, hand it over."

Undressing to his waistcoat and shirt, he tossed it to her, and watched her dart the needle in and out of the buttonholes. He picked up the pillow from the chair and smelled it. "Did you put some perfume on this? It smells amazing. Where did you buy it?"

"It just appeared one day. I guess it came with the apartment."

He tried not to notice the curve of her breasts, or her sweet scent of jasmine and cloves. On Samhain, Fiona had looked at him like he was already unfaithful. And now...maybe he was about to become what she feared.

Shite. An erection grew beneath his breeches. Shifting towards the window, he watched her reflection scratching a missive on a scrap of paper. As she blew on the ink, his manhood throbbed. *Another letter to Lord Hallewell? Why canna she write a letter for me?*

The window flung open, and wind howled through the room. As he closed it, he saw a reflection in the window pane of an old woman glaring over his shoulder. He spun. No one was there but Eleanor humming softly as she wrote. His arousal vanished. His shame remained.

"Your coat's done," she said, slipping the note into his coat pocket.

"Thank you, lass," he said, impulsively kissing her cheek. They both blinked in startlement.

The key unbolted the lock and Lord Hallewell walked in. "MacLeod?"

Eleanor wrapped her arms around Lord Hallewell, planting an excited kiss on his lips. "You're back? I worried you'd never return. MacLeod says I've graduated."

"If only exams were that easy at Oxford," Lord Hallewell joked, patting MacLeod's back.

The servants came forward, ready to attend.

"Put on your coat, darling. The Thames has frozen solid, and they're having a Frost Fair. Have you ever skated before?"

"No, but I canna wait to try it," Eleanor said, giddily. "Do you truly want to be seen with me so openly?"

His face fell. "Our next outing is a long way off. I barely arrived, and already received a letter from my mother's physician. She's dying."

"I'm so sorry." She hugged him again, clinging. "You're sure you willnae forget me being away so long?"

"I carry you with me," he said, showing her portrait in a golden locket. "Let's enjoy the day. Will you join us, MacLeod?"

"No, I've work to do. Someone has to make sure money keeps flowing into your pockets," he said, only half joking. "I'll say a prayer for your mother."

"When I return, we'll start the proper divorce proceedings. That gives you ample time to work your magic with the members of Parliament, to get them to our side."

The happy couple embraced, and MacLeod quickly departed.

Icy wind stung his face, and he raised his collar as he jaunted in the opposite direction from the gaiety of the fair. Snow crunched beneath his boots as he lumbered toward the inn.

He drowned his bitterness in tavern ale for several hours, then stumbled up the creaking stairs, and fell onto the rented bed, not bothering to remove his coat. Reaching for a handkerchief to wipe his nose, he found a note instead.

Eleanor's note.

My dearest Mr. MacLeod,
Thank you for teaching me to read, oh strict headmaster.
Your obedient servant,
Eleanor

Chapter 26

Eleanor

London—Ostara fire festival

Eleanor dashed into the street, clutching her cloak, and George's hand. In the fresh air, all her fears melted away, and the world seemed alive with possibilities. New snow dusted everything, making even the dirty streets appear like a dazzling palace. The scent of fires and roasting chestnuts wafted from makeshift stalls and tents set up on the ice. Rich and poor commingled on the ice, laughing and chattering.

"Have you ever been to one of these?"

"Not much time for leisure at the workhouse."

"Times have changed, darling. This is the coldest March I can remember in years. It's incredible to have a Frost Fair during the spring equinox." He led her past entertainers performing a puppet show for children, and vendors selling souvenirs commemorating the fair from a local printing press. They stopped in front of a tent filled with smoky fumes making her mouth water. "Two frostbites please, and some hot gin."

"Frostbite?" She crinkled her nose.

"It's gingerbread," he said, paying the vendor.

Sweet and spicy flavors mixed in her mouth as she watched a group of people scrape their skates on the ice, then fall laughing.

"There was a magnificent fair back in '17. Was Fiona with child at the time? She likely was, unbeknownst to others. We were staying with my parents for the holidays, back when we lived at Whitehall, before the South Sea scandal. I even invited my former friend Matthew Crowan.

He was from Virginia Colony, and was freezing his arse off. God, I miss those days. Do you want to skate?"

"I've never done this before," she said, teeth chattering.

"Well, I shall give you your first lesson today." He stroked her wind-burned cheek. "You poor creature. Stand by the fire and warm yourself, while I find a merchant who's selling skates. You'll quickly get warm once we start. God, I love winter. I'll be back shortly."

She hugged him tightly. Even though the fresh air was clearing her head, she kept worrying he'd discard her. *Do I tell him about the baby?* She was only two weeks late, but he was leaving tomorrow. *Would a baby keep him here, or scare him off? What if the divorce didn't go through?*

Honestly, since Christmas her emotions had been a jumbled mess. She thought she might be losing her mind, but even the servants seemed on edge. They'd be exploding with anger one minute, then acted terrified they'd lose their job the next, bringing even the butler to full-on sobs. And Jane shifted from almost drunken joy, to complete distrust, whispering with the other servants, then going mute when Eleanor entered the room. It felt like every night had a full moon making them moody.

Sipping the hot gin, warmth spread through her body until a wind swept across the frozen Thames, fluttering the colorful banners lining the Frost Fair. Her heartbeat stopped.

Walking with deliberate grace, Lady Margaret's fur-lined cloak trailed behind her as she blazed a path down the middle of the ice, ignoring the joyous revelers around her.

Every muscle in Eleanor's body tensed as she awaited the inevitable confrontation. "Lady Margaret," she whispered, involuntarily curtseying to her former mistress.

"Eleanor." Lady Margaret's lips curled into a wintry smile. "He took you to the Frost Fair. How quaint."

Lord Hallewell was nowhere in sight. *Shite, shite, shite.* "We'll stay out of your way."

"Will you? I was under the impression a marriage only included a husband and a wife, not a mistress in the bed, too. You are decidedly in my way."

Why am I acting helpless? He loves me and we're trying to follow the law. "Divorce will cure that. Perhaps if you loved him better, he wouldnae have sought me out."

"Darling, he might have bought you a new gown, but you'll always be a workhouse slut, which I will make known to every member of Parliament, every newspaper, nay I'll spoil your reputation to anyone who will listen. You're simply an ambitious whore."

Eleanor stood taller. "You wee spoilt aristocratic bitch. You dinnae even like him."

"Sod your love. Do you think I'd let a servant win? I'll put your head on a spike."

Eleanor raised her chin. "I'm not afraid of you."

"Yet." Lady Margaret stepped closer.

Some onlookers raised their eyes from their cider.

"George loves me," Eleanor said.

Lady Margaret spoke in a low, menacing voice. "You're but a worthless plaything, soon to be discarded when the novelty wears thin, like all his other mistresses running around London."

Eleanor blinked.

A harsh laugh escaped Lady Margaret's lips. "Surely, you didn't opine you were his first mistress? Good heavens, you're more ignorant than I assumed. And when he leaves you, what then? Do you imagine Mr. MacLeod will find you a new home? He might offer you a ride back to the workhouse."

"Curse you and your lies," Eleanor hissed.

Lady Margaret's gaze narrowed, her next words slicing through the cold air as a black raven flew overhead. "Dearest Eleanor, you know nothing of the curses about to befall you." With a flourish of her cloak, Lady Margaret strolled off towards a young man with platinum hair. Together they stood in front of a patch of crocuses trying to burst through the snow. The raven perched on a branch above them.

A flash of a raven chasing her through a misty forest rattled Eleanor's memory. She rubbed her temples. *Was it a dream?* She was positive the raven was wicked.

Amidst the frozen festivities, a black cat appeared out of nowhere, racing up the tree, swiping at the raven. Eleanor felt dragged by her lower back towards the tree. The raven pecked at her before flying off. Eleanor was so consumed she dinnae notice where Lady Margaret had disappeared.

"Two sets of skates. These aren't top-quality, but they'll suffice."

Nausea spread as she leaned on a nearby table littered with mugs. "Let's go home. It's bitter cold." She rubbed her head where she had been pecked.

"Leave? We've only arrived. The fair goes on for miles. Let's go this way. There's a band of glorious musicians."

Do I tell him about his wife? Is she going to have the witch of Pye curse me? I canna possibly tell him about my trip with his wife to the witch last year. He'd think me utterly stupid. Fighting her stomach, she noticed children standing around a barrel, warming their pink hands by the crackling fire. "I'm going to be sick." Sinking to all fours, everything came up and splattered on the ice. The children pointed and laughed at the steaming pile.

"Good heavens," he said, kneeling, rubbing her back. Tears dripped down her cheeks. "Let's get you home, darling," he said, helping her stand. "The hot gin was rather strong even for me."

She tightened her grip on his arm, trying to get a foothold on the ice. *Do I ask about the other mistresses? Dinnae be stupid, of course he's been with other women, he's told you as much. But now I have a bairn... a bastard. If he leaves me, then what? I have no money, no family, no source of employment. I'm so stupid. Keep him happy.* "I'm much better now. Let's stay. Tell me more about the fair from your Oxford days."

"I'll tell you on the way home. You look like you've seen a ghost."

A pounding thumped in her head, and her knees wobbled.

"What was I talking about? Ah, yes, Oxford days. What a scandal. I went to the fair with a group of friends, including MacLeod and his newlywed wife, Fiona. She was a gentle dove, but eccentric."

"What does eccentric mean?"

"Strange. She thoroughly convinced herself she could tell people's fortunes, which was all fine and well, until she traveled down a dark path."

"What do you mean?"

"Well, remember my friend from the colonies, Matthew? She predicted his children would die violently, and he got offended when I laughed. In my defense, I thought it was nonsense. One event triggered another, leading to a brawl and souring our relationship. No great loss in my estimation. I suppose it doesn't matter. He's in the colonies. I believe

MacLeod ran into a man who worked for Mathew the other day. He wanted to expand his tobacco trade."

Queasiness overcame Eleanor again. "Did Fiona say anything about you?"

"Yes. She correctly predicted that I'd be rich, but her prediction I'd have a redheaded daughter proved utterly wrong. Elizabeth's hair is as dark as her mother's. You're only as good as your last omen."

What about the witch of Pye's prophecy? She foresaw I'd get tangled with nobles, which came true. She said I'd have a daughter. Lord Hallewell's daughter? They arrived at her apartment, and went inside. Sitting on the couch, she hugged the throw pillow, and a strange sense of dread crashed over her, like a heavy weight that crushed her chest. *He'll find out I'm pregnant and leave.* "Lady Margaret is young. You have lots of opportunities to make more bairns. I'm sure you'd love to bed her to make Fiona's prediction right so she dinnae curse you."

George gave an incredulous stare. "Is everything well with you?"

No. Nothing is right with me. "Must you keep talking of witches?"

"Fiona's not a witch, she's a healer. Honestly, it's all rubbish. I've been speaking with my friends in the House of Lords about revising the Witchcraft Act. Eventually, punishment will change—whipping instead of death. One hopes the law will catch up with reason."

"Dinnae you believe in spirits?"

"My membership at the Hellfire Club tells you exactly where I stand on the matter of religion. Get some rest." He kissed her cheek, then spun to go.

Eleanor grew sweaty, hugging the pillow tighter. Her worst fears grew louder in her mind. *He's never going to divorce her. He dinnae really love me. Why would a baron risk it all for a workhouse girl?* "Dinnae you want to stay with me?" she asked in a panic.

"No, no, darling. Get some rest." He frowned at the pillow, then began rubbing the back of his neck. "I need to get ready for my trip to my mother's. I'm just... it feels like she could die at any minute. What if she dies and I'm not there? I'm the worst son in the entire world."

Liar. Did Lady Margaret have the witch cast a spell for him to abandon me? Is he leaving me to meet an old lover? "Is that how it is, then? In sickness and in health is only for your legitimate family, but if I get sick, you'll leave?"

"Why are you so upset all of the sudden? Didn't you want to rest?"

"I want you to spend time with me, but no, you have to leave for god kens how long. I'm sure you'll run into one of your many former lovers visiting your mother. Is your mam even sick?"

"What are you talking about? My goodness, how much did you drink? You know my mother is ill; you were the one encouraging me to spend as much time as possible with her." He began to scratch beneath his cravat. "You wanted me gone, but now you want me here? Is there a reason why you're changing your tune? See any good plays while I was away?"

"Stop changing the subject. I dinnae want to be..." Eleanor grew beyond agitated, throwing the pillow aside. She began to cry and clung to him. "I want to be your wife. You're real one, but it willnae happen, will it?"

He pulled her in to his arms, hugging her tight. "Darling, the law. MacLeod is researching divorce proceedings, but it takes time, and affects many people." He wiped away her tears with his thumbs, looking more upset than she'd ever seen him. "I have to go. My mother is dying. When I come back, everything will be better." He stopped at the door and turned back. "Eleanor, you know I love you. Isn't that enough?"

She thought of the bastard growing inside. "Is it?"

Chapter 27

MATILDA

London

Something was wrong. Matilda hovered in the rafters, thinking it through. When Lord whatshisname left to help his mother the first time, Eleanor became anxious, suspicious and scared. But after the Frost Fair, she acted downright paranoid, like a sky pregnant with Satan's child had cracked open, allowing every horrible feeling to gush and flood. Eleanor's behavior twisted completely out of character. With her lover away to be a dutiful son, the lass grew despondent. Each day she lay in bed longer and longer, her mood growing as dark as the drapes covering the windows.

An unnatural force must be stirring these overwhelming emotions, but what?

A key clicked in the lock, and William stormed inside. "Leave us, for an hour at least," Mr. MacLeod ordered the servants.

Eleanor left her bedchamber, clinging to her pillow like a child clings to a doll.

Snowflakes stuck to his overcoat, which he draped over the chair, and a blush rose to Eleanor's face as the servants bundled up and left.

"What's the meaning of this?" He waved her letter, reading it. "'Meet me at three o'clock. Dinnae tell George.' I'm not your damned servant, Eleanor. Why are you sending me notes? You want to get servants gossiping?"

"Stop scowling at me, Mr. MacLeod." Her lip quivered. Her eyes were red and puffy.

"Jesus, Joseph and Mary, a weepy mistress. Why are you crying?"

"Lord Hallewell dinnae love me."

He squinted his eyebrows like she was crazy. "So?"

"So? He says he loves me, but is it a trick? He says he wants a bairn with me, but what if he stops being attracted? Even learning to read dinnae help. He's too talented and worldly for me. I stay in bed for the money, thinking it'll be enough, but I feel dirty because I ken he'll leave."

Where is this coming from? Their relationship isna based on money—they're a happy couple in love. It's as though something is stoking unworthiness and fear. Then it hit her. At the Frost Fair, Lady Margaret declared curses would befall her, just as Elspeth's raven appeared. *Of course! Elspeth made an ill wish. How could I have been so oblivious?* But what could it be? A potion? Eleanor drank gin at the Frost Fair and got sick. Was it that?

MacLeod uncorked a whiskey bottle and brought two glasses from the cabinet. "Ah, Eleanor, you're young. Do you want my advice? Keep lying with him, and if you feel dirty, take a bath." He handed her a dram. "Slàinte Mhath."

They drank. Matilda pursed her lips. She examined the bottle. *No telltale signs of tampering. Still... Nothing good ever came from a married man drinking with a bonny young lass.*

"Lord Hallewell adores you. If you play your cards right, you'll be his proper mistress for a long time, and stay in this nice apartment. But dinnae get with child, no matter what he says."

"What if I already am?"

MacLeod stiffened. "Are you?"

Are ye? Matilda's eyes moved to Eleanor's stomach. The prophecy was coming true. Lord Blackmere would surely want to kill Eleanor before she had a child.

"No." Eleanor traced the glass rim, avoiding his eye.

Methodically untwisting the cork from the corkscrew, he said, "If you become with child, I'll place the bairn in a suitable home. The bastards are always cared for."

Oh no. If the child is sent away, how can I protect her?

"Bastards? How many are there? I willnae care for my child?" Eleanor sat, hugging the pillow.

He stopped twisting the corkscrew. "I shouldna have mentioned it." Tugging the cork, he stopped again, putting it down. "You're in a delicate condition, aren't you? My wife had four sons. I ken what the signs are. If you're with child, I'll know in a month when your tits get full." MacLeod grabbed her breasts and squeezed.

What the hell are ye doing, William? Matilda smacked him, but her hand went straight through.

"What the hell are you doing? Get off me," Eleanor said, smacking his hands away. It was such an awkward moment they both started laughing.

A twisted energy pulled at their wounds like a puppeteer.

"Perhaps you'd like to examine my diddeys further?" Eleanor untied her bodice, freeing them from their confines and seemed to enjoy his shocked expression.

What the hell is this about? Stay away from Fiona's man, ye Jezebel. If she took a love potion at the Frost Fair yesterday, the effects would have faded by now. She hadn't been doing much of anything but crying.

"Eleanor, you take things too far." He tossed a nearby shawl over her. "That looks like the shawl I gave Fiona."

That's right, good lad. Time to go home to Fiona and your sons.

He pitched the cork in the fire, committing them to finishing the bottle, and Eleanor grinned. "Keep Lord Hallewell happy, because he'll ruin you if you cross him. Rather, I'll be the one to do it, and I dinnae want to hurt you, lass."

He approached the window, furrowing his brow. Outside, snowflakes blew in the wind, sticking to the tall windows. He rubbed his temples.

Why did he act like his head throbbed? Was he affected by the curse, too? Then it canna be a love potion only she drank. Plus, Lord whatshisname seemed a bit off at their last meeting too.

"I have to get home, or Fiona will bite my head off. A month from now, I'll be sure to squeeze your tits," he said, putting on his overcoat, buttoning it deliberately.

"I dinnae understand you. You say you love her, but make her sound like a hag."

Aye, William. Why?

His hand rested on the door. "It's complicated."

Pouring two more drams, Eleanor said, "I'm talking with my lover's solicitor about whether I should stay in the affair for the money. I think I understand complicated." She held out the drink.

What I understand is if I dinnae find the charm Elspeth created, it's going to get ugly fast. Would it be a wax doll with a pin through the heart?

They're both heartbroken, separated from their true loves. But where was it? Matilda lurched through the room, checking beneath every piece of furniture. She only found dust.

He released the door handle and came back inside. Dropping his coat on the chair, he took the glass, and they brushed fingers. "Sometimes people grow apart, even when they dinnae mean to." Emptying his glass, he moved to a stiff-backed armchair with the fireplace burning behind.

Eleanor reclined, with a whiskey-induced blush. "What's your full name?"

"William George Henri Alasdair MacLeod."

"George is so boring. I like fancy names. French people have the best-sounding names."

Her shawl slipped ever so slightly to expose her right nipple. MacLeod feigned indifference, yet his eyes lingered before he refocused. "Enough whiskey, lass," he said, sliding the glass away. "My mother, God rest her soul, was French."

Speak of your mother to end the flirting. Well played.

"Oh? What was her name?" Eleanor retrieved her glass and finished it.

"Elise."

Matilda blinked, remembering the prophecy. She focused on Fiona and Eleanor, but William also figured in the prophecy. Was he going to protect Eleanor and her baby? Dark shadows were going to threaten Eleanor and her daughter—that must be the dark magic Elspeth used to make the hex. But what was it? Without the ability to taste, touch, or smell, Matilda wouldn't be able to find a hidden charm. She needed to transfigure. *Where's a damned cat when I need one?*

"Elise. Now, there's a fancy name." She turned the glass upside down on the table.

"What was your mother's name?" he asked, amused.

"Anna. Not nearly as fancy as your mam."

He chuckled. Eleanor started removing the pins from her hair. "I hope you dinnae mind if I let my hair down. Can I do that? Let my hair down with you?"

His eyes held mischief. "I'm not the king of you," he said in a lazy, masculine way.

Beautiful blonde hair cascaded down Eleanor's back.

Joining Eleanor on the couch, he poured another dram for each. Even big as he was, the whiskey was working its magic. She tucked the pillow behind his back. "My fair maiden," he said, moving some strands behind her ear.

Planning to blame it on the liquor, are ye, William? Whiskey provides a simple excuse for stolen kisses. And more. Please resist the wicked pull.

William cleared his throat. "My wife has brown hair."

"Does she? Why does she avoid London? Tell me about your complicated relationship, William George, six other names MacLeod."

She laughed. He laughed, then studied her. "I think you're oot yer tree," he said, his true burr escaping.

She's trying to make ye her Plan B, William. Canna ye tell? In her curse-addled mind Eleanor must believe Lord whatshisname will leave her. Matilda slipped through the apartment walls like water through cracks. No cats, rats, or mice to be found. She grunted in frustration.

"Ack, I've nowhere to be, and I sorely need good conversation," Eleanor said.

"I think you sorely need more than that," he said, with a dimple in his cheek. Then his face looked like a cloud passed over it as he rubbed his temples again. Finishing his dram, he pushed the whiskey aside and sat forward. "I've told no one this, so I trust you to hold your tongue."

"Now, that's how to start a complicated conversation."

"My wife, she's the opposite of you."

"Oh, she's ugly and stupid?" she teased.

"Shy." MacLeod adjusted Eleanor's shawl, covering her more. "I arranged Lord Hallewell's marriage. My reputation as a valuable barrister was growing. Nobles expected to meet my wife, so I forced her to come to London, even when her visions warned her to stay home."

"Your wife sees the future?"

"She thinks she has second sight."

Fiona has second sight; there's no question. And why are ye telling Eleanor about Fiona's magic? Are ye mad, man? You're putting her in danger if gossip gets out!

He turned away with a haunted look, rubbing his temples. "I forced her to come to London, then left her to the wolves. I should have been dancing with my wife, but I left her alone while I negotiated a deal. Fiona danced with another man."

"Colonel Wilkes."

MacLeod went slack-jawed.

"All the servants gossiped your wife cast a love spell to make you jealous. They said Fiona and Colonel Wilkes were playing at rantum-scantum during Lord Hallewell's wedding."

MacLeod sat stunned, shaking his head, then drank directly from the bottle. "Bloody servants. I'm sure Lady Margaret promoted those rumors, too, bitch that she is. Colonel Wilkes was her lover. Lady Margaret lusted for another man at her own wedding." He stared forward, staring into the past. "I quizzed everyone, 'Have you seen Fiona?' 'Dancing with the colonel,' Lady Margaret said. Fiona's not in the ballroom. 'Have you seen my wife?' 'Drinking with the colonel.' 'Walking with the colonel.' There were a hundred rooms. 'Where is my wife?'"

"Where was she?"

"Colonel Wilkes had raped her. Left her bleeding on the library floor like a lamb at slaughter. I snuck her out before anyone discovered her state."

His eyes welled. Matilda had never seen him cry, never heard him speak of the rape.

"The bruises between her legs—I'll never forget them. It was all my fault. I forced her to come to London. She warned me, and I—"

"William, I'm so sorry—"

Matilda flew to him in a panic. *William dinnae tell her about the murder. Please, ye risk everyone's safety.*

"I dinnae need your pity," he said. "The cowardly colonel went missing before I could run a sword through him."

Matilda breathed a sigh of relief at his lie.

"Rumors spread I must have killed him. Wilkes' powerful friends closed in to have me arrested, and there wasna even a body."

MacLeod rubbed the back of his neck. "Now Lord Hallewell had to fix something for me. He saved me from the hangman's noose, thanks to his connections, and the lack of a corpse, but he's reminded me about it ever since. So now whenever something illicit needs to be done, I fix it. He'll let me do a little side work here and there for his friends, but he keeps a tight leash." Slouching, he rested his chin in his large hands, the pillow resting against his back.

Eleanor sat up, wrapping her shawl tighter. "You're a barrister. Why dinnae you clear your name? Even if you had killed Wilkes, no one would blame you. Raping a man's wife is a capital offense, no?"

He took another swig. Now she moved the bottle away. His eyes were glassy, and he spoke with a slur. "Oh, you dinnae ken the half. God laughed by making Fiona with child. Can you imagine my wife at the Old Bailey with a bulging belly? Hearing the Lord Mayor say, 'Truly forcible violations don't result in impregnation'? Put her through public shame? Never."

He's protecting her reputation, even though exposing the rape and honor killing would have improved his own stature. He truly does love her. Matilda wished she was able to squeeze his arm, to comfort him.

"I dinnae understand. Why didn't she take pennyroyal?"

"She tried ... One day I came home early with the preacher, hoping we might pray together for comfort. We found her crying like a banshee in the garden, holding the pennyroyal." His eyes welled. "Fiona had made a salt circle around herself."

Eleanor covered her mouth. "Your wife really is a witch?"

"Fiona's not a witch. She's—her aunt was a wise woman—taught her Druid traditions."

She's a wise woman, too. Why did ye have to bring Reverend MacDonald to the garden?

He slammed his glass upside down. A brown drip wet the table. "How was I to ken she'd be doing that? I made matters even worse for her. Reverend MacDonald accused her of witchcraft. She never worshipped Satan; she just prays differently. He said God was punishing her, and we must raise the bastard as our own when he was born as a penance for her witchcraft and the rape."

"How is rape your wife's sin?"

"Why else would she be with child? She must have wanted it." MacLeod ran his fingers through his thick hair. "And by God did he make us repent to keep things quiet. Took my best land, made her do the most degrading penance each Monday in a burlap sack for a year. Trust me, any lingering desire to follow Druid traditions was stomped out of her soul."

Ye dinnae try to take her magic—Reverend MacDonald did. Every fire festival while I harped and prodded Fiona to keep up her magic, ye were actually trying to protect her from both the church and the law. I'm not protecting Fiona at all, am I? I'm the one putting her in danger.

"We named the bastard Broderick." He bit the boy's name as though it tasted of vinegar and ash. "What a puny, pathetic excuse for a lad. Looks exactly like his rapist father. Dark hair, mud eyes, a complete coward. Always sniveling and crying. I sent him away to school, so I dinnae have to stare at the bastard's face. Fiona hates me for it."

"William, it's no' his fault. What's the Bible say? Sins of the father?"

"I'm done with bastards, and witchcraft, and bloody Lord George Hallewell, holding it all over my head. If someone had raped his wife, I would have fixed things out of friendship, out of honor. The man has no honor, so he has no friends. No real ones. I'm the closest he's got, and God, I hate him and his bitch wife."

Matilda tilted her head, surprised at the intensity of his resentment. It was as though a dam had been broken, letting volatile feelings flow unpredictably. *Where is the damned ill wish hidden?*

He left the couch, glancing out the window for a long minute, letting the falling snow cool his temper. "I shouldna have spoken."

She hugged the pillow. "Stay till the storm's passed." Eleanor stood and stumbled. "I'm dizzy."

"You're blottered." Lifting her like she weighed nothing, he carried her to her bedchamber as she clung to the pillow.

William, no. Dinnae go in there. Ye love your wife. You're drunk, and angry, and the lass is throwing herself at ye.

He laid Eleanor on the bed. A fly buzzed around the room, catching Matilda's attention as it landed on the pillow. She narrowed her gaze as it seemed to grow wobbly. The haphazard stitches along the seam were loosened just enough to reveal a blood-soaked raven feather piercing the fabric. *It's the pillow!* Lady Margaret must have purchased an amplifier charm from Elspeth.

Sorry, fly, I'm going in. Holy hell. Matilda grew dizzy staring through the fly's bulging eyes wrapped around its head. A high-pitched ringing emanated from the hexed pillow. Had it been sounding all along at a lower volume? As she flew chaotically, the room became a shifting mosaic of color and movement. She bounced along the uneven seam of stitches.

Buzz. Buzz. Look here! Look here! Matilda flew in front of MacLeod, catching his eye. A wave of vertigo slammed into her, and she crashed into the nightstand on top of some jewelry. He fixated on the earrings. *Not the damned jewels, MacLeod. Look at the cursed pillow!*

"Those are Lady Margaret's earrings. Lord Hallewell gave them to you?"

"No," Eleanor smiled, naughtily. "When Lady Margaret was out of town, I snuck in her bedchamber and wore her gowns and jewelry. I kept one souvenir. She'll never notice." Her fingers stroked her throat. "See? Now we both have secrets about each other."

Eleanor's fingers trailed toward her breasts, and she let her shift fall off her shoulders as he swallowed. Her breath quickened as she gazed at his lips.

Matilda hadn't suffered heart palpitations in years, but blood rushed through her insect body, making her fly off-kilter as she struggled to get his attention.

His body stilled. "I'm married," he said, as much to himself as Eleanor.

Eleanor laughed. "So is Lord Hallewell. He mentioned how he was on the brink of poverty, and you were laird of a manor. You were the smart one, the successful one, on track to be King's Attorney. You could have married a rich widow with connections yourself. Bought your way into the aristocracy, and then Lord Hallewell might work for you instead. I might be your mistress."

His eyes threatened violence. "Shut it, Eleanor—"

"But you married the wrong woman, dinnae you?" Eleanor kissed the whiskey off his tongue, grazed his rough whiskers with her fingertips.

Matilda watched him battle his desires, then succumb.

He kissed her back.

The foulest dark magic released, making Matilda's skin crawl. The bristly antennae between her eyes vibrated from the waves of the hexed pillow, forcing her to transform back into her ghostly form as the fly neared death. *Damn ye, Elspeth, are ye determined to ruin everyone's lives?* Her anger flared for Fiona, shaking her head at William's weakness.

The kiss was clumsy, hollow, confused, already crumbling before it had properly begun. Tears rolled down Eleanor's cheeks mid-kiss. This wasna seduction. It was two broken people caught up in a mistake.

MacLeod pulled away, panting like he had run through a storm. "I canna do this."

"Why are you stopping?" she asked resting on the hexed pillow.

He stood on the threshold, holding the door handle. "I love my wife more than I hate George."

Thank the goddess he came to his senses before it got worse. Oh, William, how will ye ever fix this mistake?

Eleanor ground her teeth, seething, as she leaned against the amplifier charm. "Fine. Go home to your witch wife, and her bastard son. You better hope I dinnae accidentally call George by your name next time we hump."

MacLeod stared at Eleanor with raised eyebrows, then away, then back with utter disbelief, realizing the mess he was in. Standing with ramrod posture, William traced his fingers over Lady Margaret's earrings on Eleanor's nightstand and left.

Elspeth won this round. But I willnae let this mistake willnae break Fiona's heart, too.

Chapter 28

William MacLeod

London

What the hell did I just do? William's boots slipped on the rough and uneven stones of London Bridge. A surge of vomit came as he retched over the rail. Bile and whiskey splattered on the frozen Thames below, steaming faintly in the winter air. He stared at his own filth, his shame frozen in place for everyone to witness.

Her perfume still lingered on his coat. Jasmine and cloves. He kissed her. Just a kiss, but he knew it almost became more.

If Fiona finds out... She'll never trust me again.

"I have to fix this," he said aloud, wiping his arm against his mouth as a passerby scowled with disgust. His mouth tasted like acid.

I stopped. That counts. Dinnae it?

If George finds out...

He turned from the bridge. Snow clung to his lashes. All around him, London's spires and timbered buildings leaned at drunken angles. The city rang with the clang of church bells judging him.

"I never wanted to leave." His breath hitched. Fiona had kicked him out, but he'd given her every reason. Broderick. The arguments. Forbidding magic.

"It meant nothing," he whispered, but part of him knew that wasn't quite true.

He needed to get home. Apologize. Burn Eleanor's note. Beg forgiveness.

Oh, God, I'm turning into such a horrible man. What's wrong with me? I put Fiona in incredible danger, telling Eleanor about the salt circle.

Unless—

Unless he made the problem disappear.

He straightened, a plan forming. Risky. Dangerous.

But it just might work.

Chapter 29

Eleanor

London

Eleanor was awoken by the pounding on the door, almost as loud as the pounding in her head.

A deep-voiced man argued with the butler.

She rubbed her eyes as the knocking continued. A sharp point scratched her cheek. Peering closer, she discovered dried blood on the end of a feather protruding from her pillow. Flipping the pillow, she noted the messy stitches of coarse twine and pulled the seam apart. Dozens of black, blood-soaked raven feathers fell onto the bed. She shrieked.

Jane burst in. "They've come to arrest you!"

The constable came in and lifted Lady Margaret's earrings from the table. "Stealing from Lady Hallewell, are you? That's cause for a trip to the gallows."

"This is a mistake," Eleanor said. "Those were a gift from Lord Hallewell."

"Tell it to the judge."

"Jane, find my Lord Hallewell, please!"

Eleanor barely slipped on her petticoats and gown over her shift before the sheriff shackled her in irons, hoisted her on a cart, and dragged her off to Newgate Gaol.

Chapter 30

Matilda

London—Newgate Gaol

Matilda floated above Eleanor and watched her scratch at the brown serge prison garb as she lay listless. The scroll's prophecy had literally come true. At least the mystery of the connection between Eleanor and William's family tree was solved—he was the one who put Eleanor in chains. *I dinnae realize I'd play a part in getting the cuffs clasped to her wrists, though.*

She pushed her guilt aside. Eleanor had threatened to throw Fiona in harm's way by exposing her witchcraft after all.

Eleanor curled in on herself. Her friend, Jane, had sold off her silk gowns to pay the holding fees at the Newgate Goal. Two shillings per week bought her the 'privilege' of resting her head on a log at the top of the prison cell.

Where was Lord whatshisname? Still caring for his dying mother? It had been a month. What did MacLeod tell him to make George forsake her? *Eleanor and George love each other. I should have ken it was an amplifier hex making her do strange things. I should have protected her.*

Matilda floated away from Eleanor, too guilty to pore over her dirty face, and wavered like a heat haze over the hundred unfortunate girls with no money laying at the bottom of the heap, where urine puddles collected. It reminded her of her own arrest and torture at the hands of Lord Blackmere and Admiral Goring. She shivered at the memory.

William isna his grandfather. I ken he loves Fiona. Why dinnae I stop to consider only a hex would make him betray her? And I call myself a wise woman—I'm the biggest fool there is, she thought. *Elspeth kens my flaws, and took advantage of them. I canna believe that witch tricked me again. I let my anger cloud my judgement instead of working with Eleanor to form a coven as the goddess commanded.* If her head wasn't transparent, Matilda would have banged it against the stone wall.

The turnkey guard drank a glass of spirits before entering the cell and inhaling the foul stench to gather the disorderly girls. "Dead Man's Walk," he said, "at least for some of you."

A heaviness settled in Matilda's ghostly soul. She'd never wished for Eleanor's execution, and yet, she was the reason William noticed the stolen earrings.

The guard permitted no speaking as he led the accused through the underground tunnel past a Bible and candlestick chained to the wall. Sniffles and coughs mingled with the pelting rain as Eleanor shuffled in her irons into the courtroom.

"It reeks of vinegar and burned herbs," Eleanor muttered.

"Think we want to catch gaol fever from you?" the guard said.

Rickety seating creaked as people in the galleries craned to hear the girls' sob stories while the Lord Mayor, acting as judge, sat high above. Eleanor's hands rested over her stomach.

It all came back to Matilda. The Kirk session where her neighbors turned against her, inspired by Reverend MacDonald's sermons about dangerous women. Lord Blackmere's smug grin at the sentence condemning her to be partially hung, then burned alive at the stake for heresy and witchcraft. *If only someone had defended me.*

Then she saw him.

William MacLeod wore a powdered wig and black robe, a true barrister. "Keep your gob shut, and for God's sake, look contrite," MacLeod whispered to Eleanor.

Thank the goddess, Matilda called to the heavens. *William will free Eleanor, she'll reconcile with Lord Hallewell, and I'll stop interfering in everyone's life for the rest of eternity.*

"George is saving me?" Eleanor searched for him in the crowd.

"Eleanor, I'm here by my accord." MacLeod caught the Lord Mayor's gaze. "She pleads guilty, your Honor." He tapped his chin with two fingers.

Guilty?

The Lord Mayor mimicked the gesture and nodded. "Never have I met a more proper subject for parts beyond the seas."

Eleanor stood in shock.

"You may be a thief, but I willnae let you die for it."

She spit in his face. "Did you expect kisses? You told George about the stolen earrings. Why?"

MacLeod wiped his face with a folded handkerchief. "My job is to protect the family. Here's your half of the indenture contract. Dinnae lose it."

"I can ruin you. Tell the world about what you and your witch wife did to Colonel—"

He covered her mouth. "Think before crossing the person who saved you from hanging."

Eleanor nodded reluctantly, and he let go.

Matilda grew frustrated. 'Twas difficult to pity Eleanor when she kept threatening Fiona. She hated to admit it, but MacLeod had come up with a decent solution.

"You'll be working at Matthew Crowan's plantation in Virginia Colony. I negotiated a reduced term of four years, and at the end, you get your freedom and ten acres. If you want a clean break, this is how to do it."

"I think it's you who wants the clean break, Mr. MacLeod."

"It's for the best, Eleanor. Lord Hallewell already has a wife and legitimate children. I wager you'll want your own children someday, and not have to send them away like all his other bastards."

Her hands crossed over her stomach as her face paled.

Handing her a carpet bag, he said, "Here's your plaid shawl, a journal, some quills and ink, smoked meat, and forty shillings. You might have to bribe the guards."

"How can you be awful and good to me at the same time? I dinnae understand you." Eleanor kept holding her stomach, and walking a few steps before interrupting herself and changing direction. "Can I write a letter for you to give to George?"

"May I, and no." He nodded to the bailiff to remove Eleanor.

"And if I write to him, anyway?"

William MacLeod grew serious as the grave. "Dinnae contact Lord Hallewell, or I guarantee you will regret it. Understood?"

"I understand completely," she said with angry tears streaming. "I ken too much about your witch wife," she said in an obvious attempt to hurt him.

As he was adjusting his legal papers, a letter fell from his pocket. Matilda, now able to read thanks to his lessons to Eleanor, saw it was a letter from William.

Fiona,

I know I've made mistakes. I was too hard on Broderick, sending him to school alone. He deserved better from me—you all did. If you wish, we can send Lachie with him in the autumn. It truly is an excellent school and they'll have each other, so it won't feel like punishment. That will make things right.

As for your...gifts... I may never understand them, but I know they are part of you.

Most of all, please I know that I love you.

If you'll have me, I'd come home, not to change you, but to stand beside you.

Yours,
William

At the bottom Fiona had scrawled a note.

Come home.

Chapter 31

Fiona

Scotland

A draft of cold air stroked Fiona's face, and William's musky scent drew her eyes open. He stood half frozen in front of the fire, taking off his snow-dusted coat and cravat.

"You're home?" She sleepily lit the candle beside the bed, wanting to hug him, but not sure where they stood. These past few months were incredibly rough without him. *Does this mean he accepts who I am? Magic and all?*

"I dinnae mean to wake you. I can sleep in the guest room."

Something was different about him. Not only the presence of a newly grown beard, but his demeanor had changed.

"Dinnae be silly." She chuckled at her lopsided bun. "Ack, my twist is a mess." Untying the ribbon, her brown tresses dropped in soft waves. "I hope you dinnae mind if I let my hair down."

Averting his eyes, he shifted on his feet, returning to the fire. "I'm not the king of you."

What an odd thing to say. "You're better than king; you're my husband."

He curled his hands inward, darting glances at her and then at his feet.

Sliding from the comfort of the bed, she rubbed the outside of his arms to warm him, not sure if he'd accept her touch. "Is everything well with you?"

He kept fidgeting and clearing his throat. The top of his shirt was open now, exposing a tuft of his chest hair, and Fiona's fingers ached with the need to caress him and recover everything the past few years had stolen from them.

He reached out to touch her cheek, but pulled back. "*Tha mi air do ionndrainn.*"

She tilted her head. "I've missed you too," she whispered. They used to speak their native tongue when they were newlyweds, and when the boys were young. "I haena heard you speak Gaelic in years."

Not since the rape.

Silently, she leaned her head against his chest, feeling her heartbeat slow. He wrapped his arms around her. The heat of his chest surged through the coldness of his shirt, and a gentle warmth spread. She felt safe in his arms.

His whiskers tickled her cheek. When was the last time he kept a beard? He shaved it before heading to Oxford to study law. *Did he grow that for me?*

When she pulled back, his eyes were welling.

She hugged him tighter, longing to erase the distance between them. She'd been the one who kicked him out, after all. "I wish I could be who you want me to be," she said, tilting her chin up to meet his gaze.

Slowly, he brushed soft kisses against her neck. "*Tha mi duilich.*"

"I'm sorry, too." The words caught in her throat.

They both spontaneously laughed and hugged deeper, relieved to forgive and be forgiven. She cupped his face, even more handsome today than when they first met. He touched his lips against hers in a soft stroke, as if testing their connection. Closing her eyes, Fiona's fears melted as he deepened the kiss. Like she was home. He moved her long, chestnut hair back, kissing that spot on her neck, just behind her ear, that always made her melt. Heat spread through her body.

"God, I missed you." She tugged off his shirt and reached for his breeches, but he pulled her hand up, gently pressing a kiss on the inside of her wrist.

"Let me take care of you first."

She lay back on the bed. He kissed down her tummy, hiking her shift to her waist, then lazily stroked her inner thighs with feather-like brushes, driving her mad.

"Is this an apology or a reprimand?" she giggled. His whiskers caused such delicious friction.

"Canna a husband appreciate his wife...slowly?" he said with a smirk. He kept the heat of his mouth over her private, just hovering, then pulled away, kissing her inner thigh again. She could kill him for such torture, except it felt too good. He kissed slow circles everywhere except her private. She writhed in anticipation. He blew fervently at the crevice of her inner thigh.

"You dinnae apologize fair," she whispered.

"No, I dinnae." His tongue suspended right over that spot. He caught her eyes and whispered, "I'm sorry."

He went down on her until she shuddered loud enough to make even him blush.

He undressed, and climbed in bed beside her, folding his arms around her. She rested her head on his chest, drawing idle patterns on his skin with her fingers. *I want to stay here, in this space, forever.*

She pulled him on top of her, wanting all of him. As their bodies pressed to become one, they knew a child would come of this night.

Chapter 32

ELEANOR

London—The Mercy

The surgeon doing the cursory medical inspection seemed more interested in her ability to survive the voyage than discovering any secrets growing in her womb.

Guards rowed Eleanor across the Thames with the other shivering prisoners to Galleons Reach. Nausea rolled through her, and she wasn't sure if it was the rough waters or the new bairn growing inside. *I should have pleaded the belly, but Mr. MacLeod would have taken my child away.*

Brackish water burned her nostrils as the sky threatened more spring drizzle. Too numb to cry, she focused on balancing as the boat shifted. Her irons scraped through muddy puddles on the boat floor. She kept replaying the events in her mind.

'Twas only an instant ago I drank claret in the theater while Lord Hallewell's capable fingers traced my inner thighs. I've utterly botched my chance at a good life with the one man I truly loved.

"Oye, how long's the trip to the colonies?" shouted a boisterous harlot recently snatched up by the Reformation of Manners and sentenced for prostitution.

"Shut your jaw, woman," growled the guard. Eleanor might have guessed at his rank, but it didn't matter much, did it? As always, every man was above her.

"Eight weeks at sea, with stops along the way," said the young carpenter seated beside the guard.

The rowboat pulled beside the prison ship, and she squinted at the masts scraping the sky, like the ship that brought her to the workhouse almost a decade ago. Another wave of nausea hit. Her skin grew clammy as she retched over the side of the boat.

The bile stung her throat. Someone groaned beside her, but no one helped. She tasted salt and copper, and hated herself for crying. Eleanor rubbed her temples, but nothing soothed away her self-loathing ruminations. *Why did I imagine I could win against any of these powerful people? The ill wish in my pillow must have come from Lady Margaret...and the witch of Pye. Lady Margaret was right. I'm only a workhouse girl, only fit to clean the grime from soiled linens.*

"The ship's carpenter will remove your irons before you board *The Mercy*," said the guard. *Mercy? The jokes from God never cease, do they?*

The rowboat shifted as each woman stood, one by one, to get her shackles unlocked, then hiked the gangplanks. The youngest convict appeared twelve, the oldest about seventy. One woman acted proud as a noblewoman. Everyone called her Lady Grace back at Newgate Gaol. She made her living stealing rolls of fabric beneath her petticoats. Another woman with frizzled hair muttered aloud about people throwing bugs at her. Most women kept to themselves, casting a wary eye at the ship taking them over troubled waters into seven years of hard labor.

Well, four years in Eleanor's case. Perhaps MacLeod's conscience made him negotiate the reduced sentence. Reflecting on her life brought her to heave again, as the head prison guard in charge of transfer casually tapped his club against his fist.

"All right, miss?" The young carpenter was full of pity. "Stare at the horizon to settle your stomach."

Did the carpenter's kindness mask flirtation? She stopped trusting her own ability to read people. Head throbbing, stomach churning, she wiped her wet eyes and mouth, and glanced at the growing pile of irons at the carpenter's feet.

Each woman carried a carpetbag of her belongings. Eleanor's bag felt as light as the one from the workhouse. Some things never changed.

"What'd you done to get yourself here?" asked the young carpenter, scarcely old enough to shave, blue eyes shining. He jostled the key down by her feet.

"Murder," she said. Her irons dropped with a clank. His face fell, and she laughed, defaulting to a flirtatious smile. "Dinnae fash yourself. I stole earrings."

The gruff guard tapped his club in his hand. "Reckon that's funny, do you? Let's see how much laughing you do working on a plantation."

Lowering her head, she cursed her impulsive nature to make up such a fanciful lie, but the guard didn't need to shame her for joking. Eleanor considered mouthing off, but had a wean to consider, and didn't want her brain bashed in. Her priority was figuring out who was important and cozying up to them once on board.

"You seem a little woozy. Do you need some help?" the young carpenter said. "Careful now, the gangplank is slippery."

She smiled gratefully at this schoolboy. It might be the last bit of kindness she got for a while. She was about as worthless as a girl could be in society.

With each wobbly step over the murky waters, a million ideas ran roughshod in her brain. *Should I jump into a watery grave and join my father in Hell?*

The callous hand of a navy man gripped her wrist, yanking her forward onto the deck. To her surprise, the young carpenter came aboard after her, and saluted the officer in charge. Glancing over the rail, she watched the prison guard get rowed back toward Newgate Gaol. At least she wouldn't have to see the brutal bastard's pox-dented face anymore.

Crew mates sweated profusely as they carried goats, chickens, and sheep from the delivery ships onto the deck for the long journey. They even hoisted a few cows aboard using a canvas sling and ropes. Soon the deck steamed with piles of manure.

"Attention," said the captain, adjusting his tricorn hat as he stood before the sloppily assembled prisoners.

"It's a long journey to parts beyond the sea. You disorderly girls have two choices: Become a 'wife' for the weeks-long journey, or sleep six to a shelf in the dark orlop, splashed in vomit and shite. If you decline, someone will step in for you, as there are three of you for each of us. If a sailor selects you, you'll warm his bed. Everyone else goes to the orlop until we're sea bound."

The crew walked through the crowd of convicts, assessing their beauty. A balding sailor grabbed a skinny redhead and licked his lips. She turned pale but nodded. The line moved down. Eleanor tensed. The young carpenter practically tackled the other men to grasp her hand. "I choose her."

"It's about time someone helped clear the spots from the boy's face," a sailor teased.

Sure. I'll warm the lad's bed. Sizing him up, she guessed he was a virgin, or nearly one. He'd judge her tits were naturally firm, not realizing they were filling with milk. She needed to survive the voyage.

"We set sail in the morning. Enjoy the festivities tonight."

The captain had chosen Lady Grace, the shoplifter, as his wife, and led her to a room behind a giant wheel, while the crew rolled barrels of gin on deck stamped with the imprints of riverbank inns. Unfortunates not chosen as a wife marched to the orlop below, as the prettier girls began carousing.

She supposed there was a certain logic to such maritime privileges. 'Marriage' would end male infighting, and at least the girls weren't at the mercy of every drunken ruffian; only one. At least, that's what she told herself. It was important to make the best of whatever situation she found herself in.

Her 'husband' squeezed her hand with his sweaty palm, giddily pulling her towards the forecastle. "What's your name, then?"

"Eleanor."

She should have asked his name, but it didn't matter, did it?

His rank afforded him a cramped cabin with a door, unlike the other men sleeping in hammocks slung from bolts in the ceiling. The wall contained a built-in bed with a drawer below. A patchwork quilt peeked from it. She guessed his mother had lovingly sewn it so he wouldn't miss home.

He wasn't much of a talker, and soon his breeches were round his feet. "Ah, do you want to take your own dress off, Eleanor, or should I untie it, or...?"

The last thing she desired was to get naked, have him suspect her delicate condition, and switch wives. It was easy enough to distract him. She released her breasts from her shift and his wee face lit up like the first time a person tasted cake.

"I never thought I'd see such bushel bubbies up close. God, I love being married."

Jesus Christ, I hope the milk waits till Virginia.

"What's your name?" she asked.

"Peter Carpenter." The poor lad blushed something awful.

"You've never done this before?" she asked gently. "Neither have I."

He exhaled in obvious relief. The lad dinnae ken his arse from his elbow in bed but eventually he figured things out. Ninety seconds later, he snored soundly with drool dripping from his smiling, spotty face.

Slipping from his arms, she did her best to balance on the shifting ship, and sat on the floor. Her trip to America felt more like a journey to her grave.

George would have divorced his wife. We might have lived a happy life together. Curling over her knees, she felt like she was ten again, abandoned on the ship.

There was no point in crying. Sniffling then wiping her eyes with the back of her hand, she vowed to distract herself. Opening her carpetbag, she pulled out the thick, black journal, surprised to see an inscription: *Remember to reflect, William.*

Uncorking the ink, she dipped the quill in, then crossed out his name in bold strokes. That was her day's highlight.

Aye, there are things I'm going to reflect on, and Mr. MacLeod better hope my musings dinnae become public.

For the next eight weeks she scrubbed the ship with the other prisoners, warmed the carpenter's bed, marveled at her changing body, and filled pages in her diary while her husband snored.

She wrote angry rants against MacLeod and his betrayal, and her pure hated of Lady Margaret. After the rage left, she wrote about George, how they met and fell in love. The texture of his muscles. The heat of his skin when he held her. The way his passionate music entranced her. Their quiet conversations before falling asleep.

But when she considered her many mistakes, she lowered the quill. Her choices led her to be nineteen, unmarried, and pregnant on a convict ship. She put away her diary, steeling herself to face the consequences of her actions. She curled into a ball, wishing she could be someone worth saving.

Chapter 33

FIONA

Scotland

Fiona stretched in bed, completely content. Broderick was home from school for the summer, a new bairn kicked inside her belly, and William just climbed in bed ready for a roll in the hay.

Urgent pounding echoed from beyond the door. *Bugger.*

"James, is that you?" he called.

Salty sea wind rushed inside. Another knock.

"Who's there?"

They sat. It had been years since it happened. Both Matilda and Elspeth taught her how to raise her shields. If only she had access to her crystals, or even pumice to absorb the negative energy, she might block the path.

William grabbed his claymore, *Justice*, from the pegs, narrowing his gaze on the sound. "I checked all the locks before coming to bed. I was just in the hall," he whispered. "It was empty."

Eisd rium a Dhia. Raise your veils. Please block the undead from my room, she prayed.

The banging, initially at the door, travelled up to the ceiling with an intensifying sound of gasps, like a person drowning. William recoiled, eyes wide and staring, as his grip tightened on his weapon.

Why me? Why now? Will the Otherworld ever leave me alone?

The knocking came insistently, like a frantic parent searching for his child. She had to help. Sliding from the bed, Fiona gently tapped William's arm. "He's not here to hurt us."

He gave her a slight nod, never leaving her side.

Fiona placed her outstretched palm on the door, whispering to the spirit. The banging from the ceiling shifted down the wall, then lessened to only light scratching sounds until it disappeared, carrying the scent of the sea away with it.

William's mouth hung open, speechless.

"Sometimes they get lost," she said.

Chapter 34

MATILDA

The Mercy—Litha fire festival

While Eleanor and the carpenter had another romp in the cramped cabin bed, Matilda levitated over them growing angrier by the minute. Leaving Kirkhaven to go to London was one thing, but travelling to parts unknown on a convict ship was infuriating.

Cut off forever from Fiona. My only chance at revenge against Elspeth and Lord Blackmere ripped away. And the tart already has a new lover fawning all over her? Why am I suffering more consequences than her?

At last, the fire festival Litha arrived, the sun went down, and Eleanor made the mistake of looking into the lantern flame. Matilda's voice unleased.

I've been waiting for a fire festival and a flame to give ye a piece of my mind. Husband stealer. Whore. Ye deserve every bad thing coming to ye.

"Who are you?" Eleanor said in her mind. She covered her ears and pinched her eyes shut to block Matilda's taunting while the carpenter rode her like a mare.

Ye canna escape thoughts, lass. I'm in your head.

"Who are you? Why do you hate me?" Eleanor screamed in her mind.

I might have been willing to excuse your attempted seduction of William while raven feathers were in your pillow, but I'll never forgive ye endangering Fiona, Matilda snarled. *What did Fiona ever do to ye? Good gods, Fiona gave up her own shawl to cover your nakedness the first time ye met.*

Eleanor glanced at the plaid shawl beside her. "What are you talking about? I never met Mr. MacLeod's wife in my life."

Ack, that's right. We put a memory charm on ye. It dinnae matter now. She raised her right hand over Eleanor's head. *Cuimhnich.*

In a rush, the memory charm was broken. Eleanor remembered vividly everything that happened night at the Hellfire Caves, the masked man trying to stab her womb, the wise woman asking her to join a coven, the vengeful ghost who scared the shite out of her promising revenge. "Oh my God," Eleanor shouted aloud.

Pete grinned. "Yes? I'm a better lover then?" He went harder at his task.

"I ken his witch wife would curse me for flirting," Eleanor said mind to mind.

Ye did more than flirt, honeylocks. Fiona dinnae ken anything about your stolen kiss. Or that ye threatened to let Lord Blackmere condemn her to execution to get yourself out of gaol, but I do. No one should threaten an innocent person.

As Matilda's righteous indignation bubbled over, things plummeted around the room. Young Pete, too engrossed in his lovemaking, didn't notice, but Eleanor hugged him tighter, shutting her eyes.

"You're one to talk. You've been throwing hexes at ravens, and plotting murder since the day we met! If you want to haunt someone, go after Fiona's husband. He threw me in prison over goddamned earrings Lady Margaret dinnae even wear. I'm banished to a plantation to serve four years of hard labor, and you're scolding me? Go back to Hell, evil spirit."

Ye denied me my vengeance against Lord Blackmere and Elspeth. I'm your nightmare now, lass, Matilda cackled. *I'll cast a spell to raise a storm. Sailors are superstitious, and maybe they'll strangle ye, then throw ye overboard. Then we'll meet in the Otherworld.*

"Leave her be, witch," a clansman barked.

Matilda blinked, startled to be interrupted. Since boarding *The Mercy*, a ghost wearing a Highlander plaid kept watching Eleanor from a distance, as though he knew her. Whenever Matilda went near him to talk, he cast himself overboard into his watery grave. *How many ghosts are going to attach themselves to this wee bitch? Who are ye, man?*

"Ah, Nellie," cried the carpenter, as he released and collapsed on top of Eleanor.

"Who are you talking to? There's another ghost in here?" she said aloud, trying to look around the room, but Pete blocked her view.

"Sorry. I didn't mean to call her name. She was the first girl I loved," Pete said.

"I said, leave her be," the Highlander ghost said.

Through walls, shaky stairs, and a hatch, Matilda pursued the Highlander. As her anger intensified, the waves grew, splashing foam as sailors clung to the ratlines. He was almost within her grasp until the magical bounds yanked her back.

Pointing where she stood, Matilda used her most wretched voice. *I've made many a wave sweep away a guilty man. Dinnae cross me, Highlander. Even in death, I can do ye harm.*

He scoffed. "You've no powers over me. Your charms mean naught here."

Ye imagine ye can stop me from tormenting Eleanor? I'll kill her, and everyone on the ship. Let them all become ghosts.

Matilda's rage manifested into a thunderous storm as she drew on her knowledge of the dark arts Elspeth taught her years ago. Sailors rang the bell, and a panic fell over the ship as sailors rolled like cannon balls on the deck. Dark waves rose, lurching the vessel, and sending terrified screams from the passengers below.

"For God's sake, stop, you wicked witch." The Highlander crossed right through her, an obvious attempt to enrage her further. And it worked.

Matilda pursued him as he went down to the 'tween deck, then one deck further into the orlop, but Matilda stopped short when she realized they were in an orlop of another ship, in a different time. The temperature dropped and the magical leash disappeared from her waist, allowing her to walk freely.

Have I walked inside a memory? Matilda asked the ghost beside her. *Who are ye?*

"I'm Eleanor's father, Ned Cameron."

Eleanor's Memory—Scotland—1718

"Watch out, Eleanor! Dinnae let them see you." The living version of Ned pulled young Eleanor, aged ten, into the dark alley, away from the redcoats. Young Eleanor slipped on the heaps of rotting fish as she gagged at the stench.

"Da isna himself," Eleanor thought, watching her father scratch at the fading pox marks on his neck. "Is he mad at me?"

Matilda faced Ned. *Do ye hear her thoughts and understand her feelings, too?*

"Aye," he said, looking confused.

Peeking around the corner of the alley, living Ned grabbed young Eleanor's forearm, and they dashed past the fishwives toward a small ship crewed by the royal navy. Eleanor bit her lip as she stubbed her toe on the cobblestone.

Sailors carrying wooden crates hustled from the ship's gangplank toward a warehouse. Once past, she and Ned snuck aboard. She hobbled in pain but felt excited about going on an adventure. "What's Da up to?" He squeezed her arm tight as he led her past a giant wheel. Silently, they climbed down a ladder into the empty ship reeking of ropes and salt, then crept down a second ladder into a dark place filled with barrels with tar drips, cannon balls, and boxes with royal seals.

"What are we doing here?" Eleanor whispered.

Ned put his finger to his lips. "Wheest."

A sliver of light glowed through the hatch above, showing the outline of his face now grown thin since her siblings and Mam had died. Eleanor wished she were younger than ten, so Da might lift her up in his brawny arms in this strange place.

Wedging her between crates, he pulled cheese and a thick bread crust from his plaid's pocket, and handed them to her. "This has to last all week. Only eat a bite or two when your stomach hurts. Stay hidden," he said, wrapping one of her blonde curls around his finger, and kissing it. "I'll be back soon," he whispered. He crept back up the ladder as she watched bravely in the shadows. "Everything will be better in London, aye?" he called over his shoulder.

Matilda confronted Ned. *Ye abandoned your own daughter. Why?*

"I canna watch." Ned tried to leave, but Matilda cut in front of him, frustrated he would walk away again.

I heard Eleanor weep over what ye did. I shouldna be hearing it, ye should. Face your sins. Listen to your daughter's memory.

Young Eleanor hugged her knees, glancing around, training her eyes on the ground to let them adjust to the darkness. "London? I wish Mam were here. I even miss my brothers."

Men shouted above. "Did they catch Da?" Goosebumps came to her arms and legs in the damp cold. She strained to listen. "Should I go up? What if he needs help? But he told me to stay hidden."

More shouting followed, and her stomach sank as she made the sign of the cross. A rat squeaked nearby, scratching for food.

Suddenly, screeching noises came from all directions, and she clapped her hands over her ears. A putrid stench filled the air as water sloshed beneath the ship, and she realized they were moving out to sea. "Where's Da?"

Each board of timber beneath her moved in a different direction and soon she was on her hands and knees, spilling her stomach from sea sickness. "Please, please come back, Da."

Matilda's heart broke staring at the terror in the little girl's eyes, wishing she could hug her.

Tremors traveled up and down her arms. Crawling to the darkest corner, she found a handgrip in the wall, and she clung to it until her muscles ached.

Everything shifted, and a box hit the back of her head.

When she woke, the ship was quiet. "Da?" she said in a hoarse voice. How long had it been? Hours? Days? Heavy boots creaked down the ladder as yellow lantern light threw violent shadows against the walls. Diving behind a large barrel, her heartbeat thrashed in her ears.

Two Sassenach sailors pointed and shouted. They dragged her from her hiding spot. She shook uncontrollably as they hauled her up both ladders and into the blinding sunlight. She squinted, blocking the white rays with her hand as a crowd of men in breeches and loose shirts surrounded her. Beyond them was nothing but shifting blue waves.

A man wearing a red coat and tricorn hat stared her down.

"Why did Da leave me?" she thought. "He hates me because I should have taken better care of everyone. It's my fault our family died. No wonder he thinks I'm worthless."

The Mercy – Present Day

Ned moved away from the memory, panting. "I never meant for her to think such lies."

They were back on *The Mercy's* deck, in the midst of the storm Matilda had created. The Otherworld disappeared again, hiding Eleanor's memory.

No wonder she acts as she does. Always afraid of being abandoned if she dinnae please everyone. The storm calmed, no longer violent, but the rain continued.

Ned stood beneath the downpour a broken man. "They tell you in church God decides who gets into heaven. They dinnae tell you that after death, you sit in judgement on yourself."

Why did ye jump? Matilda asked cautiously.

His shoulders rounded, and he cast his eyes down. "I brought the pox home and killed my entire family. How could I live with that?"

Ye had Eleanor, she said with mounting frustration.

"She'd be better off without me, so I stowed her away to London." Ned took a deep, painful breath and shut his eyes. "Then I jumped. It seemed sensible then."

Mist rolled in as pity replaced Matilda's anger. They remained quiet for a time, staring into the choppy waters.

Ned finally spoke. "I remember as a lad hearing my uncle say he almost died once and watched his whole life flash in front of him. For me, it wasna quick. I walked through the important memories. Marrying my wife. Holding my bairns. And most moments were good. I expected to be reunited with them in death. Instead, I've been stuck in a fog, searching for the light. I believed I might wander lost forever, but then I heard a kind mother kissing her sons goodnight. Her golden eyes were glowing through the mist, and I ken at once she'd help me."

Fiona?

"When I approached her, she was behind the veil. She clearly wanted to help, but her man was standing there, and she hesitated. I kept banging until she whispered..." His voice cracked. "'Return to the ship where you left your heart.' Well, now, I'm on this prison ship, but my Eleanor is all grown up, and you keep haunting her. You're making her sick. Dinnae you see that?"

Shamed, Matilda twisted away.

"I dinnae realize how much pain I caused my daughter by abandoning her until now, walking through the memory with you." His voice trailed off as he scanned the horizon.

Matilda shifted. Until this moment she viewed Eleanor as a spoilt mistress, someone who foiled her plans for revenge, a vixen who threatened Fiona. She never imagined Eleanor as someone's abandoned daughter.

He spoke in a quiet but firm tone. "You need to stop bothering my girl. I ken you're a bitter old hag, and this is fun for you, but Eleanor's been hurt enough."

Why protect her now, and not then? Matilda said. *Ye ken she hates ye. I heard her curse ye myself, back in London on the night she learned the truth of your suicide.*

He nodded. "I deserve her curses." Ned climbed on the rail, on the verge of jumping, staring over the gray horizon as waves crashed beneath.

It's neither me, nor the sea, making the lass sick. A star-crossed bairn grows in her belly that needs protection. If ye truly want to protect her, convince her to join my coven. If I haena been so bent on revenge, we would have formed the coven when Beira originally wanted us to.

Ned looked confused. "Why would she ever trust me again?"

Eleanor needs ye right now. There's a man named Lord Blackmere who'll stop at nothing to kill her child. She'll listen to ye, Ned.

The sun rose over the horizon, making the veils shimmer in the light.

"No. I canna help anyone."

Stop running away, Ned.

He jumped.

Matilda reached out to grab him, but the binding to Eleanor reappeared around her waist, pulling her back. Heavy rain poured down on what was left of Matilda's soul.

"Land ho," called a sailor. "Virginia colony straight ahead."

Pete and the rest of the crew gathered the convicts on the slippery deck, locking them back in irons.

Why am I being so harsh to Eleanor? Aren't we merely two lost souls trapped in our pasts? Matilda studied Eleanor, beyond the feisty mistress, and saw the abandoned child. *I need to stop haunting Eleanor, and start helping her.*

Chapter 35

Eleanor

Virginia Colony

Dirty, shaking, and sweating in the heat of a foreign sun, Eleanor stared into the crowd of curious onlookers. Gentlemen in perukes, and lowly stableboys alike, grew aroused by the collection of fallen girls bound in chains, ready to be sold.

Black faces in homespun wool lifted barrels onto wagons, women shopped for eggs in the open market, and children pointed and laughed as she pulled in her arms closer to her core, crumpling under their scrutiny. "I am nothing to these people."

A cold wind blew through the summer day.

I can sympathize with ye, Matilda said in her mind. *The villagers all spat on me as I walked to my execution.*

"Good," Eleanor said mind-to-mind.

Ye can hear me? It isna a fire festival.

"Afraid so. Feel free to go back to Hell and leave me in peace, you foul spirit."

I suppose I deserve that. I haena been kind.

Eleanor snorted. "But you'll be kind to me now? You must want something."

It's the goddess, Beira, who's wanting us to talk. I'll no longer fight ye. I aim to protect ye and your bairn. The best way to do that is for ye to join our coven.

"I ken you wanted something."

"Get a move on." The auctioneer wiped his sweaty forehead, then shoved her towards the wooden block, irons still clamped over her wrists.

"Wait, this one's already sold to Mr. Crowan," said the auctioneer's man, reading off a list. He unlocked her cuffs, but then tied a rope around her wrists, and handed the end to her master, like a leash.

It was awful to realize she would be owned by anyone, even if only for a few years. Her new master, a man in his thirties dressed in beige and donning a white wig, inspected his investment. Now four months pregnant, she showed a rounded belly, and her breasts strained her shirt.

"Damned MacLeod," he said, frowning. "Don't even try to use the bastard in your belly to wriggle out of work. I paid 13 pounds for you, and I'm getting my money's worth."

George was right to end their friendship. He seems like an arsehole.

Eleanor tried to shield her burning cheeks with her hands, but they were bound, and he walked her towards his coach. Her throat felt thick and scratchy. "I had the world at my fingertips, but I played too many games," she muttered.

No good comes from berating yourself now. We all make mistakes, lass.

Eleanor blinked at the unexpected kindness.

Master Crowan rode in the coach while Eleanor jogged behind, now tied to the carriage. She feared the horses would spook and drag her to her death. Despite her yearn to sob, she didn't have the luxury.

She expected the colony's capital to be as large as London or Edinburgh, but it was only the Governor's palace, a church, a courthouse, the market area beside the armory, and a few rows of shops and houses. It barely took ten minutes to walk outside the capital. Soon there was nothing but farms and forests.

The tight stays chafed her breasts, and her movements were off-kilter. She still had her sea legs, and her ever-expanding belly made her clumsier than normal.

Everything here was different. Trees. Homes. Animals. And the sun scorched her face. Matilda tried to talk to her a few more times, but Eleanor was in no mood. Master Crowan only stopped the coach to relieve himself. He barely waited for her to empty her bladder before moving again.

Two long hours trudging through the heat later, Master Crowan called from his coach window, "This is Sweetwater Plantation."

Eleanor rubbed her sweaty face against her sleeve as they rounded onto a dusty road shaded by oak trees. Ahead loomed a three-story mansion with eight columns, considerably smaller than Astwick House, but quite impressive compared to the other houses she had seen in Williamsburg. Dozens of African slaves sang in the fields leading up to the Big House. They stared at each other.

I suppose ye seem odd to them too, walking on a leash behind the master's wagon, Matilda said. *Or not. I've no idea what's customary in the colonies.*

Two white men rode on horses through the field. "Git back to work," said the tall, thin man, cracking his whip against the back of a woman. Eleanor flinched at the noise, raising her bound wrists to cover her face.

"This canna be happening to me," she kept repeating.

It is happening, and ye need to face it head on.

"I dinnae need your help, witch."

Ye need all the help ye can get, and your daughter needs magical protection. As Elspeth told ye, your bairn is powerful only if she survives her childhood.

Eleanor's limbs shook under the weight of reality as they stopped in front of the Big House. A fashionable lady with powdered hair sipped iced tea on a wraparound porch. A boy, about ten, pulled a stick with a ribbon, making a top spin as his little sister watched from a safe distance.

"I canna put my finger on it, but the lad seems sneaky."

Aye. I get the same sense.

Master Crowan untied her wrists, and she rubbed them. He handed over her carpetbag. A long drip of sweat ran down her spine, and she noticed her own body smell.

"Daniel, go get Rob," he said to the gap-tooth boy, who took off running towards the fields.

"Matthew," said Mistress Crowan, "it's bad enough you've bought a convict, but you bought one in a delicate condition? Can we afford another mouth to feed? For the life of me, I don't know why you keep buying these ignorant Irish hooligans. Slaves are the only sensible investment these days."

She's Scottish not Irish, ye daft cow.

"I'm as surprised as you," he said. "I bought her from an old friend from Oxford. William professed she's an excellent laundress with great skill. He must have a soft spot for her for a reason."

"His soft spot is inside her belly, I'm sure." Mistress Crowan snickered, as though Eleanor weren't standing in front of them.

Eleanor's daughter will grow up to topple a king. Noble blood runs through her veins, ye pompous glorified farmers, Matilda said, spitting on the ground.

While appreciating the spectral defiance, Eleanor felt wary about Matilda's sudden change of heart.

"If you steal here, girl, there's nowhere else to banish you to but the hangman's noose. At least we get eight years out of her instead of seven thanks to her condition."

"That's not what the contract says," Eleanor said to Matilda in a panic.

Tell him.

"Why would he listen to me? He's the master, I'm a worthless convict."

Ye have to take a stand for something, or they'll knock ye down for anything.

"Excuse me, sir?" Eleanor extracted her half of the indentured contract from her carpetbag and appealed to Master Crowan, who at least appeared reasonable. "With respect, sir, my contract is for four years, and punitive damages wouldnae apply." She read.

IN Pursuance of Transportation of Felons to his Majesty's Plantations in America, I do hereby assign unto Mr. Matthew Crowan, a Convict, Eleanor Cameron, to serve him, his Heirs or Assigns, for the Term of four Years, commencing the Day of the Ship's Arrival. If she breaks said agreement, one year will be added as punitive damages.

"How could I possibly face punitive damages for something occurring prior to the commencement of my servitude? My delicate condition clearly originated in England."

The master and mistress' mouths gaped wide. "Are you a washerwoman or a solicitor?" he asked. "It's going to be an interesting four years."

Good job, lass.

Eleanor stood a wee bit taller to win the battle. "Thanks for the push."

He looked over her shoulder, "Ah, Rob. Here's the convict. Get her situated, then I'll give you a ride back to Riverside. Eleanor, this is Mr. Rob Birch, the overseer at my other plantation."

"Yessir, boss. Come on with me, Eleanor," Rob said.

Eleanor turned to see a solid dose of smoldering masculinity swagger toward Master Crowan with a coiled whip on his hip, and a musket strapped to his back. His dark hair, muscled torso, and intense brown eyes gave the impression he dinnae take shite from anyone.

He's rather sure of himself. He's undressing ye with his eyes, lass.

Eleanor turned away from him, resting her hands on her belly. "The only man I want is back in London."

She followed him towards a large barn with a wagon inside, and various tools hanging on the walls. A tiny wooden desk with a farm book sat beneath a window. Jingling a key, he unlocked a sizable cabinet and pulled out one coarse woolen petticoat, one linen shirt, two pairs of hose, one pair of the wrong sized shoes, an apron, and a mob cap to cover her hair.

Handing everything to her, his dark brown eyes trailed to her lip before he cleared his throat, then rested his gaze on her belly. "Not sure how long your petticoat is gonna fit. Looks like you had some fun in London."

She wanted to crawl into a hole. "That's one way to describe it." Thinking of George nearly brought her to tears, and she furiously blinked them back.

Rob locked the cabinet, and headed back into the blistering sun while she lagged, trying to shove all the clothes into her carpetbag. As she raced to catch up, she stared at scores of people with skinny black arms hoeing dirt around green leafy plants stretching towards a forest. Behind the Big House, past the long grass dancing in the breeze, flowed the James River.

As Rob strode down the path, everyone gave him wide berth. They'd rather step into puddles of muddy water than be in his way.

Careful of this one, Eleanor. People fear him. I need to read his palm to gain clarity.

"No more fortune-telling, no more cursed pillows, no more prophecies. I wish I never met the witch of Pye," Eleanor bit out, "And I wish to Christ I never met you."

Her name's Elspeth. Not the Witch of Pye. That makes her sound more mysterious than she is, and trust me, she dinnae deserve any respect.

"If any blackbirds bother you, tell Smitty," Rob said. "He's the regular overseer."

"You mean ravens?" Eleanor said, crouching as she peeked over her shoulder.

"I mean Negroes. It's against the law for a white woman to lie with one. The woman goes to gaol, the blackbird gets hung, and the baby most likely gets its brain bashed in with a rock."

Eleanor covered her mouth.

Apparently, cruelty exists on both sides of the pond.

As they moved on, Rob kept a brisk pace, and she grew winded as she squinted at the bright sun, shading her eyes with her hand. She felt unbalanced, and not only from the bairn growing inside. This new world was shockingly different.

"Hey, sugar. Where's my cornbread?" he called as they entered a two-story red brick kitchen building. Her mouth watered at the aroma of tangy spices.

A beautiful woman, about thirty, with mocha skin, full lips and an hourglass figure, wiped her flour-covered hands on her apron. "Baked it fresh for you, Mr. Birch." She smiled the way all servants do, then faced Eleanor. "I'm Hannah. You the new girl from London?"

Instinctively, Eleanor curtseyed, and the woman started laughing. "I ain't the mistress, honey. How's the king?"

"We're not on speaking terms at the moment, ma'am."

Hannah laughed, and Eleanor liked her immediately.

I like her too. She's got a good aura about her.

"No one's talking to you. Go back to the graveyard."

Nothing to bury, lass. I burned on a stake, thank ye.

The well-organized kitchen had been whitewashed, but some of the red brick was exposed due to time and humidity. Hannah took a long wooden paddle to pull bread from the brick oven built into the back wall, and placed it on a table covered with bowls of flour, eggs, and vibrantly colored vegetables.

Rob cut himself a thick slice of cornbread and slathered it in butter. "Eleanor needs rations." He lowered his voice. "Got any corn whiskey?"

Hannah winked at Rob, handing him the jug. "Don't tell Mistress Crowan."

Sunlight beamed in from three large windows held open with a stick, as Hannah rummaged through shelves stocked with herbs, spices, and other sundries. She measured out a peck of cornmeal, one pound of pickled pork, some dried herring, and salt, and handed them to Eleanor. "Everyone gets rations on Saturdays."

Ye could use the salt for protection. I can teach ye everything I ken to keep your child safe.

"Here, have some cornbread," she said, offering a steaming slice. "You're eating for two."

"Thank you." Closing her eyes, Eleanor focused on all the flavors twirling on her tongue as Matilda's offer turned in her mind. "At least I'm far away from Lord Blackmere and Elspeth in the colonies."

Ye think they canna find ye?

Eleanor rubbed her belly, her queasiness growing.

"Time to get to work," Rob said with his mouth full. "That's the smoke house, dovecote—they serve a lot of doves for dinner parties—tobacco shed, and lots of storage sheds."

"Are there many wild animals here, Mr. Birch?"

"Not so much on the plantations, but further west."

"Then why do you carry a musket?"

He chuckled. "Here's The Quarter, where the blackbirds live."

Nestled beneath a canopy of oaks, two rows of neglected cabins stood facing one another, their sagging rooves propped up by mismatched two-by-fours. Each had a single door, a set of worn steps, and one shuttered window, long weathered by time.

"How you doin', Old Betty?" Rob said, loudly.

A Black woman covered in freckles with her hair wrapped on top of her head, nodded at him as she balanced a bairn on her hip. She kept muttering, "Thomas. Mary. Harriet. Thomas."

"She lost her mind years ago. That's why Master Crowan has her watching the little ones. We tried to sell her, but no one wants her 'cause they think she's a witch."

"My god, am I a demon magnet?"

I wasna expecting there'd be witches in the colonies.

"Who are the people she keeps mentioning?" she asked him.

"Her sold-off children. Crowan bought a new plantation and needed cash for the mortgage."

Eleanor grasped the sides of her head, feeling faint. "Master Crowan can sell my child?"

"Don't seem like you're married," he said with a chuckle. "All bastards get indentured to the church for twenty-one years."

If they sell your daughter, and I'm bound to ye, who will protect her if Lord Blackmere finds her?

Eleanor leaned over, resting her hands on her thighs, and panted hard as two children toddled after a chicken through a puddle.

"You got a visitor," Old Betty said, staring above Eleanor. "Ain't that right?"

Ye can see me?

Old Betty gave a slight nod in Matilda's direction, then went back to chanting the names of her lost children.

"Crazy old lady." Rob moved on, and Eleanor hurried to catch up.

"Why can some people see you and not others?" she asked Matilda.

Betty must be some sort of diviner who can speak to spirits, like Fiona. Matilda rushed like wind through a keyhole, getting in front of her. *Eleanor, ye have to join the coven. We dinnae ken if Betty's a good witch or a bad witch, but she's clearly a conduit to the Otherworld.*

Eleanor frowned, scratching at her temples. "Stop talking. It's all too confusing."

"Here's the laundry building," he said, opening the door.

An enormous copper pot dangled in the hearth. Two large barrels stained white rested on the floor beside several buckets with flopping rope handles.

"Work starts at first light, and ends when it's too dark to see. You get a half day off on Sundays, unless the mistress needs you. You do a good job, ain't no one gonna bother you much. If you a problem, well..." He lightly stroked the coiled whip hanging off his belt.

She frantically tried to think of something to say to prove her capability as a laundress, but words escaped her.

Wee Daniel came up and tugged on Rob's elbow. "Mama says the lady thief gotta sleep with Hannah and Nancy above the kitchen."

Rob took a breath, and rubbed the back of his neck. "You sure your daddy's gonna be happy with that?"

"I don't know. They're fighting now. Seems like mama's gonna win this one." He ran off again.

"Listen, I'm gonna tell you some gossip, you ain't heard it from me. Mr. Crowan likes humping the blackbirds, especially Hannah. Nancy is his yellow baby, but ain't no one is supposed to talk about it, hear?"

Eleanor's head hurt. "Yes, Mr. Birch." She moved to a long table by the open window and dropped her carpetbag beside various brushes, an iron, and a jar full of ashes. Beneath the window rested several chamber pots, making the air reek as the piss changed into lye.

"Rob, let's go," hollered Master Crowan, with flushed skin and a tight jaw. "Goddamned wife," he muttered. "Can't wait to sell that bastard to shut her up about the investment."

"Well, good luck, I guess." Rob left.

Eleanor slumped onto a stool, head in her shaking hands. "I might get whipped and suffer a miscarriage; if my daughter's born healthy, Master Crowan will sell her; and Old Betty sees ghosts, so God help us if she guides Lord Blackmere to us." Her breathing grew shallow. "Ah, fuck."

Matilda glided over, kneeling at her feet like a shimmering mist. *Let me help ye. Ye canna do everything alone. I was wicked to ye in the past, but ye have my oath I will protect ye and your bairn.*

Eleanor gasped, resting her hands on her belly. "The baby just kicked." A cool breeze blew through the window, taking away the stink of the lye. She took a shaky breath. "I believe in God. If I become a witch, do I have to sell my soul to the devil?"

Gods, no. We're healers, not trying to do evil. We follow the old ways, the path of the Goddess Beira, and we honor the eight fire festivals.

Eleanor closed her eyes, nodding. She grabbed the ration of salt from her carpetbag, and drew a circle around herself and Matilda. "I'm ready to join the coven."

Chapter 36

William MacLeod

Scotland

William MacLeod turned over the black-sealed letter and braced as David played bagpipes around the hearth.

Dearest MacLeod,

I write to you with much urgency. I returned from Sussex, ready to go forth with divorce proceedings, only to find my beloved Eleanor gone.

No note—Nothing.

I asked the servants where she went, and the butler and ladies' maid pled ignorance. The younger one, Jane, was obviously holding something back, so I questioned her thoroughly until she revealed a most grievous betrayal. But I'm sure you're well aware, since you played a part.

MacLeod held his breath. He'd paid handsomely for silence, but Jane was always a question mark. He continued the letter.

Jane confessed Eleanor ran off with an actor. You visited Eleanor almost as often as me. Did she confide in you? Is this why you warned me to distrust her? Were you holding back information all along from your truest friend and brother?

Or was I entirely to blame for this abandonment? Did I push her away once too often, stupidly assuming she'd always be there when I was ready to amble home?

I'm begging you to help me track down this actor. Was it the brute who played Oberon—the actor from the Hellfire Club?

William, I love her. Help me find her. I'll search every theater in England if I must.

Your most humble servant,
Lord George Hallewell

It took a bag of gold pieces for her family, but thank God Jane stuck to the story. Finally, the threat to his family was gone. No more torrid love affairs to sort out. No more ridiculous talk of divorce through Parliament leaving everyone vulnerable to ruin.

Fiona and the boys applauded as David finished the lively reel. She patted her growing belly, eliciting his grin. David started to play a lament, *Flowers of the Forest,* about the famous betrayal at Glencoe. Its dark and foreboding notes played on his own guilty conscience. It was a rotten thing to do to both Eleanor and George, but sometimes rotten things needed to be done to protect the greater good. He pitched the letter into the fire.

Eleanor could have destroyed me and my entire family as collateral damage. A pang of fear struck MacLeod. *She still can. Where did I put Eleanor's flirtatious note? I need to burn the evidence.*

Pressing a kiss to Fiona's forehead, he slipped away into the study. Quietly, he tore through his trunk and papers. No sign of it. *Hold fast. I probably left it at the inn, and someone discarded it there.*

He and Fiona were on good terms again. Despite the knocking on the ceiling the other night, she hadn't mentioned magic once, and they were acting like themselves again. He even kept his beard to please her.

But what if Eleanor's note was somewhere in the house? Would Fiona deduce something more than tutoring happened? *It's not like we coupled. We only kissed, and we were drunk.* His excuses sounded pathetic to his own ears. He swallowed as the melody darkened into betrayal. *Have I murdered my marriage? I dinnae ever want to get kicked out again.*

Chapter 37

MATILDA

Virginia Colony

It was Sunday, Eleanor's half day off, and no one bothered her. The master granted each slave and indentured servant three square yards for a garden. The generosity masked the reality—no one would need a garden if rations were adequate.

For coven purposes, however, it would do.

"What other ingredients do we need for protection charms? I already have ash inside. I've been dicing, drying, distilling, mincing, boiling, and hanging herbs nonstop, but will they be effective? The one spell you taught me dinnae work, by the bye."

Which one?

"The ricochet spell. When Mistress Crowan snapped at me, I whispered *ath-bhualadh,* but nothing happened. I hoped her nastiness would come back to haunt her three times, but she's as prickly as before."

It only works if ye say it for an honorable reason, not because ye dinnae like the overbearing lady of the house. How are your plants coming along?

Eleanor knelt on a small towel to keep her petticoats clean as she showed Matilda the dill, garlic, onion, and sage, beside the standard vegetables. "I canna believe Mistress Crowan made me pay for the seeds. Her time is coming, though."

Matilda floated over the plants, inspecting them. *Och, ye more than made up for it, using Master Crowan's lustful pursuits of Hannah as a time to shop the kitchen spice rack.*

"I hope no one finds out I stole them. It's bad enough I'm indentured. If I'm executed for pinching allspice, I willnae be a help to anyone."

Aye, ye must be on guard. Beyond the church and the law, you've got Old Betty, and the Crowans to avoid. Matilda sighed. *Will there ever be a day when wise women aren't hunted?*

Eleanor clapped the dirt off her hands, and went inside to stir the bubbling cauldron on the fire, adding Mistress Crowan's petticoats and shifts into the mix.

What have ye got there? It dinnae look like your typical washing.

A mischievous grin crept up Eleanor's face. "Mistress Crowan is such a vicious hag to everyone. Since the ricochet spell dinnae work, I came up with the next best thing. It's not quite a hex, but I've added nettles and poison oak to her laundry to make her itch in all her private parts for weeks."

The spoon flew from the cauldron and smacked Eleanor's hand, leaving a red welt.

What guff is this? Leave revenge and comeuppance to the goddess. Dinnae dabble with the dark arts because I promise it leads to nowhere good. Matilda planted her fists on her hips, indicating further room-wrecking was imminent. *Dump the cauldron. Now.* Matilda quite enjoyed the random powers of an angry ghost to make things occasionally go bump in the night.

Eleanor rubbed the sting from her hand as a blister formed. "You tried to hex people the day I met you," she mumbled.

That was entirely different. They deserved it.

Eleanor rolled her eyes but dumped the cauldron.

Grab your basket lass, we need to find birch, cedar, elder, elm, heather, juniper, mugwort, oak and rowan, and I dinnae ken if it even grows here.

"I'm busy."

If you dinnae move, I'll make better use the spoon on the back of your head to knock some sense into ye.

Eleanor grabbed her basket and stormed down the road in a huff while Matilda continued to lecture and scold.

As they headed toward the forest on the other side of the tobacco fields, Eleanor stopped under the sycamore tree to clear a rock from her shoe. They watched everyone in The Quarter go about their meager half day of rest.

Eleanor rubbed her blistered hand. "I canna believe I'm training to be a witch with a cranky old hag."

You're learning to be a wise woman, a healer. People once revered women like us for divination, tending the shrines, guarding the sacred knowledge. They called us bandrui before they branded us as witches to be burned. She sighed. *'Twas long ago.*

Old Betty opened a weaved cloth as one of the field hands held cowrie shells with closed eyes, asked a question and threw them on the cloth.

Matilda glanced at the cowrie shells, tilting her head at the pattern. *I've never seen it done that way before.*

"You in Virginia now, spirit. Scotland ain't the only place they do divination." Eyeing Eleanor's blistered hand, Old Betty glared directly at Matilda with the contempt a headmaster has for a schoolyard bully and dressed her down. Ain't life tough enough for Eleanor without you hitting her?"

Mind your own business.

Eleanor's heart pounded in her ribcage as she left quickly. Becoming involved in a feud between the two old crones was her last desire. Heaven forbid they drew the attention of Lord Blackmere.

They made it to the forest, stopping in front of a small tree with smooth gray bark mottled in pale patches. Bright scarlet-red berries dangled in dense bunches against the feathery green leaves fluttering in the breeze.

This is rowan. Crush a wee bit of young bark to make a paste and spread it over your rash, then bind it with linen. If it still itches ye can boil a handful of berries, strain the liquid, let it cool and dab it on your skin.

Eleanor looked down at her hand.

Dinnae mistake my scolding for hate. If I dinnae care about ye, I'd have left ye to ruin yourself. Dinnae allow cruel people to take the light from your heart. The world needs more lighthearted people like ye in it.

Eleanor pretended to fan herself to prevent from fainting. "Are you admitting to...liking me?"

You're daft, reckless, and proud. Just the sort of witch I'd want beside me in a fight against Lord Blackmere. Come now, we've much to do to prepare for the initiation rituals.

"Will I ever get to learn anything fun? Will you teach me to fly on a broomstick?"

Flying on a broomstick is another kettle of fish. Learn deeply about the earth before you attempt to glide on air.

Chapter 38

William MacLeod

Scotland—Lughnasadh fire festival

Laughter filled the air as William MacLeod knelt and made a show of talking to Fiona's belly, holding the gift behind his back. "Good evening, fifth son," he said in a silly voice, "We canna wait to meet you." He kissed Fiona's belly as Lachlan watched and laughed. MacLeod moved up and pressed a kiss behind her ear. "Your predictions are never wrong. Even I ken that," he whispered, "But dinnae tell anyone."

With a loving touch, Fiona tugged his beard.

"Surprise," he said, handing her the package. "To replace the shawl you lost during Samhain."

Her eyes lit up, and she hugged him in thanks. He took a large, deep, savoring breath. Ever since Fiona realized she was with child, it was like they were newlyweds again.

James and David laughed as they practiced their caber toss in the hall, trying to flip a small log end-over-end.

"I want to play," Lachlan said, joining his brothers. Broderick watched silently.

"Next year, Lachie," James said.

"No fair. I'm bigger than Broderick now," he said. He was right.

"Dinnae throw a log inside the house. Are you daft?" MacLeod said, walking into the hall. James put the log in the corner.

Fiona put her arm around Broderick. "The fair offers something for everyone. Maybe we can help your da choose the cattle from the summer pastures."

"Are we going to bury the first sheaf of grain in the field?" Broderick asked.

Leave it to Broderick to bring up the fae. MacLeod said nothing to keep the peace.

"No love. Lughnasadh is a pagan custom," Fiona said, giving a nod to both William and James. "I'm sure Reverend MacDonald will give a fine blessing of the fields."

James' shoulders relaxed, and he smiled…then snatched David's glasses and ran as the younger boys joined in the chase, making a wild ruckus.

"Stop running in the house," MacLeod called. "Save that vigor for the harvest games." He checked the window. "Ack, it's dreich outside. Do you ken where my coat is?"

A crash in the kitchen prompted Fiona's investigation. "Check the trunk in your study," she called over her shoulder.

While Fiona busied herself with the boys, MacLeod pulled his trunk from the corner. Throwing on his overcoat, he dug into his pocket and brushed a folded note. *Eleanor's note.*

Closing the door, he quickly lit kindling in his fireplace. Despite the crackling flames a cold sweat broke over him. Was the note in his pocket all along? How long had it been since her banishment? Seven months? His throat tightened as he grimaced. He peered over his shoulder again. Fiona and the boys were in the kitchen, and the servants never entered his study without knocking.

'Twas an innocuous enough note thanking him. But if Fiona found it, would she read it the same way? It hinted at more than thanks. Smelling Eleanor's jasmine and clove perfume on the note had him blushing at the memory of her teasing a feather quill over her breasts.

A loud pop came from the fire.

Ack, Eleanor is probably Matthew Crowan's mistress by now. The lass had a special combination of amorousness and ambition. He held the note over the fire.

The flames cast eerie shadows. It was strange, but he had the sensation of being watched.

Eleanor thought she'd tell everyone Fiona was a witch, did she? A malicious grin spread as he tossed it into the fire. *Who'd believe her in Virginia Colony? No one, that's who.* Wetting his lips, he chuckled. *I told her I can be quite the devil.*

Chapter 39

Matilda

Scotland—The Otherworld—Lughnasadh fire festival

"Ye wee smug bastard," Eleanor said from within the flames in MacLeod's study. "Burning the evidence of our flirtations?"

Throw the nettles into the fire, Matilda directed.

"This one?"

Matilda nodded, and raised her hand over the letter. *Fuasgail an luaithre.*

"Fuasgail an luaithre—Unburn the ashes?"

Your love note will remain unburnt until amends are made. Matilda left the fireplace, and walked through the mist. *I willnae let either of ye off the hook for kissing.*

Eleanor stumbled to keep up. "Why are you blaming me? Lady Margaret put an ill wish in my pillow."

Wheest. Matilda held her finger to her lips. *'Twas an amplifier charm, not a love potion. Magic dinnae take away all your self-control. Even without the charm, ye tend to flock to married men,* she whispered.

Eleanor lowered her voice. "Why were married men philandering with me? They broke their wedding oaths; I broke no vows. And why are we whispering?"

I dinnae want to upset Fiona, in case she walks into the room.

Now, they gazed into the fireplace in the main parlor, watching the boys chase each other. William grabbed Lachie, tickling him until the boy burst into belly laughs, then he caressed Fiona's cheek, and kissed her gently. "I dinnae ever want to fight again."

Eleanor stared at Fiona's rounded belly, matching the size of her own. "Maybe we should keep the note secret. They look happy." She reached for Matilda's arm, forgetting it was transparent, then pulled back. "If Fiona finds out I kissed her man, she'll never let me into the coven. I ken you want proper revenge for her, but what about my baby's safety?" she whispered.

Matilda glanced between everyone before resting her eyes on Eleanor's womb. *You've made a solid point. There's no need to share you've ever met William, nor that Lord whatshisname is the father of the bairn. It might inspire Fiona's curiosity. Go back in the other room, sprinkle sage over the letter, raise your arm, and say, Falaich airson a-nis.*

"*Falaich*—hide...for now? Thank you," she whispered. "I'll make it right."

Matilda nodded, inching closer to the parlor fire. *Fiona?* she called. *You're having your fifth son? Congratulations.*

Fiona's smile faded as she deliberately ignored Matilda.

The veils are down. Willnae you speak to me? I've found the maiden, and she's ready to join the coven. I promise I willnae speak of revenge tonight.

"Can she hear you?" Eleanor asked.

Matilda jumped back, and placed a hand over her missing heart. *Why are you sneaking up on me, ye damned pain in the arse? I dinnae ken who's more boisterous, ye or William.*

Fiona pretended to be interested in her Bible, but it was apparent by the arch of her eyebrow she was trying to eavesdrop.

"Fiona's your niece, right? She acts more like your daughter. You love each other something fierce." Eleanor chuckled. "You can tell by how hard she's ignoring you. I miss that. I miss my mam," Eleanor said with a homesick longing to her voice. "I miss George, my brothers, my sisters..." She sighed.

What about your father?

Eleanor snorted. "He can rot in Hell."

We're getting sidetracked. Listen to me, Fiona, I found out Lord Blackmere isna only a witch hunter anymore. Elspeth is teaching him magic, the bad kind. Be angry with me all ye want, but the prophecy says Eleanor's child is chosen. If we dinnae protect her, he'll kill her for sure before Ostara of the child's fifth year.

William wrapped his arms around Fiona. "I'll get the boys in the coach."

Hmpf. Stop interrupting, William, Matilda said, as though he could hear her, then gave a ghostly elbow to Eleanor. *Why Fiona ever bothered to marry Admiral Goring's grandson is beyond me.*

"Is everything out of your mouth designed to sting? You might not like him, but it's apparent they love each other, and he seems like a good father," Eleanor said.

"Agreed," Fiona said, winking at Eleanor. To William, "I'll help you with the boys. It's too hot by the fire." She left in a huff. William squinted into the flames, clearly seeing nothing, then chased after his wife.

Gods, will we ever form this coven properly? Matilda complained.

"Matilda, your bitterness is the reason why this coven canna get formed. How am I to protect my baby if your foul temper keeps causing problems?"

The door flew open.

"I'll be there in one minute. I forgot my shawl," Fiona called as she ran back into the room, jumped through the flame, and landed in the Otherworld. "Let's do this quick. I have to sit through a three-hour sermon. You've brought the mugwort? We've got an incredibly special baby to protect for Beira." She rested her hand on Eleanor's tummy, feeling it kick.

Eleanor nodded, and quickly poured a salt circle around them, ready to do the rituals she practiced all summer with Matilda. The three women exchanged expectant glances as they stood before the goddess.

Teine ag èirigh, Matilda called, and a blazing fire rose to the darkness, sparks floating to the sky. They made a circle around the bonfire, adding juniper, mugwort, and elder leaves while chanting the sacred rituals.

Eisd rium a Dhia. Beira, Queen of Winter,
First *Cailleach*, Goddess, Destroyer, Protector.
Flesh to flesh,
Blood to blood,
And bone to bone
May our coven be bound to protect your throne.

Chapter 40

ELSPETH—WITCH OF PYE

Hackney Marshes—East London

In a vast expanse of swamp filled with reeds and small pools of stagnant water, Lord Blackmere stood in the fog, attempting to transfigure into a toad. "Why do you always want me to shift into such hideously undignified creatures? My power is meant to manifest into something greater."

"If you can't hop, how can you expect to fly, lord?"

He managed to get inside, but the poor creature seemed to want to move in both directions, making him roll rather than hop.

He spoke through garbled *ribit.* "I find it annoying people like Hallewell always end up on top. He married his way out of poverty, weasels his way out of scandals, and his pretty little mistress will bear him the child that will overthrow the king. Can you imagine the debauched state of the world if George Hallewell somehow became king? I'd die before I let that happen."

"Who cares about Lord Hallewell? Kill Eleanor at the next fire festival. I don't know why you're waiting."

"Would that I could. While Lord Hallewell was caring for his dying mother, Eleanor left. She's doing a stellar job of staying hidden, too. You think Matilda is helping her hide?"

"Mayhaps."

He seemed to be frustrated with his animal carrier. "Let me out, already. I detest lying flat on my belly."

The toad hopped to a stone, flinging him into a muddy puddle then hopped away.

Elspeth bit her lip to keep from smirking. While she cared next-to-nothing about the maiden, she delighted in thinking the raven feather pillow caused Eleanor's disappearance. But since Lord Blackmere hadn't asked her about it specifically, she was under no obligation to confess her role in the disappearance. *I'll distract him just in case.* "What if the prophecy was wrong? Maybe the blonde woman isn't Eleanor at all, but some other woman?"

"It's her, I'm certain. I've been studying the movements of the stars, and it confirms the vision. The prophecy declared the blonde would be in chains. I know it means she'll be arrested. And I am the head of the Reformation of Manners, yes?"

Elspeth tilted her head. She knew nothing of stars. Cycles of the moon, sure. She didn't like that he was learning things on his own. It directly threatened her own survival.

Lord Blackmere shook out his arms and cracked his neck. "Let's try a different spell."

"Concentrate, my lord. Move the mist with your mind."

"*Ceòthach*," he said, raising his hand. The fog rolled in thick.

"No, lord, that draws fog to you, not away."

"Don't you think I see that, old woman?" he snapped. The fog covered him in a syrupy cloud, leaving a muddy mess on his waistcoat. "Damn your Gaelic words."

"*Bidh falbh*," Elspeth said, clearing the field. "Blame the Druids, not me. I prefer English."

"Give me Latin and Greek over your pagan Gaelic any day. There was a time when only learned men controlled sorcery, but then you witches got ahold of it, and see how society became degraded? You know, you're not the only one who can teach me. I've been studying *Malleus Maleficarum*, seeking other ancient texts. I've found rare editions of *The Greater Key of Solomon*, and *The Sworn Book of Honorius*. Soon my powers will eclipse yours in every sense."

Not for a while, but in a few years, he'd be right, and then he'll string me up, sure as sunrise. "Before you challenge Lucifer to a duel, best focus on the battle before you. Matilda is cunning with storms, and I wouldn't be surprised if Fiona don't have some tricks up her sleeves, should you ever face her."

"Who's Fiona?"

An overwhelming sense of dread fell over Elspeth as the sigil heated above her heart. 'Twas a slip of the tongue, but a betrayal just the same.

He trudged to her, the mud sucking in his boots with each menacing step. Transfiguring into Jessop, she flapped her wings, but the damage from Matilda's hex made her flight unsteady.

A large, black and copper pit viper coiled around her, hissing in her raven ear. She gasped, surprised he managed to transfigure into the larger animal, but a serpent familiar suited him. "I don't like secrets, Elspeth," he hissed.

Over the years she had protected Fiona in her own way, sacrificing Matilda and keeping it secret Fiona belonged to their coven, but her need for air outweighed the burning sigil. "Matilda had a niece," she gasped. "Fiona." The sigil sizzled and smoked.

"The babe held by Matilda in the prophecy was Fiona? Not her daughter, but her niece? If Fiona coupled with Admiral Goring or one of his sons, that means there were two babies I had to hunt and kill?"

"Yes, lord." Elspeth writhed in pain. The sigil glowed like embers in a dying fire.

"You should have told me years ago," he said, showing his fangs. "I would have executed Fiona the same day I killed Matilda."

They both returned to their human forms as his grip around her neck grew tighter. He plunged her head into the stagnant water as she wrestled to keep from drowning. He pulled her head out, still squeezing her throat. She spit up as the stench of dying river fish and decayed vegetation burned her nostrils. "Who did Fiona couple with? Not Admiral Goring, nor his sons, they died."

Elspeth's knees went weak, and she saw black spots. He released her, and she dropped into the muddy marsh, gasping. Slimy mud slipped through her old fingers as the water soaked her petticoats.

"Did the admiral have a bastard son?"

Holding her neck with her wet hand, she shook no. "Daughter. Elise," she rasped. "Elise had a son."

"The babe Admiral Goring held in the prophecy was his grandson?"

She nodded.

"So the real meaning of the prophecy isn't the lie you've been pedaling to me all these years. There are actually two babies able to overthrow the king. One is Eleanor's baby..."

Elspeth nodded.

"And the other is from the union of Matilda's niece, Fiona, and Admiral Goring's grandson?"

The eye in her sigil began to bleed as she grunted in agony.

"Tell me his grandson's name or I promise I'll torture you worse than the sigil ever could."

"William. William MacLeod."

Chapter 41

FIONA

The Otherworld—Samhain fire festival

"Happy Samhain." Fiona jumped through the flame to the Otherworld to find Eleanor and Matilda practicing a ricochet spell. "Reverend MacDonald drank too much whiskey and passed out on the couch, but I'll have to leave once he wakes. What are you working on?"

"A ricochet spell. It's hopeless," Eleanor said.

Nonsense. It merely takes practice and righteous indignation. I'm going to cast a spell to push ye back. Block me. Matilda pushed the air with both arms. *Brùth!*

Before Eleanor could raise her hand, Matilda knocked her back ten feet, suspended her in midair, and then softly set her down.

"Why aren't you defending yourself?" Fiona asked.

"I dinnae ken. She's old?"

I may be old, but I'm kicking your arse, honeylocks. Try again. Brùth!

Ath-bhualadh, Eleanor said, raising her arm, but she got knocked back into a tree. "Aw," she called, rubbing her skinned elbow. "I'll never do it properly."

Fiona moved beside her, pulling rowan bark from her pocket and pressing it on the wound. She held her hand over Eleanor's belly, as the baby happily kicked inside. "Matilda you ken spells can be tricky. Try teaching her easier defensive magic."

"Defensive magic...Like making fog? Like the first time we met?" Eleanor checked her elbow, noting how quickly it healed.

Fine. Ye teach her if you're so good at this.

Fiona squeezed Eleanor's shoulders in encouragement. "Come on, honeylocks. Let's move some clouds."

Eleanor hesitated. "No, I'm not a real witch, like you two."

It gave Fiona a flutter of pity to see Eleanor so utterly down on herself. "You're in the Otherworld. Most 'normal' people canna ever do that, let alone do it by choice, multiple times. Just because you dinnae ken as many spells yet dinnae mean you aren't a wise woman. You're in our coven. You're one of us."

Aye. Matilda nodded, standing beside her. *If ye can learn to read and write, ye can chant invocations and spell cast. Trust yourself.*

Eleanor rose on her toes, a shy smile spreading across her face. "I'm finally learning the fun part of magic?"

"Close your eyes. Relax your shoulders. Breathe. Imagine a cloud. What's its texture? What does it smell like? Can you taste it on your tongue?"

"I guess?"

Matilda watched Fiona patiently teach and smiled, remembering giving Fiona her first magical lessons. It seemed just a moment ago.

"Hold up your arm and say, *Falaich.*" Fiona demonstrated, creating mist.

Eleanor took a deep breath, and raised her arm. "*Falaich.*" A dense gray cloud fell on Fiona's foot like a heavy stone.

Matilda laughed. *For once, transparency proves beneficial.*

"Sorry! I'm so sorry," Eleanor said.

"It's fine," Fiona said, limping away. "You're learning." She rested her hands on her own belly, and swore the bairn inside was giggling.

"You're resisting nature, trying too hard to make it perfect. Let earth's energy flow through you. Try again, only this time picture a soft cloud, like a cotton ball unraveling."

Eleanor nodded firmly, raising her arm. "*Falaich.*"

A white cloud appeared, slowly spreading as it floated away. Eleanor stared in awe. "I did that? I did magic! Did you see?"

Fiona nodded encouragingly. "Now that you've proven to yourself you can do it, you need to call it up on command. We have to make the most of the fire festivals to train. You need to learn blocking spells, banishing charms, how to raise mental shields—"

"And what about transfiguring? Can I change into a cat like Matilda?"

"Not everyone can transfigure. I never could."

If ye tried harder, ye might.

"My strong suit is clairvoyance and herbs," Fiona said.

And thunderstorms, when ye get your feathers ruffled enough. As a child, Fiona lit my roof on fire with a lightning bolt once because I wouldnae let her ride my broomstick.

Fiona walked away, blushing. "It was an accident, and I apologized," she muttered.

"Will our bairns be able to join the coven, Matilda?" Eleanor said. "How much fun would that be? Do you think my daughter will be blonde like me? I canna wait to meet her. But I am getting scared about the actual birthing part."

"Eight more weeks, aye? Then my bairn comes a wee bit later," Fiona said. "It's so thrilling to practice magic again, to be around women who understand."

On the other side of the bonfire, Reverend MacDonald snored loud enough to startle himself awake. He glimpsed around the room. "Someone lit a fire?"

"I better go. Love you both. Keep practicing. See you next fire festival." Fiona reentered her body. "You were shivering something fierce, Reverend, so I lit a fire just now to keep you warm," said as innocently as possible.

He frowned. "Turn to Isaiah 8:19 and read."

She picked up his weathered Bible. "Why doest thou seek guidance from mediums and spiritists who whisper and mutter? Why doest thou consult the dead to help the living?"

Scotland—Christmas Eve

Eight weeks had passed since William left for London to fix Lord Hallewell's latest financial woes. As much as Fiona wanted to meet with her coven during the Yule solstice, Reverend MacDonald made it a point to invite himself over again, preventing her from leaping into the Otherworld.

As soon as the reverend left, her sister, Mary, arrived to serve as the *bean-ghlùine* to deliver the baby. Mary set the servants about unlocking and untying everything in the manor, while Fiona knitted a blanket by the hearth.

"Aunt Mary, how come you're having them do that?" Lachlan asked, sitting on the floor with his tin soldiers scattered everywhere.

"To protect your mam and the bairn. Sometimes Beira's fairies, the *sìth*, come to unprotected homes," Mary said, throwing peat on the fire.

James cast a wary eye, shifting on his feet.

"Why would they come here?" Broderick lowered his book.

"Everyone kens fairies like to steal healthy newborns, and replace them with changelings. But we willnae let that happen, will we?" Fiona said, knitting the final stitch.

Lachlan gathered his tin soldiers and set up an elaborate battle scene. "What should we name the baby?"

Broderick turned a page. "If the birthday is on a Sunday, the name is Donald."

"If he's born on Christmas, we should name him Jesus," Lachlan said.

"The bairn isna due for another two weeks. In any case, it might be a lass," teased Mary.

"Nah. Mam told me when she was a wee girl, she had a vision they'd have five sons, and no stinky sisters," Lachlan said, making cannon explosion sounds as Mary laughed.

"Da says we're not to speak of visions," James snapped, making everyone jolt.

"Well, your Da's no' here right now, is he?" Mary offered a wry smile.

James' legs parted as he stood. "I'm the man of the house when he's away, and Da wouldnae approve any of this. It's against God."

Mary crossed her arms over her chest. "Well, man of the house, I slapped your arse when I delivered you, and we sained the house, and made sure iron was in your crib before you were born. God saw fit for you to live, dinnae he?"

A dark flush reddened James' cheeks as his brothers laughed.

"That reminds me, David, fetch a spindle, in case she has a daughter."

David set aside the sketch he was working on. "Here you go," he said, pulling one from the sewing basket. "Girls get a thimble, and boys get a sword in their hands, right? I remember Da putting *Justice* in Lachlan's hand when he was born."

Fiona smiled, rubbing her belly. "We put a sword in all your hands."

"Not Broderick," James said stonily as Broderick lowered his book again.

Mary and Fiona exchanged looks. "I ensured every one of my sons—"

"You put a knife in his fist, but not *Justice*," James said.

"Stop being a troll-bull," David said over his glasses as he wrapped his arm around his younger brother. "Why are you picking on Brod?"

"I'm not. I'm stating the facts."

Fiona winced at her eldest son's harsh glare.

"Boys, go outside," Mary said. "Do whatever it is lads do. Your mam needs some peace."

They put on their coats and left.

Fiona chuckled. "How did a single womb give rise to such varied personalities?"

"What bug climbed up James' arse?"

"Ack, he's thirteen now." Fiona straightened the parlor.

"Stop nesting, and get back to bed to rest. You have a house full of servants, and four sons who can clean up after themselves, thank you very much."

"Did anyone mention you're a wee bit tyrannical?"

"And that's why you love me, and that's why the bairns are all healthy."

While climbing the stairs, labor pangs hit, making Fiona hold the banister and slowly blow out air. "I think this baby is coming today." The grandfather clock ticked loudly from the study. "I wish William was home."

"You ken men—unconcerned by time constraints. It's probably practice pangs. It's too early for real ones."

Pain struck again, and Fiona cried out. Mary helped her into her bedchamber. Even upstairs, the ticking clock echoed ominously. The metallic scent from the chimes was inescapable, and Fiona became overcome with fear.

"Mary, I have a confession. I follow Christ, you ken I do, but I prayed to Beira for this child, and I dinnae want to disrespect her."

Mary covered her gasp. "Why would you do such a thing?"

"Unlocking and untying is something everyone does. We need to light the candles. We need to do as Matilda used to when she was a midwife. I've acquired the proper candles. They're in the drawer, hidden beneath my petticoats."

"Fiona, no."

"Please dinnae tell William. I've been avoiding magic to keep him happy for so long, surely he'll allow the old ways during childbirth?" Another excruciating cramp hit. "This bairn," she gasped, "wants to be born now."

Standing in the middle of the room, Mary split her gaze between the drawer with forbidden candles and Fiona, now curled in a ball of agony on the floor.

"Mary, please." Sweat beaded on Fiona's forehead as she moaned. When the pain passed, she panted. "William isna home... the boys willnae come into the room... Please," she whispered.

Mary pulled the candles from the hiding spot. "You better hope the reverend dinnae stop by. I'd hate to wear a noose around my neck."

"As long as William's home eight days after the birth to attend the baptism, all should be well with the him, the bairn, and James, too."

"Stop yammering, and get to the birthing stool."

Breathing easier, Fiona rose to her knees and rested her head on the mattress, awaiting the next labor pain. "You've put a piece of iron on the bottom of the cradle? I want no evil eye to harm this babe."

"I put the nail there myself this morning," Mary said, lighting the first *puir man* candle. Black smoke wafted through the air as she circled it three times over the bed.

"Do you remember the words?"

Mary nodded with a rebellious grin. "I heard you whisper them enough during my own children's births dinnae I?" She chanted the protective charms.

After all four candles were lit and placed by each corner of the bed, a calming pine scent filled the bedchamber. Taking a broadsword from the pegs above the hearth, Mary half-drew it from the holster, and placed it at the head of the bed.

Fiona's waters broke in a rush. "This is the most annoying part of childbirth."

"Take heart. If your childhood vision was accurate, this is your last bairn."

Only Matilda knew about her newest vision of the red-haired girl, and honestly, neither of them ever figured out if the lass was her future daughter or some curious fairy drawn to her. "I suppose everything will be clear soon enough."

As Fiona tried to climb into bed, an intense pang brought her to her knees again, as she tried to breathe through it. Mary brought her the birthing stool, which Fiona gripped with white knuckles.

Mary hiked Fiona's shift and gasped. "It's already crowned. That's the fastest labor I've ever seen. Maybe this bairn really is from the goddess."

Every muscle in Fiona's body tensed as she pushed with all her might. "Where's William?"

"Not here. Now push."

It felt like Fiona's insides were ripping open as her drenched shift clung to her sweaty body. "I canna anymore."

"You can, and you will. Push. I see a shoulder. Almost done. Push."

"Ah shut it, Mary, I am pushing," Fiona bellowed.

Mary laughed. "There's my real sister. One more push."

A wailing baby fell into Mary's waiting hands, and Fiona leaned against the birthing stool exhausted.

"Fiona, she's beautiful."

"A girl?" Fiona laughed as Mary wiped off the blood, and cut the cord. Tears rolled down both women's cheeks.

Thank you, Beira, for granting my wish. Finally, her home life would stay in balance. Fiona crawled into bed, exhausted, but relieved. Mary placed the wee redhead over Fiona's heart as the clock chimed the hour.

"She's perfect." Fiona kept kissing her fuzzy hair, feeling her daughter's soft skin against her heart. "Elise's prophecy was right," she whispered. "We had a daughter."

The baby opened her eyes.

Fiona expected the usual inky gray of childbirth, but her eyes were blue as a summer sky. They leaned their foreheads against each other, and Fiona couldn't stop smiling. "You're bringing our family closer, love. You're going to be a healer, like your mama, and Nana Matilda." The baby giggled, and Fiona kissed her forehead again.

Mary grabbed the fire tongs and pulled a burning peat from the fire. "A daughter. Who would have thought? Even the great second-sighted Fiona misses a thing or two sometimes." She shook some sparks from the peat into a pail of water, then returned the peat brick to the fire.

She washed the bairn properly with the sained water. After cleaning the baby, she threw some wash water into the fire for the goddess, and placed the babe back over Fiona's heart.

Kissing the top of the baby's head, Fiona inhaled the sweet newborn smell of love. "I promise to keep you safe. The goddess has noble plans for you," she whispered, smiling at the delightful heaviness of her newborn on her chest.

Knock. William opened the door with her sons in tow.

"William." She smiled, then darted glances at Mary, but no one seemed to understand the true purpose of the candles. Her family surrounded the bed. Fiona and William stared at each other in awe, laughing and savoring the moment.

"Ah, she's lovely."

Fiona grinned at her sons. "Meet your sister."

"A girl? Who wants a wee lass?" complained Lachlan.

William was beaming, moving closer to kiss his daughter's forehead.

Fiona stroked his cheek. "You shaved?"

"I had several court appearances. I was ready to come home a week earlier, but Lord Blackmere wanted to meet to discuss some legislation he's working on for the king. He's too powerful for me to refuse, but it strains my relationship with Lord Hallewell. I wish the man would leave me alone. Honestly, I think he took even more pleasure delaying me when I told him you were due, and I needed to get home."

Fiona's hair stood on end. *Why is the witch hunter trying to get close to William? Is it a ploy to get to me? Does Blackmere ken I'm in a coven with Eleanor? Is he trying to find her through me?*

"Another redhead," David said. "Watch out for her temper. Oh, here's the spindle. Her hand is so tiny. I dinnae remember Lachlan being this small."

"Broderick was the small one," James said, moving beside the cradle.

"I get the first hold," William said. "Ooch, she's a strong lass. See her grip on my finger?" He laughed.

"All you menfolk need to leave the room," Fiona said, growing anxious. Rituals needed to be completed. "We have things to do I trust you dinnae want to see."

The boys winced, making gagging noises, and rushed to the door as William handed the babe back to Fiona, giving them both another kiss.

Once everyone left, and the door closed, Mary gave a conspiratorial wink, lit a new peat brick on one end, and began drawing a circle around the bed with the ash.

"Dinnae do anything disgusting yet. I forgot my Bible in here," James joked as he opened the door. "What are you doing?" he demanded, horrified.

"Go outside," Mary said.

"Da," James called, then faced Fiona. "Reverend MacDonald wouldnae like this."

"The bairn isna safe from Otherworld harm until she's baptized," Fiona said. "You dinnae want the fae to take her and bring back a changeling, do you?" She used her most calming voice to explain. "Mary has to draw a circle thrice round me and the babe in *deiseil*, according to the course of the sun."

"This is ridiculous," James said. "It's 1730. We're a Christian family. I ken you dinnae do this when Broderick or Lachlan were born."

"You're not privy to everything, laddie," Mary said.

William came in. "What's going on?"

James grabbed the smoldering peat from Mary's hand and tossed it back into the fire, making sparks fly. "This is witchcraft. This is sin. Da, make them stop."

"We need to do this," Fiona said, clinging to her daughter. "If we dinnae, horrible things will happen." Her whole body shivered, as though the temperature dropped.

Picking up the peat, Mary started the fire-round again.

"Mary, put the peat back," William said firmly.

The baby started wailing.

"Why obey a whiskerless boy?" Mary demanded, still holding the smoldering peat.

Fiona pleaded. "You ken as well as me how difficult it is to keep a child alive before baptism. Why are you risking her life?"

"You're listening to them, Da? It's pagan."

"Stop upsetting your mother," William said. "It's not your place."

Mary started dragging the peat on the floor again. James stormed past his brothers, eavesdropping in the hall. They whispered amongst themselves.

William took the peat from Mary and tossed it back in the fire, then sat on the bed. "Shh. Sweetheart, dinnae fash, everything will be fine. Look, no one does a fire-round anymore. We dinnae have to keep following the old ways."

"We do." Fiona grew small, whispering her confession. "I prayed to Beira for a girl."

"What?" William's eyebrows rose. "What are you doing praying to a goddess? Are you trying to get burned at the stake?"

Fiona winced, drawing her shoulders up to her ears. She hugged her daughter tighter. "William, please. We have to do the ritual. Time is running out. What could it hurt?"

Mary attempted to grab the peat one last time, but he blocked her.

"I said no."

The air grew frigid.

Mary moved to the window to stop the draft. "Who's coming up the road?"

James came back inside, panting. "Reverend MacDonald is coming with another man. He looks important."

Bolting to the window, William cursed. "Mary, wash the ash from the floor." He glanced around the room. "What are those candles for? Fuck. Boys, get rid of anything pagan. Throw them into the fire. Now."

Their sons rushed inside with an air of panic.

Fiona said, "But–"

"Lord Hallewell helped us once to save you from the stake. Dinnae make me beg for the same favor twice." He pointed at his sons. "Keep this secret."

Silently, Fiona prayed. *Eisd rium a Dhia. Beira, hear me. Protect my daughter from the clutch of men.*

Chapter 42

MATILDA

Virginia Colony—Christmas Eve

Hannah placed a cloth on Eleanor's feverish head, resting her hand on her cramping belly. "Get some rest. I'll check back soon."

Eleanor faced Matilda. "Why did the bairn stop kicking?"

Matilda looked inside Eleanor's womb, then sat silent a moment. Sweat beaded on Eleanor's brow and over her lip.

I'm sorry, lass.

"No, you're wrong," she said, eyes welling. "My daughter has noble blood. She's destined to overthrow a king."

I've midwifed many a newborn. She's dying, Eleanor. The cord has wrapped around her neck, choking her.

A light came from the distance.

Ned floated next to Matilda. "Why did the veil open?"

Something's terribly wrong.

A labor pang hit, making Eleanor cry out. Her knuckles grew white as she gripped the headboard, breathing through her pain. "Da?" She looked to Matilda. "Why is he here? Get him out of here."

Ned backed away, speaking to Matilda in a hush. "Is the light coming for my grandchild, my daughter, or both?"

Matilda glanced away. Did he really want to know the truth?

"I dinnae understand. We did the protection charms." Blood stained her shift. "Why join a coven if my baby dies, anyway?" She curled in a ball, panting softly, staring at her father in the shadows. "What a cursed life I live." She stared at the knife Hannah set on the table to cut the cord. "Unbaptised babies end up in purgatory, aye? I'm not like you, Da. I'd never abandon my girl. Should I slit my wrists and be a ghost, too?" As Eleanor's fever worsened, a dark cloud gathered at the room's far end. She drifted in and out of consciousness.

Ned stood in front of Matilda. "You used to be a healer, aye? Save them."

I'll try. Matilda laid her ghostly hands on Eleanor's womb. *Eisd rium a Dhia. Beira, Queen of Winter, first Cailleach, Goddess, Destroyer, Protector. Show us your will.*

The temperature dropped, making Eleanor's unconscious body shiver as the veil opened wider. Snow fell.

Is it cold in here? Matilda asked.

"You can feel temperature changes?" Ned checked his semi-transparent arms.

Matilda held her hands in front of her in awe as they pulsed and grew solid. A rush of senses came. Her mouth watered at the scent of cinnamon apples baking. The brush of cold air made goosebumps rise on her skin. She rubbed Eleanor's hot, sweaty brow, awed at the textures and temperature she was now able to feel. She rested her old hands on Eleanor's contracting womb, sensing the slow pulse of the baby dying inside.

The veil opened fully onto a long road that led through green mounds as *sìth* played ethereal harp music.

Ned gaped. "Is that the land of the fae?"

What magic is this, goddess?

Chapter 43

William MacLeod

Scotland—Christmas Eve

"Gentlemen, what a surprise. Unfortunately, it's not a good time. My wife has just given birth."

"That's why I'm here, Mr. MacLeod." A sly grin crept up Lord Blackmere's face. "May I come in? At least to warm myself? I'd love to sample Highlander hospitality."

Do I have a choice? He invited them in, and the butler took their coats. "Care for a drink?"

"I'd like tea and a dram," Reverend MacDonald said, making himself comfortable.

"We won't be long. I must meet your wife. I suppose we met in passing at Lord Hallewell's wedding. Too bad I left before the real drama unfolded. I've heard such delightful things about her."

"She's sleeping, and the baby haena been baptized yet."

A strong, healthy wail came from upstairs followed by the faint sound of Fiona's singing a Gaelic lullaby. She came to the top of the stairs, carrying the bairn in her arms. "What's going on?"

"She looks awake to me."

Fiona inhaled sharply, as though she recognized Lord Blackmere... and feared him.

"Congratulations on the birth of your child. I'm Richard Atthill, earl of Blackmere. I'm an acquaintance of your husband. I keep trying to steal him away from Lord Hallewell to work for the Reformation of Manners, but he refuses. May I approach?"

The reverend rose with a watery smile. "We've come so I can give the child a blessing. I told him you werena due yet, but he said he had a feeling you would give birth today. Strange. Almost like he ken the future."

Fiona glanced at MacLeod, giving a tense nod, then went back to their bedchamber.

Please let everything be hidden. "After you," he said to Lord Blackmere, then narrowed his eyes on Reverend MacDonald as they went upstairs.

Fiona climbed in bed, holding their daughter even tighter. Mary and his sons were standing beside the four-post bed, making a human wall in front of her.

"What a lovely home, Mrs. MacLeod. Do I smell juniper? You must be redding the house to sweep away back luck, yes?"

"Many a Highlander decorates their home for Hogmanay, my lord," MacLeod said, standing in front of Fiona and the baby. *No one's touching my wife and bairns on my watch.*

"Is it another boy? I see a trend here," Lord Blackmere said, pointing at each individual child. His eyes lingered on Broderick.

"We've been blessed with a daughter," Fiona said, putting the babe to her breast.

"A girl?" Lord Blackmere whispered. "With red hair, like her father," he said, nodding at MacLeod.

Reverend MacDonald blessed their child, then inspected the perimeter of the room. "Quite a bit of black wax in your fire. And your floor is wet. Have you mopped it for our arrival?"

James had a panicky expression, but MacLeod gave a slight shake 'no' and the boy quieted his face. MacLeod couldn't afford a misstep. "Boys, do your chores."

Mary led them downstairs.

"With respect, Reverend, bucket loads of liquids come from a woman's body during birth," Fiona said.

Lord Blackmere upturned his nose. "Yes, I've heard. I've also heard your aunt was a midwife. I daresay some called her a wise woman. What was her name? Matilda?"

Reverend MacDonald checked the cradle for iron but found none.

Fiona glanced at him. "Matilda's been gone decades."

"I know. I signed the execution edict. I come from a long line of witch hunters," he said with obvious delight. "Interesting you never mentioned your wife is related to a convicted witch."

"Equally interesting you would travel so far north. I'm surprised you're not in London investigating the rampant sodomy you so despise."

"Didn't Matilda curse your grandfather, Admiral Goring, and kill your two uncles the same day? Yet, you married Matilda's niece?"

"Guilt isna hereditary."

"Well, I suppose if it weren't for their murder, you'd never have inherited the manor and all its lands. Love conquers all, I suppose?"

MacLeod had a complicated understanding of Fiona's aunt. His mother told him many times Matilda had given her a protection charm to escape her father's harsh household so she could marry his father. He'd only met his grandsire once, but Admiral Goring seemed the kind of man who might deserve a hex.

"I had no idea the admiral had a daughter," Blackmere said, glaring at the reverend. "And I certainly didn't realize Matilda had a favorite niece."

"You were the witch hunter, my lord," said the reverend. "I wasna privy to your interrogations."

MacLeod didn't like the direction of the conversation and stood over Fiona like a bull in the ring, ready to gore anyone who moved the wrong way. *Justice* hung on the wall peg. It would be easy enough to cut both men down to size. "As much as I enjoy discussing my family tree, it can wait until after the baptism."

"Look at that girl suckle. Incredible strength for a newborn. Too bad it wasn't a boy—he might have been on the king's guard someday." Lord Blackmere nodded at the reverend. "We'll be on our way. I'm sure you're tired, Mrs. MacLeod. Although, I'd love to speak more with you about Matilda next week."

MacLeod walked them outside, then moved to his study to watch from the window as they left his property. *Hold fast. They dinna see any evidence. He's just flexing his power over me.*

Mary and the boys rushed upstairs once they left.

His hands trembled as he poured himself a dram and drank by the hearth. He needed to be steady before facing his wife and sons. Then something caught his eye. "What the devil is that?" Kneeling, he plucked a piece of paper from beneath a smoldering log.

Eleanor's note.

He glanced over his shoulder in a panic, making sure no one observed. *How long was it in there?* It must have gotten trapped beneath the grate and never burned. *Did the servants see it? Did Fiona?*

He held the note above the blaze.

A powerful urge to confess to Fiona gripped him, but he choked it back, his throat aching. *I should be celebrating the birth of my daughter, not fighting off witch hunters, and trying to burn the evidence of a night of lustful stupidity.*

He tossed it into the fire and poured another drink. When he turned around the letter was lying on the carpet. Every time he tossed it into the fire, it flew in the opposite direction, and landed on the floor. "Why willnae it burn?"

"Did you say something?" Mary called from the parlor.

"Coming," he said, rushing to bury the note in his desk drawer. *Did Fiona find the note and put a hex on it? Why has she said nothing? Is she waiting for me to confess?* Sweat beaded his brow as he sat opposite Mary.

"Thank God we cleaned up everything in time," Mary said. "I've never been so terrified in my life. See my hands shake?"

"I should go upstairs," he said.

"Let her sleep. She's exhausted."

Chapter 44

Fiona

Scotland—Christmas Eve

Fiona lay her daughter in the cradle, rocking her as she sat on the bed. Her entire family was unraveling. She closed her eyes, vowing to do the fire-round. once everyone went to sleep, not realizing she'd dozed off.

The door opened, streaking in tapered candlelight on James by the crib. Fiona scanned the darkened room, unsure how much time had passed.

"Is everything all right?" she asked groggily.

"Between the reverend and Lord Blackmere showing up, and the fire-round..." He sat beside her. "Mam, I ken you get angry with me, but I wish you'd listen. Witchcraft is against God, and it's illegal, and what if they arrested you?" He blinked back tears as he hugged her. "I'm so scared they'll try to kill you."

A wave of guilt twisted her gut as she hugged her first born. *How heavily has my magic burdened his heart?*

"She's sleeping?" William whispered upon entering. Peering into the crib, his eyebrows drew together. He leaned in, rustling the baby. "Get Mary," he told James, lowering his voice.

James took a small step towards the cradle, then stopped, opening his eyes wider.

The baby made a high-pitched cry.

Fiona's pulse quickened. "What's wrong?"

"Now," William commanded, lifting their daughter over his heart, patting her back with increasing force as the baby jerked involuntarily. His veins stood out in his neck.

"Aunt Mary," James called, running downstairs.

The room's temperature dropped, and Fiona shivered uncontrollably as she reached out. William lain the baby on the bed, slapping each cheek with a shaky hand. The baby's face grew redder than her hair as she struggled for air, and her blue eyes widened with panic.

Mary bolted in. "Jesus in heaven. Move out of the way." Shoving him aside, she put her mouth over the baby's mouth and nose, sucking hard and spitting mucus on the ground as Fiona frantically rubbed the baby's arms. "Bring me the iron from the cradle."

The babe flailed as they struggled to dislodge whatever was choking her.

William raced, shoving aside blankets. "It isna here."

"Of course it's there. I put it back myself after the men left." Mary sat on the bed with the baby over her lap, whacking hard on her back. "Come on, breathe."

The baby wheezed as her chest moved erratically.

"She was strong." Fiona scanned the room. "Is this a changeling baby? Has Beira allowed the *sìth* to take our daughter while I slept?"

David ran to her side with a worried expression. "No one came to the room, Mam. We were right downstairs."

William flipped the entire cradle over, sending it crashing to the floor. "It isna here."

Broderick and Lachlan stepped back by the hearth, wide-eyed.

"I took it," James said, white faced, pulling the iron from his pocket.

Air left Fiona like a punch.

"You hurt our sister?" Lachlan said.

"Mam, what about your herbs?" Broderick said.

Tears formed in her daughter's eyes.

William called downstairs to the servants. "Someone fetch a physician! Go, go, go."

Fiona blinked. Pointing to her satchel in the dresser, she said, "I need rosemary...and...and..."

"Mint. You need rosemary and mint. Bring the iron nail here, now," Mary shouted.

"*Eisd rium a Dhia.* Beira...Matilda hear me," Fiona called. "Matilda, please." It wasn't a fire festival, but maybe she'd come, anyway?

"Mam, dinnae call Matilda," James pleaded. "She's a witch. Do you want to bring God's curse upon our house again?"

David grabbed the nail from James and gave it to Fiona. "Maybe we can do both, Mam? Talk to Matilda, but pray too?"

Rubbing the iron all over the naked child, Fiona sained the girl. The baby made a weak gasp. Mary waved the herbs beneath the wheezing child's nose.

Meow. Pooka sat on the windowsill, which scared Fiona even more. *Would Matilda's ghost take her bairn away? Why willnae Matilda speak to me?*

"Come on, love, breathe," William whispered.

A red rash broke over the child's back and chest as her body lurched forward for air.

"No. No. No. No. Dinnae kill my baby to punish me," Fiona said. "*Eisd rium a Dhia.* Save her from the *sìth. Eisd rium a Dhia.* Save her from the *sìth. Eisd rium a Dhia.*"

James squeezed his eyes shut, praying aloud as Broderick stood beside him. "Almighty God, we place our trust in you. Save our sister."

The baby's skin grew cold and clammy.

David's tears fogged his glasses. "Please let this work. Please let this work."

Meow. Pooka vanished, and a raven appeared at the window. *Elspeth*?

A strong metal scent filled Fiona's nostrils. A whistling sound came from the tiny lungs. "Lay hands on the baby," Fiona shouted. Everyone laid their hands on the baby's soft skin, whispering, "We love you, we love you, we love you, we love you."

As the clock struck midnight—Christmas—The baby passed.

Chapter 45

ELEANOR

Virginia Colony—Christmas Day

My dearest George—I canna bear to do this alone.

My dearest George—I wish you were here.

My dearest George—

Today, I held our daughter for the first time. She's perfect.

Our baby had the good sense to wait until Christmas afternoon to arrive, a half day off for slaves and indentured. From three o'clock in the afternoon until eleven at night, Hannah, the cook, bless her, helped to midwife me between roasting Christmas goose for the Crowans. She wiped my sweaty brow, rubbed my aching back, and gave me chamomile tea for my stomach.

But nothing would stop the hiccups. You'd think I was drunk.

Labor pains. Yet another hazard of being a daughter of Eve. Adam's descendants have it easier. You're in your mansion, probably playing at rantum-scantum with a new servant, while your bitch wife buys jewels she never wears. Then there's Mr. MacLeod. He warned me he'd be the one to lower the axe. In my stupid naivety, I dinnae believe him.

I scribbled his name from the journal's inscription. I almost ripped it out completely, except his advice was sound. Reflect. My choices led me to be exiled in the wilderness, dinnae they? George, I'm sorry. You were always good to me. I stole, and cheated, and now here I am in hell. A piece of me loved you, but it frightened me. It dinnae matter now, I suppose.

Gripping the birthing stool, I prayed to Jesus to let this bairn come out. The pain was excruciating, a burning that ripped me to shreds. I cried out for my mother, long dead and in the dirt of Inverness. No husband, no living sisters to guide me. Barely nineteen. A violent push later, and the cook pulled out our daughter, slimy and wet.

In comes the mistress with the reverend to take my baby to the orphanage. I haven't even held her, George. "No, please," I begged.

Master Crowan hears my cries. He inspects the babe, petting her fuzzy red hair. "MacLeod, you Scottish bastard," he mumbled. "I knew there was a reason he negotiated such good freedom dues." My master sighed. "I can't give away my friend's bastard in good conscience. You may keep her on the plantation. But mind, I own her indentured contract now."

What a lucky twist of nature both you and Mr. MacLeod have red hair. What might have happened if the bairn were blonde, like me?

"Since the reverend is here, let's baptize her," said my master. "What's her name?"

I remembered a conversation with Mr. MacLeod. My mother was named Anna. His mother was named Elise. Mr. MacLeod's friendship with my master saved our child from the orphanage. I hope you won't mind her name. It was the right thing to do.

Finally, I held her.

"She's beautiful," I said, tears rolling down my cheeks. "My little Annaliese, you're going to make the world a better place."

Love,

Eleanor

Eleanor put the quill down and wiped her eyes, wishing she could send the letter. She drank a healing tea to help regain her strength after such a rough birth. A purr lifted her eyes to the cradle.

"Are you going to be Annaliese's wee protector, Matilda, curled up inside the cradle and licking your paws until Ostara on her fifth birthday?"

Meow.

Chapter 46

MATILDA

Virginia Colony—Christmas Day

When Matilda returned with the baby from the veil, Ned drew back his head quickly, shocked as he watched her lay the babe on Eleanor's flat stomach. A blinding light and snow flurries burst through the room, and when it cleared, the baby was gone—nestled inside Eleanor's womb. Matilda faded back to her ghostly form.

"My girl's alive? They're both going to live now?"

Aye. You're a grandfather. He didn't seem to realize there was a changeling inside her, but it didn't really matter, did it? A mother is a mother no matter the circumstance. Ned grinned, stunned.

Matilda's smile was tinged with sorrow. *Did ye speak to her when ye were alone?*

He glanced away. "I dinnae think she'd want to speak to me." His chance at the connection had passed.

Her heart ached for him. *One day, Eleanor will be ready to forgive.*

The sound of ocean waves called in the distance. "Not now. Never." With a caved chest and slumping shoulders, he walked back to the Otherworld, and the veil closed behind him.

Eleanor rolled over in bed as Annaliese lay in the crib beside her. A smile tugged at Matilda's old lips as she gazed on her grandniece until everything sunk in.

Fiona thinks her baby is dead.

Eleanor thinks this baby is hers.

'Twas the right thing to do. Beira wouldn't have allowed her soul to manifest in flesh form to carry the babies through the land of the fae and swap them otherwise.

Those glorious moments of being tangible again—holding a new life—overwhelmed her with emotions not felt in decades. The sweet smell of the top of a newborn's head, a tiny heartbeat against her chest, the soft skin of the bairn held in her wrinkled hands. For an instant, the idea of death being life, and life being death, didn't frighten her.

She wanted to comfort Fiona, tell her the truth. But Lord Blackmere would be relentless if he discovered Matilda's deception. Fiona had to be kept ignorant. At least she had family. Eleanor had no one.

The goddess knew best to send Annaliese to Eleanor. As much as Matilda thought the lass was a pain in the arse, Eleanor was a fighter. She had found every ingredient they needed for protection spells all summer, despite the risk, and performed every ritual Matilda remembered to keep the baby safe from dark magic. With Matilda here to protect and instruct, the next five years would be the easiest of her life... or death, rather.

Having briefly experienced the tangible earth again made the restoration to her ghostly state even harder. Perhaps this was all part of her penance?

Matilda drifted toward Annaliese, studying her closely—she'd never seen a changeling up close before. Transferring Fiona and William's daughter into the womb shared by Eleanor and Lord George's child had mingled the essence of all four parents in strange, unknowable ways. The girl had Eleanor's face, and William's untamed hair. But would she inherit Fiona's magic? And what, if anything, had she taken from Lord whatshisname?

Sorry, cat, I have to cuddle her again.

Meow.

Matilda rested her head on Annaliese's heart, purring as she fell asleep.

The Scottish Otherworld

A frigid wind blew her into the Otherworld. *Why aren't I tethered to Eleanor?* Purgatory felt cold, lonely, and confusing, like wandering through a blizzard.

The sight of the crumbling castle in Kirkhaven startled Matilda. How was she allowed to wander through Scotland again? The Otherworld shifted with Beira's whims. Matilda never knew what rules applied anymore. *Is this my reward for swapping babies, Beira? Back to normal, again?* It was odd to admit, but she missed being bound to Eleanor. She sighed. While she didn't enjoy reliving her death day, at least it was familiar.

She walked down the path beside her former self as villagers chanted, "Burn witch!"

Admiral Goring made his mockery.

"He looks exactly like an older version of William MacLeod, dinnae he?"

Eleanor? Matilda spun. *How are ye here?*

"I dinnae ken. I was sleeping, then a stiff wind carried me here. Where are we?" Eleanor twisted to the left, and spotted herself sleeping. Annaliese and the cat were snoring in the cradle. "Is this a dream? Why am I here?"

This is...was...my home. Kirkhaven. Sometimes dreams can carry people to the Otherworld. I suppose Beira wants ye to see my past, she said, grimacing. It was bad enough she had to relive it, but now Eleanor was witnessing the most humiliating, painful, and consequential day of her life. *It isna pleasant to watch. Ye might want to go home.*

"We're coven sisters. I'll not leave you alone to face your past."

Together, they watched the executioner hang Matilda's living self as the crowd cheered. He cut her down and slapped her conscious. "Reckoned you'd get off easy, witch?" he said, yanking her to standing. "Dinnae fash yourself. The nobleman witch hunter's got something special planned for you."

"Christ in heaven, how cruel are people?" Eleanor said, glancing between the bruises on Matilda's neck, and the stake awaiting her.

Lord Blackmere called for it at my sentencing. He wanted to prolong the cruelty, Matilda muttered. *They revived me only to burn me alive minutes later.*

"I'm innocent," her living form said.

"I know." Blackmere grinned.

Eleanor watched in horror. "Blackmere is the same man with the viper mask who tried to kill me in the Hellfire Caves? Why would they kill an innocent woman?"

As a ghost, Matilda's suffering had been invisible for decades, known only to her. It was strange to have someone else see her perspective. Vulnerability felt unfamiliar. This time her memory seemed different. It sped up, and slowed down, and paused, allowing her and Eleanor to truly examine everything.

Reverend MacDonald took hurried steps beside her, speaking in a compassionate tone as men dragged her to the stake. "You're paying for your sins with your body, as is just, but will you not repent and release your soul? I imagine it's lonely when you dinnae allow Christ into your heart, but you're not alone." He whispered urgently. "I'm a sinner too, as is every villager here, but Christ saves us. I wish you would find God."

"Wasna the reverend one of the people you spoke about cursing at the Hellfire Club?" Eleanor asked. "He dinnae seem evil, like Lord Blackmere, or the witch of Pye."

Matilda rubbed her finger over her bottom lip as she listened. *The reverend seems...more sincere about wanting my salvation than I remembered.*

Admiral Goring said, "Thou has put down many with the fever; it would have been better for the good people of Kirkhaven, if they had knit a stone about thy neck, and drowned thee at birth."

Eleanor held her gaze. "Did you do that? Bring a plague?"

I never caused the fever; I tried to heal people. She lowered her voice. *But I did conjure storms with Elspeth. And my curses killed from the stake.*

"Why would you do that?"

I dinnae want to relive it. We should go back.

"Well, Beira clearly wants you here right now. Wait, let's go back to that bit where Lord Blackmere and Admiral Goring were talking. If they ken you dinnae cause the fever, and killed you anyway, they must have had a reason."

Matilda looked over. *I only discovered his true identity the night I met ye at the Hellfire Caves. I never even thought to listen to his conversations.*

Admiral Goring patted the nobleman's back. "Congratulations are in order on your new title. What's it like to be made an earl by the king?"

"I'm honored my investigation produced information to safeguard His Majesty." Lord Blackmere gave a small bow. "But there are yet threats to his reign. I've destroyed Elspeth's testimony records. Only the king, you, and I are aware of the prophecy."

"I'm sure the prophecy is wrong." Admiral Goring's jaw grew tight. "Neither I, nor my sons, would ever bed a witch, but it's prudent to kill Matilda in case she tries to use a love potion or some such thing. Why risk it?"

"Why indeed?" The corners of Blackmere's mouth rose with venomous grace, as he glanced at the admiral's sons.

A raven cawed in the distance. Eleanor pointed at Elspeth in human form, leaning against a cane. "What's going on over there?"

More ravens gathered on the barren tree. Elspeth raised her arm with fingers splayed towards Matilda. "*Meudaich*." Bloody feathers shed from the ravens in the trees.

"*Meudaich*—amplify? Elspeth used a spell to amplify all your worst feelings, like she did to me? That wee bitch! She must have been hoping you'd curse everyone. Can we read her memories to find out more?"

Matilda flew to the younger Elspeth. *Ye already betrayed me to spare your own life. Why would ye trick me into cursing people as I was dying too?*

"Blackmere needed a distraction, so I gave him one. Said he'd let me come back from exile if I played along. You were already bound for flames. What's one more shove?"

I was an innocent woman. Before ye entered my life, I was a healer, only practicing natural magic. I might have gone into the light. Ye condemned me to walk forever in purgatory for casting those curses.

Younger Elspeth wiped fake tears. "I'd cry if I had the tears left. You didn't cause the plague, but you weren't innocent neither. You sought what I knew, dark arts and all, long before your death day came callin'."

I was in mourning for my husband.

"You were drunk, and bitter, speaking naught but misery from sunup to down. I taught you how to hurt those villagers who hurt you with charms and ill wishes, and you didn't bat an eye. The only thing you cared about more than your petty grievances was Fiona. If I hadn't cared about her too, she'd have burned with you. I never mentioned her at all to Blackmere."

"But why did Lord Blackmere want to cause a distraction?" Eleanor asked.

What does it matter? Matilda watched herself spit on the ground, and roll back her shoulders defiantly. "This is your doing," her former self shouted from the stake at a younger Lord Blackmere. "Evil tidings come upon you. It would be better for the women of the burgh if ye are castrated."

Matilda watched Blackmere walk towards Fiona. *See? He and Admiral Goring's sons were going to kill Fiona. Only cursing them could stop Fiona's murder.* Matilda's human form shouted from the stake as the flames violently rose. "Witches take your wit and the grace from ye. Your sons shall die yet, Admiral."

"That dinnae make sense, Matilda. If Admiral Goring believed Fiona was a threat, he would have arrested her, and burned her at the stake next to you, not have his sons kill her in the middle of a crowd. And Elspeth just said Lord Blackmere dinnae ken anything about Fiona. If he wanted to kill Fiona back then, I'm positive she'd be dead."

They followed Lord Blackmere through the crowd of jeering men and women who rubbed their bits of iron for protection. As the once-strong admiral buckled with half his face frozen, everyone shrieked in mesmerized horror.

The glint of a knife redirected Eleanor and Matilda's attention as Blackmere held it waist high and took quick steps towards young Fiona. They gasped as he came right beside Fiona...then passed her, to the admiral's oldest son.

Lord Blackmere stabbed three quick jabs, right below the ribcage and into the kidneys of the admiral's oldest son. The lad never had the chance to reach for his sword nor wipe the smirk off his face.

As he rotated and collapsed, his younger brother caught his arm in confusion, not seeing the blood darken his brother's navy frock coat. Lord Blackmere spun to meet the younger, slipping his blade upward and forward from behind his victim's ear.

The younger brother's chapped lips parted but no words came. A thin crimson thread of blood ran down his collar, disappearing beneath his cravat. Soon he lay dead beside his brother, a frightened look on his boyish face.

Was it my curse or Blackmere's knife that killed those young men? Or both?

By the time the crowd noticed their murder, Blackmere had escaped on his waiting horse.

The memory froze in time, allowing both Matilda and Eleanor a chance to fully absorb all they witnessed.

"I feel sick." Eleanor knelt by the murdered brothers, and squeezed the hand of the younger son, then looked at Matilda. "Elspeth betrayed you twice, and Lord Blackmere let you take the blame for his planned murders." She looked at the sons. "Poor things. They were pawns in a game."

I've been such a fool to let myself be manipulated so easily. The sons were innocent.

"How did you get mixed up with the likes of Elspeth, anyway?"

Matilda paused, unsure how to begin. *I was married once, if you can believe it.*

"I can."

My husband, Angus, loved me. Respected my magic. When he died, I drank ale to numb my pain. Unfortunately, it loosened my tongue against powerful men. My rage consumed me, and only Elspeth understood. She was an outcast like me, banished from England, and angry at the world, too.

"Why did you hate the admiral so much?"

The man had a heart black as flint. I canna tell ye how many pennyroyal tinctures I made for the poor scullery maids he raped. He dinnae care for his tenants, either. If a father fell ill, or his harvest failed, and he wasna able to pay rent, Admiral Goring threw all the poor wretch's possessions into the front yard, and burned his croft house to the ground while the family watched. Wicked man.

"But why would he say you caused an illness?"

He was too ashamed to say the real reason he wanted me dead, even before the prophecy. I sunk his ship. A gleam came to Matilda's eye, and she didn't even pretend to be remorseful.

"Why?"

After Angus died, I worked for Admiral Goring's merchant business as a day laborer, rolling barrels of salt on his ship from dawn till dusk. He paid all the men forty shillings but gave me only eight. I appealed for just wages, but he sent me away as his sons laughed. Elspeth offered to teach me to make storms to get back at him.

"Like the storm you raised on the convict ship when you were angry with me?"

Aye. When I encountered him on the dock, I raised my finger and said, 'Your ship will sink along with your pride.' The next day he set sail, and a storm came, sinking the ship and all his profitable salt. But he and his sons swam to shore. The villagers respected me after that. I relished scaring powerful men to claim justice. If I'm being honest, killing Admiral Goring gave me a satisfying pleasure.

"It felt good? The admiral treated you wrong, Matilda, it's true. But you hexed him to death, and his sons did nothing."

The memory unfroze, showing Admiral Goring's fall, and the slaughter of his sons again.

Matilda left the crowd and glided back to the Admiral. She hovered in the air over the Admiral's French wife, Cécile, seeing everything from a different angle, watching her cling to her collapsed husband in her arms. But then—she experienced Cécile's feelings as though they were her own. Not rage. Not terror. Grief, raw and unrelenting, pouring from the woman's throat. "My sons..."

I never paid attention to anyone's cares but my own during the past twenty years. Why am I hearing them now?

Eleanor's demeanor softened. "Maybe Beira waited until you were ready to listen."

I meant to punish powerful men, not shatter a mother. Nor kill her boys.

The ghosts of Admiral Goring's two sons suddenly stood beside their dead bodies. The younger held the back of his hand against his nose and looked away from his slit neck. He joined Matilda and Eleanor. "My brother and I've been wandering lost for ages. How are we here?"

The older brother's ghost held no such confusion. Nostrils flared, his breathing grew noisy. "You damned us for nothing, and then watched us die, witch."

I was wrong, Matilda whispered. *I—I was angry, and I'm so sorry—*

"You're sorry?" He barreled towards Matilda, uttering a war cry as the ground shook around them. Matilda backed away with her shaking arms held up as he pursued her, landing each accusation like a punch. "Sorry won't get us into heaven. You bound us to this fate forever. You should have spared my younger brother. He never hurt anyone."

I dinnae mean—

"Why?" Touching the base of his neck, the younger kept repeating himself. "Why? Why?"

The crowd came unfrozen, and Matilda heard everyone's thoughts in a rush.

"Stop cursing people, auntie," young Fiona pleaded. "You're a wise woman. Look how much you're hurting everyone."

Children stared at Matilda unable to blink. She covered her ears, trying to block the sounds of the villagers hyperventilating, to stop experiencing their pounding heartbeats thrashing in her own ears. The stench of her own burning skin and hair choked her. Rasping breaths of terrorized fishwives grew louder. The admiral's wife crumpled to the ground, pulling her stricken husband tight. The hatred of the townspeople came in a wave thick enough to touch. She absorbed the shaking fists, bared teeth, spittle flying, while villagers yelled, "burn witch!"

Overwhelmed, Matilda pulled away from her furious former self. Her ghostly body ached as a wave of shame dragged her to her knees among the castle ruins. Matilda covered her mouth with her hands.

As the crowd emptied, she watched the flames char her body to ash.

It's a miracle I wasna cast into Hell outright. Matilda wiped her eyes. *What's the point of watching these memories? Of understanding other people's thoughts? My soul is lost.*

A soft snow fell, calming everyone's emotions, taking away the heat of the rage. The admiral's sons kept glancing between their corpses and Matilda's obvious grief.

Eleanor's eyebrows furrowed. "I dinnae claim to understand this realm of the Otherworld, or what Beira is trying to teach us, but perhaps you can help the admiral's sons get to the light?" Her brows released. "What if you did a counter curse?"

A sliver of light cracked through the clouds.

"What's a counter curse?" asked the younger brother.

"Don't trust her, she's a witch. Come on, Will." The older son began walking back up the road. "We're leaving."

"No. I've been wandering for ages. I'm tired of being lost," he said tugging at his cravat, revealing the deep scar from Blackmere's knife. He faced Eleanor. "Can she truly help us?"

"Matilda, think," Eleanor said. "Why did your curse make them stuck?"

Matilda tugged at her ear. *I said, 'Your sons will die yet.' That must be why they're both trapped here. Yet is a lingering word. They need a proper burial. I can say incantations, but I have no limbs to work potions with.*

"I'm in human form. Let me help," Eleanor said.

"Edward, what do we have to lose? Please," whispered the younger brother.

The older brother gave a wary nod.

We need iron, cheese, salt, and green earth.

Villagers left in such a rush, many dropped their bags as they fled. Eleanor scoured the grounds, finding as many items as possible. "I found a lot of iron bits along with a lump of cheese, but couldna find any salt. I can scrape moss off the stones for green earth."

"The loch is salt water," said the younger brother. "Might we use salt from there?"

Aye, that should work. Put those items on the lads' chests, then grab some loch water.

Eleanor reappeared with a flask of water and some mossy stones.

Lay the bodies straight and place the iron, cheese, and stones on their chests.

She did as prescribed.

The older brother's ghost stood with his hands crossed over his chest, pursing his lips as the younger brother hovered behind him.

"I've never seen a witchy ritual up close," said the younger. "Elise told me Matilda made a charm for her to elope with Rory MacLeod and it worked, so Matilda must know what she's doing,"

"That... and she killed us with a curse," quipped the older.

"Lord Blackmere was the one who stabbed us. I hold him to greater account."

Matilda waited for silence. *Eleanor, anoint each brother's forehead, eyelids, and wrists with the water, while saying their names and an incantation.*

Eleanor knelt, sitting back on her heels and rocking nervously. "I dinnae ken any spells for this."

Ye are a wise woman. Listen to your heart for the words.

"I don't want to be trapped here forever, and you're the only one who can do this part. Please," said the younger. "I'm Will, by the way."

Eleanor took a shaky breath and nodded. "I'll do my best."

A bright light inched closer, just over the horizon. "I'm Edward," said the older with a dubious look.

Eleanor knelt beside the younger's corpse, poured some water from the flask into her palm and made a fist, concentrating. Opening her palm, she let the water drip from her fingers as she anointed him and whispered. "Will Goring, you are seen. You are innocent. You are free." She moved to the older. "Edward Goring, you are seen. You are innocent. You are free."

Eleanor and the boys stared into the distance as a warm, peaceful glow washed over them. Matilda explored the sky as flurries fell, and the light grew closer. She chanted the incantation.

Eisd rium a Dhia.
Beira, Queen of Winter, first *Cailleach*,
Goddess, Destroyer, Protector.
Unwind my wicked curse,
Allow my hatred to reverse.
By ancient fire and sacred rite,
Guide them through the veil into the light.

Cécile appeared from the light, opening her arms to her sons. "I knew you'd come."

"Maman?" Edward said in disbelief.

"I couldn't find you, till now." Will ran into her arms, hugging her. "Edward, come into the light," he called. "It's beautiful here."

Edward and Matilda locked gazes as he clenched his hands. "I want the truth from your own mouth, witch. Did you cause the illness sweeping through the village, like Father said?"

No.

Edward absorbed her answer. "I suppose you weren't the first innocent woman Father killed. I suppose I can understand your anger at him, but why curse me and my brother?"

I was weak. I let hatred rule me. Matilda knelt before him, bowing her head. *I ken I dinnae deserve your forgiveness. I'm truly sorry for what I've put ye through.*

"She's not the same woman as before," Eleanor said, standing by Matilda.

The light glowed brighter.

His fists unclenched. "No soul is beyond redemption, I suppose. If you mean it." He walked into the light, and the veil sealed in a flash.

Matilda blinked and found herself back in the attic at Sweetwater Plantation where Eleanor slept peacefully next to Annaliese's cradle.

Beira, will I ever be worthy of the light?

Chapter 47

Fiona

Scotland

Fiona moved in a daze as though she were underwater, watching others above as the rites began. Someone—William? had lifted her daughter from the bed. She now lay on a plank beneath a plaid canopy, her face unnaturally still.

How many people visited their home each night during the *feille* to mourn?

This wasn't her daughter. Strawberry-blonde, not redheaded. Mary switched the subject, not wanting to admit it either.

James avoided her since the death, and for once in her life she didn't bother to keep the peace by reaching out to him. She felt too betrayed. James with his religion. William refusing to listen to her warnings about Beira's wrath. Lord Blackmere threatening their entire family. Mostly she was furious with herself.

I failed. If only I did the full saining, Beira wouldna have punished me.

William kept busy as usual, strong and composed, arranging everything for the *feille.*

Cam, William's brother, came down from Skye, bringing the clan piper. David asked him a million questions, and his face lit up when the piper tutored him on his old set of bagpipes. David had done his best to cheer Fiona and care for his younger brothers all week. She was thankful he got a rest from acting like a mother hen.

Reverend MacDonald led the prayers, then the men drank and danced, as tradition demanded. Everyone knew music guided souls safely through The Otherworld to *Tìr nan Òg*—the land of the eternal—even if they didn't say it aloud.

When the wake ended, the bagpiper played the death march as they carried the coffin to church. William and her sons were pallbearers. They walked a circuitous route to the church to confuse the evil spirits. If James had an objection, he kept it to himself.

No coffin should be small. It wasna right. What goddess would allow this?

The women moved in a cluster, leading a dirge of wails and tears. As the procession wove through the valley, other women joined the *coronach* along the road, sobbing for the lost child, as was expected.

"Why isna Fiona crying?" The whispers circled her.

They lumbered to the unconsecrated section of the graveyard for unbaptized children.

"Why isna our sister in the good graveyard?" demanded Lachlan.

"Wheest," Mary said, pulling him closer, whispering the answer.

Fiona stared blankly as the village men took turns with the shovel. The tiny hole was hard to dig.

Mary sobbed.

James was utterly distraught, pounding his thigh with his fist. Everyone consoled him. Not her. She felt numb.

"Why isna she crying?" everyone kept whispering. "It isna natural for a mother not to cry."

Reverend MacDonald prayed over the grave. Lord Hallewell sent his condolences, promising a large donation to the Kirk, and a proper tombstone with their daughter's name. They named the bairn Elise, after his mother.

Fiona suddenly remembered the scroll. Elise had written, 'The tree began to bloom, but then frost covered the ground.' She touched her fingers to her lips. *Beira is punishing me, taking away the fruit of my womb, leaving our family cold.*

A raven's caw lifted her eyes. *Elspeth.*

Fiona froze. Lord Blackmere stood at the corner of the church, beneath a barren tree. *Why is he still in Scotland? Our baby's death isna enough? He wants to terrorize us?*

Elspeth picked at the entrails of a dead pigeon. Lord Blackmere squinted at the guts in the steaming snow. Whatever the fortune, it made him smile. What other magic had he learned?

Blackmere joined Reverend MacDonald, and came to the grave where she stood. "My deepest sympathies for your loss," he said, laying his cold hands over her own.

Instinctively, she pulled away. Elspeth must have told him about the prophecy. *That's why he came the night I gave birth. That's why he's gloating right now.*

William gently moved her behind him, making a human wall to protect her. "My wife needs rest. Surely, you'll not bother us with nonsense questions about her dead aunt when we're in mourning?"

"Of course not, my dear man. Just wanting to pay my respect. By the bye, I see no evidence of witchcraft in Fiona. I'll leave you to mourn. I'm sure we will meet again in London."

William nodded, but everyone understood Blackmere's ever-potential threat to their family.

Lord Blackmere giddily strode down the icy road and into his coach.

More relatives circled William to offer condolences, interrupting his attempt to stand by her. She wandered to the barren tree.

Caw. The raven spoke with Elspeth's voice. "Pity you had to stop the saining rituals. The babe might have lived. You know how testy the goddess gets with disobedient witches."

"You suppose the goddess is happy you're teaching black magic and divination to a witch hunter? Betraying Matilda wasna enough? You send him into my home?"

"I betrayed Matilda, it's true, but not you, love," she said, wincing as the sigil gave off an eerie glow beneath her feathers. "Not on purpose. I walked through fire for you over twenty years, keeping your role in the coven secret."

"You're lying. Stop bloody lying to me." Fiona's breathing became shallow. "Why do you taunt me at my daughter's funeral?"

"I've come to comfort you. Matilda mentioned you discovered Elise's prophecy. You can see other people's dreams now?" Elspeth flew closer, tucking her beak into her wing.

"Not that it's any of your business, but she wrote it on a scroll, and we found it."

"If you know the prophecy, then you know the babe's death is for the best. Kings don't like prophecies, especially ones where girls bring down their empire." Elspeth nudged the pigeon entrails. "I see Eleanor dies in childbirth of a daughter. The king will sleep easier tonight."

"Both our babies?" It was like a punch to Fiona's gut. Sure enough, the entrails pointed to death of mother and child. *Everything we did was for naught?*

Elspeth flew to Fiona's forearm, like she used to do when Fiona was a child. "I've convinced Lord Blackmere to leave you alone. With your burden lifted, can you return the favor for your old coven sister? Have mercy on me, and forgive me?" Elspeth winced, the sigil glowing red.

"I've lost my daughter, my true coven sister, Eleanor, and probably Matilda too, and all you can talk about is reducing your own pain? Begone," she said, flinging her off.

Elspeth flew over the crowd as everyone watched, leaving Fiona even more unsettled than before. *They'll whisper about my daughter's death. Will they blame me?* All the people blurred together, their voices muted. It didn't matter. Nothing mattered. Both babies were dead.

Sleet fell as everyone walked home. In a few days, everyone would celebrate Hogmanay. Some people discussed their New Year's plans, keeping their voices hushed to speak of pleasant things during dark times.

"Mam." Broderick tugged at her skirt. She picked him up and kissed him. William didn't like her babying him like this, since he was practically five, but she cared little about anyone's opinions these days.

"Did James kill the baby?"

"No, no, love. Elise is in heaven." *I killed the baby through my willful disobedience*, she wanted to scream.

"But if she's not baptized, how can she get into heaven?"

Fiona bit her lip. "I think..." Words left her, and she blinked rapidly. Everyone had gone ahead.

Broderick whispered, "Baby Elise isna in heaven because the fairies have her, right?"

Fiona nodded.

"Will they take me too?"

Hugging him tightly, she said, "No, love. The *sìth* like taking strong babies and leaving dying ones."

"Do they ever send anyone back?"

"Sometimes?" Fiona gazed around, confused. "Where is everyone?"

"They've gone home, Mam."

Fiona lowered him and rubbed the back of her neck. "How do I get home?"

Broderick blinked. "We're over the hill. You ken where we live."

"No. Get your Aunt Mary. I dinnae...I'm lost."

Broderick tilted his head, then ran down the path.

A tightness spread across Fiona's chest, lowering her to the ground. She couldn't get a lungful. Spreading her fingers against the wet earth, she gripped the muddy rocks as the rain soaked through her clothes, chilling her.

"Fiona?" William raced over with Mary and James. "Broderick said you were lost?"

His words sounded muffled, and a coldness spread throughout her body until he lifted her from the ground. Willing her limbs to move, she said, "Dinnae touch me. I can walk on my own. Mary, help me home."

"Fiona, you're disoriented," he said.

She punched his arm. "You'd love to carry me home, wouldnae you? Big, strong William MacLeod to the rescue in front of all the villagers."

"Fiona, you're upset," he said calmly. "You haena cried once since she died."

"You'll beat Broderick for crying. How do I ken you willnae beat me? Wouldnae that make everyone happy? Beat the witch? Burn me at the stake?"

"Mam, calm down," James said, peeking over his shoulder. "What if someone hears you?"

"Haena you done enough?" she said, cutting James to the bone. "I want him gone. Send him to Skye with your brother."

Mary swooped in. "Fiona, stop speaking before you say something you regret. You're not talking straight. William, go home, I've got her."

Fiona's fingers curled into fists as lightning splintered the sky. "I'm not a child. I'm just... lost."

Chapter 48

MATILDA

Virginia Colony

Creak.

Matilda slit her cat eyes open. After a long, emotional night dealing with her past, she simply wanted to snuggle up next to Annaliese for a long nap. Eleanor had returned to her laundry work, leaving the attic empty.

Creak.

Old Betty walked toward the cradle with a horseshoe.

Meow. Matilda hissed and scratched her.

"Ouch." Old Betty dropped the horseshoe with a loud clank. "You best stay away from this girl, spirit, or I'll cook you in a pie."

Raising on her tiptoes, Old Betty hung the horseshoe on a rusty nail over the crib with the ends pointed down. The horseshoe immediately sucked Matilda in, freezing her within the amulet.

Baby Annaliese wailed, as Old Betty lifted her over her shoulder, swaying with her hips as a trickle of blood rolled down her forearm from the scratch.

"Don't you worry none, baby. Old Betty gone protect you from that nasty witch."

Chapter 49

ELEANOR

Virginia Colony—1734

Dear Diary,

It's been a while since I wrote, but in fairness, three-and-a-half years of indentured servitude beneath a blistering sun, combined with being a new mother, dinnae leave much time for writing.

I'm soon free, land awaits, yet worries plague my nights. How will I farm ten acres by myself with no money for seed? Where will I even live? Beneath a tree? I can take in more laundry jobs, but will it be enough?

Too bad Matilda dinnae cast a prosperity charm before she left.

Without a man to provide, how will I feed Annaliese? If I sell some land, can I buy her contract?

Some witchy advice would be helpful, because my daughter is no typical child. Matilda taught me herbs, but Annaliese is witchborn, I'm sure of it.

A few months ago, musicians were setting up in the Big House for a Christmas party. Harp music, beautiful and mystical, filled the air, like a fairy's tune. It made sense Master Crowan would only hire the best musicians.

I snuck inside to listen. Behind the harp, Annaliese played with her eyes closed, as naturally as if she had a lifetime of practice.

Everyone swayed to the music, getting lost in the notes as I had done my first night at Astwick House.

Thunderous applause sounded as she finished. I hugged her tightly and took her back with me. How on earth did such a young bairn play an instrument she'd never seen before so gloriously?

"The fae taught me," she said, as though she read my thoughts.

Thank God the master and mistress were at the other plantation that morning, or they might try to sell her to travelling musicians.

I think she sees the future. She cried the other night, telling me she dreamed a man from The Quarter was hanging from a tree. Sure enough, he tried running away, and was hung a week later.

How am I to raise such a child?

The prophecy said she would overthrow a king, but which king? King of England? King of the Fae? This magical realm is vast and confusing, and the whole situation frustrates me. Such a rush to form a coven to protect Annaliese, and then no word from my coven sisters for nearly four years?

Did I do something wrong? Why cut me off from the coven? I ken I'm not an experienced witch, but why leave me without warning?

Matilda and Fiona were just like everyone else. Full of promises until they left, leaving me to protect my girl alone. Even the witches cast me out.

I am worthless, worthless, worthless.

Eleanor ripped the page from her diary, and burned it. She had to be careful writing about witchcraft. Besides, the shirts would be done with their final soaking by now. She hid her diary, and went outside to hang the clothes on the line.

Annaliese, her three-and-a-half-year-old hellion, escaped the watchful eye of Old Betty to run amok beneath Eleanor's feet.

That wee creepy shite Daniel Crowan, now in his awkward and gangly age, leaned against the sycamore tree, spinning a horseshoe in his hand, then dropped it to pull a silver flask from his waistcoat. After taking a sip, he coughed, still learning how to hold his liquor.

"Daddy gave me this for my birthday a little early. It's genuine silver."

The party was next month, and everyone scrambled to make the Big House ready. Eleanor closed her eyes, remembering her dance with George a lifetime ago.

"Daddy says he's gonna set up a maypole for my party. The blackbirds already set up the horseshoe pit. I took the horseshoe hanging over your bed so I can practice."

"So, I see," she said, hating the fact the master's family barged into her room whenever they wanted, although mostly it was Matthew Crowan who came visiting at all hours to lie with Hannah.

"Stay away from the clothesline, Annaliese. You'll get mud on the wash."

"I can mind her," Daniel said, with his gap-toothed grin.

My arse. I'd never leave her alone with you. "Your mother wouldnae approve." She hung another shirt on the line. "Ack, it's been years since I danced around a maypole. I dinnae think they celebrated Beltane here in the colonies?"

"We don't. But Daddy has important investors coming from Ireland. He always finds a way to increase tobacco sales." Daniel put away his flask, and left to play horseshoes.

Escaping the kitchen heat, Hannah came outside.

As Eleanor beat out stains from Mistress Crowan's gowns, a hard tug on her skirt drew her attention to the mess of red curls beneath her. "Mama, who him?"

Master Crowan approached with a familiar looking man. "Eleanor, Hannah, this is Mr. Robert Birch from my Riverside plantation. He's going to be the new overseer to help establish some discipline in the field, aren't you, Birch?"

Mr. Birch drank Eleanor in, staring at her bottom lip. "We met once before."

She curtseyed, flushing. "Aye, 'twas my first day."

That was the precise moment Annaliese got tangled in the clothesline, dropping all the clean, wet clothes into the dirt, making the entire morning's work wasted. "I told you not to play there," Eleanor yelled, feeling inadequate as both laundress and mother.

Annaliese took off running toward the massive sycamore tree, and climbed it quick as a squirrel.

"That little rascal is Eleanor's daughter," Master Crowan said. "She's in the corner more than she's out of it."

"Ah, she's a hoot," Rob said. "I'll leave you to your work. Afternoon." Mr. Birch tipped his straw hat at them with an unfaltering stare.

"Birch, you'll sleep here in The Quarter to monitor things at night," Master Crowan said as they strolled toward the rows of dilapidated cabins.

Eleanor gathered all the linens and dumped them back into the steaming cauldron, then beat the dirt from the mistress' shift with her washing bat. Again. "My shoulder will ache something awful tonight, but not nearly as much as wee Annaliese's backside when she gets down from the tree."

Both women laughed as Eleanor stirred the lye with a long stick.

"The new overseer be sweet on you," Hannah said. "What did Old Betty say the cowrie shells predicted? A dark-haired man would come into your life and marry you?" she teased.

"What? No. That was a bit of scrying for fun." She lost all faith in magic when her coven sisters abandoned her, and she'd never thought about anyone romantically since George. But Rob Birch was a strapping fellow who looked like he could be devilish between the sheets.

"Be careful, though. Take a certain personality to be overseer. There's a reason no one rents out their field hands when he's in charge. My cousin works over at Riverside with him. He beats the slaves something terrible."

"Well, the law says masters aren't allowed to whip indentured servants anymore. My solicitor put it in my contract to make sure." MacLeod might have been a backstabbing bastard, but he was an excellent lawyer.

"There's laws for indentured servants maybe," Hannah said, "but not for wives."

"Wife?" She laughed out loud. "I barely met the man. Besides, my only focus is counting down my days to freedom," she said, hanging the mistress' shift on the clothesline.

"Must be nice," Hannah muttered, returning to the kitchen.

Clank. Daniel split the horseshoe against the metal stake. "Damn. Now I need another horseshoe."

As he sulked off, a cold breeze blew.

Eleanor rubbed her arms, watching Mr. Birch reappear and amble past the cabins, their rooves drooping with decaying leaves, and down the oak alley towards the tobacco fields. He was undeniably handsome in an unpolished sort of way. After her four year draught of companionship, she finally felt thirsty enough to drink again. Mr. Birch must have sensed her watching, because he veered around, catching her eye and grinned. Not even a cool breeze off the river stopped the burning sensation growing inside her.

"Hey, Red," he called, eyeing Annaliese in the tree.

"Yeah?"

"Git down an' help your mama. Now."

Annaliese scrambled down, and hid behind Eleanor's skirt, clinging to her legs. Mr. Birch tipped his hat at Eleanor and winked, then sauntered away as a raven flew from the fields against the darkening sky.

"I ain't like him, Ma."

Chapter 50

Matilda

Virginia Colony, The Otherworld—1734

Wind rattled. The horseshoe clanked against the iron stake—then snapped. Matilda gasped as her spirit unfurled like smoke. After three-and-a-half years sealed inside the cold amulet, she was free.

A raven landed on a tree branch. *Oh shite.* They locked stares.

"Thought you could stay hidden forever, sister? The eye sees both ways. And it never closes." The sigil beneath the ravens' feathers hissed, releasing a curl of steam.

Matilda lurched like a puppet cut from its strings. *Please dinnae tell the witch hunter about her. She's the last hope of our coven, Beira's miracle.*

The raven cawed loudly, flying straight through Matilda's head before flapping her wings back to her master.

Matilda flew to Eleanor, who was hanging shirts on the line.

I'm free!

Eleanor passed through her like mist. No gasp, no flicker of awareness. The bond forged in the Hellfire Caves had snapped with the horseshoe. Matilda called after her, but her words died in silence. Forgotten. Alone again, now in a strange land.

A girl with wild red curls sat high in the tree, her blue eyes fixed on Matilda with an intense curiosity. Matilda floated up. Magic hummed between them like a plucked sting of a fairy's harp.

"Who are you?" the girl asked, not with words but thought.

Matilda blinked. The child could see her. A seer. A witchborn.

My name is Matilda, and I'm here to teach ye how to fly.

Chapter 51

Fiona

Scotland—1734

The April wind bit through Fiona's shawl as she stared at her daughter's grave. A shadow passed over it, more like an omen. Three and a half years had passed in a blink. James and David lived with their uncle on Skye. Broderick and Lachlan studied in England. William buried himself in work. Fiona just felt numb.

As she stared at the tomb, her thoughts drifted. Eleanor and her baby were dead, too. If Eleanor's baby had survived, she might have toppled a king.

Matilda was as good as dead, too. The few times Fiona looked to a flame during a fire festival, she saw nothing but mist. Maybe Matilda's ghost extinguished when Eleanor did. They were bound, after all. Fiona repetitively swallowed, wishing to go back in time and change what happened.

Fiona's fifth and final son, Hamish, toddled beside her daughter's tombstone, a lovely marker Lord Hallewell commissioned.

"They'll be here soon." William picked up Hamish.

She stayed planted, feeling both empty and heavy. "You go ahead."

He exhaled slowly before speaking. "You canna freeze him out forever."

"I'm not freezing him out, I'm preventing an argument."

"Fiona, he's our son," he said, loud enough to make other parishioners glance over.

Standing in a huff, she brushed past him. "I suppose you're the authority on how to treat sons with compassion. Just ask Broderick."

"She was my daughter, too." His eyes welled before he quickly blinked them dry. "The awful truth is sometimes babies die, and neither prayer nor bits of iron would have saved her. God called her home, and it's incredibly unfair for you to blame anyone for her death."

Guilt flushed her cheeks. Hamish reached his arms out, and she cuddled him close, happy for a distraction. Hamish was a bright spot at home, a constant reminder that goodness did come from their marriage.

They walked the winding path from church to their manor. William touched her back, guiding her over a rocky patch, always being the one she could lean on. She and William loved each other but couldn't seem to put back the pieces.

Conflicting thoughts rolled through her brain as James and David arrived from Skye, dressed in tartan, and riding as though the horses were part of them. As they dismounted, she was shocked to realize they'd transformed into young men.

"I've missed you." Fiona hugged David and adjusted his glasses, which kept slipping off his nose.

"They're taller than me." William mock punched them. "I guess I have to pay attention to you now," he joked. "How's your Uncle Cam? Tell us about your adventures on Skye."

"You look good." She politely kissed James' cheek, now furry with a red beard. "My bairn has grown into a man."

"Who's this wee redhead?" David scooped up the boy.

"Your youngest brother, Hamish."

James was standoffish, but nodded. "Glad he's healthy."

It was odd to see James dressed as a Highlander, but she knew it would be short-lived. He wore the clan MacLeod brooch on his shoulder, a bull with the motto, *Hold Fast*. She tapped it. "That's an appropriate animal spirit for you."

"Da, do you have breeches and a cravat I can borrow? I'd like to dress properly when we go to Glasgow. I dinnae ken why you want to open a law office there and not Edinburgh," James said.

"I told you, we'll handle English law, and David will focus on Scottish law so we can expand our client base." He put his arms around his sons' shoulders. James looked up, and David looked away. "Edinburgh might be the head of Scotland but mark me, Glasgow will become the hands. You dinnae need second sight to observe all the merchants relocating there. They'll need lawyers to write the contracts."

"Hm," Fiona murmured. "I'll be in the garden while you menfolk talk business. Dinnae fash, I'll only be picking vegetables, not magical herbs. I wouldna want to break any laws."

An uncomfortable silence fell as William shot her a scowl. James shifted on his feet before going inside. The garden remained choked in winter's grasp. Not a single herb, sacred or ordinary, dared bloom.

"Are Broderick and Lachlan home?" David followed Fiona and William to the garden while playing peekaboo with a giggling Hamish in his arms.

"They are learning the finer points of ancient Greek and Latin at Lottington Hall. I suppose you'll have to settle visiting with me and your da."

"Will they be home to celebrate Beltane? They used to love decorating the maypole."

"They'll be home in July. Even if they were home, there's no maypole celebration to attend."

"Ack, you ken the Kirk," William shrugged. "The Reverend banned every fire festival after the explosion." Another uncomfortable silence hung in the air. "I better help James tie his cravat properly."

Once William was out of earshot, Fiona leaned in. "Anything from the old ways must mean it's got to do with devil worship. I suppose they fear I might cause an earthquake next," she chuckled bitterly. "I'm sure James would agree."

David lowered Hamish. "Mam, I wish you and James would talk with each other. He's told me how guilty he feels about baby Elise's death."

Fiona winced at the mention of her daughter's name, then composed herself. "Why would he feel guilty? It must have been God's will."

"Mam. I love you both, and I hate being in the middle. Remember how close you and James used to be?"

"That was before he started spying on me to the preacher."

"Spying? He loves you. James would never betray you to the Kirk. Do you really think that?"

"No." Her face blushed. "It dinnae matter."

"You seem so bitter, Mam, and that's not like you."

It felt like a slap, because it was true. *Am I becoming like Matilda?* She didn't like being unforgiving, holding tight to her hurts, but was unsure how to fix herself. "I dinnae want to fight, either. I'll be quiet. You two have the interesting things to talk about, anyway. You've the whole world ahead of you."

"That's what I wanted to talk with Da about when the timing's right." He chewed on his bottom lip. "I dinnae want to be a barrister. I want to apprentice myself to the MacCrimmons and become a piper. It's seven years, but I'll get paid my final year as a journeyman, and I'll get to play at Agegdun Castle."

"Oh, that's wonderful. You'll have to play the pipes for us after dinner."

"Maybe make me a good luck charm before I talk with Da? I can start next autumn if he needs me to help with some legal filings at the new office this summer."

James came out clean shaven and in breeches.

"That was fast," Fiona said. "Were you crawling out of your skin in Highlander clothes, like your da?" She gave a forced laugh, but no one found it funny.

"Da received an urgent letter from Lord Hallewell. He needs to leave for London tomorrow. I'm heading to Glasgow for a look around. Can I borrow a fresh horse?"

A pang of guilt struck Fiona. *What's wrong with me? Why am I running off my own son?* "You dinnae want to stay for dinner?"

"You seem busy."

She squeezed his hand, trying to connect, despite the anger she tried to keep bottled inside. "This is your home. You dinnae have to go."

"That's not what you said at the funeral."

Fiona let go, unable to meet his eyes. The wound between them cut too deep to heal.

James forced a smile as he nodded. "David, you can keep my sporran and tartan—I left them on your bed. Wee Hamish, it's nice to finally meet you." He pulled a cross from his pocket and handed it to her. "I had the smith forge an iron cross from nails to safeguard Hamish."

Iron and faith, fused together. Fiona held the cross in her hand, staring at the blended traditions, her son's olive branch.

James headed to the stable before spinning to face her. "I'm trying to do the right thing—for everyone."

Fiona's heart ached, wanting to close the distance between them. "Old ways aren't evil, just different."

After waving goodbye, David lowered his voice. "I dinnae mind if we follow the old ways. Many clansmen on Skye do, and James dinnae say shite to them. He's just scared for you, Mam. When Beltane comes next month, we'll make a bonfire."

"Dinnae you hear what I said earlier? All fire festivals have been cancelled."

"I'll light a small one in the woods, and none will be the wiser. There's nothing magical about wanting to warm yourself in the forest, aye?"

She chuckled. "I've missed you, David."

"It's not like we're making salt circles," he said with a grin.

Chapter 52

Eleanor

Virginia Colony

Rob Birch hit a pebble against the window. Eleanor crept from the bed, as giddy as when she snuck out of the workhouse. It had been years since she felt desired.

Her foot sank into a rotten wooden step leading from the attic to the brick kitchen as she slowly descended the stairs, slid past the table stacked with pots and bowls ready for tomorrow's cooking, and crossed into the night air.

The Big House loomed large as she followed Rob into The Quarter. She'd been in the shadows of enough plantation balls to watch the courting rituals of the gentry. Fathers spoke of dowries and settlements. Women chaperoned their daughters. Young couples exchanged modest tokens of a fan, locket of hair, or—gasp—a love letter. No public touching until engagement. No risking a reputation for being a demure maiden.

Rob's courting had been a wink and a nod towards the river. Hidden by the tall grass, they kissed, and groped that first night, and knew they wanted more. But how far would she go? It was risky, and she was older, wiser, and had more at stake now.

Rob nodded toward his cabin. The Quarter was quiet, but ears were always open. Once inside, he flung her against the wall, wrapped her braid in his fist, and gave it a wee tug. A breath hitched in her throat before he kissed her. Rob's skin had the sweet aroma of tobacco, and his tongue had the flavor of corn whiskey. Blood rushed through her veins, spreading heat throughout her chest.

Soon his breeches were down.

Every worst-case scenario passed through her brain until she blurted out. "Please, Mr. Birch. I canna get in a delicate condition again." Slowly, she twisted from him and pressed her forearm against the wall. In a forward-tilted posture, she lifted her nightshirt, feeling the night air on her bare flesh. She peeked over her shoulder at him, curious if he'd comply.

"Well, shit, never used that hole before." He chuckled. "We can do it your way, I reckon," he growled in her ear.

He pulled off her shift. It had been years since she was naked with a man. Slapping her ass hard, he took her from behind, pounding her good and rough, pressing his fingers in all the right places. When they finished, he moved to his narrow, unmade bed.

Eleanor unbraided her hair, letting it fall in soft waves over her breasts. Men had always been drawn to her hair, and she needed to look pretty. *Perhaps he would marry me? He makes a steady living, maybe enough to help me buy Annaliese's indentured contract. And he's not married. My coven sisters would be proud.*

"Damn. Never git tired looking at you. How'd I get so lucky to meet someone like you?"

She laid beside him, propping herself against her arm. "No one has ever called meeting me lucky." She traced her fingers over his scars. "When did you get these?"

"Some from being a soldier. Most of them scars are from my father. We ain't seen eye to eye much. I deserved plenty though." Rummaging through a drawer cluttered with keys and loose change, he retrieved a silver flask wrapped in a handkerchief.

She read the engraving. "D.C.? Your name's Rob Birch."

His eyebrows raised. "You can read letters?"

"Aye. And books too." She took a swig. The expensive bourbon burned down her throat. *Was it only four years ago I drank the finest claret at the theater?* "Who's D.C.?"

Rob smiled impishly. "Daniel Crowan, I reckon."

Eleanor covered her gasp. "You stole it from the master's son?" The irony of the situation wasn't lost on her.

He laughed, quite pleased. "He needed to be brung down a peg."

"This is good liquor." She smiled. They passed the flask back and forth as she scanned the messy cabin: muddy footprints, damp wood next to the fireplace, abandoned hose balled up near a chair. His neatly coiled whip was lovingly hung on a shiny new nail though. "Was your father an overseer too?"

Rob drank. "My great grandpa came as an indentured, like you. You hear of Pocahontas? He married a Powhatan girl, like her, but we've only married English since then, praise Jesus. But the Indian blood in me is what makes me so good at catching runaways before they git within a mile from here. I can track damn near anything. Saves Crowan a ton of money."

He took another long swig.

Is his drinking a concern? I suppose it's not my problem to solve.

"Used to be there was mostly English here, then the slaves come from Africa and now, shit, it's like an invasion. There's five slaves to one indentured. It's disgusting. They take all the jobs. Why hire me when they can buy a slave once and have him work forever? I hate them damn blackbirds."

"Everyone has been friendly to me. Seems like everyone in the Big House work hard."

"Crowan likes to treat his house slaves real nice. He should, he's related to half of them." Rob propped his head on the yellowed pillow.

"If you hate them so much, why not find a different job? You dinnae have to be an overseer." She took another swig.

He grabbed it back. "Does it look like I can buy my own farm? You think I want to go trapping like my Uncle Hal? Spending weeks in the forest like some savage? No thank you, ma'am. Here I got me a roof, steady pay, and you warming my bed. How's a pretty Irish lass get to Virginia on a convict ship anyway?"

"I'm not sure how an Irish lass does it. I'm from Scotland."

"Same thing."

"You truly are from the New World, aren't you?" she said, drinking. She stayed quiet for a long time. "I had an affair with a married baron. I stole his bitch wife's earrings and got caught, so His Majesty gave me a one-way ticket to Sweetwater Plantation, and here I am with you. I get my freedom in September."

"Damn. Then what?"

"I dinnae ken. I have my daughter's indentured contract to buy, and then I'll figure it out. Ken any good men?" she joked. They held eye contact, then broke away.

"Listen, if I want to fuck you, I can do it right now, and ain't no one gonna say a word about it. I can fuck all the slaves and indentured. You pretty, but why would I marry a thief with a bastard?"

A hot flush crept across her cheeks. "Yes, Mr. Birch," she whispered, wishing to shrink into the background "'Twas just a joke." *What a stupid thing for me to have said. Why would any man want me?*

"Besides, I got to try you out, make sure everything works the normal way a man takes a woman."

"But my contract—"

"I'm the only master you got to worry about." He stared at her bottom lip, then pressed his fingers over her private parts with a wicked grin. "Someone likes breaking the rules. You a bad girl, Eleanor? Want a firm hand?"

Her breath grew ragged as her body and mind warred. He mounted her, plunging harder as her hips rose to meet him. Rob thrust deeper, making her back arch in a hazy line between pleasure and pain as he released his seed. *George had always been so gentle. Maybe roughness is all I deserve these days.*

The door slammed open, spilling moonshine across the room. Annaliese appeared like an angry ghost in her white shift, hands balled into tiny fists. "What you doin' to my mama?"

"Jesus Christ, ain't you learned to knock?" He rolled off Eleanor and covered himself with his hands.

Her daughter was having none of it. Annaliese stomped her foot, and wagged her finger at Rob. "You's a bad man."

"Let's go, Annaliese." Eleanor threw on her shift, picked up her daughter, and fled before the situation got even more humiliating.

"Better be nice to me, Red," he called strutting to the doorframe, covering his cock with a towel. "I might be your pa one day."

Chapter 53

WILLIAM MACLEOD

London

Lord Blackmere strutted like a peacock on the raised platform with the other nobles, while the executioner adjusted his black hood. Thousands had assembled to enjoy the hangings at Tyburn Tree. The Reformation of Manners group was on a rampage. Eight ox carts carrying dozens of men and women slowly made their procession to the gallows.

William MacLeod slipped into an alleyway across the street and re-read the letter.

Dearest MacLeod,

It is with great humility that I seek your help. Blackmere's relentless pursuit to harass me is boundless. He wasn't content destroying my father, his retribution now targets me. His Reformation of Manners henchmen have been bringing up Wilkes' disappearance. He's trying to get the king to revoke my title. I'm terrified he'll throw me in prison, as my father before me. God, I wish I escaped all this noble backstabbing and lived with Eleanor in peace. I beg of you, find a way to direct his attention away from me.

Your most humble servant,
Lord George Hallewell

He pocketed the letter. The past four years he and Lord Blackmere had played a stupid game. Blackmere dangled royal connections that never came to pass and MacLeod handed him a list of sodomites—who had already been executed. Finally, they left each other alone. But now he was threatening George again, MacLeod knew he had to bash him hard in the teeth to end his harassment.

He weaved through the cheering mob and weighed his choices. *How do I distract his attention without getting him angry with me or setting him off against Fiona? If George is arrested, he'll crack under the pressure of Lord Blackmere's infamously rough interrogations and expose the truth about Colonel Wilkes' murder.* MacLeod stared at the gallows with nooses waiting for necks, and rubbed his own.

"My good people of London," Blackmere said, basking in the crowd's affections, "I stand before you today, as defender of His Majesty's great realm against the vermin before you: Whores. Sodomites. And witches."

"Put a pear up the bugger's arse," called an alewife.

Lord Blackmere grinned. "Yes, madam, those defying God through depravity will face ultimate justice."

"Give him a good flogging first," a farmer said.

"Followed by a close shave," said a boy dragging a finger across his neck. The crowd burst into laughter.

MacLeod saw Joseph Pate from *The Tatler* paying rapt attention and joined him. "Planning to publish the confessions?"

"We've already published the pre-written ones today, but you never know. Occasionally a condemned man will say something unscripted and interesting. But not as interesting as the whispers I heard about Lord Hallewell being arrested next."

"For what?"

"Questioning about the disappearance of Colonel Wilkes again. The man's long gone, there's no body, so technically no crime. The investigation itself is the punishment. Blackmere's such a petty man. Those who brag the most about their piety tend to be the most debased. I'm sure there's more rot to Lord Blackmere beneath his gleam of morality. I've heard your relationship with Blackmere is rather touch and go."

"Leave my name out of your pamphlets, if you ever want any information from me."

"You've never given me any tips. Why start now?"

"Who says I'm starting now? We're just two men enjoying a hanging." MacLeod folded his arms over his chest.

"Stephen Rose, step forward."

MacLeod squinted before he recognized the condemned man as the artist/lover who paid for Charles Jamison to escape several years ago. He'd lost touch with the painter, busy with other things.

Their eyes connected. He wanted to shout, *Why save your lover but not yourself?*

"Do you have any final words of confession, sir?" Lord Blackmere asked.

The artist shuffled forward with slumped shoulders and wrists bound behind him. He addressed the crowd, but it seemed he was explaining himself to MacLeod. "My niece and nephews have been taken away, my true love is exiled, and my warehouse of paintings has been set ablaze." He gave a half-hearted shrug. "When the government steals everything from a man with such cruelty, the only blessing is death."

MacLeod felt a rush of regret. *Why dinnae he tell me? I would have helped him escape.*

Lord Blackmere made a mock sympathetic face at Stephen's statement then laughed. *What was he so damned smug about?*

"Cut off his cock," shouted a man.

People spit and jeered as the executioner placed the rope over Stephen's neck. A woman reached up and pulled on Stephen's foot, throwing him off balance. Soon more hands reached up, and he was dragged into the bloodthirsty mob. A crush of thousands pressed forward, shoving MacLeod and the journalist back.

Lord Blackmere did nothing but grin. Stephen screamed helplessly as the mob beat him to death as MacLeod tried to buck the crowd to rescue him. The soldiers managed to extract Stephen from the crowd. MacLeod had to shield his eyes from Stephen's pulverized body.

"Jesus Christ," Pate said. "Has our society reduced into mere beasts?"

The crowd cheered for Lord Blackmere, who appeared to thrive on their violence. "May this sodomite's fate be a warning to others," he shouted as they hung Stephen's corpse.

A bitter tang of disgust filled MacLeod's mouth. He leaned in. "Methinks the earl doth protest too much."

Pate glanced up at him, eyebrow arched as the next terrified condemned man stepped forward. "Is this a rumor, Mr. MacLeod, or do you have evidence?"

"You're the one who likes to investigate things. All I ken is Lord Blackmere is unmarried and frequents coffee houses rather than taverns as real men do. Leave my name out of your paper. Good day, sir."

As he left the angry mob, MacLeod's rational brain took over. *Am I insane? I just picked a fight with Lord Blackmere.*

Still. He was glad he did it.

Blackmere made a serious miscalculation when he threatened Fiona, and now it returned to bite him. Let's see how much he likes being investigated.

Chapter 54

Elspeth—Witch of Pye

London

Lord Blackmere leaned in. "You've been withholding from me again, Elspeth."

"Never, my lord," Elspeth pleaded as she sat strapped into her chair facing away from the hearth fire. *What did he discover?* The sigil pulsed quick as her heartbeat.

"I thought squeezing your throat and dunking you in the Hackney Marshes might have kept you in your place longer, but you're a strong-willed hag, aren't you? Some women never learn."

He'd kept the flames low and out of her direct sight, just enough light for him to savor the panic in her bulging eyes as he revealed his little toy. "You remember the caspie claw, don't you?"

"Mercy, lord. You've already crippled me. What more do you want?"

"I want to kill William MacLeod and his insidious tongue...slowly." He knelt in front of her, fitting her crippled leg between the two boards then gave the metal knobs a twist as she winced.

It felt like she'd been run through.

"Do you know how many satirical pictures of me getting buggered are appearing in the papers? I'm positive he started a rumor about me that's spreading like wildfire."

Twist.

Anger flashed at the unfairness of her torture over this. "A rumor, or the truth?"

He took her cane from the ground and cracked it against her crippled leg, making her scream out as though the devil were coming for her.

He threw it against the wall, knocking over jars on shelves filled with festering liquids that dripped to the floor. Jessop cawed from within a birdcage with a towel over top. *No chance for escape. Is this the day I die?*

Lord Blackmere's eyes glistened. "The king discussed my replacement as head of the Society of Reformation of Manners. If enough people turn against me, I'll be the one hanging from Tyburn Tree. They'll kill me before I learn enough defensive spells to protect myself," he shouted.

Elspeth smiled, picturing him belly down on a rack, getting a taste of his own torture. He was too busy ranting to notice her glee.

"I'll be damned if I let some Highlander take away everything I dedicated my life to achieving. Haven't I protected the king from potential usurpers? Haven't I proven my loyalty to His Majesty, yet he threatens to revoke my power?" He paced the room "Damned witch. You should have warned me this was coming. You peek into my teacup enough."

"I can only reveal what the goddess shows me."

With another twist of the claw, she cried in agony.

"I should have killed you years ago." He picked up her cane, ready to strike a death blow against her skull.

"Eleanor is alive," she shouted, bracing for the pain. "Her baby's alive," she panted. The sigil grew hot and started pulsing, but there was no other way. She tightened her muscles, trying her best to prevent the caspie claw from digging deeper into her flesh and crushing what was left of her bones. "Mercy, lord, I beg you, let me go."

"You can pray for mercy, just don't expect to get it." He tapped the cane against his hand as she watched with rapt attention. "Don't you think that would have been an important thing to mention four years ago?"

"I only found out," she panted. "The eye Matilda seared into me," she gasped, "works both ways. I saw Eleanor with the changeling girl but yesterday."

He held the cane mid-air. "What changeling?"

Every breath twisted like a knife in her ribs. "You said yourself Fiona's baby was strong. We both read the pigeon entrails. Eleanor's real daughter died. Beira must have switched babies, as goddesses are known to do. Kill the baby, save the king."

"What do I care if the king is overthrown? He's ready to hang me."

Sweat rolled down her forehead. *Think fast, before it's your last thought.* "She's a threat to the king," she swallowed, "but an opportunity for you, lord," she said licking her dry lips, "Keep the girl alive," she gasped, "and in your power." Tears rolled down her wrinkled cheeks.

"Why?"

"A powerful changeling can end your hex," she panted. "Or god forbid Matilda's curse comes true and you're castrated."

He stared at her suffering, his pupils narrowed to slits.

She bit her lip, tasting her own blood. She spit on the ground, leaving a long watery blood drip dangling from her mouth. "Only blood magic fixes that fate. You can curse other people dead too. Think how powerful a changeling's blood is."

He lowered the cane. "Powerful enough to overflow a king," he whispered.

"Constant source of blood," she panted, "for dark magic. I swear I'll never cross you again. Just give me another chance. I'll teach you. I'll teach you everything I know about blood magic. And I'll bring the girl under your control."

Lord Blackmere had broken enough women to know when they were telling the truth. He tossed the cane in the corner and removed the caspie claw. The sigil's eye wept blood, making him smile.

He released Jessop from the birdcage. She transfigured and flew up the chimney with a furiously unstable wingbeat.

"Find my changeling, Elspeth," he called.

Chapter 55

Matilda

Virginia Colony

Old Betty was supposed to keep an eye on the children in front of her. Instead she searched the Otherworld for her sold-off children, chanting their names to the orisha. "Thomas. Mary. Harriet. Thomas." When she finally nodded off in her rocking chair, Annaliese snuck out to Matilda waiting outside to teach the next bit of magic.

"I've got the salt in a secret spot, Nana Matilda," Annaliese said aloud.

Wheest. Only speak mind-to-mind, child. Ye dinnae want the master to see ye sneaking off. How about Old Betty? Does she ken I'm free?

Annaliese slipped through the tall grasses to the river. "Nah. She's busy looking for her children."

Tell me what the air feels like, lass.

"Air."

Cool breeze? Warm sun on your face? I miss that. The scent of wildflowers after a rainfall.

Annaliese picked daisies. "Look. They smell flowery."

They're bonny, like you. Tie the stems to make a wreath for your hair.

"Why?"

Beltane, a fire festival, is coming soon. Perhaps I'll find a way to speak with your mother if she looks into fire or water.

Matilda toyed with the idea of having Annaliese be the mediator, but she didn't know how Eleanor would react to her nearly four-year absence and feared Eleanor might lock her in a horseshoe herself. The first conversation had to be face-to-face. There was too much at stake.

Remember why we celebrate Beltane?

"Spring comin'?" Annaliese knitted her brows, struggling to tie the stems.

Matilda smiled at her determination. No wonder Beira chose her. *Aye. But what's the most important fire festival?*

"Samhain."

And who comes at Samhain?

"Beira Winter," Annaliese said, clapping.

A gentle breeze rippled the water. *Ye ken your mam's birthday is on Samhain.*

"Mama ain't born then, silly." Annaliese made a sloppy knot, and steadily grew the flower chain.

Eleanor is your earth mother, aye. But ye have a magical mother back in Scotland. A white witch like me.

"Witches are bad."

Not all. We're healers, as you will be one day.

Annaliese tilted her head. "Mama ain't my real mama?"

Ye are blessed with two mothers who love ye.

"Two mamas?" She puzzled over it, finishing her flower wreath. She placed it on her head. "Can I meet my Scotland ma?"

When it's safe.

"Is the bad man coming for me too? The one who burned you?"

Matilda gasped. *Ye saw my memory?*

"I see lots."

Both your mothers and I will protect ye. Get the salt.

Annaliese pulled a hidden bag from a hollow tree. "When you gonna teach me to fly?"

When the time is right, and ye willnae even have to leave the ground.

Annaliese wrinkled her freckled nose. "That don't make no sense."

Matilda laughed. *Let's pray to Beira.*

They gathered flowers, rocks, and sticks as an offering. Annaliese dumped the salt in a lump and had to spread it to make a circle around themselves. She sat cross-legged as Matilda led the prayer.

Eisd rium a Dhia. Beira, Queen of Winter, first Cailleach, Goddess, Destroyer, Protector—Thank ye for protecting us through the past winter. May our coven reunite, and be reborn in spring.

A breeze scattered their offerings. *We should return before Old Betty notices you're gone.*

As they passed the Big House on the way back to The Quarter, a caged wagon with two shackled Africans arrived. Mistress Crowan dabbed sweat from her bosom with her handkerchief as she chatted with Rob Birch.

"Matthew, your new Negros are here." She darted a side eye at Annaliese as the girl tried to run past. Rob caught her arm.

"Why ain't you with Old Betty?"

"I was playing with Matilda, Mr. Birch."

"Old enough to sneak off, old enough to work the field," Rob said.

"Who's Matilda? Did someone from another plantation wander over?" Mistress asked.

"Matilda knows my real mama."

Wheest, child. Ye talk too much.

"Real mother?" Rob chuckled. "I'll bet Eleanor would be curious to meet her too."

"Ah, right on time." Master Crowan jaunted outside to meet the slave trader and inspect his chattel as they were brought out. He seized the taller African's face. "He has an intelligent intensity, doesn't he? There's a certain magnetism about him. Janet, record the sale in the farm book. Name him Moses. The other's Tom."

Rob slung his musket over his back. "Ain't sure how much magnetism a blackbird needs to pick tobacco," he joked.

"I'm expecting a record harvest, Birch. I see you've got a new field hand." Master Crowan patted Annaliese's head and returned inside with his wife.

Annaliese pointed at Rob. "A bullet to your brain."

"What the hell?" Rob yanked her arm. "Is Old Betty teaching you hexes now?"

Blame me, child.

"No, sir. Matilda told me."

"I ain't got time for this childish shit. Come on, Red." He strode towards the fields. The new men were clearly assessing threats with each step. Matilda wished she could warn them. On the other side of the tool shed, Rob pulled his hidden jug of corn whisky and gulped it on the way to the fields.

"How come you wanted me to lie, Nana?"

Keep your visions secret for now. We must protect your magic.

"Hey, Jacob, come here, boy. You a Bite?"

"I am from Bight of Biafra."

"Good. You can talk to these new blackbirds. You play your cards right, I might promote you to enforcer one day."

Jacob gave an unsure nod.

"Nana Matilda," she said in her mind. "What smells funny?

I have no senses anymore, lass. Maybe it's the corn whiskey.

"It smells like metal."

Matilda blinked, surprised her gift would manifest so young. *You'll find out soon enough.*

"Know what we gonna do today?" Rob asked.

"Teach them to weed, sir?" Jacob guessed.

"Well goddamn, you is intelligent. Must be all that reading you do." Birch kneeled by a plant and spoke to Annaliese while Jacob translated to the others. "See here? This a secondary shoot. You need to cut them off each plant. Now look at the stalk. That's a goddamned tobacco worm. Peel every worm and beetle off the stalk and the leaves, and kill 'em. They'll eat through a whole crop like it's they own Sunday dinner. I'm gonna to check everybody's work."

Rob watched the twelve-person squads work in the fields for hours, drinking steadily. Annaliese peeled off the worms, thicker than her thumb and two inches long, careful not to break the leaves. Rob swayed on his feet as he took longer gulps.

Annaliese tugged his shirt. "I'm thirsty."

"Swallow your spit." He staggered towards Jacob. "What books you read, boy?"

"Nana, how come Mr. Birch's eyes is glassy?"

He's fuddled, lass.

"Cat got your tongue? Guess you ain't that smart then, is you, boy?" he slurred. "What you lookin' at, Red?"

"A worm," she said, staring directly in his eyes.

"Moses, git your ass over here."

Jacob translated, and the new man came. A lone worm clung to the underside of the plant's smallest leaf.

"Reckon you gettin' an extra meal today, boy. Tell him to eat it."

Jacob translated. Moses stood tall in his refusal.

Rob held the gun to his head. *Click clack.*

Moses's eyes bulged, unable to blink. Everyone in the squad froze, or flinched at the cock of Rob's musket.

Goddess in heaven, what's wrong with the man?

"Eat it."

Moses plucked off the worm and shoved it in his mouth, gagging as he swallowed. Everyone kept their heads down, returning to work as the sun shifted in the sky.

Rob grinned. Once the corn whiskey jug was empty, Rob pulled out a silver flask. Annaliese scratched her neck. "How come you got Mr. Daniel's birthday gift?"

"Hush your mouth before I hit you."

Wheest, child, Matilda said gently. *He's dangerous.*

The sun beat down, making Annaliese's skin burn. Rob disappeared. Everyone stretched their sore backs.

Annaliese wandered and found him face down. "He dead?"

Jacob peeked. "Drunk."

Moses rushed towards the James River to escape, still holding his grubbing hoe.

Bang.

A plume of smoke left Rob's musket. Everyone dove for cover as blood sprayed over the tobacco. "He was trying to kill me with that hoe. You seen that?" Rob's entire body trembled.

Moses's soul rose, blinking in the light. "Who are you?"

Matilda. She smiled kindly. *Your family is calling ye.*

The light opened to reveal an Igbo village. The colors were brighter than anything Matilda had ever seen. Vibrant green palm trees, crystal blue sky. A woman in a headscarf came out with open arms from a red clay house with a thatched roof. "You've come home, Chinedu."

"What's Chinedu mean?" Annaliese asked.

He smiled. "It means 'God has answered my prayer'." He rushed home, hugging his mother.

"When did he learn to speak English?"

In the Otherworld, everyone understands each other, Matilda explained.

"Can you go into the light, too, Nana Matilda?"

With a longing gaze, she felt the light's pull. *Mayhaps. I still have work to do.*

The veil snapped shut, leaving them nowhere to focus but at his brains splattered over the tobacco plants.

Rob stumbled to standing then patted Annaliese's head. "A bullet to the brain. How'd you known about that, Red? Or maybe I should thank your pretend friend Matilda, huh?"

Chapter 56

Elspeth—Witch of Pye

Virginia Colony

Elspeth soared above the tobacco fields in raven form, stretching out her wings and letting the wind carry her. *If only I was able to stay a raven.* The world was more expansive, colorful, and full of hidden patterns easier to spot as a bird.

Circling above the decaying flesh of the slave left to rot, she noted the shadows and light reflecting off his body, and the broken tobacco stems splattered with blood. She followed the footprints leading away from the body, seeing most returned to the rickety cabins, but those weren't the footprints she was interested in.

With a slow, powerful wing flap, she found her prey on his knees panting by the river. Ravens didn't have a strong olfactory sense, but even she smelled the fear rolling off Rob Birch. Elspeth landed on an oak branch, narrowing her gaze. She took a deep breath, sore but grateful to be alive. "You've had a bit of a fright, haven't you, love?"

"I reckon so," he said, rubbing the back of his neck. He spun, searching for the speaker, confused to find no one there. No human at least.

"Up here," Elspeth said side stepping along the branch, squeezing her talons to balance her shifting weight.

"Jesus," shouted Rob, falling back. "What the hell was in that flask?"

Elspeth dove, doing a barrel roll and flying upside down for a short burst as he scrambled to reload his musket. She landed on its barrel, and stared into his eyes. "You'd kill the one who can give you everything you want?"

Rob swallowed. "What?"

"Annaliese ain't no ordinary child."

"How come you sound like an old lady from England? Do all crows talk like you? How come I understand you? This a dream?"

"It's a proposition."

"I don't known your big words."

This addle brain will do quite nicely for my purposes. She spoke in a soothing voice she might use on a distracted child. "Listen to me closely. My lord can give you anything."

Rob backed away. "Aw, shit, is you the Devil's familiar?"

"Not exactly. But my lord wants Annaliese."

"Always thought that girl was trouble. You want me to kill her or somethin'? Not sayin' I would—I'm only askin'."

"My lord very much needs her alive, and under his power. Name what you want."

Rob lowered his musket, searching if anyone was watching, then stared into Elspeth eyes. "Respect."

Elspeth hopped to the ground, tilting her head at his answer, which was far more interesting than she expected—she pegged him as someone who merely wanted money. "What does respect look like?" she asked, silently mouthing the malevolent incantation.

"It's me owning my own land, with a pretty wife, and a son. It's Uncle Hal coming to my cabin, and seeing I ain't need his help no more."

She saw him get drawn into the seductive mirage, beautiful and hollow, with a too-perfect sky, and birds singing the same loop, but he didn't notice.

"Ten acres, that's what Eleanor gets for freedom dues. It's there for the takin', if you've the spine to serve my master. You've scraped and bowed to Crowan long enough, haven't you? Time you were treated with the respect you deserve."

He rubbed the back of his sweaty neck. "I get everything I want, plus the bastard goes away? Shit, where do I sign?" He laughed, opening his hands as he relaxed.

Elspeth pecked his open palm with her sharp beak, puncturing his skin as he howled. Flying right above him, she tasted his blood as he closed his fist, looking as scared as the slaves he whipped.

Flapping her wings, she became airborne again. "The master will be in touch."

Chapter 57

Fiona

Scotland

Fiona wanted her sons home for Beltane, but not like this. Fever spread in Lottington Hall closing the school at the start of April, forcing Broderick and Lachlan to come home. David began sneezing, then baby Hamish. James came back from Glasgow to help.

She huddled outside their manor with the few servants not stricken with the fever as William's coach pulled into the drive and he stepped out.

James came outside, coughing into his fist. "Good afternoon, Da." He handed William *The Tatler*. "Did you read the paper? It's full of stories implying Lord Blackmere is a sodomite. The king is publicly defending him, for now, but there are calls for him to be replaced as head of Reformation of Manners until the matter is sorted out."

William squeezed Fiona's hand and gave her a wink.

Broderick and Lachlan came outside with David close behind, holding Hamish. The bairn shivered beneath a blanket in the spring air.

"Why is everyone coughing?" William advanced inside the manor. "Where is the governess?"

The maid took his hat and coat as they walked inside.

"I gave her the week off to care for her mam, and gave her some herbs to help with the cough going around," Fiona said sitting by the hearth. "'Twas a tonic with honeysuckle and water from the clootie well."

William eyeballed James.

"They were healing herbs, Da." James wiped his red nose.

Fiona tilted her head. "What other kind of herbs would they be?" *Had William told James to spy on me again?*

"Damn it, I wish you wouldn't do such things without consulting me first." He planted himself in his armchair across from her as he warmed his hands. "James, fetch me a dram."

"Why would I consult you?" Fiona took Hamish from David and rocked him. "What do you ken of herbs?"

"What happens if their illness gets worse? They willnae blame the herbs, they'll blame you, like they did your aunt Matilda."

Fiona grit her teeth. "Lachie take Hamish back to bed."

"Why canna people understand the difference between healing and harm?" David said.

She turned to William and James. "Do you suppose Lord Blackmere's scandal ends our risk or will it make it worse? A wolf is most dangerous when he's cornered."

"Mam," Lachie called from upstairs, "Hamish is coughing."

"I'm aware. We can all hear him. I'll bring some tea in a minute."

David went upstairs to check on them.

William reached over and squeezed her hand reassuringly. "Look, I ken you only mean to help. I admire that part about your nature, and you clearly have healing skills, but it's too damn risky. Tavern keepers told me grim news: eight fell to the fever in Inverness, and ten bairns in Glencoe. I hoped our village might escape it."

"Is it because Beira's angry they banned the fire festivals, Mama?" Broderick said.

"No, love. Dinnae interrupt when adults are talking," Fiona said.

"I dinnae want to hear any magic or fairy nonsense in this house. Understand, boy?"

"You're not mad at him, you're mad with me, and you shouldna be. I haena done a thing but try to help bring the fever down for the villagers."

Lachlan came back and tugged on her skirt. His eyes were watery and red. "Mam, I dinnae feel good."

She pulled him onto her lap and kissed his forehead. "Lachie, I think you've got the fever too. What about you, Broderick?" She touched his forehead.

He shrugged. "I'm fine."

"Boys, go to bed and rest."

"Mam," David called, "Hamish threw up on himself."

A knock came at the back door. Fiona moved toward it, but William cut her off, opening it himself. Two boys with watery eyes waited and a procession of weary villagers came up the road. Stepping back, the younger boy coughed then hid behind his older brother. They both craned their necks as they looked at William.

"Beggin' your pardon, laird. We came for some herbs. Our baby brother died, and Mam's got the fever something awful."

How could he have died? Fiona covered her gasp with her hands as her chest tightened. *Everything William feared was coming true.* "Did you follow the instructions I gave with the tonic?"

The older brother scratched his neck. "Da dinnae want us using potions from a witch's niece. He let us dab the tonic on the baby's head but dinnae allow him to drink it."

Fiona grew exasperated. "Healing herbs only bring the fever down if they're swallowed. It canna get absorbed through the skin. Tell your mam to drink it before it's too late."

"Go home," William said. "There's sickness in our house too. I'll stop by later with the reverend to pray for your mother."

Closing the door on them he spun to Fiona. "We have to get ahead of this."

Scotland—Beltane fire festival

Death lurked around every corner. All her sons but Broderick had the fever. Each night she touched her lips to her sons' foreheads; their fevers burned hotter as her own stomach churned, terrified they might not live through the night. Thank the goddess it was finally Beltane, and she would have a chance to scry once the sun went down to find out if the fever would get worse in the village.

Fiona diced and boiled and mixed all manner of herbs in her cauldron for her sons, but not the villagers anymore. *Are my neighbors my enemies now?* William didn't want her to visit anyone without him present. They might whisper behind her back, but they'd never confront the laird.

With a fixed jaw, she went about her tasks, bitter William couldn't even be with their boys because he had to waste time tamping down rumors she caused the illness. Sick with fear, she just wanted him close.

At last, she heard a horse come up the road. She flung open the door in relief.

"Good afternoon, madam."

"Lord Blackmere? Reverend?"

She cursed herself for being unprepared. She'd been so busy healing, she hadn't bothered to put a protection charm over her threshold. Covering her face with her shawl, she wondered at the thick leather-bound book Lord Blackmere carried. "There's sickness in this house. You should stay back, gentlemen. My husband isna here right now."

"It's you I'd like to speak with, Mrs. MacLeod." He shot her a crooked smirk, eyes glinting.

Who am I dealing with today—the witch hunter or aspiring dark lord? Both sides to his personality were dangerous. She invited them in, and the butler took their coats. "May I offer you a drink?"

The reverend sneezed into his handkerchief. "I'd like tea and a dram."

Broderick burst into the room. "Mam, Lachie threw up again."

"I'm sorry, gentlemen, but I must care for my sons," she said, willing her hands to stop trembling. "Perhaps you can return in the morning?"

"We'll wait," said Lord Blackmere. "This boy is quite healthy. Who does he take after? Certainly not William."

"Broderick, come help mam." She held out her hand.

"He's fine with us. How old are you now, son, seven?" Reverend MacDonald waved off Fiona. "Take care of Lachlan."

Her heart pumped loudly. *Where is William? Please, please come home.*

Upstairs her sons were a mess. Hamish was crying. James, David and Lachie were sweaty and vomiting. She needed the two vultures downstairs to leave so she could make a proper tincture for her boys.

The sun would soon set. It was a fire festival, so perhaps someone in the Otherworld could help. But her coven sisters, Matilda and Eleanor, were as gone as her daughter.

Fiona finished cleaning up the boys, and then went into the parlor. Reverend MacDonald whispered something to Broderick, who nodded nervously then left. She darted her eyes around the room, looking to escape from her rigid chair.

"I assume you're well read, Mrs. MacLeod. Perhaps you've seen this before?" Blackmere handed her the large tome he carried.

"*Malleus Maleficarum*? Of course."

He pulled out a clay pipe and snuffbox from his waistcoat pocket. "Do you know why it was written?"

William always told her it was helpful to listen more than she spoke in matters of interrogation. "Tell me, my lord." *Come on sunset. I'll look in the flames and escape.*

He pinched the tobacco leaves and pressed them into his pipe. "Heinrich Kramer, a German noble, got into a dispute with a witch named Helena Scheuberian. She told the elders he made unwanted advances, and that's why he started rumors about her."

"Aye, to taint her reputation."

"Something your husband knows a considerable amount about." His cold smile tried to cool his own temper. "Being a barrister, I mean."

Is this about some argument with William, or my witchcraft? Did he realize William planted the rumor of his sodomy in The Tatler? Am I to be the proxy for Willim's punishment?

Striking flint from the box, Blackmere lit the leaves, inhaling deeply as the embers burned orange. "Helena went to trial for witchcraft and an interesting thing happened. Can you imagine what?"

"The jury ruled in her favor."

The reverend sneezed several times in a row.

"Precisely, because no lawful definition of witchcraft existed. Mocked by his peers, undone by a woman who dared oppose him, he would not suffer obscurity. No, he cloaked his vengeance in Latin and wrote the *Malleus Maleficarum—'The Hammer of Witches.'* A masterstroke of cruelty, that book. What a gift. Now any fool can identify a witch, recite her crimes by rote, and slaughter her with the blessing of scripture and science alike."

Hair rose on her arms. *Where is William?*

Lord Blackmere took another puff, then relaxed in his seat. "At the time of its printing, most men possessed only two books: The Bible and *Malleus Maleficarum.*"

"You are certainly full of historical insight today, my lord." *He's trying to scare me. Turn the tables.* "There's an entire section dedicated to what witches do with their victim's penis. How did the story go? When a man claimed a witch had stolen his member, she allegedly told him she hid it in a nest with several others. The man climbed the tree and found them wriggling inside like worms and the largest one leapt up and cried it belonged to the parish priest. Dinnae Matilda say at her execution the village would be better off if you were castrated, my lord? How terrifying for you."

Both men exchanged nervous glances, shifting in their seats. Lord Blackmere leaned forward. "The woman's initial mockery went unpunished. However, Heinrich had the last laugh over... everyone... didn't he?"

"If you consider burning innocent women alive a laughing matter."

He inhaled deeply, then blew three smoke rings that floated around her neck. "I want to protect women. I want to protect the realm. Nothing is quite as threatening to our glorious society than a woman with strong opinions, don't you agree, Reverend? It leads to unfettered sex, maleficent magic, and the slaughter of babies."

Fiona felt claustrophobic. *Why is he speaking of babies? My daughter is dead.*

The door swung open. William raced inside with Broderick panting behind. "What brings you here, my lord? Reverend?"

Fiona exhaled in relief. "Our boys are very ill. I should go back to them."

"It's shocking these fine gentlemen would keep you from your maternal duties. Broderick, go with your mam to check on your brothers." He gave Broderick a pat on his back, clearly pleased to have been warned.

Broderick took Fiona's hand and led her to the top of the stairs. He was beaming. "Da said I was a good boy for protecting you."

She hugged him then listened in.

"We were merely asking your wife a few questions," Reverend MacDonald said.

"Regarding?"

"I have evidence she gave herbs to the Barclay family," Lord Blackmere said. "Both the mother and the baby died, and the father is livid, saying Fiona used enchanted water from the clootie well." Lord Blackmere steepled his hands, leaning forward. "Intriguing Matilda caused an illness to sweep through this same village nearly thirty years ago. She burned for it."

"What I find intriguing is you would speak to my wife without me being present," he said shifting his gaze, "given I was delivering baskets of food to the villagers at your bequest, Reverend."

Fiona peeked at Reverend MacDonald rubbing the iron cross between his aging fingers. "Lord Blackmere was quite insistent we shouldna trouble you, William."

"No trouble at all. As to the Barclays, the father refused to let his wife or bairn drink the tonic, but when he got the fever himself, he drank it and was better the next morning. My wife's a healer. She's not a witch."

"People died, Mr. MacLeod. A baby died." Lord Blackmere exhaled smoke.

"Tragic as it is, death is as natural as life. God calls us all home, eventually." William's legs casually spread into a fighting stance, and he towered over the seated men. Even hidden Fiona sensed tension in the room.

"His Majesty believes my attention to sodomy detracts from the more pressing matter: eradicating witchcraft."

The reverend's skin grayed. "Forgive me gentlemen, I'm going home. I feel sick."

"My lord, I've uncovered something relevant to the important work you do on behalf of the king. I've recently been in touch with young Charles Jamison through third parties. Do you remember him? It seems he read about Stephen Rose's grisly death at the hands of a mob. His father is on his deathbed, apparently. Charles wishes to come home from exile, and is willing to name names. He wishes a face-to-face meeting in London."

"No, that time has past."

"Has it?"

Lord Blackmere hesitated. "He best provide a lengthy list, MacLeod, or I promise your wife will face the Reformation of Manners on witchcraft charges. And I keep my promises."

"Done and done. We can meet at your favorite coffee shop in London."

Blackmere dumped his pipe ash on the threshold. "See you next week in London." He left to his waiting coach.

Fiona came downstairs and hugged him, her entire body trembling. "Did your client really say he'd betray his friends?"

William swallowed. "Not exactly." He stroked her cheek. "I had to stall him. I'll always protect you, or die trying. I have to go to my law office in Glasgow, there might be a way out yet. If anyone comes to question you, James kens the law well enough to protect you."

David came downstairs coughing. "And I can protect Mam with my dirk."

Giving a quick nod, William snuck out the back door. "We'll get through this, I promise."

Once gone, David checked out the window. "The moon's out now. Lord Blackmere, Da, and the reverend are gone, James is upstairs snoring. I'd say that's divine intervention. Let me light a quick Beltane fire in the garden. I think you need to scry."

Chapter 58

Matilda

Virginia Colony—Beltane fire festival

Beltane had at last arrived. Matilda counted down the seconds until sunset when she would finally reunite with the coven.

Coaches carrying Virginia Colony's elites rolled up the dusty road, and deposited them into the celebration. Ladies wearing expensive gowns imported from England mingled with wealthy merchants and politicians in silk coats and powdered wigs. Alcohol flowed like a waterfall as the enslaved hurried to keep up with their masters' demands.

In the midst of children dancing around the maypole, she heard Old Betty's chant. "Thomas. Harriet. Thomas."

Ceòthach, said Matilda, creating a fog to keep her hidden from Old Betty. It unnerved her to be seen when she didn't want to be.

Rob carried a satchel, and tapped Eleanor's shoulder. "Come on, let's sneak away," he said pulling her hand.

"Now? Mistress Crowan—"

"Is drunk off her ass thinking she can win a drinking contest with a bunch of Irishmen. She ain't gonna be looking for nothing but a bucket to puke into." He tugged Eleanor toward the stable.

I need to talk to Eleanor and reunite the coven. How am I to do this if she's busy playing at rantum scantum with Rob Birch? Annaliese, try to stop them, Matilda called.

"Mama, don't go." She hugged Eleanor's skirts, glaring at Rob Birch.

"You'll have lots of fun dancing the maypole. Mama needs a break," Eleanor said.

"Too bad you ain't like me much, Red, 'cause I brung you something."

Annaliese raised her head.

"This is for you," he said giving her a rag doll. He pulled a new pair of children's shoes from his satchel and gave it to Eleanor. "And this will make your mama happy," he winked.

"You got me a baby doll?" she squealed, grabbing it from his hands and hugging it tightly. "Nancy," she called to Hannah's daughter, "look at my baby!" She was off with the other children.

A lot of good that did.

Eleanor tilted her head. "That was quite kind of you, Mr. Birch, but I canna accept expensive gifts like these."

"Call me Rob, at least when no one's around."

She dropped off the shoes in the laundry building, and he led her to the stable where a horse was ready and waiting for them.

Matilda glanced between mother and child. *Where do I go? Whom do I protect?*

A crisp wind blew in Eleanor's direction.

Eleanor it is. She called to Annaliese. *Put an iron nail in your pocket. Nana Matilda has to go with your mam.*

Annaliese groaned but obeyed, then rejoined the other children at the maypole.

The black cat was in the corner stall licking her paw. Matilda locked eyes on her. *Sorry cat, Beira says I need to follow them. He's far more charming than I thought, and I dinnae trust him.*

Meow.

Rob tied the satchel to the saddle, leaving the top open. Matilda's cat form dove right in, staying hidden.

They rode past the gentry drinking, dancing, and sneaking off for stolen kisses. The sun set over the horizon, and the sky lingered in twilight. The witching hour.

"One of the Irishmen told me all about Belltrain."

Beltane, ye eejit.

"That maypole is like a giant cock, and you're supposed to fuck in the fields or somethin' to bring a good harvest."

"I was a bairn the last time I celebrated. I only remember the ribbon dancing."

He veered off onto a dusty road, and Matilda peeked out of the bag, with the breeze on her whiskers. *This isna town.*

"Where are we going, Mr. Birch? Rob?"

"The York River, on the other side of Williamsburg."

Birds chirped as they made small talk along a meandering path into the forest. The pine trees grew taller. Fireflies blinked. Matilda had to fight the animal urge to chase a mouse scurrying under the shrubbery.

As the sun descended towards the horizon, they stopped near a grassy clearing between a thick forest and the riverbank. It cast golden sunlight on the brown waves making a soothing lapping sound against the driftwood-covered beach.

If only Eleanor looked into water or a flame, I could warn her about Rob's dark heart, pull her into the Otherworld, find Fiona, and practice defensive magic again to protect Annaliese. So much needed to be done.

"Oh, it's lovely, here," Eleanor said with wonder.

"I'm glad you think so, because it's yours. Eleanor Cameron, these ten acres are your freedom dues."

A slow smile built to beaming. "This is my land? To the river and back?" Circling gradually, she took it all in, tears pricking the back of her eyes. All restraint left her as she ran through her virgin land with her arms open, laughing.

Matilda, jumped from the bag and watched Rob race Eleanor until they were in a dead heat, neck and neck, through the forest as wild as them. They stopped at the riverbank, bent over panting as the moon rose. "Guess this is about as good a place as any to ask. I want you to be my wife. Will you marry me?"

Finally, the river mirrored the vibrant, moonlit sky. Matilda's ghost separated from the cat, and she stared at Eleanor with worry from the river water.

"You?" Eleanor gasped.

Rob scrutinized her. "Of course, me. Who else would you marry?"

I've come to warn ye, Eleanor.

Eleanor backed away from the water. Rob grabbed her hand and walked, not waiting for her answer.

Sorry, cat, I'm coming back in. Meow! Dinnae talk out loud, Eleanor. Now we've connected, I can hear your thoughts, but only during fire festivals.

"You left me. Sisterhood of the coven my arse. You dinnae only abandon me, you left my bairn vulnerable to Lord Blackmere. How dare you, how dare you come back now and act like nothing's wrong," she nearly shouted in her mind.

"This here's a good piece of land Crowan gave you," Rob said. "I'd build a cabin right there, protected in the forest, and far enough from the river in case it flooded during a big rain."

Listen to me. I'm not like your father; I dinnae abandon ye. Old Betty put a witch's horseshoe over the bed and trapped my soul inside the amulet. I wasna released until the master's son hit the horseshoe against the stake and broke me out.

Eleanor stared at the cat, with bulging eyes. "That happened weeks ago. Why dinnae you speak to me?"

I tried. The binds between us from the Hellfire Caves are broken. We're back to regular order of living and dead only able to speak directly during fire festivals.

"You dinnae leave me?"

Gods, no, Eleanor. You're my coven sister, like a daughter. I'd never leave you on purpose.

"Does Old Betty realize you're back? We have to tell her you're a wise woman so she dinnae trap you again."

I dinnae want to risk meeting her again. The good news is Annaliese can see me, and lets me ken when Betty is asleep so I can avoid her.

"Those back areas would be perfect for tobacco," Rob said. "Plant a garden right over here to feed you for the winter and spring."

A distant voice came from the river. "Auntie Matilda?"

He grew more animated, excited by the future. "After a harvest or two, we can buy us some slaves and then, shit, this land becomes a money maker. Ain't like Crowan to give up something so good."

Fiona? Matilda's heart beat faster. *I'm coming.* Matilda turned back to Eleanor. *Can ye give me a few minutes of privacy with Fiona before ye join us?*

Eleanor smiled at Rob and nodded.

Fiona? Matilda looked into the river and was pulled into Scottish Otherworld. *I've missed ye. Oh gods, I've missed ye child.* Matilda longed to embrace Fiona.

"Where were you all these years? I thought your soul was extinguished when Eleanor died. Thank the goddess you're here. Lord Blackmere almost arrested me for witchcraft, saying I caused the fever in the village."

What? Why is he after ye?

"He's angry with William. Where were you?"

I've been trapped in an amulet, but that's neither here nor there. Matilda stared directly in Fiona's eyes, keeping strong contact. *Ye must listen. Your daughter is alive.*

"Alive?" Fiona covered her mouth. "How? Is she among the fae?"

I had to do it, Fiona. I swapped your daughter for Eleanor's dying child.

"You stole my baby?" Fiona stepped back, absorbing the news. "All this time I thought Beira took my baby to punish me."

Punish ye? Beira rewarded ye for calling out to her in your darkest hour, despite everyone wanting ye to deny the old ways. Your coven sister, Eleanor, has been raising your bairn as her own. She dinnae ken Annaliese—that's her name now—is a changeling.

"That's what the prophecy in the scroll meant? When frost fell, it was my daughter that appeared in Eleanor's arms? I should have realized it. Frost represented Beira, and the shift from William and me to Eleanor meant she'd raise *my* child, now a changeling." Fiona sank to a fallen log. "I've been furious with James, blaming him for my baby's death—"

Why would ye blame James? He has no control over life nor death.

"I dinnae ken…I…oh my God, I'm a horrible mother. All this time Eleanor has been raising my daughter, and you never told her the truth?"

I would have told her years ago if I werena stuck in a damned horseshoe. But I dinnae want to tell her now and risk scaring her off, because the stakes are rising, and time's short. Fiona, we haena much time. Annaliese is in danger.

"What was the prophecy?" She paced. "The sun rose and set five times, and ended with a struggle for the crown. My baby died…became a changeling…almost four years ago. That means—"

Lord Blackmere is coming for her.

"He's coming for all of us. Does he ken my baby is alive?"

I think so. Eleanor is going to need our help to protect herself and Annaliese.

Eleanor slipped into the Otherworld from the river. "Fiona?" She beamed a beautiful smile as they hugged. "Where have you been?"

"Reverend MacDonald invites himself over every fire festival to keep me cut off from the Otherworld. After the baby's death…I've felt so alone these past few years to lose both daughter and coven."

"Your baby died?" Eleanor's face dropped. "Fiona, I'm so sorry. I canna even imagine what you're going through."

Fiona glanced between Matilda and Eleanor. "No, I dinnae suppose you can."

Matilda reached out to both with ghostly hands. *Eleanor, Fiona, listen to me, Elspeth took the form of a raven and found Annaliese. Lord Blackmere will soon learn Annaliese is alive...and a threat to the king. Ostara of Annaliese's fifth year is fast approaching. We need to prepare. But he isna the only threat. Now listen properly for once, Eleanor. Ye might consider Rob attractive, but his heart is encrusted with darkness. Distance yourself.*

"Rob may be rough around the edges, but you're wrong about him. There's kindness underneath."

Dinnae trust him, lass.

"Matilda, he just proposed. I'm free in five months with nothing but unplowed land, and a daughter indentured until twenty-one. Master Crowan can sell her any moment, I've no money coming in, no idea how to farm, and I'm pregnant again. I need a husband. You should be happy for me."

"Do you love him?" Fiona asked.

"I dinnae need love, I need stability."

He isna love, lass. He's chains around ye.

"You dinnae even ken him. And why am I listening to you? You're always bashing Fiona's husband too. You clearly dinnae like men."

I loved my husband for thirty-five years, thank ye very much. I walk with the dead, and even they pity the path you're on, Eleanor. He'll beat ye.

"Have you brought me here to gang up on me? I'm done with this conversation."

Fiona grew agitated. "Stop fighting and think of Annaliese." The other women fell silent. "Can we please focus? You need to practice defensive magic. Agreed?"

"It's been years since I did any spell casting."

"It'll come back to you." Fiona squeezed her shoulder. "It has to."

How's your ricochet spell? Ye were starting to get the hang of it before I was trapped inside the amulet.

"I haena needed to practice it. No one directly threatened me. I dinnae even remember the words."

"*Ath-bhualadh*," Fiona said. "You should commit it to memory."

Rob called from the tangible world. "Eleanor? You keep staring off into the river. Eleanor?"

Fiona grabbed Eleanor's hand. "You dinnae owe your life to the first man who offers a ring."

"This may be the only offer I get. Who else would want me?"

Matilda's heart sank to hear such a thing. *Eleanor, you're smart, and funny, and kind. Anyone would be blessed to have ye for a bride. Why dinnae ye realize it?*

Rob shook her on the other side of the river as a raven circled above.

Eleanor darted glances between her coven sisters and Rob with tight lips. "I better go." Eleanor leapt into the water and disappeared.

Fiona peered through the lapping waves with deepening concern. "What's he pulling from his bullet pouch?"

Matilda squinted. *Please, Beira, let my magic be up to the task.*

Chapter 59

ELEANOR

Virginia Colony—Beltane fire festival

"Eleanor? Honey, you bein' awful quiet, staring into the water. Are you even listening to me?" He was staring at her with knitted eyebrows.

"Sorry, I get lost in thought sometimes. We should head home. It's late."

The forest silhouettes became more pronounced against the moonlit sky, and night sounds became clearer—frogs croaking, the rustle of animals through the underbrush, and the caw of a raven.

"You still ain't answered me. Listen, I known you wanted to find a man in London, but Virginia Colony's got good men, too. I want you to be my wife." He pulled out a ring. "It was my mother's."

She held the ring between her finger and thumb. *Heed Matilda's warning.* "I'm flattered Rob, it's just...sudden. We barely ken each other."

"Why you looking for reasons to leave, when I'm the only man who's promising to stay? It ain't just a ring. It's a bond that cain't be broken. Ever."

She squinted at the inscription. "What are these symbols?"

"Old Betty carved some love drawings in African. I ain't known what they mean. I wanted to impress you, I reckon."

Eleanor tilted her head. The crowing above her grew louder, trying to drown out her thoughts. *Elspeth.* She handed back the ring.

Falaich, she called, doing her best to picture clouds blocking the raven. A torrent of cotton balls fell from the skies, bouncing as they landed. She drew in her arm, wide-eyed.

"What the hell?" Rob gazed into the woods, then went motionless.

A low growl from behind caused hairs on the back of her neck stand on end. A wolf bolted straight at Rob, biting his arm. He bashed it with the butt of his musket, but it was ready to eat him alive. Suddenly the raven flew down, frantically flapping her wings.

Sprinting, Eleanor stumbled through the brush. A gun went off, followed by a howl. She had a single-minded focus to get on the horse. A minute later, Rob mounted behind her and beat the reins.

Galloping back to the open road, the forest blurred around them as they heard another howl at the moon. Breathless, they stopped in a clearing. Dozens of ravens cawed and circled above.

She absorbed the vast beauty of the Virginia wilderness that surrounded them. Beautiful...but hollow somehow. The moon reflected off a too-perfect sky. Raven feathers began to fall around her. The raven flew closer, whispering.

"Why listen to Matilda, love? She knows a workhouse girl like you will never do better than Rob. She don't care about you, only the coven, so she can do her curses."

"No." Eleanor shook her head. "Matilda's right; I can find someone kind."

The raven laughed. "Like your precious Lord Hallewell? Where's he now, love? Abandoned you, just like your father. Knows all the wicked things you done. Stole his wife's earrings, stole a kiss from MacLeod. How do you think your coven sister, Fiona, will like that? He saw you for the worthless piece of rubbish you are."

"I've made mistakes, but—"

"You've got a brand new mistake in your belly right now, right? The master will love that. Trapped another year in servitude. Another child to be sold off. Do you really think Rob will stick around if you make him wait? He'll leave you quick for a better woman." The raven's voice shifted, mimicking Lady Margaret's voice. "And now your deepest fear comes true," she whispered. "Cast out forever, my worthless girl."

Eleanor wanted nothing but the safety of Robs arms around her. *Matilda is wrong—Rob protected me from the wolf, dinnae he? If he ever threatens me, I can use the ricochet spell.*

Rob held out the ring again. It sparkled in the cold light. "Ain't this everything you ever wanted? Old Betty told me you was casting cowrie shells to find a husband. I'm here." He was smiling but his eyes seemed blank. "I ain't no lord or nuthin' but I'm offering you my name, a roof, and a pa for your little girl. I ain't gonna ask again. Will you marry me?"

She pictured Annaliese running at their farmstead with flowers in her hair. A large family around the table. Rob never letting her go.

"Yes."

He slipped the ring on her finger. An unnatural heat came from the metal, making her both lightheaded and euphoric. Rob kissed her, claiming her as his own.

She was spellbound.

Chapter 60

Fiona

The Otherworld—Beltane fire festival

Fiona pulled the hobbling wolf back inside the flames, holding a healing hand over the gunshot wound, but it didn't seem promising. Matilda's soul slipped out just before the wolf passed.

I tried to stop him, Matilda panted. *I've never*, she gasped, *transfigured into anything larger than a cat before.*

"Did Rob give her poison?"

No, Matilda said, catching a lungful. *He held a wedding ring. It must be a hexed token.*

"Do you think Rob proposed on his own? He might not be part of Lord Blackmere's plans at all."

No, Elspeth was there. I saw her raven. Matilda stood, glancing back into the river, now showing nothing but the reflection of an empty forest.

"We need a plan. Can we pull Annaliese into the Otherworld and keep her here?"

Fiona, she's a girl, not a ghost. Ye ken as well as me the veils only open and close during fire festivals. But she has hints of clairvoyance, and has already spoken with spirits. I haena seen power at such an early age. No wonder Lord Blackmere wants her.

"I'm helpless on this side of the earth. My magic is no match for theirs. There's no one here to guide me. I'm imprisoned by the church and the law. Sneaking out tonight was a miracle."

The little girl I raised wouldnae let anyone stop her. Matilda caught Fiona's eye. *It's a prison of your mind. There are no irons over your windows. Ye are Druid. The earth is your teacher.*

Fiona stood taller, remembering herself. "I'll find a way to channel my power."

Practice your conjuring, come to the Otherworld when ye can. I have to return to protect Annaliese. Matilda glided towards the York River then vanished into the Virginia wilderness.

Fiona knelt by the dead wolf, placing her hand over its heart. "Thank you for your sacrifice. I willnae let it go to waste."

"Mam?" David called from the Scottish side of the flames. "Are you well?"

With a rush of wind, Fiona returned to the tangible world, quite flustered.

"We best get back before someone sees the smoke," he said. "I'll take this torch back to relight the hearth."

"I'll join you in a few moments. I feel a storm brewing."

David smiled. "It's good to see the real you again. I'll keep watch." He stomped out the remaining embers and headed toward their manor under a clear sky.

Fiona hung back a few paces, absorbing the moonlight on her face, allowing it to energize her spirits. The forest buzzed with life, and she touched each tree to thank it silently.

As she thought about all she discovered, her daughter being alive, and the dangers to her posed by men and dark magic, lightning charged the air. "I'm not going to let anyone hurt my baby." Thunder clapped as she felt the rage grow inside, releasing a torrent of rain.

"As the Druids before me, teach me the wisdom of nature. Show me how to control and camouflage my powers. Guide me to understand the nature of my enemies, so I can destroy them."

Chapter 61

MATILDA

Virginia Colony

From her place in the shadows, Matilda watched Eleanor's new life bloom—then wither. At first, all seemed well: freedom from servitude, a cabin on ten acres, her son born beneath the pines. But rot spread slowly.

Eleanor only came to the coven once, hiding her wedding ring, embarrassed she invited a hexed totem into her life.

Ye think ye chose him? Aye. Like a lamb chooses the butcher.

Eleanor stopped coming to the Otherworld after that.

Matilda shook her head in frustration. *She's bewitched herself with lies. How do I break a spell she refuses to see?*

Then Eleanor stopped writing in her diary, as if she stopped trusting her own voice. Rob criticized her cooking, her clothes, the way she held the baby. Called her stupid. Lazy. Too proud for a convict. And she believed every word.

And then he hit her.

When Eleanor was busy with baby Sam, Matilda sat beside Annaliese. *We need to uncross your mother, to get this love hex removed. Got your wand?*

"Uh huh."

Go into the darkest corner of the room, away from Rob. Your mam is busy nursing Sam, she willnae notice ye, and she canna see or hear me except on fire festivals.

Annaliese took her rag doll and stick to the corner.

Good job, lass. Draw a straight line top to bottom. One day, when you learn to read and write, you'll have lovely penmanship. Draw a line across it.

Annaliese dragged the pointed stick across the dirt floor, making deep grooves. "So, it makes a cross?"

Aye. Your ma is at a crossroads and dinnae ken her own worth. Now draw a circle in the middle. The circle is your ma. Draw arrows from the circle to each corner. Eleanor needs clarity so she can make a choice—herself and her family instead of Rob's lies.

Rob's eyes narrowed.

Quick now, kiss your poppet. Make it look like a game.

Annaliese kissed her doll, then moved away from the uncrossing sigil, and sat by the hearth to warm herself. "I hope we leave here. He's mean, Nana Matilda."

Aye. Are ye ready to practice flying?

"That ain't real flying."

Deep breath. Go inside yourself. Find the castle in Scotland. Fly to it.

Annaliese closed her eyes. With each breath, she floated inward.

There will come a time when magic willnae be available, but even so, ye can always escape in your mind. He can bruise your skin, but I'll guard your soul. Nana Matilda will always be right here with ye, when ye need to fly.

Chapter 62

Eleanor

Virginia Colony

Eleanor twisted her wedding band. *I should be grateful,* she thought, inhaling the fresh pine scent of her cabin as Sam slept in his cradle. *I own land, have a husband, two children. He's raising my bastard child. None of my joy would be possible if Rob Birch haena stooped to wed me, a lowly convict. Why canna Matilda and Fiona see that? Most men would have run from us. We're the lucky ones,* she thought, twisting her band again.

Annaliese sat on the dirt floor, head down, fingers laced behind her neck, like a war prisoner. Her rag doll lay beside her. "Mama, please?" she whispered.

Eleanor's head ached as a vision of herself in chains flashed in front of her. *Matilda is right. I'm acting like a prisoner, not a mother. What would Fiona do?* Eleanor snuck her a few carrots from the stew pot, and the ring grew tighter around her finger.

Rob swigged corn whiskey. "What're you doin'?"

"She hasna eaten all morning, Rob. She's only four."

"You spoil your girl, then wonder why she a brat. My pa beat me, starved me, I'm fine."

It's my fault. If I were a better mother, he wouldna be so angry with her.

Sam screamed his wee lungs out until she lifted him to her breast.

"Knock, knock," said a deep voice sounding like gravel scratching along an old dirt road. An old man filled the doorway, leaning on his long musket, with a basket hanging from his arm. "Here's a cradle board for the boy. Shawnee say it helps 'em grow straight."

Rob beamed. "Uncle Hal. Ain't expecting you till tomorrow. Eleanor, uh, cover yourself."

She tucked her breast inside her stays, and gave a quick curtsey. Rob put his arm proudly around her shoulders, swaying lightly. "Uh, this my boy, Sam, and my new wife, Eleanor."

"I don't remember hearing nothing about a church wedding until last week." Hal eyeballed the baby.

"I was indentured at Sweetwater. We hid my pregnancy and held off on our church nuptials to prevent Master Crowan from extending my term for another year as punitive damages."

"Punitive damages? You pretty and smart? What you doin' with my fool nephew?"

Hal laughed. Rob didn't.

He propped his musket in the corner, and inspected the tidy cabin. "When'd you learn your letters?" Hal nodded at the diary on the table.

Rob flushed, shoving the diary in the cupboard. "Aw, that's Eleanor's scribbles, but she's too busy for that shit now. Ain't that right?"

She grew quiet, twisting her ring. *He's taking my voice too?*

"All them clothes on the line outside yours?"

She laughed, relieved to switch subjects. "I'm a laundress. Gentry pays quite nicely for clean shirts. Rob drives them into town on the way to Sweetwater."

"You finally got a horse?"

"Well, an ox," admitted Rob, "but it do the trick. Ain't want my wife deliverin' to other men. You known where that leads. She needs to be home."

Her lips smiled on command, as though magically masking the implied rebuke.

"Mm. You let your wife work?" Hal crossed his arms.

"Oh, it's no bother—"

"He ain't talking to you, Eleanor," Rob muttered, gripping the sole chair.

I shouldna have spoken. She cowered into the corner where Annaliese liked to make stick drawings.

"After the baby git older, I'll decide what's best for my family."

Hal peered outside. "You got land now?"

"Yessiree. Ten acres. Haven't plowed much yet."

"How'd you afford that?"

Standing in the shadows, suddenly there was a fire in her belly, a bit of the old Eleanor feistiness she hadn't felt in years. *Why does he claim credit? I earned my land.* "My solicitor, Mr. MacLeod, arranged for my freedom dues."

Rob's lips went taut as the ring pinched her. She winced, and felt the ring yank her away from the dark corner.

Why did I speak? Stay calm. It's a pleasant visit. She swayed with Sam to steady herself. *Rob willnae slap me in front of his uncle. Will he?*

Hal chuckled. "Oh. This her land then. I known you ain't have the cash. Trying to get money from Rob's like trying to get milk from a witch's tit."

A giggle sounded. Uncle Hal spotted Annaliese, huddled on the floor. "Who's that?"

Rob cleared his throat. "You can git up, Red. That's Eleanor's daughter. Paid thirty pounds for her. She ain't raised right, but I'm learning her better."

"You? You gonna learn her?" Hal snorted.

Annaliese ducked behind Eleanor's skirts.

"Aye. Rob stole Daniel Crowan's silver flask to raise the money." She locked stares with Rob who grew visibly angrier by the minute.

"What'd you do to get put on the floor like an attemous?" Hal asked.

"What's a attemous?" Annaliese said.

"Powhatan for dog. How come you git punished like a dog, Red?"

"My name ain't Red. It's Annaliese," she said, haughty as a princess.

"That's why she on the floor. Got her a fresh mouth," Rob said.

Annaliese hugged Eleanor tighter. *Keep the peace. Rob's easily soothed by flattery.* "Beg pardon, Hal—my wean likes to blether. Rob's been quite good to us. He built this cabin all by himself. Isna it grand?" She laid Sam back in his cradle. Annaliese grabbed her hand, pulling her into the darkest corner of the room by her stick drawings.

"Ain't her accent somethin'? Eleanor uses Irish words like wean, and blether, to show off," he said with a cold smile.

Was that a compliment, or a reprimand? Her lips pressed together in a slight grimace as the ring heated. *Sod the ring.* "I'm Scottish."

Hal walked the cabin's perimeter, gathering empty bottles. "It's somethin' all right. Patch them chinks in the walls, or opossums gonna move in. Make sure you mix it good with long grass and dried dung. Cain't be too wet."

"I known it. Just ain't got time yet 'cause Crowan made me head overseer." Rob puffed out his chest. "Got the Sweetwater slaves to outproduce every plantation within ten miles of Williamsburg."

The room grew lighter, as if the sunlight wanted to come through the cabin but was muted by the wax paper covering the sole window. She felt drawn to it, drawn to Rob.

"Well, you got it all figured out, boy. Only took you twenty-seven years, but you done it. You got a pretty little wife, a son, some land, decent job."

Rob stood taller as he wrapped an arm around Eleanor and even tussled Annaliese's hair.

Eleanor tilted her head seeing Rob's heart for an instant. A flash of a little boy wanting desperately to matter. In this moment he had everything he ever wanted, and she was genuinely happy for him. *Dinnae we share the same dream after all? To be worthy of love?*

Then the raven nesting in their chimney began to crow. One by one, Uncle Hal lined up a dozen empty liquor bottles on the table. The sun passed behind a cloud, darkening the cabin.

"I known you got demons, Rob, but don't piss it all away like your pa."

Rob's face flushed to the roots of his hair as the men faced off for a long silence. In an outburst, Rob's arm swept the table, sending all the bottles crashing on the floor, glass shattering. "Why cain't you be happy for me once, old man? I got a wife—"

"You got a whore, and her little bastard you paid too much for."

"I got land—"

"No, she got land. I give it a year before you drink yourself into a stupor and lose everything, and I have to bail you out of debtor's prison again."

"Git out my house, old man."

Hal left, casting a long shadow behind him. The sky grew overcast and gray as the raven cawed from the chimney.

Rob slammed the door, kicking shards against the wall. "Why you got to tell him this your land? We married now. This is my land."

Her thoughts twisted in confusion as the ring cut off her circulation. *I shouldna have boasted, but I only stated facts. Am I causing the fights?* The ring pinched tight enough to make her finger throb. "I'm sorry, I—"

"You supposed to love me. Why you got to embarrass me, too?"

He slapped her hard enough to force her to stumble to the ground. Her hand brushed a faint symbol—a circle, a cross, arrows.

A fury roared to life. Rising, she shoved Rob hard. "Dinnae touch me or my daughter again. Get out. This is my land!"

Caw, caw, caw. The raven's calls were deafening. She tried to pull off the ring, but it clamped down tighter, burning.

"You want me to leave?" He grabbed Annaliese. "Fine. I'm taking your girl."

All the air left her lungs. "You said she was my wedding gift."

"You acting like you ain't want to be married. She indentured to me till twenty-one. You ain't gonna play me for no fool, Eleanor. The boy's mine, the girl's mine, the land's mine by law."

"You only married me for the land? You dinnae love me, you own me."

He snorted. "Shit, you just figuring that out now? You reckon you smart 'cause you can read? I'm the smart one."

The raven swooped inside.

"Your dark lord broke his deal," Rob shouted. "She has to love me."

"You got everything you asked for, love. You got your wife, your land, your son. You showed your uncle you ain't need him none. Respect don't last forever, and I never guaranteed love."

"You can understand the crow too?" Eleanor asked. "How is she here? It's not a fire festival."

"I'm a witch, Wanderwit, not a ghost like Matilda. I don't need a fire festival to talk."

Eleanor held up her bruised ring finger. "Is this your work? An amplifier curse wasna enough?"

Click clack. Rob pointed his musket at the raven. "You tell your dark lord if he don't give me what he promised, I'm gonna find someone who'll pay a king's ransom for the fortune-telling brat. That girl's got real magic in her."

The raven flapped wildly where the uncrossing symbol had been drawn. "You need to sever Matilda's ties to Annaliese, or she'll help both escape," she hissed.

"I'm getting sick of all your little charms you like to use on me, Elspeth. *Ath-bhualadh!*" But as she raised her hand the ring scorched her skin, making the spell miss its mark. Eleanor grabbed a broom in the corner and swung, knocking the raven to the ground.

The raven blinked, disoriented, and scrambled up the chimney, shedding feathers from her wounds as Eleanor took a final swing. She swept the feathers into the flames, sending blue sparks up the chimney. "Sod your blood magic."

Rob shouted after the raven. "Tell your dark lord I ain't playin'."

Chapter 63

Elspeth—Witch of Pye

London

Lord Blackmere entered the hovel. "What's going on with my changeling? I tracked down the plantation owner only to discover Eleanor is free and the changeling has been sold."

Elspeth swallowed, pouring a cup of tea to calm herself. "I've handled it, my lord. They're both bound to a violent man named Rob Birch. He'll make sure they won't escape. I've got a hexed ring on Eleanor to keep her pliant. They're in a cabin in the wildness, and she's pregnant with her third child now. We've got a bigger problem: Matilda. She can still talk with the changeling—Annaliese. Matilda's teaching her how to make uncrossing sigils to reduce the power of the hexed ring, and gods knows what else."

"How can a child so young have such skills? It took me three years before I was able do basic spells."

Arrogant nimwit. "She comes from a long line of the witchborn, my lord, plus Matilda has decades of experience, and is teaching her. I can only guess what additional powers she picked up travelling through the land of the fae. Is it any wonder she's powerful already?"

"We need to get rid of Matilda."

"I've got ideas." She fidgeted with her teacup.

He studied her for a moment. "Why are you avoiding my gaze?"

"There's another problem."

He drummed his fingers on the table. "Yes?"

"Rob wants to use the girl's magic for his own purposes. If you don't give him what he wants—more money, and Eleanor's love—he threatened to sell the girl."

"That bumpkin gravely overplayed his hand if he believes he can make demands of me. We need him and the entire coven out of the picture. I killed Matilda once, I can do it again. I just need to be able to enter the Otherworld. Why can't I pierce the veil? I've looked into flames and still waters for hours on end every fire festival, but nothing happens."

"You've got power, but you ain't a full wizard yet, m'lord, and I can't form no new covens to bring you in proper. Beira don't hand out access to the Otherworld lightly. And thanks to your Reformation lads, the local witches are either hangin' from trees or scattered to the wind."

She braced to hear him yell, but he smiled smugly instead.

"Oh, I'll find a way to get invited in. It's not that hard to outsmart a witch, or a king for that matter. I'll destroy my enemies in the process."

As his lithe fingers steepled beneath his chin, Elspeth sensed she might be among the destroyed if she didn't act.

Chapter 64

WILLIAM MACLEOD

London

William MacLeod shook off the rain from his coat as he joined Lord Blackmere's private table at Jonathan's Coffee House. *It has to work.*

"You're missing the most important person. Where is Charles?"

"He sends his regards. He feared your Reformation of Manners henchmen were waiting to arrest him on the spot. He did leave me with a bargaining chip, though." He opened his satchel.

"Ah, the list of sodomites." Blackmere folded his newspaper and dropped it on the table with a grin. "I've been so busy hunting witches and getting married, I nearly forgot."

"Congratulations on your nuptials, my lord. *The Tatler* mentioned your fortuitous match."

The earl smirked. "Indeed. My wedding to the king's cousin should tamp all the wicked little rumors you started. Honestly, I should have married years ago. Care for some crow with your coffee? Or is a coffee house too effeminate for the likes of William MacLeod? They do serve tarts here, after all."

Let Supple Dick enjoy his victory. It's good to let people believe they're in control.

Blackmere held up two fingers. A waiter presented a tray of two coffees and two spiced apple tarts, each with a dollop of cream. MacLeod left his dessert untouched.

"I'm really quite disappointed. I took you as a man of your word. I might have found a way to persuade the king to forget young Charles' daring prison escape. But now?" Supple Dick dug his fork into the layers of buttery crust, fruit, and cream of his tart and ate it, thoroughly pleased with himself. "His Majesty will be most happy to learn my progress on the Scottish witch investigation, given Fiona's links both to a condemned witch and to dear Colonel Wilkes. I heard she was reading his palm before he disappeared. I'm excited to call in witnesses." Lord Blackmere licked his lips. "That's the difference between us. You persuade potential witnesses to stay mute, while I break people until they confess loudly. I'll be sure to hang you, your wife, and Lord Hallewell close together so you can watch each other die."

Casually, MacLeod pulled a rolled-up canvas from his satchel, opened the watercolor painting, and lay it on the table just out of the corner of Blackmere's eye.

"I have an update on my client, Charles Jamison. He used to frequent the Holborn area of London. I'm sure you're familiar with the location through your work."

"I am." Lord Blackmere glanced at the watercolor and his smile froze while he pretended not to notice it.

"How many men were arrested at Mother Clap's? Before Charles became the exclusive lover of Stephen Rose, the painter you let the mob rip to shreds, Charles was friendly with quite a few artists. Many gifted him paintings, including portraits secretly sketched of the masked men at the molly houses.

Blackmere rocked in his chair, slightly shifting away from the painting. Beads of sweat formed on his forehead.

"You probably thought you got rid of all the evidence, burning down Stephen Rose's warehouse, not realizing Charles dinnae keep his private collection in there. See?"

MacLeod lifted the painting of Lord Blackmere in pink petticoats and a flowered bonnet, holding a viper mask in his hand.

Lord Blackmere's eyes bulged when he realized it was a painting of him. His body coiled tighter, posture rigid and poised to strike. MacLeod snatched the painting before he grabbed it.

"What slander is this?" he demanded, eyes darting around the coffee house for potential threats. "Are you trying to frame me? It's a lie."

"Dinnae fash, I'm in the business of solving problems, not making new ones. I'll keep this hidden...for now." He returned it to his satchel. "But I have more. Loads more. You must have realized your mask slipped and someone painted you at Mother Clap's but dinnae ken who. That's why your Reformation of Manners people keep targeting artists, right?"

"I don't—this is preposterous—"

"Poor young Charles dinnae realize the identity or stature of the nobleman's portrait he owned, until your face was plastered all over *The Tatler,* and spread to other newspapers in other cities. Your portrait sat unnoticed with his other belongings at my law office this whole time. I wonder what the king would think? Or *The Tatler*? Or any number of your victim's families when they discover you killed their loved ones for the exact 'crimes' you committed yourself?"

Lord Blackmere's entire demeanor changed. He withdrew, curling inward, seeming to calculate escape routes.

MacLeod leaned in. "Look, I dinnae give a rat's arse if you like wearing petticoats or enjoy a good buggering, you damned hypocrite, but your new wife and her royal cousin very well might."

Lord Blackmere's voice lowered to a hiss. "What do you want?"

"If you fucking threaten my wife or Lord Hallewell over Wilkes again, I swear to Christ I'll reveal the hypocritical scoundrel you are to the world, and let your self-righteous mob cut off your cock before killing you. I have dozens of paintings ready to be sent if your Reformation of Manners henchmen try to arrest any of us."

Supple Dick's shoulders caved in as he gave a hypnotic nod.

MacLeod finished his coffee, then stood. "Enjoy your tart."

Chapter 65

Lord Blackmere

London

Lord Blackmere wandered Covent Garden, frowning at all the woman of loose morals calling out to drunken gentlemen, like sirens leading them to drown into debauchery.

"Looking for a good time, sir?" called a middle-aged woman, sporting an old wig and white face-paint thick enough to frost a cake.

"Keep your pox-ridden cunny away from me," he grunted to the chuckles of a collection of youths standing outside a brothel. He sized up the men waiting to gain access, locking stares with a quiet young man with chestnut hair. The door swung open to muted chatter punctuated by laughter. All the youths stampeded inside, save the one.

"Waiting your turn?"

The young man shrugged. "Waiting for my mates to finish." He leaned against the wall, letting his strong arms hang loose at his sides, legs slightly wider than hip distance apart. "Watching people walk."

Lord Blackmere leaned against the brick wall beside him, noting his pulse accelerate. Dangerously close, he slid his foot next to the young man's, tapping his toe. "Interesting street. It runs both ways."

The youth stared straight ahead. "So, it does." His soft, chilled fingers lightly brushed Blackmere's hand for an instant. "I need to piss." He wandered into the darkened alley beside the brothel.

Blood rushed so thunderously through his ears, he could barely concentrate.

I shouldn't do this.

Hungrily he took in the youth's physique—his slight but healthy frame, the rounded lift of his buttocks, the strong-muscled calves so clearly defined below his breeches.

Drunken sailors walked by with women of the night on their arm. *Come on, come on, move away.* When the street cleared, he slipped down the alley, hearing his heeled shoes echo with each careful step.

Don't do this. This is wrong. You don't need to do this.

Facing the brick wall, the young man held his hard cock in one hand. A window from the brothel gave off some candlelight, and the alley stank of chamber pot.

Glancing up, the youth curled his thick lips into a smile. Lord Blackmere checked over his shoulder again before grabbing this forbidden kiss, feeling his age seep away. "I'm yours."

The young man's smile grew more sinister, understanding the role he was to play. "Turn around then."

Blackmere's heart raced as his erection grew. The young man swung aside the earl's smoky charcoal coat, and tugged down his breeches exposing his skin to the cool spring air. Contradicting emotions flooded Blackmere's brain, overwhelming him.

The young man put one hand on Lord Blackmere's back and the other on his hip, expertly controlling his movements, forcing him to submit to each thrust. Heat spread across Blackmere's cold body as every sensation intensified. Hot tears rolled down his cheeks as his spine arched in a sudden jolt before releasing into the dirty gutter, and he panted hard to catch his breath.

"Are you crying?" The young man stroked Lord Blackmere's too-smooth face. "I haven't hurt you, have I?"

"No," he said, with a lump in his throat, pulling up his breeches. "I'm just terribly sorry."

"For what?"

Pulling a dagger from his waistcoat, the earl struck without thinking, allowing instinct to take over. He stabbed the youth's kidneys multiple times until the young man collapsed, bleeding out in a dirty puddle.

Across the alley, Elspeth emerged, horse in tow, and nodded. They had to go to the Hackney Marshes to make the potion in secret. He needed the ability to navigate the Otherworld, if he ever hoped to eliminate Matilda's coven and kidnap the girl.

Lord Blackmere kissed the dead youth's lips, then cut out his heart. The realm would hardly miss a sodomite, and blood magic required sacrifice.

Imagine what I'd profit with the girl as my pawn, draining her blood in small doses for decades?

Chapter 66

ELEANOR

Virginia Colony—Samhain fire festival

Rob had made a tidy profit the entire harvest season, hiring Eleanor and Annaliese out to the Crowans to help in the fields. At the end of each night, Eleanor collected Sam as Old Betty chanted. "Thomas. Harriet."

What about her other two children?

And so it went through harvest.

Finally, the end of October had come, a month filled with twelve-hour days. Eleanor and Annaliese pulled the last dried tobacco leaf from the barn ceiling, crammed it into the barrel, and waited for Rob to let them out.

Annaliese tugged on Eleanor's skirt. "Nana Matilda says its Samhain tonight. If we look in a flame she'll find us," she whispered.

"He barred the door, we'll use the window. There's always a way. Let's get out of here." Eleanor twisted the ring to stop the bruise from spreading as they rolled the barrel beneath the high window. Eleanor lifted Annaliese on her shoulders, and the girl quickly climbed outside. Eleanor dragged herself up, praying her ever-growing belly wouldn't get stuck. It was a leap down, but freedom was worth facing the fear. "We must be cats with nine lives," she whispered to Annaliese with a wink.

Three waiting ships with full masts docked behind the Big House. Rob cracked his whip as the enslaved rolled the tobacco barrels up the gangplanks to take them off to Europe.

Eleanor stared at the tall masts and raised sails. *Should I do as my da did and make Annaliese a stowaway?* Anything would be better than being bound to Rob. Eleanor grabbed Annaliese's hand, striding in the opposite direction. "I'll never abandon you. We have to get Sam."

In the twilight, they spied Master Crowan and his wife share a kiss on their wraparound porch decorated with jack-o'-lanterns as the river sparkled behind them. A raven circled then landed on the hanging tree.

Eleanor's heart pounded at the thought of a confrontation with Old Betty, but she was out back in the garden chanting, "Harriet. Harriet. Harriet."

Eleanor grabbed Sam, who was crawling on the floor of the cabin, took hold of Annaliese's hand, and fled. Her mind raced. *Steal a horse? If we get caught, I'll be hanged. Go further down the river and use the Crowan's fishing boat? No, too many other ships today, they'd catch us, and send us back to Rob. The fields were barren, we'd be too easy to spot. Go to the forest.*

The sun set, casting an eerie orange light as they ran with all their might. The forest grew closer with each step. Eleanor stumbled over the uneven dirt, clinging to Sam as she fell. He let out a wail.

"Shh, Sammy." Annaliese kissed his bruised forehead.

Eleanor scrambled to her feet, as the blood from her skinned knee wet her petticoat. She picked up Sam again and ran limping.

"Ma, Elspeth is coming," Annaliese called. "Do your," she panted, "hiding charm," she gasped.

Caw. Caw. The raven's wings spread wide leaving the Big House, and cut the distance between them by half.

Eleanor stopped, raised her hand, and tried to spell cast, but the ring around her finger burned, forcing her to lower her hand.

Annaliese raised her own small hand to the sky. *Falaich.* A thin fog blocked Elspeth.

"Matilda says get to the river. If we look into the water, she can pull us into the Otherworld."

A cramp stabbed at Eleanor's side, either from the hard run, or from the new baby growing inside. Bile rose in her throat. They dashed into the forest.

Caw.

"The river's down there," Annaliese gasped.

The slapping of small waves on the riverbank grew louder, and the briny scent intensified. Annaliese's sweaty hand gripped Eleanor's like a vice as the water was mere yards away.

Click-clack. Rob pointed his musket at them from his horse. "Afraid I cain't let you two near bonfires or reflective water till sunrise. I'd hate to lose you to the Otherworld."

The ricochet spell was their last hope. The ring burned so hot she thought it might sever her finger. Eleanor raised her arm anyway. As she started to say, *Ath-bhualadh*, the raven broke through, shifting the trajectory. It hit a nearby tree branch, rattling the horse, but not enough to throw Rob. The ring glowed orange as it heated, bringing her to her knees. She spit on it, trying to cool the metal.

"Please stop hurting her, Pa," Annaliese begged.

"I ain't hurting her none, the ring is," he said with a self-satisfied grin. "You chose to be bound to me, Eleanor, till death do us part. Ain't that what you wanted? I told you I ain't never gonna leave you."

Virginia Colony—Christmas

Winter gnawed at the colony like a starving wolf. No field work meant no pay. The forests were picked clean. Even the animals hid, leaving behind the hollow trees and frozen mud. What little money Eleanor scraped together laundering was wasted by Rob on cards and beer before they could buy food.

Rob drove them to Sweetwater, their wagon creaking. The Crowans were hosting dozens of guests for Christmas, and Rob hired her and Annaliese out to help scrub the Big House's linens and clothes. Inside the drafty washing house, Eleanor wrung dirty water from a shirt with aching hands while Rob pissed into a chamber pot in the corner.

"Dinnae dump it. I need it to make lye."

"Mind your own damned business," he muttered hitching up his breeches, leaving with the pot. Eleanor winced at the sharp stink he left behind. She and Annaliese crouched over the pounding stick, battling filth from sleeves.

"Happy fifth birthday, sweet girl." Eleanor pressed a kiss to Annaliese's forehead.

Three months till Ostara. *If I can keep her alive, the prophecy says she'll grow strong enough to topple a king. I dinnae even care about the throne, I just want my daughter safe.*

"Mama," Annaliese whispered, peeking out the window. "He's headed to The Quarter."

Eleanor's heart drummed low and hard. If he got drunk, they might have a few hours of breathing room.

If not...

The night thickened around them. Candles glimmered in every window of the Big House, sparkling on the holly and mistletoe decorating the porch columns. Drunken carols drifted from inside while someone played the harpsichord. For a heartbeat, Eleanor thought of Lord Hallewell's music, of another time lost forever.

"Mama, he's coming," Annaliese whispered, folding a linen fast.

Rob came inside. "Follow me."

"Should I get Sam?"

"He fine. Move."

He shepherded them off the plantation. Their skirts brushed dead cornstalks as the half-moon cast shadows from the dark sky. Behind them, laughter spilled from the Big House. Ahead, the forest loomed large. Despite the newest bairn kicking in Eleanor's belly, she carried Annaliese, who was exhausted. If only Rob hadn't kept them trapped in the dark cabin on the winter solstice a few nights earlier, Matilda and Fiona might have helped them escape into the Otherworld.

The sting of the cold caught in her throat as white mist escaped her lips, but Annaliese stayed asleep in Eleanor's arms.

"Tonight, we gonna get some answers about just how magic your girl is." Rob sauntered down the path as a murder of ravens flew into the dark skies. The moonlight shimmered off the barrel of his musket as they trekked over the dead ground.

A puff of smoke billowed from a makeshift shack beneath a sycamore tree at the crossroads beyond the plantation. Eleanor froze at the sight of a dead chicken surrounded by a collection of bones, feathers, and iron nails, recognizing them at once as an offering, but to which gods?

Old Betty had transformed from a broken woman muttering the names of her sold-off children, into a wise priestess wearing a necklace of cowrie shells, and a red scarf wrapped around her silver braided hair. She sained the air with burning roots. A drum rested by the fire.

Eleanor's hands kept shaking. "What are we doing here?"

"You brought what I told you?" Old Betty asked Rob. Sparks flew as she rotated a jug in the flames. A faint clink of metal tapped from within.

"Yep." Rob dropped a fistful of coins, and handed over his bullet pouch.

Annaliese rubbed her eyes awake, walking around the shack with interest.

"Is this why you needed the piss?" Eleanor glared between the two. "You're making a potion to keep me trapped?" Her pulse raced. *Matilda?* she shouted in her mind as she stared into the flame. *Fiona, are you there?*

No coven sisters. No answer. No time.

"Why would you help him and not us?" she asked Betty.

Rob answered instead. "'Cause I found her lost children. Ain't that right?"

"The raven did," Betty said. "Three of them dead, and Harriet lost her mind after what they did to her in Georgia. She'd be better off dead."

"But they ain't lost no more, is they?" He grinned.

Old Betty's eyes rose towards Eleanor. "Your child ain't never been stolen. I do what I gotta do." Betty sat on a tree stump. "Come here, baby, we gone call the orisha." Betty pulled Annaliese onto her lap.

"No," Eleanor cried, but Rob's hand clamped over her mouth.

"What's orisha?" Annaliese asked, not understanding the potential danger.

"Ancestral spirits to guide Matilda here."

Smoke coiled from the fire as she opened Rob's pouch. The black cat's hair burned first. Then Annaliese's fingernail clippings.

Eleanor thrashed, but Rob held tight.

Old Betty's fingers blurred, tapping a drum as she chanted softly, until Annaliese's head lolled. Sparks rained down on the ground. The jug roasted, hissing. Soon, her daughter's hands hung limp, and Betty lowered the drum. "Old Betty wants to talk with your friend, Matilda. She here now?"

"Uh huh." Annaliese grew unnaturally still, eyes open, but unseeing.

Matilda's Scottish crone voice came through Annaliese's mouth. *Where am I?*

Eleanor's eyes grew wide, as she shouted in her mind. *Matilda? Can you hear me?*

Matilda didn't answer—but the raven flew in.

"Spirit, why you inside this child?" Betty asked.

Annaliese's flushed skin grew sweaty. *To protect her. Dinnae trust the whisperings of the raven, Betty. She'll trick ye, as she did me in my life, and Rob right now.*

"The only way to protect her is if you leave," Elspeth said to Matilda. Old Betty pulled a horseshoe from her pocket.

Fear fluttered inside her chest, knowing what she was about to do could cost her dearly. Eleanor bit Rob's hand anyway. "Matilda, run, it's a trap," Eleanor shouted, knocking the horseshoe into the flames.

Annaliese's eyes rolled back, and she shook her head back and forth, still in a trance, but without Matilda inside anymore.

"Why would you help a bad spirit?"

"She isna evil, she's a healer, a protector, my coven sister, and I willnae betray her."

Rob grabbed Eleanor by the collar, craned back his fist and punched.

Dazed, Eleanor opened her eyes finding herself knocked full length to the dirt. The bairn in her womb tumbled. Eleanor's head turned sideways, squinting through blurry vision at Rob's mud-caked boot hovering over her face.

One kick away from oblivion.

"Do it," hissed the raven as her sigil glowed above her heart.

"You gonna fuss and fight till daylight?" Old Betty stood between them, holding Annaliese in her arms. "I ain't gonna save my child, then watch you beat your own baby to death."

"Wait a minute." He trained his musket on the raven. "Why do you want me to kill Eleanor all of a sudden? I think the bastard's power comes from Matilda and Eleanor's coven. You trying to take away the girl's power source, and think I'm too stupid to figure what you doin'? You think I ain't gonna fight keep my girl's magic?"

Dùisg, the raven hissed, knocking Rob back three feet with his gun on the other side of the room. Laid flat on his back, Rob was completely stupefied.

Eleanor lifted her head an inch, bracing for what might happen next.

"I don't know what to believe," Betty said.

"I own you now, Betty. If you ever want to help your daughter escape Georgia, you'll finish what I commanded."

Old Betty looked at Eleanor and they both realized the impossible situation. "I'm sorry," Betty said, then waved smoky mugwort leaves over Annaliese three times before tossing them into the fire. She put Annaliese on the ground beside Eleanor then poured a bucket of water over the fire, extinguishing the flames.

Did she extinguish Matilda too? Eleanor squinted one eye open to watch.

"What have you come up with?" the raven asked Betty.

Old Betty lifted the jug. "A witch's bottle. It needs to be buried upside down in front of their threshold. Ain't no one, not even Matilda, gone be able hex anyone on their property after that. Annaliese cain't do spells neither. And Eleanor's got her ring. But Rob ain't gone to want to give up magic power. You heard him."

"He don't have a say in the matter, love." The raven hopped to the ground. Rob was curled in a ball moaning, holding his head. "He's dazed right now, not understanding our conversation. Go to their cabin, Betty, and bury the witch's bottle. Your daughter will come back to Sweetwater by the year's end."

Old Betty left with the jug.

Elspeth flew beside Rob, now beginning to stir. "My Lord Blackmere didn't take kindly to your threat, love. And now it's time for your punishment. *Mu choinneamh*."

Mu choinneamh—opposite? What's that supposed to mean? Eleanor's entire body throbbed, and she struggled to stay still.

The raven hopped near Eleanor, and she braced for death.

"Don't worry love, I won't kill you. I've read your fortune. You'll die in childbirth soon enough. Between the ring and witch bottle, you're powerless." Elspeth flew to Rob, walking on his chest. "An oaf like you doesn't deserve to be aware of the powerful magic inside Annaliese. *Na dìochuimhnich*." The raven pecked his head as he yelped, then flew off.

Na dìochuimhnich—forget. Eleanor inched forward, through the lingering smoke, pressing up to her hands and knees. Blood dripped out the gash beneath her eye. She fought the rising vomit. *I'm going to die in childbirth? Before or after Ostara? What about my children?*

Annaliese woke from her trance, and glanced around. "Nana Matilda? Where did she go? Ma? Why you on the floor?"

Rob rubbed his head as he sat. "Where are we? Was you trying to run off again?"

She gripped Annaliese, as she sat back on her knees, hugging her tightly.

How can I protect her at all?

Chapter 67

William MacLeod

Scotland

William MacLeod took the letter from Lady Margaret into his study, noting the black seal rather than her usual red. *What mess do I need to fix now?*

Mr. MacLeod,

Without meaning to sound like a novelist, I must alert you to an appallingly calamitous situation requiring your immediate departure to London. Specifically, what do you know about the witch of Pye? Given your wife's background, I'm confident you will handle this matter with the utmost discretion, which can only be discussed in person.

Regards,

Lady Margaret Hallewell

Ah, shite. He crumbled the letter and tossed it into the fire. *Another fucking witch.*

London—ten days later

"How bad is it?"

The curtains were drawn, stacks of past due notices piled on top of the desk, and Lady Margaret hid in the shadows of Lord Hallewell's study.

She lowered her hood. Even in the darkened room MacLeod gasped at the cluster of warts on her forehead, chin, and tip of her nose, and the crusty blister on the corner of her lip.

"You're sure it isna the French disease?"

Her nostrils flared. "I'm telling you, the witch of Pye tried to extort me, then hexed me."

"Have you seen a physician?"

"He gave me a salve which did nothing. Powder and rouge only make it worse. I can't leave the house looking like this. People might whisper I caught a peasant disease."

Her lips bared in a snarl, and he noticed her rotting teeth. It took everything in his power to not glimpse at her and wince. Or smirk.

"What is the plan, Mr. MacLeod?"

"Dinnae fash yourself. I'll fix this."

Lord Hallewell stumbled in with his coat misbuttoned and wig sitting askew. "You two are planning a party? What's all this?" He picked up a creditor's notice. "Oh."

"Oh, indeed," she said rising, covering her face with the hood. "To think, I might have been divorced by now if Eleanor hadn't left you."

Lord Hallewell stood gaping as Lady Margaret stormed off. The stench of port on him knocked MacLeod back. It wasn't even noon and he could barely walk. "I'm fine. I just need some tea, and some—"

"Sleep it off, my lord." MacLeod helped him stagger to a guest bedroom, and pulled off his boots, then pulled the covers over him and turned to leave. It took every ounce of restraint to not punch the eejit.

George grabbed his arm with a pained expression. "I searched everywhere for her for years, William." His eyes were reddened. "I followed any lead promising a positive outcome. I prayed. I offered a reward, I..."

A pain spread in the back of his throat. "Maybe Eleanor dinnae want to be found."

"She's vanished. Like a ghost." His chest hitched as he openly cried. "What did I do wrong? I would have given up literally everything for her."

MacLeod's posture went rigid as he went on the offensive. "That's what you're doing now you bloody fool, drinking away your fortune, too drunk to raise your bairns."

Lord Hallewell sat, wearing a shocked, pained expression. "You never helped me look for her. And I helped you with everything."

"Goddamned it, George, man up. Eleanor's made a cuckold of you. She's with some actor in Paris by now. Find a new whore and move on." MacLeod stepped back, remembering his place. "I'll be back when you're sober, my lord."

Slamming the door behind him he almost toppled Lady Margaret, eavesdropping in the hall. She offered a begrudging nod of approval.

"What was the hex the witch put on you? Dinnae lie."

Lady Margaret blushed crimson as her favorite gown. "She said, 'May the poison in thy soul rise to meet thy face, till the world sees you as I do.'"

MacLeod ducked under the doorframe of the witch of Pye's cottage and immediately felt uneasy. He didn't always carry *Justice* on his person, but a claymore seemed prudent when entering a witch's dwelling.

The old woman sat in her rocking chair, with a calm grin. "I've been waiting for you. Care for a fortune?"

He had better things to do than have tea with a crazy old woman. "Lady Margaret tells me you've been extorting her. Her face is now covered in warts and she's terrified they'll never leave. I'm not sure what you slipped in her tea, but I'm told you require money to disappear. Let's settle terms and we can both be on our way, madam."

"How official you sound. Exactly like Admiral Goring."

He squinted at her. *How would she ken my grandsire's name? Ack, she's must have heard from Lady Margaret.* He pulled a bag of coins and a contract from his satchel. "Here's forty pounds and an agreement to keep your silence about any dealings. Plus, you need to do a counter charm to remove the hex."

"The price was one hundred pounds. Forty for the charm she never paid for, and sixty to get rid of the hex."

"You've made quite the enemy of Lady Margaret. Dinnae tempt her to send the Reformation of Manners men on you. Is that what you want?"

She acted remarkably unconcerned by the threat. A raven watched him from its perch in the rafters. "Only one person can give me what I want."

"What do you want?"

"Forgiveness for a betrayal. You have some knowledge of that, I'd wager. How is your friend, Lord Hallewell? Still believing Eleanor ran off with an actor?"

Caw.

Every aspect of this meeting made him morally uneasy. The room seemed to shrink, as his cravat constricted his neck. "I'll give you your price old woman. Sign the paper and be gone. I'll need your real name. I canna imagine 'the witch of Pye' would hold up in court." He counted out the cash on the table.

"Elspeth Rogers." She took the quill and signed. As she clawed at the money, he slammed his hand over hers, pinning it in place.

"And the charm to remove Lady Margaret's hex, Elspeth?"

Her wrinkled smile went to her eyes. "It will take at least three days time..." she winced, clinging her heart which seemed to pulse beneath her shawl. She sank to the ground.

MacLeod rushed to her side. "Are you well? Are you having a heart attack?"

She shook her head, panting. "Nothing as simple as that."

He helped her onto a stool then noticed a carved ivory comb on the mantle. He grabbed it. "Where did you get this?"

"From your mother, of course."

His fingers itched to unsheathe *Justice* and slash her top to tail. "My mother never came to London," he said slowly.

"No, but I've been to Kirkhaven, before your mother ran off with your father." The witch rubbed some wound above her heart. "Thank the goddess Matilda made that protective charm for you mother, right love?"

Lord Blackmere had sentenced Matilda to death, and now I find Elspeth knew Matilda too? Are they cohorts? "Why would you have this?"

"She paid me to interpret her dream. A lot of good it did me." She rolled up her woolen skirt, exposing her crushed leg.

"What happened?"

"The witch hunter happened. Some people are noble, others are brave." She let her skirts fall. "I'm neither."

He examined the comb. "What was my mother's dream?"

"That you'd marry a witch. I knew you'd marry Fiona before either of you were born. And that your family line would grow powerful."

He circled her. If she threatened his wife he'd charge, ready to gore her through.

She grunted, squeezing her hand over her heart then scowled at the ceiling. "Fine, I won't stall him anymore."

He glanced around the room. "Who are you talking to?"

"Beira, bitch goddess that she is." Elspeth pulled her hand away, grabbed a wax doll, and removed pins from its face. "Lady Margaret's warts will be gone in a week, but I'm leaving her teeth rotted to mark her. The only way they'll come clean is if a barber-surgeon plucks them out and replaces them with new ones. She needs something to remember me by."

"Done." He moved to leave.

"Won't you stay and chat?" Her lips made a white line. It was clear she was in pain. "Fiona was a sweet child. Such untapped powers at her fingertips." She began to writhe in her chair. Beneath the shawl he swore he saw the outline of the embers of a fire on her chest. "Matilda never wanted to teach her about her full potential." She clung to her heart, as a moan escaped her.

"What have you got under your shawl, witch?" He let the comb fall, then ripped back her shawl. Her worn shirt was soaked with blood. Her old hands grabbed his wrists but were no match as he tore open her shirt enough to expose an extraordinary branding he'd never seen before. A snake eating itself was glowing orange and an eye in the middle of three Celtic loops cried blood.

He unleashed his claymore, gripping it in both hands.

She raised her arms above her face. "I protected Fiona from burning. If only she would forgive me."

A sinking feeling came over MacLeod. *Why did Fiona never mention Elspeth?* "Protected her from whom?"

"This is a ruse, Mr. MacLeod."

"A ruse? What are you talking about?"

"I put a hex on Lady Margaret because my master, Lord Blackmere, wants me to trap you here. He's hunting down your wife."

He pointed the blade at her neck. "Why should I believe you?"

"Matilda might hate me, but I've always protected Fiona from him. He knows you were the one who told *The Tatler* about his unnatural lust for men. He's going to kill her the night of Ostara to hurt you."

"That's in less than a week." He lowered his claymore and narrowed his eyes. She appeared to be telling the truth.

"Leave now. I foresee the wind at your back."

He stormed out of the hovel, calculating the quickest way to get home.

Elspeth called as he left. "If Fiona lives, she has me to thank, MacLeod. Tell her that. I've earned her forgiveness."

Chapter 68

Eleanor

Virginia Colony—Ides of March

Five more days to Ostara, then I can finally sleep. But as soon as Rob came home, danger hissed in the air. Holding the mantle and swaying, he stabbed the logs with a fire poker, making sparks fly up the wattle and daub chimney as Annaliese sat in her shift on the hearth playing with her rag doll. Wind whistled eerily through the chinks in the cabin logs.

"Did you stop at the tavern?" Eleanor asked softly, wrapping her worn plaid shawl over her thin shoulders. *If only Fiona or Matilda were here. How can I protect Annaliese on my own and without magic?* She scratched her belly, big with the new baby.

Flexing his fingers on the poker handle, he spit tobacco juice into the flames before setting the poker against the wall.

Annaliese whispered with her doll and giggled.

A shock of greasy hair fell over his once handsome face. "What'd yer doll say?"

Annaliese covered her mouth and looked to Eleanor, who shook her head 'no.' Swallowing hard, she said, "Nuthin', Pa."

Rob's crooked smile faded. "Nuthin', huh? Don't lie to me, Red." His nostrils flared.

Eleanor moved closer. *Keep things light.* "The wean was just playing, Rob."

"Ain't no one talking to you, Eleanor," he snapped. "You think I'm gonna deal with slave bullshit all day, then come home to sass from your five-year-old?" Rolling up his sleeves, his fingers moved to his buckle.

Annaliese inched back from his sweaty face, and lowered her eyes to be respectful, but he snatched her doll, anyway. "No!"

"Whatdyer doll say?" His bloodshot eyes narrowed, and they knew what he'd say next. "Little bastard."

Annaliese spat out, "She called you a witch's tit."

Rob hurled her baby doll into the fire. Annaliese reached for it, but he grabbed her wrist and held it against the chimney, thrusting the poker in the blaze with his other hand.

"Rob, no!"

Annaliese twisted in terror when she understood what was coming. He pressed the red-tipped iron into the back of her hand, making her writhe and shriek as it hissed and sizzled her skin. "Mama!"

Eleanor pulled his arm, and his elbow bumped hard below her eye. The poker clanked on the floor. "Why do you torture her?"

She picked up Annaliese, backing into the corner. Her eye was already bruised. Annaliese buried her face in Eleanor's hair, sobbing onto her neck. *Is he the one to kill us?*

He yanked her from Eleanor's arms. "You hush your mouth, girl," Rob growled.

Annaliese gulped back her tears, terrified of what he'd do next, and wiped her runny nose on her arm. He grabbed her shaking hand and smiled at the branding. Squeezing her eyes shut, she twisted from him, as if wishing him away.

Rob pressed his lips to her ear. "Now everyone will know how bad you is."

Later, Rob fell asleep with a whiskey bottle beside him. Eleanor opened the door, stuck. Terrified to run, and get caught. Terrified to stay, and get beat. She wrapped herself in Fiona's shawl—the one given to her the first night they met—and stood on the threshold. Sinking to her knees, she prayed. "*Eisd rium a Dhia.* Beira, Queen of Winter, first *Cailleach*, Goddess, Destroyer, Protector. Please protect my daughter. Please let her survive Ostara. I cannae do this alone. I need my coven. Your will be done."

It began to snow. Through the flurries, a white wolf appeared. "Are you Beira's wolf?"

She crossed the threshold. The wolf licked her palm, breaking off the hexed ring, then dug with both paws until she unearthed the buried witch bottle. Eleanor dashed it against the wood pile, shattering it to pieces as the wolf returned to the wilderness.

Eleanor returned, rubbing her skin where the ring once pinched, and eyed Annaliese asleep with her bandaged hand. *We're not going to run away again just to get caught. I've got a better plan. I'm going to rescue you, or die trying.* Tiptoeing past Rob, she pulled her diary from its hiding spot, ripped out a page, and scratched a letter to Lord Hallewell. *Even without magic, I've got power at my fingertips.*

Chapter 69

Fiona

Scotland—The Ides of March

Fiona jolted awake in the early darkness with echoes of *Mama!* shrieking in her ears. A monster on the other side of earth was hurting her bairn. *Would Annaliese survive it?*

Moonlight streamed through the window. Ostara was days away, but she had to do something. Quietly going downstairs into the kitchen, she took a pinch of salt from a bag hidden behind the bowls, and heard a cough.

James was working by candlelight in William's study to prepare for a court case. *Shite.* She forgot he was home. He blew out the candle and headed upstairs as she hid in the shadows holding her breath.

"Mam?" He lingered for a moment then went into his bedchamber and closed the door.

She slipped inside the study, smelling the tallow from the extinguished candle, opened the grandfather clock and pulled the scroll from the chime.

Please dinnae hear my footsteps, she prayed, pulling on her boots and wrapping a shawl over her shoulders. She snuck out the back door, grabbing her satchel of herbs, and headed straight for the privacy of the castle ruins.

Cold dew made the well-worn stone path slippery. Only her sense of purpose kept her balanced. She descended the pitted steps, passing the water gate, then the tower on the upper bailey before reaching the cliff overlooking the Firth of Clyde. Closing her eyes, she set an intention for clarity.

A pinch of salt was hardly enough protection. Spinning, she tossed what she had and acknowledged the ancient gods. *If I can scry and focus on the scroll, maybe I can capture Elise's vision and discover how it ends. Please gods, let Annaliese survive.* As she lit the mugwort leaves a dark shadow behind the ruins rattled, startling her.

"James?"

"Funny, I was about to come knock at your door," said Lord Blackmere from his horse.

"*Bolt dealanaich*," she called, doing her best to summon lightning, striking beside the stallion. It reared, hooves pawing at the sky as it threw Lord Blackmere to the ground, gaining her enough time to flee.

Gasping, she strained every muscle to get away while he sprinted toward her.

"*Ceòthach*," she panted with a raised hand, blanketing the land with a thick fog. Sprinting with no clear destination, she kept looking back, terrified he might catch up.

"*Aotrom*," he hissed, causing a ball of light to shine on her.

Leaping over crumbled rocks and chunks of weeds, Fiona's blood rushed in her ears as the unmistakable rattle encroached from all directions. Her entire body felt constricted as something coiled around her legs, her waist, her breasts, her neck. Before she knew it she was magically bound and writhing.

He unfurled the enchanted scroll in front of the ball of light, revealing the full prophecy. "Oh Fiona, aren't you a naughty little witch, hiding this from me?"

Chapter 70

ELEANOR

Virginia—Ostara fire festival

Rob was missing for days. He never told Eleanor his whereabouts, leaving her uncertain when to attempt escape. Today was the spring equinox—Ostara. The final day to survive.

One of her customers pulled up his wagon in front of her cabin. Annaliese rushed to help carry his basket of laundry, and he noticed her bandaged hand. "What happened to you?" He kissed it.

Her cheeks became bright red. "I was bad," she muttered, slipping inside their cabin to sort the clothes on the table. Before Eleanor could correct her, her customer interrupted.

"You know Rob was arrested, right?"

"For what?"

"Not for what he should have been," he said scanning Eleanor's black eye. "Cheating at games, at Black Swan Tavern, and causing a drunken ruckus at all hours. Twenty-five lashes, and locked in the pillory until noon."

Noon? She checked the sky. *Now's my chance to send the letter. He'll be stuck an hour at least.*

"What's a pillory?" Annaliese called from inside.

"Stop eavesdropping, and mind your brother."

Sam was walking now, and getting into everything. Annaliese grabbed Sam by his strings from the back of his shirt to keep him safe. The man paid Eleanor, then left.

"Put your brother in the wagon, we only have until noon."

Eleanor shoved the letter she wrote to Lord Hallewell into her pocket, hitched their ox, then hit the reins and headed into town. The sun filtered through the pine trees making the ice-trimmed banks of the York River glisten as the newest bairn tumbled inside her belly.

"What's that coppery smell, Mama?"

Eleanor squinted at a washer woman in the river, and she could swear the woman was washing her blood-soaked shift and a baby's birth gown. Annaliese's shift was crumpled on the ground beside it. *Did the washer woman steal our things?* Her mind shifted to the tales Da used to tell. *'If you find the washer woman washing your shirt, you're going to die soon.'*

She shook off the memory. *Those aren't our clothes. My mind is playing tricks.*

More wagons joined the muddy road. Eleanor stopped on Nicholson Street, tying their ox to a post, then checked the sun. "We're running out of time."

She waddled with Sam on her hip to an alley lined with shops. The queue inside the brick building stretched long. Eleanor surveyed the clock, tapping the letter against her big belly.

Two women gossiped. "This is the second time that drunk got caught cheating at cards. There's his wife. Indentured convict," the lady in the blue cloak said to the skinny one. "The whole family's a disgrace. Look at her black eye."

Eleanor's cheeks blushed, but she kept staring forward.

"Next." The man with glasses behind the counter took Eleanor's letter. "Only one, madam? You usually write three letters in case they get lost at sea." He raised his bushy caterpillar eyebrows. He said it like he thought she was stupid.

"God must safekeep this one, then."

The clock struck noon.

Something across the street drew Annaliese's eye. "Look!" she cried, dashing into the bustling road—barely missing the wheels of a rushing carriage.

"Careful," Eleanor called, finally caught up. She took shallow breaths as Sam squirrelled in her arms. Annaliese pressed her hands against the window to view the dolls. "Them babies is so pretty!"

"Maybe your father will get you one."

"Pa ain't never gonna buy me nuthin."

Slaves stared at her as they walked past, like they knew something. Eleanor walked across the street with her children, past Englishmen in powdered wigs, lobster-backed soldiers marching on the green, and Powhatans trading furs at the market. The jeering from the courthouse drew them closer. She balanced Sam on her hip.

"That's a pillory," Eleanor whispered touching her finger to Annaliese's lips to be quiet. Annaliese peeked through the legs of the heckling crowd.

Rob's back was a ruin—strips of skin hung loose where the whip had peeled him open, human meat glistening in the cold light. Blood slid down his sides and darkened his breeches.The bailiff slammed the nail through Rob's ear into the wood with a brutal thunk. Rob grunted but couldn't free himself. He was trapped on display for all to mock.

A pack of boys hurled rotting tomatoes with savage glee. As it smashed open on his face and splattered, the stench of rotted fruit, sweat, and Rob's fear soured the air.

Annaliese's fingers tugged Eleanor's skirt. "Why'd they nail his ear?"

"To mark him as untrustworthy."

A raven landed on his head to the laughter of the onlookers. Eleanor then understood Elspeth's curse from the night with Old Betty. *Mu choinneamh*—opposite. Rob got the opposite of respect, a most public humiliation. The raven pecked his head, as if to punctuate the memory charm would forever clear every magical memory about Annaliese from his thick skull.

Eleanor doubled over as a sharp cramp stabbed her side. A rush of water fell from between her legs. "Oh no. The baby's coming early. We have to get home. I canna die yet and leave you."

Chapter 71

FIONA

Scotland—Ostara fire festival

Where am I? Fiona woke in pitch blackness completely disoriented. *How long has it been?* She tried to rise, only to discover herself bound. Her involuntary gasp was met with the stinging piercing of the spike on her tongue, followed by the metallic tang of blood in her mouth. With no way to swallow, it trickled down her chin, to the apparent delight of her tormentor, whose soft laugh echoed against the stone walls.

A single candle was lit in the back of the room.

Clack. Clack. Clack. Clack. The disembodied sound of Lord Blackmere's footsteps echoed on the stone floor.

And then he touched her.

"Stroking your cheeks makes me understand why your husband keeps you hidden in Scotland. Mark me, your husband will know I came to visit," he said in a deep baritone.

It suddenly dawned on her she was in the same dungeon where Matilda had been tortured, her own family's crumbling castle. Panic seized her. James and David must have gone to the Glasgow law office by now. William was in London.

"No one is coming for you, although I do appreciate the fog you made still clinging to the air. I never could figure out that spell."

Fiona panted, eyeing the room for any hint of escape as Blackmere slowly dragged his index finger down her cheek.

She tried to turn from his breath, hot against her ear, but the cold metal of the scold's bridle glued her face in place, and the shackles cut deep into her wrists and ankles, allowing only her eyes to defy him. *He wants me to cower and cry. Sod that. I'm a witch.*

He adjusted his velvet cuffs. "There's a certain satisfaction watching the spike pierce through the tongue of troublesome women, like your Aunt Matilda. Long after the lock came unbolted from her face, it kept the other women quiet too. But you, Fiona, are getting too mouthy with your spells. We need to silence that."

A drip of sweat rolled down her forehead, following the line of the metal down her nose. In the corner, a raven cawed by the lone burning candle. Visibly uncomfortable, Elspeth ruffled her feathers as the sigil steamed until she transfigured back into human form.

Staring into the flame, Fiona scrambled to remember an unlocking spell. *Eisd rium a Dhia–*

His body blocked the candlelight. "Uh, uh, uh. We wouldn't want you to use magic, now, would we? Your aunt thought she was special with her little Druid tricks, but I broke her, just like I did with Elspeth, and every other barren hag with their roaming cats and incessant opinions."

Fiona tried to protest his lies—Matilda never confessed—but the spike prevented it. Angry tears fell unbidden down her cheeks.

"And you, thinking you were so clever, threatening me, reminding me of Matilda's curse to castrate me, as though I'd forget. Ever since then, my member only grows hard with other men. I can't even pretend to be interested in women, like before," he snarled. Even in the dim light, his eyes glistened as he restrained his tears. "I'll fucking find a way to kill every goddamned witch I find, even the ghosts."

Clenching her fists, she struggled against the rusted metal scraping against her skin. A flicker of light caught her attention. She squinted and spied a small bed with a child's dress and a doll, guarded by Elspeth.

The fire festival. He's going to kidnap Annaliese and keep her here.

The cage around Fiona's face seemed even more claustrophobic as she tried to control her rasping gulps.

"I can tell by your reaction you've figured out my plan. You probably thought yourselves clever, but actually you're rather stupid making me mistakenly believe both daughters died, not merely one. Matilda's little trick of switching babies was a blessing in disguise. What a waste it would have been had I killed a girl as powerful as that. Now that it's finally Ostara, it's time for you to call everyone home."

With bowed head she feigned submission, letting her weight sag against the chains. Slowly, carefully, she tested the give in the old iron links. Matilda was the last person held in the dungeon, nearly thirty years ago. Surely, she'd find a weak point worn thin. As Fiona lifted her head, the weight of the bracks caused a searing pain in her jaw that made her see black spots.

He attached a rope leash to the bottom of the scold's bridle, wrapping it around his hand several times to keep a firm grip. "When I unlock you, you will obey, or I swear to Christ I'll tug the rope and sever your tongue in two."

She nodded, experiencing nausea as she heard the clank of the key unbolting her ankles and wrists. He led her outside into the courtyard, same as he would any lowly beast. She squinted at the full moon; its brightness in sharp contrast to the dungeon she'd been locked inside the past few days.

The spring air caused goosebumps to appear on her flesh.

Fiona's eyes opened wide, and she nearly collapsed at the sight of what awaited. The yard held a stake on the same spot where Matilda had burned.

"*Aotrom*," he chanted, lighting the bonfire a few yards in front of the stake. Flames rose twenty feet into the night air. She tried to flee, but a tug of the bridle brought her to heel.

"Tie her," he commanded Elspeth.

This canna be happening.

The old woman tried to avoid Fiona's intense, cold stare. "I tried to stop him, love," Elspeth whispered.

Fiona's vision blurred as she fended off her betrayed tears. The same hands that once taught her magic—how to mix herbs, and cast spells, and move the wind—were now binding her to a stake to be burned alive. *Why was I so stupid to think she'd betray Matilda but not me?*

He walked to a blackthorn tree growing between broken rocks and cut off a shillelagh. "I've been studying up on natural magic. Time to banish the ghost."

The rope rubbed her exposed arms raw, and she shivered staring at her manor in the hills above, wishing she was able scream for help.

"Don't worry, you'll be warm soon enough," said Lord Blackmere gliding beside her. "Look into the bonfire flames, Fiona. Call your coven."

Shutting her eyes, she refused to lead them into a trap.

"Fiona MacLeod," called Reverend MacDonald coming up the long road. "Are you lighting a bonfire?" He stopped in his tracks. "My Lord Blackmere?"

Lord Blackmere recoiled, momentarily startled. "This doesn't concern you, Reverend. She's a witch."

Fiona tried to scream, but the spike pinched her tongue.

"There's been no arrest. No trial at the Kirk. You canna execute people without following the law, have you gone mad?" He narrowed his gaze. "Elspeth Rogers? Why are you here?"

"Walk away, Reverend," Blackmere hissed.

Reverend MacDonald darted his gaze between them. In a flash, he reached for his iron cross, but Lord Blackmere raised his hand. "*Bidh falbh.*"

The reverend was thrown across the yard and knocked unconscious against the crumbling stone wall. He had landed upside down, and the iron from his pockets fell into the weeds next to his cross.

Lord Blackmere twisted Fiona's face to the flames, and they were swept into the Otherworld, with Elspeth transfiguring into raven form, flying above them.

Chapter 72

WILLIAM MACLEOD

Scotland—Ostara fire festival

William MacLeod raced against borrowed time on horseback from London to Kirkhaven. Ten days later he galloped through the forest and finally made it to the private road to his home where the mist disoriented him.

"Da," called James riding from the opposite direction with David, who held a lantern. Their faces were lined with worry. "Thank God you're back. Mam's been missing for days. The fog has been thicker than soup ever since she left."

"Has she been arrested? Did Reverend MacDonald come with the Kirk?"

"Reverend MacDonald's been searching for her too. We've no idea where she is," David said.

"Lord Blackmere is using your mother to get to me, because I'll expose his hypocrisy. It's time for my own *Justice*," he said nodding to the claymore strapped to his back. "I'm going to carve the bastard limb to limb when I find him."

The scent of burning wood filled the air as the fog cleared. Down the hill, past the forest, a bonfire burned by the castle ruins overlooking the loch.

"There!"

Chapter 73

Matilda

The Otherworld—Ostara fire festival

The veils were finally thin. With the witch bottle gone, Matilda came through the cabin hearth, shocked to discover Eleanor with sweaty hair matted against her forehead, and her children beside her as she lay dying from a miscarriage.

Eleanor's soul began to separate from her body and rise to the ceiling. "What happens when Rob comes back? She isna safe here with him. We have to take Annaliese into the Otherworld."

It's even more dangerous if Lord Blackmere claims her. She has to stay on this side. Cover the bairns with iron so no one can hex them. Gather as many herbs as ye can.

Eleanor forced her soul to stay in her body, and left the bed on wobbly legs to find two iron nails from the jar, placing them in each child's sleeping fist. Grabbing a satchel, she shoved every healing herb she had inside, then leaned against the bed to catch her breath. She pulled Rob's hunting knife from the mantle above the fireplace, and put it in the bag, too.

What's burning? Matilda crossed into the hearth fire. *Eleanor, come quick.*

Eleanor slung the satchel over her shoulder, entering the flames.

The Otherworld was cloaked in disorienting smoke, but a burning odor guided them to Kirkhaven where Matilda's memories, past and present, folded into one.

The crowd from Matilda's death day stood shouting, "burn witch!" Patches of mud shown through a thin layer of snow covering the terrain.

Matilda shoved past the torch-bearing men from her memories, only for the illusion to dissolve, revealing the sickening truth: present-day Fiona was the one tied to the stake.

Fiona, she cried, racing forward.

Wildly shaking her head 'no' Fiona gasped as Lord Blackmere slid from his hiding spot in the tall grasses, shedding his cloak like a second skin.

"Silly women," he hissed. "Did you think you could outwit a witch hunter?" His body twisted into a monstrous viper, twenty feet long, scales glistening black and gold.

Stoirm-thàirneanaich. A surge of energy coursed through Matilda's ghostly body, summoning a thunderclap as a spring blizzard rose around them. The gales knocked him back, pinning him against the ruins of a stone wall.

Eleanor raced to Fiona, unlocked the scold's bridle and removed the spike. She took rowan from her satchel and pressed it inside Fiona's mouth chanting, *Slànaich a theanga*—heal her tongue—then sliced her free from the ropes with Rob's hunting knife. Fiona rubbed her jaw.

He struck back without warning. Just a blur of serpentine speed passing through Matilda like smoke and knocking Eleanor hard into the rocky ruins with his tail. She held her womb, screaming as a labor pang hit. Blood soaked through her shift as her skin grew ashen.

Matilda hurled a curse at the partially collapsed tower beside them. *Sàthadh deigh-chnàimh.* Icicles sharp as daggers fell from the windows above, stabbing his winding tail as blood splayed across the snowy ground.

His tail coiled around the shillelagh of blackthorn and then threw it at Matilda, banishing her powers momentarily. "*Congelo*," Lord Blackmere hissed, and Matilda's ghostly form was frozen in the air, unable to move. Unable to help. Panic and defeat etched across her face.

He hissed, glancing through the bonfire to Annaliese sleeping on the other side.

Fiona tried to spell cast, but the rowan was still absorbing the blood on her tongue. No sound could come, though she tried.

"No," shouted Eleanor. "Not my girl. Not any of us."

Lord Blackmere slithered against the wind, and lunged straight for Annaliese as snow swirled in every direction. "You'll all die a torturous death, once I claim her. *Tormentum.*" Blackmere's searing bolt roared through the air. And just as his fangs stretched wide—

Ath-bhualadh, shouted Eleanor, rising from the ground with shaking fingers splayed. The ricochet spell flared, raw and unstable. At the last instant it ricocheted like lightening off glass, rebounding into his heart, thrusting him back, locking him in agony. A strangled hiss raked the air, punctuated by gurgling spasms as his body thrashed, knots tightening into unnatural shapes. He transfigured from monstrous serpent to mere mortal, crying out in pain from the ground. The foul, sulfurous stench of his ruptured innards rose as his pooling blood grew dark and tarry. His glassy eyes were rimmed with red as he blinked rapidly, unable to escape.

The icy hold on Matilda melted, and she drifted down, jaw agape staring at Eleanor. *Well, I'll be damned. Ye outwitted the witch hunter.*

Eleanor swayed, drained, but still standing.

Fiona dropped the rowan to the ground, her tongue now fully healed. "You did it," she called, hugging Eleanor, her golden eyes gleaming. The coven, shaken but alive, circled close in relieved victory.

On the tangible earth, William and their sons arrived to see Reverend MacDonald unconscious, and Lord Blackmere's human form zigzagging in front of the stake in agony. David cut Fiona free, and James unlocked the bridle from her face, and carried her unconscious body near the bonfire.

MacLeod thrust *Justice* through Lord Blackmere's heart, pinning him to the stake. "Elspeth told me about your plot to kill my wife. Guess the witches had the last laugh," MacLeod said as Blackmere sliced his own fingers trying to pull the claymore from his chest. "I'm laughing too, you wee bastard," he whispered, twisting the blade.

Back in the Otherworld, Matilda nodded her approval. "You've wed yourself a bull-headed man, lass, thick-skulled, iron-strong, and ready to gore the world itself if it threatened you or the bairns."

Fiona laughed in agreement, then blinked at Elspeth. "You werena lying to me at the stake...you really did try to save my life?"

"Mercy," Blackmere squealed, voice cracking, drawing back their attention.

And now, said Matilda, *we deal with him.*

Matilda, Fiona and Eleanor formed a circle around him, raising their hands as Elspeth watched outside their coven.

"*Bolt dealanaich*," Fiona shouted.

He twisted, and squirmed as lightning coursed through his veins, lifting him from the ground and pinning him to the stake meant for them.

How about a wee bit of divine justice? Matilda said.

"As described in your favorite book—*Malleus Maleficarum*," Fiona said. "Shall we cut off your manhood and keep it in a nest?"

"No, no!"

Matilda, Fiona and Eleanor inched closer, chanting.

Eisd rium a Dhia. Beira, Queen of Winter wild,
Hear thy daughters—witch and child,
Blood to blood, and breath to breath,
We give him over to rightful death.
No Kirk, no crown, no prayer can save,
He burns beneath the curse he gave.

An explosion of blue fire shot up into the sky. The ghosts of everyone Blackmere murdered stood in judgement over him. The admiral's young sons, the painter Stephen Rose, the young man from the alley, and dozens of women wrongly killed for witchcraft. The wind whipped upward with the echo of every single victim he'd condemned.

The air howled.

The scroll with the prophecy ignited, burning to ash.

As Lord Blackmere recoiled before his victims, Beira's wolf leapt from the flames, castrating him with one bite.

On the tangible earth, a spark from the bonfire lit the kindling beneath the stake, quickly setting it ablaze. MacLeod left Blackmere to burn, and joined James and David kneeling beside Fiona's unconscious body. "Oh God. Is she dead?" He cradled her in his arms as the night sky faded in the horizon. "Fiona?"

In the Otherworld, the flames beneath the stake caught hold, and Lord Blackmere writhed in the same sick dance he forced on so many others.

Enjoy your last dance with the Devil, Matilda shouted.

Caw. A scream tore the sky. The raven swooped in fast and sharp. Its talons struck, blinding him. Thrashing in further agony, blood wept from ruined sockets.

Matilda connected eyes with Elspeth. The sigil still showed through her feathers but no longer steamed.

Blinded, bested, and betrayed, Lord Blackmere let out one final screech of rage. As his body charred black on both sides of the veil, his soul separated and was pulled under, vanishing into the utterly horrific eternal inferno of Hell.

Eleanor, Fiona, and Matilda's ghostly form embraced, panting.

"Annaliese is safe now, aye?" Eleanor shivered with chills.

Fiona laughed. "That viper's been cooked body and soul."

Annaliese survived Ostara of her fifth year.

Eleanor had a gleam in her eyes. She stood taller, more confident. "And one day our girl will topple a king."

Matilda gasped at the blood soaking Eleanor's shift. Her form kept flickering between flesh and spirit. Eleanor looked down, touching the glistening blood, watching her own hands begin to become transparent in front of her. "We're running out of time."

Fiona and Matilda touched Eleanor's belly, and were transported back to Virginia, on the other side of the flames in the cabin's hearth. Elspeth's raven flew in with them uninvited. Eleanor's body lay feverish in the bed between her children in the tangible world.

"Is that—?" Fiona's words hitched in her throat.

"Your daughter?" Eleanor said. "You both taught me herbs and natural magic, but Annaliese...She's a changeling, isna she?"

Matilda nodded. *You've raised a good girl.*

Annaliese woke. "Nana Matilda?" she squealed, leaving the nail behind, jumping from the bed, and running toward the fire. She stopped short, staring at Eleanor inside the flames, then spun to see Eleanor's body also in the bed. "Mama? How come you in two places?"

Eleanor held out her hand. "Come step through the flames, sweet girl."

Annaliese hopped through the fire. Raising her head she took in the vast grayness of the Otherworld, then glanced between the women. Eleanor placed her hands on Annaliese's shoulders and smiled at Fiona. "Meet your daughter."

Fiona's shaking hand covered her parted lips, as she laid eyes on her daughter for the first time since birth. She knelt to Annaliese's eye level, studying every feature of her face to etch it into her memory. "It's lovely to meet you, Annaliese."

The girl hid behind Eleanor's legs, suddenly bashful.

"You're a lucky girl." Eleanor twisted a red curl around her finger. "Do you ken why? Because you have two mothers who love you."

"You're my magic ma?" Annaliese took a tentative step towards Fiona. "You gonna teach me to fly for real?"

"Someday." Fiona pulled Annaliese tight for a hug, smelling the top of her hair. "I've missed you. I've missed you so much," she whispered.

"I can teach you to fly better than anyone, love," said Elspeth hopping on Annaliese's arm, like she used to when Fiona was a child.

Matilda narrowed her eyes.

Fiona took a tentative step towards her. "And you, Elspeth...What was it William said? You tried saved my life?"

Elspeth bowed her head, wings dragging. "I told your husband about Blackmere's plans. Sent him rushing home from London, with the wind at his back. Ask him. Without me, that devil would still be hunting you."

Fiona's voice cracked. "But you tied me to the stake."

"I knew your man was coming," Elspeth said softly. "I always tried to protect you, in my own way, love. Didn't I peck out Blackmere's eyes? How long am I to be cursed? Can't you spare me a drop of mercy?"

Holding her elbow while the opposite hand made a fist against her mouth, Fiona weighed everything. "You protected us, after betraying us."

Elspeth avoided her gaze. "I never wanted you burned. Did my best to protect you so Blackmere would leave you be."

Fiona's lips pressed together in a tight grimace as a light was cast over her, only it lacked any warmth. She remembered—years ago—Elspeth teaching her to make healing balm while Matilda was too busy getting drunk on ale to notice or care. A strange buzzing filled her ears. She remembered being scared she might be arrested too, but Elspeth had whispered, 'They'll never find out you were in the coven.' She wanted desperately to believe in her. "You dinnae deserve forgiveness," Fiona whispered. "But maybe that's the point." The stark light grew nearly blinding.

Matilda and Eleanor raised their arms. *Fiona, no—*

"Beira teaches mercy, dinnae she?" She stepped closer, heart pounding. "I suppose... I forgive you."

A purple cloud whipped up around Elspeth as she laughed. The cloud shifted into fingers plucking off the sigil from her skin and making it vanish into thin air as Fiona watched horrified.

Wings now completely healed, she swooped over the wise women, and pecked Annaliese's hand where Rob had burned her. Annaliese shrieked in pain.

Ye backstabbing witch! Matilda called.

Both Fiona and Eleanor put their bodies over the girl to protect her as Matilda threw a hex, but it missed.

"Till we meet again, sister," Elspeth hissed to Matilda. "Next time as a sorceress," she called beating her strong wings out of the Otherworld, through the bonfire into Scotland, past William trying to wake Fiona on the tangible side.

"A sorceress?" Eleanor looked sicker by each minute.

Matilda grunted in frustration. *She might have helped us kill Lord Blackmere, but only because it served her purposes.*

Fiona covered her mouth with both hands. "What have I done?"

"The raven's mean." Annaliese rubbed her poor hand. Fiona kissed it, but it was marked beyond healing.

Dinnae blame yourself, Fiona. Elspeth's a cunning one. She tricked me more than once. If she wants to be a sorceress, no doubt she'll use blood magic. Matilda knelt beside Annaliese. *Ye must go back inside with your brother now, child. Do ye remember how to fly?*

"Uh-huh. Go inside my mind. No one can hurt me there."

Fiona's heart seemed to break at her words. She gave Annaliese a final hug and kissed her cheek. "I promise I'll find a way to get you home."

Annaliese gave a small wave and hopped through the flames. "You coming, Ma?"

"In a minute." Eleanor leaned on Fiona, panting. "What do we do?"

A bright light glowed in the Otherworld horizon, and dark storms with lightning flashes formed at the opposite end. Eleanor's weakening hold on life flickered in and out like a candle on its last breath.

"Will Elspeth," she panted, "try to kill Annaliese?"

Why kill Annaliese when she can have an unending supply of her magical blood to drink? Surely, she'll try to kidnap her to gain power. We need to seal the veil and make an enchanted wall around Annaliese.

"Canna Fiona protect her?" she panted.

Elspeth will always have links to Fiona as a coven sister. If Fiona comes here, Elspeth will be able to find her...and Annaliese, Matilda said.

"But how can we leave her with Rob?" Fiona said. "He might not have magic, but he'll harm her."

Rob is the lesser of two evils. Elspeth's lust for control is boundless. It must be done.

Nodding, Eleanor hugged Fiona and whispered, "I know you'll rescue her someday." Her flesh flickered, and the blood stain on her shift grew wet on the other side of the flames in her deathbed. "I need to confess... back in London," she panted. "I'm not proud of what I did..."

"Whatever it is, it dinnae matter right now. Go with your children these final moments."

The dark cloud moved closer, as more lightning bolts spiraled through.

Fiona ye have to go too. The sun will soon rise at home, and we need to seal you off.

A guttural moan came from Eleanor's body on the other side of the flame.

"How can I watch myself die and...just leave them?" she said to Matilda. "It's too soon. I want," she gasped, "my children." Eleanor's soul, through sheer willpower, went back inside her body.

Na dìochuimhnich Matilda whispered memory spells over Annaliese. *It's best if she forgets her magical powers. Beira will open the veil when Annaliese is strong enough, and the time is right. Raise the wall, Fiona.*

Fiona exhaled, a pained expression on her face. She shook out her arms and hands before kneeling, and placing them on the ground as Matilda recited an incantation.

Eisd rium a Dhia.
By Beira's breath, the veil be sewn
With threads of frost, and ice-bound stone.
To call her home when time is safe.

In the goddess we place our faith.

Misty plumes curled into the freezing air as Fiona exhaled. Frost flowers bloomed across the earth, then vanished as the ground cracked, and a gush of blue liquid rose to the sky, then froze, blocking all view into the cabin.

Fiona knocked on the ice sheet, touching its cold wetness, then put her ear close, but heard nothing. A lonely wind chilled her as snowflakes landed on her eyelashes. "It smells like snow and juniper," she said in a daze.

Her knee buckled and everything that happened came to her in a rush of bottled up emotions. It felt like her daughter died again. For the first time in years, Fiona wept.

Let it out, love. Let it all out, Matilda whispered softly.

After every last tear drained from her soul, Fiona gazed up at Matilda with those golden-amber eyes, as she did as a child seeking comfort.

I ken it's hard, especially when ye just held her, but ye did the right thing.

Fiona stared at her feet and nodded. The mist shifted as they walked the uneven path, and a dim light shown from the earth side of the veil revealing the burning stake in Scotland.

On the other side of the bonfire, William, James and David shook Fiona's unconscious body as the sun loomed on the horizon. Lord Blackmere burned to ash behind them as Reverend MacDonald crawled through the weeds, praying aloud as he searched for his iron cross.

Were any of the men aware of magic taking place? Do we need to wipe their memories too?

"I dinnae think so. They probably assume Lord Blackmere kidnapped me to get to William. He exposed Lord Blackmere's hypocrisy in *The Tatler.*" Fiona looked at her husband, sighing. "We have so many secrets and lies between us weighing down our marriage. How would I even begin to tell him our daughter is alive—and a changeling?"

There's something cleansing about telling the truth.

"Confess I'm still doing magic? He'd never understand."

Fiona, do you wish to become a bitter old woman as I was?

"I'm not bitter."

Ye are, only ye show it differently. I unleash my hurt as anger against the world. Eleanor directs the hurt at herself, believing she's worthless. But ye, Fiona, when ye get hurt, ye pretend nothing happened, and that isna good either. Ye have to face the wickedness Colonel Wilkes thrust upon ye, the rape, his killing, Broderick, and why magic is important, not just in general, but why it's important for ye, Fiona—

"I have."

Ye can pretend everything is fine in your marriage, but I've seen visions of the future and trust me, there's going to be a reckoning. I hope ye and William will be up to the challenge. It's clear ye love each other, and I want to see ye happy again, and with Annaliese home.

Fiona stared at the castle ruins as the last charred remains of Lord Blackmere blew to the wind, past William and her sons beside her human form, as Reverend MacDonald prayed nearby.

"I'm not ready for any of those conversations. And I dinnae ken how to keep our daughter secret," she confessed. "I'll need a memory charm too. I canna risk slipping during a fire festival to see her, and putting her in danger."

Aye. But the charm willnae last. Your visions will return when it's time to guide her home.

As Fiona's soul left the Otherworld and reentered her body, she regained consciousness, hugging her husband and sons tight.

Matilda crossed into the tangible world, and raised her hand over Fiona. *Na dìochuimhnich.*

Reverend MacDonald was on his knees, completely vulnerable. No cross. No iron. And unmistakably able to see her ghostly form for the first time.

I always predicted this would happen one day, Reverend, she said mind-to-mind. *Beira is granting me my chance at revenge.*

He raised his arm over his head, bracing for the curse she had waited decades to cast. They locked gazes, and Matilda held her head high. *I am a healer. I was innocent.*

He nodded.

Matilda walked away from revenge, leaving the reverend untouched, and her burning stake in the past. A burden lifted from her soul. She returned to the Otherworld, where Eleanor would need her.

Chapter 74

ELEANOR

Virginia Colony

Although Eleanor's soul had crawled inside her body, she sensed herself slipping. Her dry mouth tasted the salt of her own tears.

The washer woman she'd seen by the river knocked at the door holding a basket. Annaliese slipped out of bed to meet her. The washer woman kept Eleanor's and the miscarried baby's gown, but silently returned Annaliese's unwashed clothes and left.

Eleanor lay back exhausted on the bed, panting. *Annaliese survived the prophecy. That's all that matters.*

The scent of damp fire logs and fresh earth came on the breeze as the snow outside melted. Beira's season had ended. Annaliese plucked something from the ground.

"Look Ma." Annaliese climbed under the covers, handing Eleanor a wild crocus, the first flower of spring. "It smells flowery."

All around, Eleanor inhaled the sweet aromas, knowing it would be her last season on earth. She hugged her children tight.

Annaliese put her head on Eleanor's chest. "It's making a rattle noise like Sam's toy."

"Protect your brother," she whispered, hugging Annaliese close. "Mama loves you," she gasped. Her lips were dry, and cracked, and the room began to fade. "George will come."

Annaliese lifted her head, confused at the name. Eleanor tried to focus on her face. Blue eyes. Red curls. Nose dotted with freckles.

It's time, Eleanor, Matilda called from the other side of a thick icy wall.

Eleanor floated above her body with her children, now asleep, snuggled beneath her arms.

A white light appeared in the distance, pulling her away from her children, halfway through the icy veil.

It's all right to let go, lass. Dying is like being reborn.

Eleanor's eyes darted around the room, clinging to its walls. "I'm not ready to die." An overwhelming taste of metal filled her mouth as she tried to lick her lips. "It's too soon, Matilda. I have too many things to tell her. I never taught her to read. I never told her how much I loved her father, or that he wanted her. I need more time. I want to see both of them grow up."

The children left her bed. Rob walked into the cabin where her dead body lay. "No!" he shouted, kneeling by the bed, the small piece of him still able to love now devastated.

The light drew closer. The ice melted barely enough to let her through.

"No." She ran from the light—she ran through her life.

Past Rob making a fist as she cowered from him. Past Annaliese laughing with Sam when he took his first steps, and back to the brief moment when Rob was sober, and hugged everyone in their cabin scented with fresh cut pine.

She floated past Hannah putting Annaliese in her arms at Sweetwater the first time on Christmas morning, when it smelled like roasting goose and baked cinnamon apples, and Matilda in cat form licked her paw beneath the window.

She lowered her eyes in shame, watching MacLeod touch Lady Margaret's earrings on the nightstand. Stumbled back through the Hellfire Caves, remembering how it led to her joining the coven.

Warmth grew inside, she was there—at Astwick House the night of the ball, feeling beautiful, inhaling George's musky scent. Music swirled, people clapped, but all she noticed was his warm touch as they danced. His hazel eyes held the promise of 'I love you.'

Past the workhouse. The shame. The fear.

Until she ended in the belly of a pitch-black ship, cold as ice, hugging her knees as the stench of salt air and tar overpowered her.

A light glowed from the hatch and familiar steps came down the ladder.

"Eleanor, where are you love? I've come for you."

"Da?"

Refusing his outstretched hand, she rose on her own. "I hated you for leaving me."

"I ken." Casting down his eyes, he held his hat in his calloused hands.

It's time, Ned, Matilda said.

Bright light warmed Eleanor's cold, aching heart. More rays slipped into the orlop.

"I'm sorry," he blurted, "for everything. For giving up on you, and myself. For making my problems yours. You dinnae deserve the childhood I condemned you to. Can you ever forgive me?"

They shared a prolonged gaze. She opened her arms, and they hugged, finally letting go of their pain as the fog of the Otherworld moved behind them. The light grew brighter, casting a warm glow and clear path in front. Her mother waited, holding her miscarried babies.

"Mam?"

Her siblings came forward, reaching out to welcome them. Beyond, was a field of purple heather, beside her childhood home in Scotland.

Ned grasped Eleanor's hand and squeezed. "It's time to leave the darkness."

As bright and as loving as the light felt, her sleeping children on the other side of the ice wall pulled stronger. "You go on. I'll meet you eventually, I hope," she said with a full heart.

Are ye sure ye want to be undead, lass? Matilda said.

"I need to stay for my children."

"You're a good mother, Eleanor. I couldna be prouder of you if I tried." Ned gave a final nod and rejoined their family.

As the veil between worlds closed, Eleanor faced Matilda in the dim forest of the Otherworld.

"So, tell me how this ghost life works. We've got time before we rescue our little witch and topple a king. Might as well learn how to haunt with style."

Enjoyed the Book? Leave a Review!

One of the best ways to show your support is to leave a review on Amazon, Goodreads, BookBub or where you purchase your books.

Don't know what to say? Just leave a sentence or two about what you liked.

Sneak Peek

To continue the adventure, I've provided an exclusive preview of the first three chapters of *To Rescue a Witch*, delivered to your email immediately by signing up for my newsletter at www.lisatraugott.com. Be the first to receive exclusive previews, special deals and book contests.

Cast of Characters

Scotland

MATILDA, burned at the stake for witchcraft, Fiona's aunt. Now a ghost, she is bound to live in the Otherword except during the fire festivals when the veil between the living and the dead is thin.

FIONA MACLEOD, part of Matilda's coven, married to William.

—WILLIAM MACLEOD, Fiona's husband, laird in Kirkhaven, lawyer and fixer to Lord George Hallewell.

—their children:

—JAMES, their eldest son, twelve years of age.

—DAVID, sweet boy, age ten.

—BRODERICK, the bastard child of rape, age three.

—LACHLAN, age two.

—HAMISH, born later in the story.

—Fiona's family:

—MARY, Fiona's sister.

—MALCOLM, Fiona's brother.

—William's family:

—ADMIRAL GORING, William's English grandfather, cursed to death by Matilda.

—ELISE, William's mother, had the prophesy which she wrote on the secret scroll. Matilda gave her a protective charm to help her elope with William's father, RORY MACLEOD.

—CECILE, Admiral Goring's French wife, William's grandmother. She watched Matilda curse her family.

—EDWARD GORING, Admiral Goring's eldest son, cursed to death by Matilda. William's uncle.

—WILL GORING, Admiral Goring's youngest son, cursed to death by Matilda. William's uncle.

—CAM MACLEOD, William's half-brother, lives on Isle of Skye.

REVEREND MACDONALD, helped execute Matilda, punished Fiona for witchcraft years later. Cursed by Matilda.

London

ELEANOR, abandoned at a workhouse, rises to become Lord Hallewell's mistress. Joins Matilda's coven after she's sent to Virginia Colony. Her daughter, Annaliese, is destined to topple a king if she can survive her fifth year.

— LORD BLACKMERE, the witch hunter who executed Matilda to gain political power. Now an earl and head of the Societies of the Reformation of Manners in London. He and Lord Hallewell's father used to be business partners in a fraudulent venture, but Blackmere made Lord Hallewell's father the scapegoat. He is learning blood magic from Elspeth to gain more power.

—ELSPETH, WITCH OF PYE, betrayed Matilda's coven, condemned to serve Lord Blackmere, cursed by Matilda. Now lives in London. Likes to shapeshift into her pet raven.

LORD GEORGE HALLEWELL, a baron from a scandalous family, he is Eleanor's lover, married to Lady Margaret and is William MacLeod's best friend and employer.

LADY MARGARET, his vicious wife fond of red gowns.

—their children:

—ALEXANDER, age four, the heir to Lady Margaret's first husband's fortune, he is the secret bastard of Colonel Wilkes.

—THOMAS, age two.

—ELIZABETH, their baby daughter.

JANE, a scullery maid and Eleanor's friend.

Virginia Colony

ANNALIESE, the bastard daughter of Eleanor and Lord Hallewell, and is also a changeling with links to Fiona and Matilda. Lord Blackmere and Elspeth are trying to capture or kill her.

—ROB BIRCH, overseer at Sweetwater Plantation, Eleanor's husband, Annaliese's stepfather/owner.

—OLD BETTY, an enslaved Nigerian diviner searching for her sold off children.

—MATTHEW CROWAN, owns Sweetwater Plantation and is Eleanor's master when she becomes an indentured servant. He went to Oxford with William MacLeod and Lord Hallewell.

—JANET CROWAN, Matthew's wife and the mistress of the plantation.

—DANIEL, their ten year old son.

—HANNAH, the cook, Eleanor's roommate, and Master Crowan's mistress. They have a daughter, NANCY.

—UNCLE HAL, Rob's uncle.

ACKNOWLEDGEMENTS & HISTORICAL NOTES

The first book, *To Rescue a Witch*, was a love letter to all the father figures in my life. This book celebrates the wonderfully messy relationships of women – mothers, daughters, grandmas, aunts, friends and frenemies. Let's hear it for the coven of women who pick us up, call us out, and cast a little magic when needed.

If you read *To Rescue a Witch*, you noticed it was historical fiction with magical elements that could technically be explained away. For this prequel, I went all in on fantasy: *Ghosts! Witches! Spells!* Because every time I watched the news I wanted to escape into a different world for a time, and nothing does that better than fantasy fiction. Thank you, readers, for travelling this expanded story path with me.

Matilda was inspired by a real woman, Alison Dick, accused of witchcraft and burned at the stake along with her husband in 1633. Known for cursing her neighbors, sinking men's ships over financial disputes, and an uncanny knack for accurately predicting the future, she had a reputation as a troublesome woman. In court testimony it was apparent that the villagers were terrified of her. Today we understand that magic isn't real, and we view all accused witches as innocent victims. Her contemporaries had a different opinion. They believed witches had the power to harm or heal and feared for their lives if they were cursed. I thought it would be interesting to explore this idea of a witch having agency and having to face her own deeds to reach redemption.

History lovers will note that the Hellfire Caves were excavated in 1748, and my story is set in 1728, but I couldn't possibly pass up a setting as fascinating as this for my characters. As the Mark Twain quote goes, "Never let the truth get in the way of a good story."

Segments of this book deal with near death experiences and brushes with the supernatural. I'm grateful to Tiffany Keenan, H.T. and P.S. for sharing their personal stories with me as inspiration, and to lend authenticity to the Otherworld.

Many thanks to Anne Daly for her incredible guidance through Scottish history and customs as she toured me through castle ruins and croft houses in the Highlands, Edinburgh, the Isle of Skye and Raasay.

I'm grateful to the historians and re-enactors at Colonial Williamsburg, especially Lindsey Foster. Thanks to Judy from Shirley Plantation in Virginia, the Oak Alley Plantation re-enactors in New Orleans for taking the time to answer all my questions, and to history professor Dennis Johnson for additional information about witches in the colonies.

Thanks to therapists Nicole Richardson and Shawn Wood LCSW, CYC-P, who helped put my characters on the proverbial couch again, especially to help understand the complicated dynamics of domestic violence.

Thanks to editors Kahina Necaise and Pippa Brush Chappel for their sharp insight and belief in the story, and everyone in The History Quill's critique group, especially Sydney Young, Mila Evanovich and Kate Shanahan. Thank you, Stuart Bache, for another beautiful book cover and KJ Waters for the interior formatting and help with the book launch.

Dave and Katie Walters, Meghan Montague, Deirdre Ryan and Jenny Dambeck – thank you for your support. Thanks to Cindy for keeping my spirits up when I was down. Thanks to everyone at Toastmasters for always showing up and cheering, especially Lark, Barbara, Reed, Steve & Debi, Monique, Mercedes, Amy, Nicole, Marcia, Heriberto, Donna, Chelsea, Charles, Deepak and Victoria.

As always, thanks to my kids Rylee and little Henry for their love and constant encouragement, and for teaching me how to make reels on TikTok. To my husband, Henri, thank you so much for rescuing MacLeod in the 11th hour.

To the many beta readers and ARC readers, especially Shannon, Robin, Natalie, Aimee and Campbell – thank you so much for your feedback to make the characters stronger and the story stickier. Finally, thanks to you, AWESOME READER, for your kindness and support! I can't wait to share the next story with you.

The books I read included:

MacDonald, Stuart, *The Witches of Fife, Witch-hunting in a Scottish Shire, 1560-1710*

Rendell, Mike, *In Bed with the Georgians, Sex, Scandal & Satire in the 18th Century*

Newton, Michale, *The Everyday Life of the Clans of the Scottish Highlands*

Blalock, Georgie, *Historical Contraception, Pregnancy & Childbirth*

Kramer, Heinrich, Sprenger James, *Malleus Maleficarum*

Cleland, John, *Fanny Hill, Memoirs of a Woman of Pleasure*

Selected by Rosemary Gray, *Scottish Myths & Legends*

McColman, Carl, Hinds, Kathryn, *The Spirit of the Celtic Gods and Goddesses, Their History, Magical Power, and Healing Energies*

Hudson, Jr., Carson O., *Witchcraft in Colonial Virginia*

Meiklejohn-Free, Barbara, *Scottish Witchcraft, A Complete Guide to Authentic Folklore, Spells, and Magickal Tools*

Grose, Captain Francis, *A Pocket Dictionary of the Vulgar Tongue*

Hagist, Don N., *Wives, Slaves And Servant Girls, Advertisements for Female Runaways in American Newspapers, 1770-1783*

Gibson, John, Mayor and Fisher, William, Mayor, *Record of Indentures of Individuals Bound Out as Apprentices, Servants, Etc., in Philadelphia, Pennsylvania1771-1773*

Rees, Siân, *The Floating Brothel, The Extraordinary True Story of An Eighteenth-Century Ship and Its Cargo of Female Convicts*

Jacobs, Harriet, *Incidents in the Life of a Slave Girl*

Hannah-Jones, Nikole The New York Times Magazine , et al., *The 1619 Project: A New Origin Story*

Miley Theobald, Mary, *Death by Petticoat, American History Myths Debunked*

Spalter, Mya, *Enchantments, A Beginner Witch's Guide*

Vered, Annabel, Editorial Director, *Witches, The Truth Behind the Legends &Lore*

O'Connor, Anne Marie, Project Editor, *Secrets of the Supernatural*

Madden, April, Editor, *Book of Spells, fourth edition*

Deary, Terry, *Horrible Histories, Scotland*

DK London, *A History of Magic, Witchcraft & The Occult*

Olsen, Kirstin, *Daily Life in 18th-Century England, Second Edition*

Scott, Walter, *Manners, Customs and History of the Highlanders of Scotland –Historical Account of the Clan Macgregor*

Brown, Beth, *Haunted Plantations of Virginia*

Franklin, Benjamin, *Wit & Wisdom from Poor Richard's Almanack*

Raum, Elizabeth, *The Dreadful, Smelly Colonies, the Disgusting Details about Life in Colonial America*

Kalman, Bobbie, *Colonial Times from A to Z*

Murphy-Hiscock, Arin, *The Green Witch, An Enchanting Immersion into the Magic of Natural Witchcraft*

About the Author

Lisa A. Traugott is the award-winning author of *Tales of the Witchborn* series (*To Rescue a Witch* and *To Condemn a Witch*), a haunting historical fantasy saga in the realm of ghosts, goddesses, and rebellion. She double majored in history and theater (flirting with unemployment) yet somehow became a full-time author. An original cast member on *American Grit* with John Cena she also had five lines on *Buffy the Vampire Slayer.* She lives in Austin with her husband and two kids where they enjoy walking ghost tours and telling scary stories around the campfire.

On LisaTraugott.comyou can download a FREE chapter of "To Rescue a Witch."

You can also find her author social media accounts:

Facebook: https://www.facebook.com/LisaATraugott

Instagram: @lisa__traugott

Made in the USA
Coppell, TX
10 February 2026

70962432R00216